PRIVATE THOUGHTS OF
A FIERY SOUL

April 25, 1786: "Have locked my door. Somebody might try to break in."

May 10: "Cannot believe that any woman ever let herself be treated that way of her own free will and enjoyed it."

August 8: "It is so easy for a woman surrounded by slaves to give way to her whims, even wicked ones, and go unpunished."

August 18: "I admit it is an agreeable feeling, this sense of unlimited power that is given us over slaves. But it is dangerous."

Confessions of Elizabeth

Edited by
H. A. Bashlin

Published in England as
The Diary of Elizabeth Renault

CONFESSIONS OF ELIZABETH
A Bantam Book

PRINTING HISTORY

*First published in Great Britain in 1970
by Transworld Publishers, Ltd. as
"The Diary of Elizabeth Renault"*

Bantam edition / August 1979

*Bantam Books are published by Bantam Books, Inc. Its trade-
mark consisting of the words "Bantam Books" and the por-
trayal of a bantam, is Registered in U.S. Patent and Trademark
Office and in other countries. Marca Registrada. Bantam
Books, Inc., 666 Fifth Avenue, New York, New York 10019.*

Confessions of
Elizabeth

EDITOR'S FOREWORD

This strange old diary has, to my knowledge, never before been published, although the former owners of the manuscript, or of copies of it, seem to have well realized how interesting a document they were hiding from the public.

In 1955, a few months before he died, my uncle H.B. (born in 1877) handed over to me an old carbon copy of a handwritten text, about three hundred yellowed pages. He told me he had written it himself in 1906 from a text in English shorthand that had been given to him by a distant relation of my grandmother's, an old lady, the widow of a citizen of Geneva, a certain M. Rey. She told my uncle that she remembered a number of old "cahiers" with faded blue paper covers that her husband had kept locked up in one of his drawers for many years, perhaps since they were married (about the middle of the last century, I presume). They seemed to contain a journal in a woman's delicate character, but she was unable to read it as it was in English, a language she did not know. She knew that, as a young man, he had acquired the manuscript from a Frenchman. As he often went to London on business he showed the text to various London publishers, but they all refused to bring it out because of its "indecent character," which, in Victorian England, would have shocked the public and probably provoked the authorities to confiscate the book. In the eighties he sent the "cahiers" to a publishing firm in New York. Whether the manuscript got lost on its way there or by negligence on the part of that firm or it was confiscated by some puritanical American postmaster, who knows? At any rate, he never saw it again. The publishing firm wrote to him they were sorry they had

never received the parcel. Fortunately M. Rey had cop-
ied the text in English shorthand. His widow gave that
copy to my uncle as she knew he mastered English
stenography.

As I mentioned above, my uncle transcribed that text
by hand. He told me he had submitted his handwritten
copy to two well-known publishing firms in London before the First World War, but neither seemed to be interested, probably for the same reason mentioned before.

It was not until 1926, when I was a student at the
University of Basle (Switzerland), that I learned about
the existence of this document. On one of my rare visits
to my uncle's home near Lucerne (our families had
never seen much of each other) he gave me part of a
handwritten text, about fifty pages, which he asked me
to show to Prof. H., the then university lecturer on
English literature at Basle. It was an apparently au-
thentic text, my uncle said, written in the late eighties
and the early nineties of the eighteenth century. He
wished to have an expert's opinion about it. On my way
home I glanced at the text. It dealt, as I remember,
with the author's flight from Santo Domingo and her
strange relations to the octoroon twins, happenings
which I thought too extravagant to be true, to say nothing of the very unladylike language she uses, a lack of
discretion unusual in those days judging from contem-
porary memoirs by women authors I knew. Still, it was
only a first impression, based on a very cursory glimpse
at some of the entries.

As I was preparing for my examinations I did not
find the time to examine the text more minutely before
submitting it to Prof. H. Three months later my uncle
impatiently urged me to return it to him, which forced
me to call on Prof. H. unannounced. He seemed scarcely to remember the text, and when he found it he said he
doubted its authenticity, the original manuscript being
lost. Looking back, I frankly doubt if he read it at all!

Maybe my uncle was as much disappointed at my
own lack of interest as at the professor's sceptical
opinion. At any rate, he never mentioned the manuscript to me for many years. As a little cardboard manu-

facturer he had to fight hard against strong competition in the thirties, which may have diverted his interest from that document. It was not until 1939 that he once more tried to find a publisher for it. In the summer of that year he sent the diary to a publishing firm in London which had been recommended to him as very open-minded. I wonder how my uncle could have chosen such a time of political crisis, a few weeks before the outbreak of the Second World War, to separate from his valuable document. His parcel never arrived at its destination. When he tried to gather information through an English business friend of his, nobody knew about the manuscript. After the war, when my uncle was over seventy, he asked me to inquire after it while staying in London. But neither the publishing firm nor the Postmaster-General's department could give me any information about the lost text.

The carbon copy which the old man entrusted to me was in such a bad condition, some of its pages being almost illegible, that I put it aside with the intent to read it some time in my holidays. Frankly, I was not very interested, thinking it was a fake.

It was not until the autumn of 1963, when I was confined to bed for several weeks, that I remembered that old diary. Reading it I soon realized that it was really worth publishing. I started copying it in my spare time, which, however, took me much longer than I had expected, not only on account of the bad condition of the carbon copy but also because I could devote but little of my time to that task.

All my friends who have, meanwhile, read the text are astonished that such a remarkable document should have been ignored so long. I suppose the fact that it is written in English but belonged to a French family for generations may have prevented its publication for many years. Maybe the family were shocked at the frankness of the author's confessions; they did not wish their near relative to be exposed to public disapproval and scorn. It is quite possible that the author herself may have stipulated in her testament that her journal should not be published as long as her family lived. M. Rey, who later got in possession of the "cahiers," was a citizen of Geneva, no doubt an austere puritan who must have severely disapproved of the wicked woman author's views, deeds and language. It is amusing to know that his moral indignation did not prevent him from trying to make money out of his hidden treasure. My uncle, too, though widely travelled and open-minded, kept that shocking diary locked up like a piece of pornography that must be hidden from his wife and daughter.

Public opinion has changed, meanwhile. We have learned to appreciate candor in a person worthy of our sympathy. That Elizabeth Renault was an interesting character, no one can deny. That strange mixture of tender warmth and cold energy, of sensuality and sober matter-of-factness, delicacy of feeling and shocking callousness, of female vanity and shrewd self-analysis, this wide range of a rich personality make her attractive even in moments when we most vehemently disagree with her. Her knack of describing persons and emotional situations is remarkable enough to make her diary entertaining wherever we open it.

As a historical document it is unique in so far as it depicts from a white lady planter's point of view the social and human situation in Haiti on the eve of the great Negro insurrection of 1791. A young woman, forced by circumstances to run a large coffee-plantation all by herself, ruling over more than a hundred slaves, finding the best ways to keep order and discipline among them and to impress her authority on them even in critical situations, confides to her diary her intimate experiences and feelings as an enlightened despot, a frustrated wife, a dissatisfied widow, a cynical observer of her fellow-planters, men and women, of cruelty, vice and corruption behind the white façades of the rulers' mansions.

It is, moreover, a tale of human tragedy: the slow corruption of a decent young girl's mind by its daily contact with perverse abuse of power. She learns to lie and cheat and to regard her slaves as human cattle to be exploited and, if necessary, ill-treated, but valuable enough to be looked after well for profit's sake.

Being a woman the author is much less interested in

politics and economics than in personal matters regarding the intimate spheres of life: fashion, gossip, intrigues, scandal and, above all, love and sex. Her candid remarks on that inexhaustible topic are excusable considering the fact that they are confided to a secret diary certainly not meant to be read by others. They tell us a lot about the sexual behavior of women of the ruling class in slave-holding colonies of the past, at any rate in the West Indies towards the end of the eighteenth century. The women mentioned in this journal have, we admit, little in common with the sweet romantic heroines of so many historical novels dealing with those times and places, but they are, no doubt, depicted much truer to life.

It is a pity that the original spelling was, quite obviously, corrected either by M. Rey or my uncle. Whether some of the phrasing or a number of outmoded words were also altered by one of the copyists or both I do not know. Still, there is enough of that patina preserved that helps to give such private documents of the past their peculiar charm.

H. A. BASHLIN

Part I
1786

APRIL 24TH, 1786

Have made up my mind to begin a new journal, not in French like the first, but in English, so that others won't be able to read it, some prying snuffler like Mère Cathérine, that old crow!

She said it was a shame, a young girl writing such abominable things! Well, it was not meant to be read by her, nor anybody else, was it? It was no business of hers to read my most secret thoughts and feelings which I could not confide to any living soul.

What's the use of a diary if I must not write down what really happened, what I really saw and heard and experienced, not only nice things, but embarrassing and wicked ones, too, things I would not dare speak of, not even in the confessional; things I heard them whisper about at night, in the dormitory, Jeanne and Henriette and Marie and the others, those innocent virgins, and in the daytime so modest, so pure, so immaculate! I hate hypocrites! The old ones, too, Mère Cathérine, that Tartuffe in a nun's disguise! Heaven thanks that's over! If ever I have a daughter I won't allow her to be buried in a convent, not even for a month!

Mother would not have sent me there, not my mother. She did not like sanctimonious people. She liked fun and laughter, which didn't prevent her from going to Mass three times a week. All Irish women are obedient church-goers, they say, but they like to be merry, too. Singing her Irish ditties, so sweet! Dear little Mama, how I miss you! Everything useful I learned in the convent Mama could have taught me herself, being so clever, so well-read. I am glad she taught me English as a child, though Father was angry many a time when we talked English in his presence, which he didn't understand very well. It was our secret language that

9

allied us against him, and against all other menfolk with their rudeness and their domineering ways.

I meant to start this diary on the very first day on board this ship, but how could I? Sharing my cabin with that monstrous fat old woman! So glad Mme Puy left this morning at Fort de France. She will spend the rest of her life in Martinique, at her son-in-law's plantation. If it is true that daughters will grow the size of their mother when over forty he may look forward to a heavy burden in bed! Heavens! Those thighs of hers! And her breasts dropping like heavy udders when she opened her stays. And her snoring— like a drunken sailor for hours and hours with no end to it. Often I could not close an eye the whole night because of that dreadful snore. And how she would spy on me all the time! Could not have a single word with P. without her popping up, listening. Like a jailer! Thank heavens I am rid of her.

Have my cabin all to myself, perhaps for the rest of the voyage, a whole fortnight or even more, P. said, if the wind calms down. Hope there won't be any new passengers at our next harbor, which is Guadeloupe. Three will disembark there, the young couple and the pot-bellied abbé who smiled at me whenever he passed. A pity the lovebirds are leaving. Nice people, charming, and so much in love! Through the wooden partition I could hear them laugh and giggle whenever my fat old room-mate stopped snoring for a minute or two. Now she has left I am sure I can hear more of those funny noises they often make as if fighting. But they are not! May happen any time of night. At first felt quite embarrassed, but soon got used to it, the inarticulate language of love. A little frightening, but fascinating, too.

My cabin seems to be so much larger since she left. Plenty of room to write and read. And the air so much better! Hated her stale smell. So typical of old people. I would have preferred a nice young girl as a room-mate. Perhaps will get one after Guadeloupe. If not, I must keep my room locked whenever I am on deck. Imagine a man hiding below my bunk! Pierre! I would scream, scream, scream, and my neighbors would come to my rescue.

I wonder what my aunt looks like, and my uncle. He is five years my mother's senior. She was forty when she died three years ago. So he must be forty-nine now, no, forty-eight, an elderly gentleman. Well, some of them are still attractive. Hope they will meet me at the port. Their plantation is not very far away from Cap, as Uncle told me in his letter.

Saw the first slaves in the port of Fort de France this morning, pitch-black Negroes rowing boats in which sat gentlemen and ladies under white, green and red parasols. Some were very aristocratic-looking, in tinsel finery. The boats circled round our ship, the slaves were all poorly dressed, naked to the waist, some of them like skeletons, just skin and bones with their backs scarred and wincing to shake off swarms of flies. Poor creatures!

Tomorrow is my birthday, and nobody knows. Not even P. Wonder what present he would give me. Three years ago, when I was fifteen, Mother was still alive, merry and gay. It was my last happy birthday. Even Papa was nice. Kissed me and gave me my first ring, the one with the tiny sapphire. How proud I was!

APRIL 25TH

Could not find a seat on deck, everybody gathering in the shade. The heat is indeed getting almost unbearable. P. said women in these islands wear nothing below their gowns! How does he know? Either he is a lier or a rake. Delights in telling me things to make me blush. Would be very embarrassing, no underwear, in my present condition. Picture bloodstains on my frock, making everybody stare at me! How I hate these days! Headaches and feeling so disgustingly unclean. All the people I meet seem to know. There is a sneer in their smile, a twinkle in their eye. It is a real curse for us women, and no end to it till we are old and worn.

Have locked the door. Somebody might try to break

in. Pierre! Would suit his designs to see me undressed. I would not put it past him to grow daring, touch me, kiss me, force me, disregarding my cries, my protest, my desperate resistance. Men are brutes. All men are. Even Papa was sometimes. Not this way, of course, but towards Mama and me. Kept us in frightened submission all the time. Expected his women to obey him and serve him like slaves. And after Mother's death he treated me harder than before. Was afraid I might be tempted by sin if given the least bit of freedom.

I can't forget him hitting me for trifling things—at that age—fifteen! Humiliating to be treated like a naughty child. Hurt my pride more than my bottom. At such moments I would hate Father, I could not help it. That's why I felt relieved, not really sad, when he died. I know it is a sin, hating one's own parent. But how could I feel different? How can I, remembering that night when he hit Mama! Men are beasts when they are drunk. Never shall I allow a man to treat me like that, threaten me, bully me, never! Better remain unmarried than live in terror of my husband for a lifetime. Or see him run after other women like Uncle Paul.

Those months in Lyons were a nightmare. A house full of noisy, dirty brats, and me expected to replace the nurse and the maidservant and the cook all the time! Aunt Henriette was all right, poor woman. But her husband! His dirty jokes and allusions, his shameless attempts at touching and pinching me whenever his wife was away. And then the shock, the terrible shock that afternoon, when I saw him standing in the doorway stark naked, the swine!

Could not eat a bit this morning. Maybe I am getting seasick, after keeping fit as a fiddle these six weeks. But the ship does roll worse than ever. Don't feel like writing any more. Heaven, what a rotten birthday!

APRIL 29TH

Haven't opened this journal since I got sick. Four beastly days! Kept in bed all the time, trying to retch and sleep and die and could not. The captain was decent enough to send a woman to take care of me. I never saw her before. Colored. A mulatto. Calls herself Bastienne. Funny names they give to those bastards. Rather plain-looking with a flat nose. But a nice woman, friendly, very helpful. Shall ask P. what present to give her. Money? Or that funny large comb Mme Puy left me? It is too showy for me anyway.

P. was very decent, must admit. No attempts at familiarity. I must have looked too pitiful and ugly all the time. I still do, looking at myself in the mirror. That woman Bastienne must help me to have a wash from head to foot. She seems to have come on board at Martinique. A free woman? A slave? Was too tired to ask questions.

A pity I missed Guadeloupe. P. said we departed this morning. The wind sitting fair we may arrive at Cap within ten days.

Had beef-tea this morning. Feel hungry after four days starving. Maybe this evening I can try and climb up on deck. Wonder if there are any new passengers on board.

APRIL 30TH

Feel much better today, though I still look pale and exhausted. Thank Heaven the sea is calm again. The sails are full and I saw dolphins dancing around us, droll animals, charming.

P. behaved like a perfect cavalier, so attentive. He is not so bad after all.

The two lovebirds have left, but another young couple has replaced them, with a baby and its wet nurse and a colored male servant. Never saw a more beautiful young lady. No doubt very rich, judging from her dress and jewels. But terribly conceited, too proud to talk to anybody but her husband. She walks like a queen, followed by her brown servant holding a white and golden umbrella above her and the buxom wet-nurse, again colored, with the babe in arms, sucking.

Bastienne is a slave. Her mistress is a widow at Fort de France who hired her to our captain for the voyage to Cap and back to Martinique. She also hired out a Negro man, both to be used to serve the passengers. Pierre asked her if the Negro was her lover or husband. She denied emphatically having anything to do with him, saying she would never allow a dirty nigger to touch her. Said her late master stipulated in his will that she must serve his widow till she is thirty years old. Then she will be emancipated and given 2,000 livres. With that money she intends to purchase a Negro to make him work for her.

In these colonies it seems to be everybody's ambition to own slaves. P. says you are judged by the number of Negroes you own, even among the poor. They will spend the last sous of their savings to buy one or two, even if the slaves are valueless cripples, or runaways who will escape if they don't keep them in chains. It is all so terribly disgusting!

P. sent for the Negro to show him to me. A tall lanky black Senegalese, thick-lipped, his eyes soft, embarrassingly submissive, as if scared. P. told him to open his shirt to show me the letters JCT branded on his right breast, which are his mistress' initials. Tried to show him I like him, he needn't be afraid of me. Find him handsomer than that woman Bastienne. Ridiculous her treating him as her inferior, just for the difference in color. These stupid class distinctions even among slaves!

The room next to mine is now occupied by an elderly man with a withered face, pug-nosed, his monkey eyes swimming in a sea of wrinkles. He is very funny, reminds me of an old turkey. Introduced himself as M. de Courvoisier. Pea-green breeches and a long yellow coat with green stripes, silk stockings striped likewise! Never saw an old man dressed up so foppishly. His periwig is yellow, which is very old-fashioned, as all the young men are wearing theirs powdered grey. He is always strutting about like a general inspecting his troops, gripping the outmoded heavy hilt of his sabre as if ready for an attack. Nobody else on board wears a weapon like that. P. calls him an old fool. Towards me he is solemnly courteous, bowing deep, swinging his hat in a grand gesture, the perfect cavalier of times past and gone. Very amusing.

WEDNESDAY, MAY 3RD

We are sailing along the coast of Puerto Rico. This morning we passed San Juan, its white houses, palms, several brigs and smaller ships and boats in the blue harbor, no more than half a mile away. A pity our ship didn't drop anchor. But it is a Spanish port, not friendly to the French.

That queenly young lady from Guadeloupe is terribly vain. Worse than her husband who is conceited enough himself. But I must admit they are by far the most aristocratic couple on board. Their handsome mulatto servant in grand white livery stands never more than a step or two away from his idle mistress, all the time watching for her mute orders given with a quick turn of her hand or fan, suddenly, as if awakening from a dream. Once only I saw her lose her languid calm, saw her, for reasons unknown to me, hit the servant's face with her fan in sudden anger, then relapse, as abruptly, into her habitual arrogant languor. She is mostly lying in a hammock fixed between the foremast and the rail, watching the wet-nurse rocking or suckling her babe, or talking to her husband who is bending attentively over her. Very elegant, her broad-rimmed straw hat with the high white ostrich feather, scarlet ribbon and trimming, she paraded yesterday afternoon, while all the other women wore scarfs. Must be the latest Paris mode. Her hair grey powdered, not so high as they wear it in Paris. Or is this outmoded, too? But she wears muslin, not silk, even such a rich lady. Silk would be too warm in this climate, I presume. No *cul de crin!*

P. has started being fresh again! Put his hand on my buttocks caressingly, just for a moment, the impudent rake! Should have boxed his ears but was afraid other people might see us. Said he wanted to make sure that I had followed his advice, considering the hot climate. Indeed I had. And now he knows, the scoundrel!

Saw M. de Courvoisier swaying towards his door. Seemed to be tipsy, the old fool. Glad he does not snore at night. At least hasn't, so far.

SUNDAY, MAY 7TH

Had a very narrow escape last night! Was silly enough to open the door when there was a knock. Thought it was Bastienne. Instead it was P. Tried to force his way in, the blackguard!

I had the presence of mind to cry for help, whereupon my neighbor rushed out, swinging his sabre. Said next time he would carry his pistol and shoot to protect me! P. retired laughing, said Monsieur was wrong, he had not meant to do the young lady any harm. I said I was not so sure of that, I had good reason to be very grateful to Monsieur de C. for his protection. He said I needn't worry for the future as he was a light sleeper, would wake up at the slightest noise. Stared at me all the time, which made me realize that my négligé is thin!

This morning P. pleaded the penitent, said he had really meant no harm, just wished to tell me the good news that in two or three days' time we shall arrive at Cap.

He says he is depressed at my coldness, not granting him a single kiss though I must know his feelings. Called me cruel and heartless when I laughed. I know well enough I am neither the first nor the last of the girls he tries to wheedle into shame and disgrace. We girls are always the losers if we give in but once.

Talked to two young girls I never met before. It turns out they are that stern, black-dressed lady's nieces. They are sisters, twins, fifteen, very Spanish-looking with smooth black hair and black eyes and very pale, as if they had grown up in a cellar. But their Créole accent is quite amusing, and they have a vocabulary like naughty boys and worse. Their aunt's husband died

some months ago, therefore her deep mourning. She
sold her plantation and is returning to her own family
near Cap, her brother, the twins' father, owning a sugar-plantation there. The girls spent a few months with
their aunt at Guadeloupe, said it had been sad and
boring because of their uncle's death and funeral and
all that. No place worth seeing, no town like Cap, which,
they said, is by far the finest in their island, theatres,
balls, plenty of elegant people, European shops and the
latest articles of mode from Paris. They were seasick
the first three days of this voyage, therefore stayed in
their cabin till Monday, and have been lying about at a
hidden spot on deck since then. That's why I didn't
see them before.

They seem to have recovered well enough now, judging from their funny comments on everyone passing us.
They have but one servant with them, their aunt having
sold all her slaves before leaving. That servant is a
stout Negro woman to whom they seem quite attached
as she was their wet-nurse and has served them ever
since.

Their own mother died a year ago. That's why their
father sent them to Guadeloupe to be looked after by
their aunt. They said they hated going there, for it had
been great fun to rule a house full of servants all by
themselves. But their father found it dangerous for two
white girls their age to be surrounded by colored slaves
without any white person supervising them.

They had been instructed by a young lady from
Paris for years, but that silly woman had started fooling about with a slave of theirs, a handsome quarteroon boy, and got with child, which forced their father to send her back to France. Next June he will take
them to Paris for schooling.

In two years' time they hope to get married into
some good family in France, as many wealthy planters' daughters do. Odd to hear two fifteen-year-old girls
talking of marriage as of something granted so soon,
to be arranged for them like their schooling or voy-
aging or getting new hats and perfume sent from Paris.

I doubt if there are any girls their age and station in
France so frightfully precocious in love matters, talking

of bed-mates and whoring and getting with child and of
how many of their father's slaves were ruined by the
Spanish malady, which is the name they give to that infamous sickness caused by sinning flesh. And what
words they use! Must have picked them up from vulgar
slaves. Naughty brats. Though I am sure they just
pretend to be wicked, trying to act the part of grown-
ups, in order to impress me.

The way they treat their stout black maid proves they
are not really bad. They like to tease her, said they had
seen her making love to the Negro boy on board,
which she denied with indignation, bursting into tears,
whereupon they soothed and caressed her, calling her
silly big little Mammy, quite touching.

MAY 9TH

We are going to drop anchor in the port of Cap
tonight, towards ten or eleven, P. says, in the bright
moonshine. One more night on board. Tomorrow morning they will row us to land after the surgeon and officers from Cap have come on board. We are all in great
commotion, packing and preparing for the farewell
festivities after supper. The captain is offering us a cask
of brandy to celebrate the safe and early arrival. Perhaps there will be some dancing on deck in the moonshine. Must be grand!

Shall try and be cold towards P. to punish him for
his insolence. When we all were gathered on the leeside
watching the approaching coast he managed to stand
behind me, pressing against me in the most indecent
way while I could not move an inch in the crowd! An
hour before he had plunged his hand into my bosom
and tried to kiss me, which I avoided by running away.
He is the most impertinent fellow I ever met.

He has made friends with M. de Courvoisier, in spite
of the incident the other night. Saw them drinking
brandy together, the old fool bragging about some
military campaign he took part in.

Pia and Maria, the twins, seem to have an immense
wardrobe with them. They have changed garments half

a dozen times since I first met them. What a contrast to their aunt's stern mourning! Have not seen her smile even once. Can't abide people spoiling others' good humor by looking sad all the time. We must allow wounds to heal, not scratch at them day after day.

This time tomorrow I'll be on my way to Uncle's plantation, I suppose. Perhaps he is coming to town himself to pick me up. It would be awkward for me to stand on the pier alone, not knowing where to turn. But how can he know our ship has arrived? Somebody will inform him, no doubt.

Would not marry Pierre if he asked me. Could not trust him to be faithful.

MAY 10TH, AFTERNOON

I am much too upset to lie down and close my eyes after what happened this morning, and yesterday, on my arrival in Cap and during my first drive through the town. I cannot forget Aunt's strange doings there, things and people I have seen, Uncle's terrible misfortune, the last hours on board, that beastly brown woman, and the worst, the inexcusable, meanest, most brutish, most villainous wrong ever inflicted on me. The scoundrel! The dirty vulgar rogue!

Perhaps it would not have happened if I had stopped drinking after emptying the first glass. I am not used to strong drinks, so the second glass made me careless and merry, joining the sailors singing and then, all by myself, singing that old English ditty I learnt from Mama: Oh, the Oak and the Ash and the Bonny Ivy Tree. Was cheered so loudly by the men present that it made me blush.

And afterwards took part in dancing a minuet on deck, and when P. was my partner he looked at me and whispered love words each time we touched, and I was silly enough to smile and feel happy and gay.

But I retired with the other ladies, early enough, to leave the men to their carousal. Undressed in my hot cabin (the door safely bolted) but was still too much alive to go to bed. Continued packing my trunk and bags in the poor light of my lantern when suddenly I heard a loud pounding at the wooden partition separating me from M. de Courvoisier's room, and a man's voice I thought was my neighbor's shouting: "Run upstairs, the ship is on fire!"

I was so alarmed that I lost my head. I slipped into my négligé and opened the door.

The next moment I was pushed back and seized by the shoulder, and my mouth was firmly shut by a strong, big hand, and the door closed behind the intruder and was bolted by him. I saw it was Pierre, half drunk, naked passion in his face and eyes, pushing me to my bed, whispering mad things, saying it was no use screaming because my neighbor was upstairs dead drunk, and if people found him, Pierre, here, they would be convinced I had let him in, everybody knowing he was my lover. For my honor's sake I had better keep quiet.

Was so paralyzed with fear I could not move, then tried to struggle and resist, but he was terribly strong in his madness. It all happened so quickly, the brute being merciless, ruthless, not minding a bit my scratching and hitting and biting him, nor my moans and screams and sobs, till all was over and I felt I had been murdered, stabbed and crushed, oh God Almighty, have mercy on me! It was so ugly, so disgustingly ugly, all of it. Cannot believe that any woman ever let herself be treated that way of her own free will and enjoyed it.

Later, when it was over, he tried to cheer me up seeing that I wept silently. Called me a wildcat, said he liked a girl fighting him, it was more fun that way. For every young girl there was a first time, he said, only plain girls and nuns were spared this experience, and not many of them either. Having tasted blood I was sure to enjoy it better the next time, all women did, once initiated. If I had had a dagger hidden under my pillow I should have stabbed him in cold blood that minute.

When he left I lay awake for hours. Once I heard men's voices outside, laughing and cursing, and the slamming of a door, then my neighbor rumbling about

behind the partition, my gallant protector, who had
promised to shield me from that young rake. For a minute or two no more sound was heard, then he started
snoring, snoring, snoring, worse than Mme Puy, and no
end to it. Didn't sleep a wink the last night on board.

After getting up in the morning had but one desire:
to leave the ship and never see the blackguard again.
But we had to wait for the authorities and the surgeon
from Cap to give us permission to land. Up on deck I
saw a number of passengers gathered along the rail,
staring down at something below. I was not curious. I
ran to the bow from where I could see the harbor, the
dozens of sailing vessels clustered a few hundred yards
from us, and behind the forest of masts and rigs, the
rows of white houses and palm trees and above them the
immaculate blue sky. I could see people walking about
in the distance. Some rowboats were moving on the
azure sea, two or three of them—approaching us.

"The officers and the doctor, I suppose," said a man's
voice behind me. I turned round. Pierre! How dare he.
After what had happened last night!

I spun round and ran away to join the group of passengers that were still staring down. There he would not
dare to molest me any longer. They would protect me
from that brute.

The twins turned to me with laughing faces. Asked
me if I had a sous or two with me, which I denied.
But Pia had already got one from another passenger. She swung it far out into the air, and peeping over
the girls' shoulders I saw it disappear in the water, a
few yards away from a large rowing-boat below us.

A little black fellow jumped from the boat into the
water, diving for it, while three others stared up at us
with begging gestures. They were naked little Negroes,
none older than ten or twelve, I guess. At the bow
sat a fat brown woman clad in a loose pink garment
that exposed a good deal of her heavy breasts to the
spectators above her. She had a long bamboo cane in
her hand with which she would hit the shoulders of
the two black oarsmen on the thwart in front of her,
now the one to her left, now the other, as a sign for
them to move their oar. The two Negroes were the

most pitiable creatures I have ever seen. Their backs
were covered with ugly scars and open purulent wounds.
Whenever that abominable woman hit them swarms of
flies could be seen circling above their heads, ready
to drop back on their wounds the moment the cane
came to a rest. They both looked starved, just skin and
bones, and when they moved we could hear the
clinking of the fetters that chained their feet to the
planks of the boat. The woman didn't look angry. Hitting her oarsmen seemed to be a matter of routine to
her. Neither did my fellow-passengers mind her shocking behavior. Even the twins seemed to take it as a
matter of course.

On the stern of the boat, facing the oarsmen, sat a
very young girl, not more than eleven or twelve, I presume. She was lighter skinned than the fat woman, a
pale yellow. She, too, had a bamboo cane in her hand,
directing the little Negroes ready to dive.

I watched our diver reappear and climb into the boat
panting heavily. He took the coin out of his mouth
and handed it to the girl to put it into a bowl beside
her. Others jumped into the water and returned with
their coins to deliver them to their young mistress.

Whenever a boy failed to secure his coin, which happened but rarely, he would lie flat over the gunwale,
submissively waiting for her to hit him hard on his
buttocks, three or four strokes as their routine punishment.

It was a shocking sight, but none of my fellow-
passengers seemed to care. Pia and Maria giggled and
laughed when I protested. They said it didn't hurt
very much, not like whipping them. The little brats
needn't be pitied, they were used to it. It made them
work better. As to the oarsmen, they were not worth
their food. Probably runaways. Such stinkers must be
treated harshly, they were getting their deserts. In any
case, they were the woman's property, so she could
treat them as she liked; we had no right to interfere.
Everyone could see they were the cheapest offal. They
would not pay ten sous for the couple of them.

I never heard young Christian girls talk like that.

Heartless, cold little monsters, I hate them, don't wish to see them again.

Was about to turn away, disgusted, when I saw another rowing-boat approach full of fruit, melons and grapefruit, pineapples and oranges and lemons. A single oarsman was sitting on the thwart, his mistress again a mulatto woman, quite European-looking with a Jewish nose. She tried to turn our attention away from the divers to her own boat, advertising her fruit in a shrill voice.

When her boat touched the bigger boat the fat woman turned, angrily telling her to keep off. But the fruit vendor ordered her slave to keep close to our ship, whereupon her antagonist dropped her cane and seized a long whip that had been lying at her feet. She turned round, lashing her whip, which hit the other woman's slave across the back. He screamed, his mistress picked up a foul orange and flung it at her enemy. The next moment the two women were facing each other like two snarling tigresses. Never before had I heard such a continuous stream of vulgar insults, threats and curses from the lips of two infuriated females. It was a scene of such fascinating ugliness that all the spectators watched it with breathless admiration.

The big slave had been hurt by the lash: I could see blood oozing from the cut skin. His mistress cried for revenge. She said he was ruined and she was going to sue the fat bitch for damaged property, which, however, did not impress her enemy at all. She said she had warned the fruit vendor, and if she was not willing to keep off her boat the whip was ready for a second and a third and a fourth stroke to teach her nigger to react sensibly. As for suing her, she was ready to pay the ten sous that miserable cripple was worth, although his many scars and cuts proved he had been ruined long before.

Their dispute was put a sudden end to by the arrival of a long-boat rowed by four Negroes. Two soldiers in uniform sat in it, and three dignified-looking men in civilian clothes. The rivalling boats glided away in different directions, each stopping at a respectful distance from our ship. A ladder was pushed over the railing and lowered to the surface of the water for the officials to climb up. I rushed down to my cabin to prepare my departure.

It would fill a book to record all the strange and terrible and ugly and funny and fascinating things I saw this morning. The mixed, brightly dressed crowds in the streets, all shades from black to white, but the dark colored far more numerous, women wearing funny broad-rimmed straw hats or headkerchiefs most beautifully suiting their gay garments. All the blacks and most colored persons go barefoot, while even the poor whites wear shoes, and so do the wealthy mulattoes and those pretty colored girls my aunt called cheap harlots. There must be crowds of them! Wonder what they are doing in the bright morning. I thought night was the time for sinning. Pretty women seem to be more numerous here than in Paris, and more elegant ones, too, though few are dressed *à la mode de Paris*. Scarcely any *cul de crin* nor *tournure*, nor plain *jupes*, but bright-colored fichus that rather display than cover their deep bosoms. Fans and white or green or red umbrellas are indispensable accessories for ladies, a gaudy sight, like big bright flowers swimming above the crowd.

Saw several rich white ladies in sumptuous coaches driven by two or four horses. They looked like proud queens surrounded by half a dozen brown and black servants in bright liveries, with forerunners and others standing behind their mistresses on the rear step of the coach, holding umbrellas above them. My aunt's coach looked small and plain compared to theirs, nor were her servants so well dressed. Hannibal, the coachman, is an elderly Negro, kinky grey-hair, no doubt a good fellow, very submissive. César, the boy that helped me step on land asking me if I was Mlle Renault, is a handsome young mulatto, thirteen years old, he says, slim and graceful, soft-eyed, a charming lad. The mulatto maid, Helen, is his elder sister, about five years his senior. She does not bear any resemblance to him. Perhaps they have different fathers. All the three servants

are rather poorly dressed, barefoot, but nice manners.
Treated me like a princess, smiled gratefully, seeing I
was kind to them.

I felt a little shy while following the boy to my aunt's
coach, dozens of people watching me as though I were
a strange animal. It seems to be a great event, the arrival of a ship from Europe. Crowds of idlers were gathered on the pier, dozens of rowing-boats swarmed on
the water. Nor did I feel at ease when I saw her—my
aunt—sitting in the coach waiting for me. At first I
took her for a very haughty woman, cold and unfriendly, assessing me from top to toe. But she is not,
thank Heaven. She looks very Spanish, dark-eyed, pale,
severe, a little fattish round her hips, but still a handsome woman. She must have been pretty as a young
girl.

She told me her family had lived here for generations. So she is a Créole. That's the name they give to
whites born on this island.

I was alarmed to hear that my uncle had an accident
a month ago: fell from his horse and broke his spine.
He has been lame since, can't move his legs, poor man.
I shall try and cheer him up. He looked so sad and helpless when I was introduced to him an hour ago.

But I must record another incident before turning to
my poor uncle. Something shocking like what I saw
from the ship, earlier this morning.

We paid a visit after we had passed the main street.
I was disappointed to see that the houses are not all of
stone, some are of plain wood, or partly of wood, not
impressive at all, one or two storeys, no more, nothing
to be compared to the fine buildings in Paris. The
streets very dirty, and bad smells everywhere.

But I like the white awnings covering the main streets
like large sails, protecting them from the sun. Gives
them a strange effect, somehow Oriental.

Passed a group of Negroes walking in single file,
chained together with fetters hanging like festoons from
neck to neck. They were escorted by a man on horseback, whip in hand. A sad, disgusting sight, but nobody
seemed to care. There are things to be faced here which
I shall never learn to excuse. But saw funny things,

too; a man carrying a parrot on his shoulder that was continuously screaming insults at the passers-by; brown, half-naked children dancing like crazy little monkeys to the wild drumming of a boy; a furious fat mulatto woman chasing little brats that had filched a melon.

We passed the flower market. So rich, so beautiful! A pity we never stopped. I should like to lounge about there, see the other markets, the park, the fountains, the Government Palace, the church, walk along the red-brick pavements amidst the gay crowds.

Having passed the busy streets we pulled up in front of a detached wooden house. César jumped down and knocked at the door, whereupon faces appeared in the windows, the door was opened, a brown maidservant came out and showed us in, my aunt and me, while our servants were told to wait for us in the narrow shadow of the house.

Inside we were welcomed by a white woman in a morning gown. She was unkempt, seemed to have risen from bed ten minutes before. She greeted my aunt by her name, like an old acquaintance, but with respectful cordiality, acknowledging her as her superior. A little younger than my aunt, I think, handsome in a vulgar way, not a real lady.

She pressed her hand to her bosom to keep her gown from opening. Said she was sorry her husband was away, but she would be happy if she could help us.

She patted my cheek, calling me a charming young lady. Then the door opened again, and a very young girl came in who was introduced to us as Jeanne, her daughter. She was about three years my junior, a slim little person, chestnut-haired like her mother, stub-nosed, with a freckled face, pert and inquisitive. Asked me a hundred questions about France, and my native town, and Paris, and the latest fashion in hats and dresses and shoes, and the Queen of France, and if it was true what people said about her love affairs. As if I knew!

Meanwhile my aunt and her hostess had been conversing in a whisper and had gone out together, saying they would be back soon. I didn't dare to ask questions but felt highly embarrassed when the girl told me her father was a slave dealer travelling about to purchase Negroes and offer them here for sale.

So my uncle's wife had come here for the purpose of acquiring slaves. To prove she was right the girl took me to the window, from where I could see the two women standing in the large yard, while three Negroes were running towards them, followed by a young white fellow carrying a short whip.

The black men stopped at a few steps' distance from the ladies, the white man watching them from behind.

I saw them take off their ragged shirts and tuck up their short pants. Then my aunt approached them and started touching and turning them, pressing their arms and thighs and bellies and making them kneel and open their mouths for her to examine their teeth.

After a short while she dismissed two of them with a disdainful wave of her hand, concentrating her interest upon the one Negro left, I saw her inspect his back and eyes and fingers, saw him jump and squat and run to the far corner of the yard and back to my aunt who still seemed not to be satisfied. I could not hear her speak, for she was too far away, but I saw her give a sign, whereupon the other woman interfered, pointing towards the window where we were standing. My aunt turned round and, seeing me, she sent the Negro to one of the cabins that stood in a row on the left side of the yard. The two women followed him in while the young white man was kept waiting outside.

"Know what they are doing in there?" the girl asked me with a twinkle. And seeing I was perplexed she laughed, saying they were making him strip to see if he was complete! That's what they all do, to make sure the Negro is not sick. Though a dealer would have to pay damages if he were.

She said her father was very careful knowing the risk. Asked me if I had ever seen one stripped! Said she had, plenty! They were all ugly there, monstrous! She hated them, all of them.

That's what she said, a fifteen-year-old girl. I remember every single word. Lord, how modest these Créole girls are!

After a while the two ladies reappeared, followed by the Negro. Was relieved to see that he had his pants on. I saw him turn to the white overseer and precede him to the stables opposite where the two other Negroes were shoeing a mule.

Later, on our way past fields and thickets and through lush tropical woods, my aunt told me why she had been forced to try and get a few Negro hands for the crop. She said that after Uncle's accident there had been a general unrest on their plantation, all kinds of rumors having spread among the slaves. Five Negroes had run away, one of whom was killed when they hunted him down, while the others have so far not been recovered. She supposes they have joined the marooners, that is a whole horde of escaped slaves living in the woods, stealing food from neighboring plantations at night, attacking lonely travellers, and desperately fighting the soldiers of the *maré-chaussée*.

Three blacks died a month later most probably from purposely eating mud or poison. A total loss of eight valuable slaves worth about 2,000 livres each!

It was difficult to replace them at present, she said, slaves fit for field work being wanted everywhere. The three fellows she inspected this morning proved to be worthless, too old and worn and in bad health.

There will be a big auction of slaves in a few weeks, the slaver's wife had told her. Meanwhile they will have to start the crop with a reduced number of field hands, seventy-six, which, she said, means hard work for them, ten more being required at this time of the year.

She depends wholly on her overseer, a certain M. Dubrit, nobody being able to replace her husband as she cannot afford to employ a qualified *économiste,* as they call the business managers of the larger plantations.

She has to take care of everything now that Uncle is lying in bed a hopeless cripple. As a planter's wife she used to rule the house servants and inspect the slaves' quarters, take care of the sick, and Negro mothers in child-bed, and things like that, but the fields were never her domain.

She says it is disgusting for a woman to deal with crops and book-keeping and crowds of lazy field hands and runaway-slaves and all that, but there is no other way to manage. She hopes I can help her by taking charge of the house and the slave quarters in her absence, which, of course, I promised, though I have no idea how to do it. Uncle's is a coffee-plantation of middling size. His richest neighbor, who has a sugar-plantation, owns more than a hundred and fifty slaves and there are some that rule hundreds!

I told her about that wicked brown woman in the boat. Aunt said most of those mulatto women had been slaves themselves before being manumitted. She remembers the one I saw, said she had been a vulgar harlot till she grew too fat and ugly for that trade. With the money she had saved she bought a boat and a number of little Negro boys and an oarsman from an old woman who had earned her living the way I saw for many years. Little Negroes of that age are cheap, Aunt says, and so are the cripples she uses as her oarsmen. Some planters will cut their captured runaways' tendon above their right or left heel as an ultimate punishment, which renders them unfit for field work. Such lame Negroes are sold away for a trifling to people like that woman.

She chained them to the thwart to prevent them from jumping overboard to get drowned. What a monstrous fat bitch of a female devil! It is all so sordid! I cannot forget that sight, nor my aunt's handling of those poor creatures like cattle or horses, examining their teeth, pinching their thighs. What perverse wicked things for a lady to do. Cannot help feeling disgusted, scared, depressed. What a vicious world this is. And last night's disgrace, to boot! I am tired, must try and close my eyes, sleep, sleep, and forget, for a while.

MAY 11TH

I could not finish my record of yesterday's happenings because I really fell asleep. Then I spent an hour with poor Uncle, and then had supper with Aunt and M. Dubrit, her overseer, whom I don't like at all. And later went to bed, too tired to open this journal again.

I should have recorded a hundred things I noticed on our way here, black slaves working among the sugar-canes, cutting them or carrying the cut canes away. In some fields they were decently clad in short pants, some were even wearing shirts, though dirty and ragged, but some groups were stark-naked, no more than fifty or seventy yards away. A shame to expose them to the eyes of the passing children and young girls! No sense of decency.

Many wore broad-rimmed straw hats, the males as well as the females, which is quite reasonable in that infernal heat. No use fanning your face and neck all the time, the sweat runs down your armpits and bosom in streams. I felt quite exhausted when we arrived after a two hours' drive. Had to wash from head to feet and change before seeing my uncle for the first time.

Poor man! His room was so dark when we entered that I could scarcely distinguish the pieces of furniture, the heavy wardrobe, the armchairs and the four-poster in the darkest corner. The air was so stuffy I almost suffocated.

A man had risen at our approach, an old Negro servant, silent like a black ghost. He lifted the shutters a little to let a few sunbeams in, then withdraw into a corner to stand there motionless, as if part of the furniture.

"Hallo Henri!" said my aunt in an undertone, approaching the bed. I followed her. The pallid face of the patient didn't move, but his eyes opened and stared at me.

"Bonjour, mon oncle," I said, putting my hand on his, which felt limp and cool, in spite of the sultry heat in the room.

He kept on watching me while his wife told him how disappointed she was that she could not find any field hands worth their price. I doubt if he listened to her, for his eyes were still resting on me, warm and friendly. Reminded me of my mother's eyes. A handsome face, but so sad and pale. I took to him at first sight. His right hand moved slowly towards mine. I pressed it. He smiled at me, brighter, more awake than before. His wife drew me away saying we had not had

dinner yet, she was sure I was starved, I could see my
uncle again in the afternoon, while she was out in the
fields.

I am glad she was away when I saw him again. First
thing I did I ordered his old servant Jules to open the
shutters and let fresh air and daylight in, which he did
but reluctantly, saying it was against Madame's orders.
Well, he may lay the blame on me if his mistress ever
takes him to task for disobeying her.

Uncle gratefully breathed in the fresh air. He groped
for my hand and pressed it. "Thank you," he said.

"But you can speak!" I answered, surprised.

"Sometimes I can, sometimes I cannot," he answered, smiling at me with a conspirator's wink. Then
he cast a suspicious glance at the old servant. I sent
him to the kitchen to fetch us a pot of hot coffee.

As soon as we were alone Uncle pulled my hand to
his mouth and kissed it, saying he was so happy I
had come. He hadn't felt so delighted for years. Asked
me to let him feel my cheeks, my chin, my lips, caressed
me, kissed me. So touching, his hunger for love and
sympathy! Was a little embarrassed at first, but let him
touch me for pity's sake.

In the daylight his features remind me so much of my
mother's, the same clear profile, the same beautifully
curved lips, the same intelligent, long-lashed eyes. Of
course everything harder, stronger, a man's face, that
of a hermit or a monk. Maybe his long illness, his
knowledge of approaching death, has rendered it so noble. It shows the traits of suffering and disillusionment.

He says he has been a prisoner since he had his accident. His wife has taken over the rule, and she enjoys
it—enjoys her revenge. It seems they haven't been
on good terms for years. He admits he was not always
faithful to her, and when she found out she made life
in this house a hell. So he started keeping away whenever he could—until that fatal accident happened which
rendered him helpless. She knows how to make the
best of it, he says. He is sure she wishes him to die soon.

What terrible things to say about his own wife! Especially how terrible to confide them to me, a stranger
he never met before, trying to turn me against her,

against the woman whose hospitality I enjoy and depend on. His loneliness must have put these atrocious ideas into his head, made him suspicious and gloomy.

He said his wife agreed to give me Helen and César as a welcome present and, in case I should get married, six Negroes as my dowry. I felt embarrassed to have become the owner of two human beings, handsome and nice ones, to own them like dogs or cats. A pity I haven't got the money to buy them better garments.

I had a glimpse of some other servants in and around the house: a quarteroon boy called Louis, about my age, a little squat, not so handsome as César though lighter skinned. He seems to be shy, elusive, taciturn. Aunt is not nice to him, so brusque! But she is brusque to all her servants, snapping at them in a cold voice. It seems they are all scared of her. Helen says Louis is Aunt's secretary, replacing the *économiste*. But, though well educated he is still her slave.

Then there is a butler, Léon by name, a mulatto like César, but double his age. A broad friendly face, though rather plain. Dreadfully submissive. Wish those fellows showed more manly pride. But could they, being treated by her like dogs?

Two very young fellows assisted Léon waiting at table, both dark brown, probably griots. Don't know their names, nor those of the colored women in the house, except Rebecca who is Aunt's chambermaid, a comely wench, a mulatto.

Then there is a fat black woman in the kitchen, which is about twenty yards away from the house, a separate small stone building adjoining an empty barn and the stables, and the kennels where they keep six or eight big brown dogs. That funny stout Negress has a bunch of half-grown black boys and girls at her command. They stared at me in mute wonder when I entered the kitchen.

I haven't seen the stable-boy yet, nor the two gardeners, big Negroes whom Helen and César hate, saying they are brutes.

Was a little disappointed when I sighted our house for the first time. Not very stately, quite unlike the mansions and castles of the landed aristocracy in

France. A plain two-storied house, wooden frames with white stone walls between them—windows without any panes, just shutters to close them, and a shingle roof. Aunt says they don't build better houses because of the many earthquakes. Haven't seen the slave quarters, only from a distance: two rows of small white cabins some hundred steps away from our house.

I had supper with Aunt and M. Dubrit, her overseer: A tall man with bushy brows, a straight nose, hard lips and a strong chin, quite handsome in a manly way, but terribly arrogant and vain. Didn't like his rude manners, the mean names he gives the blacks, his bragging about the terror he spreads among them to keep them from idling, his vulgar jokes, his condescending smile whenever I dared put in a word. It is strange that Aunt should admire him in spite of his boorish behavior. Embarrassing to hear her laugh at his indecent jokes. If he thinks he can impress me by his good looks he is wrong. He reminds me of P.! But even that one knew how to behave at table!

Was pestered by mosquitoes the whole night. In France they leave us in peace at least this time of the year. César promised to fix a canvas to protect me for the future. Not a very agreeable first night. The air was sultry, no refreshing draught, and in the early morning there were shouts and cries and commands, and the crackings of whips from the slave quarters, and half a dozen dogs barking all the while.

This morning I offered to assist Aunt, but she said I had better get used to the climate and new surroundings before taking charge of the slave quarters, which later will be my domain. So I unpacked my trunk and bags and saw Uncle, who, too, has a very low opinion of Dubrit.

He calls him an arrogant upstart, and hinted at knowing the rascal has been his wife's lover for weeks or months, at any rate since Uncle had his accident. I do hope he is wrong. Being a helpless cripple has made him terribly suspicious. Still, remembering the way she looked at Dubrit at supper, her approval and smiles and laughter at whatever he said, you could feel, though not really see, a certain hidden intimacy between them. I would not vouch for her being a faithful wife. But I must not draw rash conclusions. She is a proud woman who certainly knows where to draw the line.

It seems Uncle wishes to make it a habit to kiss and caress me. Poor man! He must have been an ardent lover once, tender and passionate. Was she too cold for him? I don't mind his weak caresses; knowing he is harmless makes all the difference.

Afterwards it was already so hot outside that I preferred retiring to my room to undress and devote my time to my diary. Hope nobody here understands English. Fancy her reading my journal! Must keep it in my locked-up trunk. Should like—but Helen is interrupting me. Somebody calling.

AFTER DINNER

She expects me to spend the siesta in bed, sleeping. But I never feel tired at this time of day, not after the wine and the coffee. Makes me restive, excited. Cannot forget the handsome young man that girl sent me to have her visit announced. Never saw a finer man before. Eyes so attractively blue under his dark brows and hair I should not have taken him for a colored man, a slave. His face as if sunburnt, like a sailor's, not really dark, just healthy. Such a good face, intelligent and manly. How can they treat him like a vulgar lackey?

Wonder what kind of girl she is. Probably like one of those wicked twins. Forcing him to run the whole way, and run back. A mere whim of hers. Out of breath he was, exhausted, his shirt wet from sweating. Told Helen to help him take it off and wash it and bring a clean one instead. I washed his back and manly chest and shoulders with my sponge and dried him with my towel. Saw the initials DG branded over his left breast, Denise Galez being his mistress' name. Ugly old scars from a whipping on his back. What a shame! He confessed he had been branded and whipped four years ago, at the age of fourteen, for trying to run away.

George (that's his name) gave me his mistress' letter, begging me to answer it.

It was a short notice, written with a hasty hand, asking permission to call on me this afternoon, at half past four, signed Denise Galez, and with a postscript requesting me to give my answer on the same note, adding the exact time when her slave arrived and when I sent him back.

He told me she allowed him twenty minutes for the way here and the same time for the way back. Helen says it is half an hour's walk. So I altered the time of his arrival and departure in my answer to spare him punishment. Makes me unhappy to know that bitch has the power to humiliate that boy, maybe ill-treat him, and no way for him to escape her.

He is such a fine lad, so handsome, so perfect. Reminds me of one of the Greek gods in that park in Paris, only honey colored, golden, not chalky white. I had a wild desire to press his chest to mine, just for a minute, and kiss and caress him, not in a wicked way, no, out of mere tenderness and pity. I never felt that way before, not for a grown-up man. Would not have dared to touch him if he were a free man. Pity makes us bold, makes us forget out modesty, which is, perhaps, our weapon to protect us from the stronger sex. Maybe I was crazy to behave as I did on an impulse, washing and drying his fine body myself, but I enjoyed it, was sorry when Helen returned with the clean shirt (which belongs to Léon).

George . . . I like that name. I never knew a man called George before. I am glad the men I hate and detest have different names. None of them could match him, in any way, I am sure. Was drawn to him the very first moment I saw him. *Coup de foudre!* Is this love? If love means tenderness and immense pity, then this is love. Of course I know it is ridiculous, impossible, bad taste they would call it, perverse. But is it perverse to feel attracted to a blue-eyed Apollo? Everything else is perverse, here, not this. George. I wish to God he were mine, mine, mine, mine!

MAY 12TH

Yesterday at dinner asked Aunt about George. She says the girl's father purchased him from some distant relation of theirs about ten years ago. Gave him to Denise as a birthday present when she was seven, the boy being about a year her senior. He grew up with her as her playmate till he was fourteen. Then her father sent her to France for schooling while the boy learned to assist him as his secretary. The girl has been back from France since the end of March. Aunt laughed when ,I told her about George having arrived in a sweat. Said that naughty girl seemed to claim her rights on her handsome boy whenever her parents were absent. She knew they were in town yesterday.

I looked forward to her visit impatiently, hoping he would escort her. Was much disappointed to see a black coachman jumping from the box and only two young girls stepping out of the coach.

Denise looks fifteen rather than seventeen, a little person, very slim, her hips and bust no fuller than mine were two or three years ago, very blonde, her eyes a pale blue, like the color of her dress which is very fashionable, after the latest *mode de Paris,* no doubt; silk fichu, pale blue and white. Suits her hair and eyes and milky complexion beautifully. Pretty in an arrogant, impish way, her pert little nose slightly freckled like a forward boy's. No doubt her fair hair is very eye-catching in this hot climate. A proud little person, leisurely walking towards me, fanning her neck, protected from the sun by the pretty white parasol held by the brown maid escorting her.

We had coffee in the open, shaded gallery. Her accent was pure Parisian, but whenever addressing servants she would drop into vulgar Créole, sometimes using words not suitable for a young girl of her class.

She said she had found life at the convent near Paris very boring at first, but later, secretly, had a lot of fun,

We laughed a lot, exchanging our experiences of that sort of life. Before returning here she spent a few months at a little château of an aunt of hers where she met her future husband, second son to one of the richest sugar-planters in this part of the island. They have more than four hundred slaves! It seems she has not a very high opinion of her fiancé, says he is not much of a man, in spite of the rumors spread that he has contributed much to the increase of the number of babes in Paris.

It is easy for any man to produce a dozen brats, she said, whoring about with actresses and chorus-girls and cheap trollops. But whenever she saw him he looked so exhausted that she was not very hopeful about her marital outlook. Rather cynical views, considering she is not yet seventeen. I wonder if she is still a virgin? At any rate, she is not willing to be duped. Not that girl! I would hate to marry a man I don't love. I would rather remain unmarried. Well, she will find some secret lover to console herself with, like that duchess in the naughty novel I found in Uncle Paul's library at Lyon. They will be married in September when he is back from Paris.

Her father promised her thirty black slaves and four mulattoes as her dowry, which remark made me ask her questions about George.

She laughed when I apologized for changing his shirt, said I needn't be so considerate regarding a mere slave and sent her maid to the coach to fetch that shirt, clean and ironed. She remarked she was quite aware of George's good qualities, she knew that other women envied her for such a handsome servant. But returning from France she had sometimes found reason to be angry with him. In her long absence the boy had been spoiled by her parents.

"He forgets he is not our equal but a mere slave," she said, "so I am forced to remind him that he must obey me, being my property, not my parents." He was given me as a present, not a loan, and when Father took him away from me three years ago it was for a few years, not for ever.

"Next year, when my parents retire to France for good, I shall claim him as my absolute property, not part of my dowry, but mine personally, exempt from my husband's legal rights on my other slaves."

She thinks her parents are ridiculously concerned about her chastity, and therefore forbid her to admit George or any other young male slave to her private rooms. She says it is one of the advantages of being married that parents can no longer interfere. As to her future husband she is not willing to submit to any tyrannical restrictions he might try to impose on her. She is a terribly self-willed little person, no doubt spoiled from a child, precocious, and possibly wicked to the core. Who knows?

She said she had seen the Queen at Versailles, in her royal coach, very majestic, but not half so pretty as people thought. Everybody knew that the King was a *cocu,* and that she had more lovers than pearls to her necklace! Denise seems to like spreading scandalous lies like that. She says she knows France will go bankrupt in a few years!

Later, when Aunt joined us, they talked about my uncle. Denise said her father's doctor was sure Uncle could never recover. Very tactful, to report that to us! But Aunt didn't mind. They discussed him as though he were a stranger. Now I am sure she does not love him any longer. So cold and heartless!

The girl's father suffers from gout and terrible headaches. His doctor advises him to return to France, which M. Galez intends to do next year, when his daughter is married and his son Charles is of age and able to replace him. He is twenty. She invited me to pay her family a visit tomorrow morning. Hope to see George again. Poor dear George . . .

I must admit that she was very nice to me, by no means haughty. Might call her good company, merry and witty and likeable, if she were not so dreadfully mean to her servants. Was again shocked when she departed. Before leaving she had ordered her coach to be made ready for her, but when we walked out into the yard the coachman was still busy harnessing the two white horses, which delay angered her, for she was late. She told her maid to make the Negro hurry by "counting his portion," whereupon the mulatto girl approached him urging him to make haste. She started counting slowly one—two—three, and so on in a loud voice, emphasizing each number by clapping her hands. I saw the poor boy get dreadfully nervous, quite upset. It was not till she had counted up to eighteen that he was standing ready for his mistress to help her in.

Denise had, meanwhile, been talking to my aunt

affably, indifferent to her maid's counting. While getting in she asked her. "How many?"

"Eighteen," said the maid.

"Eighteen," repeated Denise, turning to the coachman. "Remind me of that number when we are back, Mister Lazybones. It is your pay for prompt service, sir. Eighteen, a suitable reward."

I suppose the poor lad will get so many lashes as a punishment, although he may have tried hard to be ready in time. She is a heartless despot, not much better than that awful brown woman in the boat. Makes me sad to remember that incident. To know George is her slave, too. Though, of course, of a higher class, not to be treated that way. I should slap her face if she ever dared to do him any harm in my presence.

MAY 13TH

I returned from my visit to the Galez's rather late; sorry I could not see Uncle this morning. Now he is asleep. Shall try again after supper. I hate to have left him alone the whole day, but I could not possibly leave before five. They were all so kind to me, such really nice people, Mme Galez above all. The nicest lady I ever met, except my own mother, of course. Not at all proud and haughty, just friendly and interested in all I said. I like her much better than her daughter, though she, too, is all right as long as she is not dealing with servants. The moment she starts giving orders or finding faults with them it changes her into a nasty brat. Even her voice is different, then, sharp and cold, like my aunt's. Seems to become a habit here, snarling at servants. Disgusting! Mme Galez is so much nicer, never heard her threaten them. Why then does she allow Denise to be so nasty? Her husband is not bad, either. It is strange that such a big, heavy giant should have conceived a boy and a girl of such slender stature.

Charles is not much taller than I am. Quite a nice boy, though not very manly, with a weak chin, pale eyes and blond hair. I don't like blond men, dark hair makes them look more virile. Like George. Didn't see

much of George, which I regret. Saw him cross the
yard from a distance. He turned and bowed to me
when he saw me smile at him. Then, just before dinner,
I passed him on the stairs. For a second our eyes met. I
do hope he knows what I felt at that moment. Poor dear
boy.

Their house is much bigger than ours, and richer as
well. The walls in the large rooms are covered with
damask and mirrors. There are flagstone and brick
floors. The furniture is not very costly, not much better
than Uncle's. But what a crowd of servants! Too many
waiting at table, standing behind you all the time,
watching you eat and drink, ever ready to change plates
and glasses and things. I hate being watched and
waited on so obtrusively.

After dinner Denise showed me her wardrobe which
is, indeed, very rich and costly. Brought all her dresses
home from Paris, one silk robe, pale mignonette,
tournure, cul de crin, white fichu, white shoes, very
elegant, the latest mode which suits her admirably. Undressed she is as slim as a boy, small buttocks, funny
pointed little breasts with pink tips, her waist so narrow
you could easily clasp it with your hands.

Her maid Marie is a quarteroon, not mulatto, in
spite of her dark brown skin. Her features are quite
European, pretty. Denise made her strip to show me
her nipples, which are thick and dark, very funny, but
her breasts are well shaped, big enough to fill a giant's
hand, as Denise remarked, though the wench is only
seventeen. She is the only slave to whom Denise seems
to be attached, kind and friendly. Shares her bedroom,
follows her everywhere like her shadow. Still a virgin, at
least Denise says so.

Both Denise and her brother welcomed me when
we arrived. Met us on horseback on the road leading to
their mansion. Charles, a perfect cavalier, kissed my
hand, and helped me alight in front of their house. The
smell of burnt sugar is everywhere, even inside, but
you soon get used to it.

Charles is a lanky fellow, narrow-faced, irregular
teeth, not very handsome, but extremely polite. His

voice is high, almost like a woman's, and his conversation not very brilliant. His sister, who is three years his junior, seems to be the wittiest of the family. She likes teasing him, and he is not quick enough to retort.

Their father is polite, too, in a dignified, solemn way. Has a portly paunch, heavy like a pregnant woman's.

Mme Galez is a little fat, too, but her complexion is still rosy, not so pale as Aunt's, and she is very fair-haired like her children. Motherly, placid, good-natured, a really likeable woman. She said she was glad her daughter had taken to me so quickly. Made flattering remarks, said Denise had never had a white girl friend before and had been too much in men's company.

Helen was missing after dinner. When she finally turned up Denise forced her to confess she has a lover here, some mulatto house-servant she met in the kitchen. Denise teased her, asking her questions that made the poor girl shed tears. Had to console her. Denise wished me to punish her, which I firmly refused to do. Why should a servant be forbidden to fall in love? She has a right to yield to her feelings like any white woman. She is a human being, after all.

Hannibal having been sent home on our arrival, Mme Galez offered me their coach and Negro to drive us back in the late afternoon. Charles escorted us halfway on horseback, which was, indeed, very nice of him. When he had left I asked the young black coachman if he had been punished yesterday, which he affirmed, saying, "Yes, madam," no more. She is a merciless little devil.

SUNDAY, MAY 14TH

Was very angry with Uncle's Negro yesterday after supper. Found he had kept Uncle in the dark the whole day, almost suffocating him in the sultry, stinking air of his bedroom. When I took him to task he said it was his mistress' orders. The doctor had been here in my absence and said bright daylight was no good for the patient, forbade him drinking brandy or rum or any other liquor. Uncle was terribly depressed. Had to comfort him, supplying him with a bottle of brandy I took from the cupboard in the dining-room.

He warned me, said I must not provoke Aunt too much. If angry she might throw me out of this house penniless. But she must not refuse him the little consolation he takes from a drink now and then, poor man.

He needs a thorough wash, from head to foot, not only face and hands, and his hairy chest and back rubbed with eau-de-Cologne, occasionally. A thorough wash every day will help a lot, take away the stale, sweaty smell.

Old Jules, his Negro, stinks even worse, has not changed his clothes for weeks, nor washed as he should, the sweating old beggar. He is a carpenter by profession, said he would like to go back to his old work. His wife is the fat Negress in the kitchen. He has not seen his family since he was summoned to come and serve my uncle. How could he, being forbidden to leave the patient alone?

This morning I asked Aunt's permission to care for Uncle myself, replacing old Jules with my own servants, Helen and César. Said Jules would be more useful to her in his old place, which she admitted. At last she consented, but said I must not disobey the doctor's orders. Of course I shall!

Uncle is terribly helpless. Must be assisted when relieving nature, his sheet being changed twice a day. Had him stripped and washed by Helen and César. Such a pitiable sight. Never saw a grown-up white man in the nude before (except Uncle Paul that afternoon for a very short second), but Uncle Henry being a patient makes all the difference. A little awkward for both of us, but creating a mutual feeling of intimacy, shame melted away by the warm breath of pity. From now on Helen and César shall alternately share his room at night. It is Helen's turn this night. In daytime, too, they will serve and nurse him in turns.

Uncle was kind to Jules, patted his cheek and kinky grey hair as the old man was kneeling down to kiss his hand. When the Negro had left Uncle said he was his oldest servant, had been trustworthy and faithful to him for many years. That's why he preferred him as his nurse to any of the brown house-servants who were all trained to obey his wife, not him. But she had put Jules in such awe that he dared not do anything against her orders, even if it meant disregarding his master's wishes. Well, if old Jules follows my advice, he will have a good wash before meeting his long-missed wife. May he have a blissful rest in her fat arms, good old Jules . . .

MONDAY, AFTER SUPPER

I am writing this in the poor light of my candles. Must try and report what happened this afternoon soberly, not distorted by hot emotions, indignation and disgust.

At five Denise picked me up in her coach. Said she was bored to death sitting about alone, Charles being out in the fields and her father busy in his office dictating letters to George.

We drove along a narrow road across green maize-fields, then dense sugar-cane, so tall we could not overlook them. Passed a group of field hands, the males in ragged soiled short pants, the females in shapeless skirts, all wearing old broad-rimmed straw hats (in fact made of palm leaves, Denise told me), a mulatto standing behind them, watching them, whip in hand.

They were hoeing the dried-out soil between the canes, stopping to stare at us while we passed, their dark faces sad, tired, suffering, no smiles, just dull apathy. Behind us I heard their driver shout and crack his whip. Depressing.

Later we were driving along a hot dusty road shaded now and again by a tree. Suddenly Denise cried: "Stop!" and then in a quieter voice she repeated. "Stop, boy. Stop."

Our coach came to a halt. "Look there," said Denise, pointing to a Negro who was walking idly along the road, about a hundred yards ahead. He was almost naked, wearing only very short dirty pants. We watched him for a while sauntering along with swinging hips as if absorbed in a happy dream.

"That's the limit," whispered Denise. "I'm going to wake him up, the lazy bastard!"

The Negro had stepped behind the trunk of a big tree. After a while he reappeared, fumbling at his pants. Denise gave the signal for her coachman to start. At the sight of our approaching coach the Negro spun round and again hid behind the tree. When we reached it Denise commanded her coachman to stop.

"Come here!" she shouted. But nothing moved.

"Come here, or I'll have thy hide whipped to rags!"

The Negro's frightened face appeared first. Slowly he moved towards us, staring at Denise with big, scared eyes. He was a tall, sturdy fellow with a flat nose and thick lips.

"What wast thou doing there?" she questioned in a sharp voice.

He shrugged his humbly bent shoulders.

"Answer my question!"

With both his hands he made a gesture of such disarming crudeness that Denise cast a glance at me trying to suppress a smile.

"Don't lie to me! Thou wast hiding!" she snarled.

"Sure no, Missus, no!"

"How dare thou contradict me! Was thou hiding or not?"

He shook his head, staring at her in mute appeal.

"No!" she said. "Well, then, I'll teach thee to tell the truth. Step aside! Turn thy back to the coachman. Stop. Don't move. Now, Gil, take the whip and hit him hard! No, that's nothing. Shall I teach thee how to handle the whip? Once more! Once more! Crosswise!"

I should have interfered, but I was so shocked I could not find words to stop her. It will haunt me for ever, that disgusting sight, her hardened features no longer a soft girl's face but that of a cold, merciless tyrant.

"That will do for the moment," she said. "It's for hiding and contradicting your mistress. And now, tell me, who gave thee leave to go for a walk on a workday? No more lies, my boy. Come here!"

The Negro had winced at each of the three lashes that hit his back, but he had not even moaned. He seemed to be used to such treatment. He obediently approached her again.

"Massa Pilet said I must fetch a barrel of water for our gang."

"Which gang?"

"Eight, ma'am."

"Thy number?"

"Sixty-seven, ma'am."

"Come here and turn round, that I can see!"

His broad black back was covered with scars. Three fresh swollen streaks were clearly visible. Denise examined the different brand-marks on his shoulder-blades. Beneath the big initials AG, I myself could make out the number 67.

"Sixty-seven. Mind the number, Gil! I wish to make sure that loafer told me the truth."

She pushed him away.

"Is it true? Did Master Pilet tell thee to walk to the well?"

"Yes, ma'am."

"Certainly not! He said r-u-n! Didn't he?"

"No, ma'am, yes, ma'am. Run, he said . . . said Master Pilet."

"Well, then, I'll teach thee what the word run means. Stand close to that horse and keep pace with it the whole way! Don't dare slow down! I am watching thee!"

She gave Gil the signal to start. "Faster!" she shouted when the horses had resumed their usual trot. Gil cracked his whip. The big Negro quickened his steps to keep pace. He started panting and choking, and from time to time he turned his head to cast an imploring glance at the young mistress who was watching him from her seat.

"Don't you think this will do?" I interfered. "The poor fellow has been punished enough."

"Don't be soft-hearted," she replied. "They must be taught their lesson. Else they lose their respect and make loafing a habit. Let me handle that nigger my own way. I know the tricks."

There was a critical moment when the Negro started tumbling as if he were about to collapse.

"Give him the whip!" shouted Denise. "Gil, give him the whip!"

The effect of the lash was instantaneous. The black fellow at once seemed to have regained his strength. For the last five minutes it took us to reach the mansion he ran steadily beside the brown flank of the horse, his own wet back glistening in the sun.

"I knew he was acting. They all try to bluff us with their old tricks," commented Denise.

We stopped in front of the house and stepped down from the coach. Denise beckoned the Negro. He looked exhausted.

"Thou knowest now what thy master means when he says run," she said with a malicious smile. "Now, get thy barrel and run! M. Pilet will tell me if thou art late. Tell him I caught thee loafing and wish thee to be punished severely. Don't forget to tell him! Else I'll take care of the whipping myself, doubling his portion! Now be off!"

I have tried to record that ghastly incident as exactly as possible in order to remember it as it really happened, not dimmed or exaggerated or distorted by my memory. It has shocked me more than anything else I have seen in all my life, worse even than that beastly woman ill-treating her oarsmen. That woman was a fat vulgar slut, while Denise is a well-bred young girl, not yet seventeen, pretty and charming, as long as she is among her equals. But what a vicious little devil she is when dealing with slaves! She ought to be spanked for her cruelty. Her mother should have done so the very first time she was so mean. No doubt she was spoiled and wicked from a child, nobody preventing her from being mean to her servants. Growing up among slaves seems to have poisoned her heart.

They are all spoiled, poisoned, these Créole girls— the slave dealer's daughter, the twins on the ship, that beautiful lady on board slapping her servant's face with her fan. It seems to be a habit among them, hitting slaves, an everyday routine, the cruelty of which they are not even conscious of any longer.

The moment Denise had dismissed the Negro she

was again in high spirits, seemed to have forgotten him, talked about her approaching birthday, which is to be celebrated in grand style, great banquet and music and ball and all that, forty guests or more. Aunt and myself will be included, of course. I am not very enthusiastic about the invitation. I haven't a dress suiting such a stylish reception. And even if I had, I don't wish to be her friend any longer, not since she showed me her real character, unmasked.

MAY 16TH

Witnessed an embarrassing scene this morning. When leaving the breakfast-table to go upstairs, I heard voices on the staircase. Standing in the partly open doorway I could see Aunt leaning against the banisters, facing a servant who was standing a step or two below her. She was speaking in an angry undertone and suddenly she slapped his face. He turned round, trying to avoid her, and I could see it was Louis, the quarteroon. I stepped back into the breakfast-room to spare him the humiliation of knowing I had watched the scene.

Helen, who had spent the night in Uncle's room, asked me if it was wicked to let her master finger her, which I denied, laughing. There is no harm in it since he is so helpless. Seems he cannot keep his hands off a young girl's skin, poor silly man! Even being lame and facing death does not change him. The very sight of a woman's rounded forms makes him lose his dignity, the noble dignity of pain and resignation that suits him so well.

For the first time I escorted my aunt to the plantation this morning. We drove along maize- and cotton-fields to the bottom of the hillside which is covered with tall coffee-shrubs in regular rows. The narrow road there turns to the right, along the green slopes, and, after a two or three hundred yards' drive, back along the other side of the cotton-, maize- and millet-fields to the slaves' quarters.

Aunt says cotton is safer though less profitable than

coffee, which must be attended to carefully, weeds
growing abundantly between the shrubs if not cleared
day by day.

Saw groups of Negroes hoeing the soil, colored
drivers watching them, armed with whips like those in
M. Galez's sugar-cane fields. The blacks all poorly
dressed, some seemed stark-naked, though they were
too far away for me to make sure. One group consisted
mainly of women and children, boys and girls between
ten and fifteen. They were controlled by a brown
wench, the only one to wear a decent garment, not just
a ragged skirt. Aunt said there were two such women
drivers who were in charge of children above ten, pregnant woman and mothers returning from child-bed, and
men recovering from some illness—all of them slaves
who could not do hard work.

M. Dubrit met us on horseback. Had a long talk
with Aunt while I was watching the young mulatto
woman from a distance. Like some of the other drivers
she had a dog at her leash. At the overseer's approach
she had started shouting at the blacks in her charge,
cracking her whip to emphasize her threats. It was
obvious she tried to demonstrate to her master or mistress how efficient a driver she was. In my aunt's place I
should forbid them to carry whips. I am sure there are
other ways to make the blacks work.

On the way out to the fields we passed the stone
floor used to spread the coffee for drying, and a low
stone building in which the dried coffee is rolled and
winnowed to remove the parchment. It is then stored in
sacks, cotton bales being stored in a separate room.

On the way back I saw the Negro cabins, ten or
twelve whitewashed wooden huts, roofs covered with
cane-tops, no windows, no more than about twenty
feet long each. Must be crowded overnight, to shelter
more than eighty Negroes.

When we passed them a few women were staring at
us, some with big bellies, others nursing tiny new-born
black babies. About a dozen little children, all of them
stark-naked, came running to watch us. Aunt told Hannibal to stop our coach. I followed her into one of the
cabins which proved to be the sick-room. A black man

was lying on a mat covered with palm-leaves. At our approach he tried to rise, but she told him not to move. She examined his eyes and tongue and lifted his cover to see if his belly was still swollen. She seems to know a lot about diseases common among slaves, almost like an expert doctor. Ordered the woman in charge to wash the sick man and bring him fresh water. Was quite nice to him, not so nasty as to her house-servants.

Those cabins are badly aired, sultry, smelling of sweat, smoke and worse things; no wooden floors, just hard-trodden earth. The blacks make their fire in the middle of the room at night to protect themselves from mosquitoes.

There is a prison beside the sick-room, empty at present I am glad to record.

Behind the cabins there are vegetable and fruit gardens cultivated by the slaves in their spare time: manioc, sweet potatoes, bananas, melons and other products I never tasted before.

Uncle feels so much happier now. He gets his glass of rum after meals, which helps to cheer him up. Aunt said she missed a bottle. I told her I sent for one to offer a glass to Denise when she called on me (which is true). I wonder if she is still suspicious. I would not like her to know I am disregarding her orders.

Before supper last night I told Uncle about Denise. He said she was right, punishing the Negro we met. Idlers must be handled roughly, else they make it a habit. Sad to know that the quality of mercy has not softened the doomed man's heart.

MAY 17TH

This morning, at an early hour, I heard horses approaching at a trot, and then stopping below my window. There were two riders on horseback, Denise and George. What a surprise! I ran down to welcome them. Denise was dressed like a boy, in white breeches, a boy's shirt and brown riding-boots; George was in a plain grey cotton shirt, breeches and black boots. But what a man!

The stable-boy was already taking care of her white
horse when I opened the door to show my guests in. I
beckoned George to follow his mistress which, however,
seemed to displease her, for she turned round and told
him to stay where he was and wait for her return. Inside the house she said I must not spoil slaves by treating them as though they were our equals. She asked me
how I liked her riding-dress. She preferred breeches to
skirts, riding astride like a man being much more fun,
though her parents would be cross if they knew. They
thought it indecent for a young girl her age. But they
were again in town so nobody could stop her from
having her own way for once. She wished to see my
uncle; said she had seen him but once since he had his
accident.

Uncle was in high spirits, called her his little Amazon,
and asked her how she felt in man's breeches. "Hot,"
she said, which ambiguous answer made him laugh so
convulsively that he dropped back into his pillows
exhausted. He asked her to kiss him for old friendship's
sake, whereupon she bowed over him, brushing his pale
cheek with her lips.

"How charming, your little twins!" he whispered,
peeping into her bosom. "Let me feel them to see if you
are really a grown-up lady!"

She withdrew, laughing, and said there were plenty
of others he might examine, glancing at me and then
Helen who was standing behind me.

"You are very naughty, M. Martin," she added. "Not
at all the repentant sinner you ought to be."

"Not repentant, my dear," he replied. "Just impotent," which made her giggle a moment, but then caress
his cheek and brow muttering: "Poor, poor man. I am
sorry, so sorry for you."

There was an awkward minute of silence which he
interrupted, saying he had heard she was engaged to
marry young M. d'Argout.

"Do you like him?" he asked.

She shrugged her shoulders.

"He will teach you to like him if he is a real man,"
Uncle said.

"If he is," Denise replied.

"If he is not, send him to me to receive my instructions," said Uncle.

"He doesn't need to be instructed, I'm afraid," she retorted. "He has spent three years in Paris and he is still there, receiving instruction from better experts than you, M. Martin, though I never doubted your qualifications in this respect."

Such was the tone of their bantering, and she was never slow in retorting to his jokes, however *risqué* they might be. I admit she is witty and quick at repartee, but she lacks the least trace of virgin modesty. I wonder where she learned that kind of conversation. Well, we didn't say prayers in our dormitory all the time, either!

When we stepped out into the hot yard, George rose from a bench in the shadow of the house.

"Where are the horses?" asked Denise in a sharp voice.

"We put them in the stable, Mademoiselle."

"Who told you to do so?"

"The horse-flies were pestering them."

"Answer my question!"

"Well, I thought——"

"You thought! You have to obey orders, and nothing but orders. You ask my permission before doing anything!"

She was facing him, slapping the handle of her crop against her boot to emphasize her words. I saw him turn rigid at the humiliation to which she was exposing him in my presence, a tall strong, handsome, young man scolded and debased by an impudent, conceited little brat of a girl who ought to be spanked for her arrogance! I am sure she did it in order to impress me, to show off the unlimited power of ownership she claims in dealing with that boy. How he must hate her. But what can he do but bow to her, keep his mouth shut and obey. I hope her father will not deliver him to that little despot when she is married.

Last night Aunt told me why she has been childless to the present day. She had a number of stillborn babes and miscarriages at the beginning of her married life, eight in eight years, which ruined her health and hap-

piness. The doctor must have advised them to stop
trying. Maybe that disappointment estranged husband
and wife for I cannot imagine Uncle forgoing the pleasures of the flesh for the sake of his wife's health. What
man would? Going astray with pretty colored wenches
may have become a habit with him. It is easy to understand her feelings. I must not put all the blame on her.
Disillusionment will harden any heart, even a weak
woman's.

MAY 17TH, AFTER SUPPER

It is a shame, the way Denise treats George. Such a
handsome boy! I never saw a finer one. In France I am
sure he would be taken for a white man, just sunburnt
like so many healthy-looking people. His lips are a
little full, it is true, but not like a Negro's, just warm,
soft, sensual, a tender lover's lips. And his eyes! I never
saw a blue-eyed colored person before, so attractive in
contrast to his long dark lashes and eyebrows and hair,
long wavy hair, not kinky like that of Negroes. Handsome indeed, with his long legs, narrow hips and graceful gait. He must be a good dancer. And clever, too—
well educated and bright. He should not be kept a slave,
such a fine man.

I wish I could purchase him from her and then
manumit him. I asked her how much she would charge.
She said she meant to keep him as he had been hers for
ten years.

"Of course he is very valuable," she commented.
"Say a thousand piastres, being so fair-skinned and
well-bred, a real fancy slave."

A lady from Charleston in Georgia told her that very
light-skinned slaves didn't sell so well in the United
States because it was easy for them to run away and
hide, being taken for whites. But here it was different,
Denise said, all free mulattoes being known to the
authorities. Seeing that George is branded and wears
scars on his back they would arrest him as a runaway
slave and soon deliver him to her father. No, she said,
George would not dare run away again because he

knows what he would risk. I asked her how runaways were punished.

"That's left to their owners to decide," she said. "Some cut their ears or right or left ankle-joint or tendon or put them in heavy chains for the rest of their days, or sell them to the mines or the galleys. My father has his male runaways gelded if they are too valuable to be crippled. You know, gelded, that is cut, like turning bulls into oxen, or stallions into geldings. It makes them tame and submissive, and if you sell them you get high prices for them providing they are handsome, because many fathers and husbands are too suspicious to allow their wives and daughters to be served by ordinary male salves, *toutes pièces*. So they prefer geldings of whom they need not be jealous."

Denise has a way of saying such awful things in such a matter-of-fact voice as if talking of cats or dogs. She is not at all embarrassed. I wonder if she is capable of any tender feelings, real sympathy, pity or love. To me she has always been nice—so far. Why can't she be nice to her inferiors? Why must she keep on humiliating George? If he were white and free and rich she would adore him. It is his station in life that makes all the difference. How cruel fate can be.

Her mother had told her that, as a little boy, George had been treated like a grandson by that old planter's widow. After her death her sons and daughters sold the boy away as if glad to get rid of him. There was some rumor about a loose sister of theirs who had run away with a colored slave, a quarteroon, leaving their babe to her parents' care. But nobody knew for sure. If it was true, why did the child's mother never claim him? I ought to try and find out. If George is a white woman's child, he is entitled to be free. That's what my uncle told me.

I cannot find a single book in this house. Uncle says books are ruined quickly in this moist climate by worms and insects and mildew. Still, in one of M. Galez's rooms I saw a whole bookcase full of books. Must beg him to lend me some for Uncle. It would pass his time, and mine, too, sometimes.

The wretched mosquitoes again! A real pest! Bigger

and wickeder than ours. Everything is wickeder here. I
hate this island.

Branding George, the brutes—his back scarred from
a whipping for trying to run away at fourteen. I am
sure that little devil is responsible for that. She ought to
be whipped herself, with a vengeance! And branded,
and threatened, and humiliated day after day, the heartless little monster!

THURSDAY

Uncle told me mulattoes are, as a rule, emancipated
at the age of twenty-four. It all depends on their owners. Some won't consent, and keep them slaves for their
lifetime, which is very cruel, and quite against the rule
in this island. Denise must set him free, at the latest
when he is twenty-four, that is in six years. A long, long
time. Poor George!

Uncle is very happy I brought him the two books
from M. Galez's library. Read to him the first pages of
Emile by the great J. J. Rousseau. What a noble mind!
How true, how sublime every single phrase of his!

I wonder why Charles picked out the *Lettres Per-
sanes* by Montesquieu. Said he was a very great political thinker, was sure Uncle would appreciate that book.
But I suppose Charles has not read it, as most pages are
uncut. From what glimpses I took it is very naughty,
very audacious, not at all suited for a young girl. But
ever so interesting. About a gelding, a eunuch, who
feels very unhappy, poor fellow. I thought of George
and what they might inflict on him if ever he tried to
run away again. It ought to be forbidden by law. I am
going to read it through before giving it to Louis to read
it to Uncle. He would not like me to know this book,
not the naughty passages!

Had a little earthquake this morning while break-
fasting. All our pottery and china clattered, and outside
the dogs barked. Funny, quite harmless. Aunt said it
happened very often, sometimes so violently that
houses collapsed. Very reassuring!

Charles offered to give me riding lessons. I said yes,

but asked Denise to join us. As long as she is present he won't dare to be forward. I hope she will take George with her.

Still no drop of blood! Am worried consulting the calendar. May heaven spare me the worst!

FRIDAY

Every morning the same disgusting noise outside wakes me before dawn: barking and shouting and cursing, and the horrible clashing of whips and moans and wails. Why can't they drive them out to the fields and workshops in a more decent way? And why so terribly early? Aunt would soon stop it if her bedroom opened to the yard like mine does. No window panes or shutters like at home to protect me from that noise, just blinds that don't help.

I had a ride with Charles and Denise, George following at a respectful distance. My horse an ambling white mare, very docile. Charles said I must not keep so tense, just relax, and indeed I made good progress in the end. Denise is an expert rider, wore breeches again and sat astride on horseback like a boy. They galloped away for a short while, leaving me behind with George. Had a few words with him. I know he likes me, saw it in his eyes!

Mme Galez is of Danish origin, from the island of St. Thomas where her father had a very large sugar-plantation, over two hundred slaves. Of course she turned Catholic when she married M. Galez, much against her parents' will. Danish . . . that's why she is so blonde and blue-eyed like Denise and Charles, a different blue from George's, not dark and intense, but like blue ice, very light. She must have been pretty as a young girl but has grown a little fat.

Most white women over thirty or forty I have met here are fat. I suppose because they are too lazy, sitting about the whole day in their hammocks or chaise-longue, ordering their slaves about, nagging and threatening them, nibbling at candied fruit and drinking sweet coffee and rum and sugar drinks.

But Mme Galez is a nice woman. I wish Denise were as kind to her servants as her mother. Never saw her hit or threaten one—as yet. Whereas Denise is so mean! She didn't speak a single word to George besides a command or two. Would snap her fingers at him the way you beckon a dog. Seems she delights in degrading him as if playing a cruel game. Too much acting. Pretending to be indifferent. But is she? I wonder what happens when they are alone. She says her parents would not allow her to have him upstairs in her own rooms. But she will watch her chances, I am sure she will! Shameless little bitch! That's why he is so nervous sometimes, so terribly frightened, poor boy. Fancy them being caught together. All her parents' wrath would fall on him, not on her. And she would coldly see him punished in that horrible way, not lifting a finger to save him. I do hate her!

Charles is not so bad. Though brusque and haughty towards George, too, he at least is not cruel. Takes his superiority for granted, though he is not so handsome; too weak and receding a chin. Would not be his match, undressed, but very attentive, I admit, the perfect cavalier. Wonder if he is just polite, or really trying to court me? I doubt if I could ever respond. Nice, but not attractive, not in any way, though I would not call him repulsive.

Having my feet washed before going to bed has become a habit I would not miss. Helen says everybody has their feet washed at least once a day, all the whites in this island, and many colored people, too. An old custom, the same as observed in biblical days, even by our Lord Jesus Christ. Uncle says the Turks and Arabs and other heathens make it a religious duty, though, in fact, Mohammed prescribed it for cleanliness' sake. In this murderous climate it is, indeed, an indispensable routine. Makes you feel relaxed and comfortable.

Since Helen moved into Uncle's room, César has taken over that duty, and he likes it. When drying my feet he has a way of massaging and caressing them that makes me think he is in love with my feet! Very agreeable, though a little excessive, almost indecent, itching my soles, watching me askance to see if he can make me laugh. The dear little rogue!

Still no signs! What shall I do if——? Ask Helen? The colored know all kinds of tricks. Must not wait another week.

SUNDAY

Drove to Mass with Aunt, which took us over an hour. But I looked forward to seeing the town again. Wondered at the half-empty church, on a Sunday. It was richly decorated, but not to my taste. People were standing in groups, talking in a loud voice, even laughing, while Mass was performed. Scandalous! Some women very richly dressed, precious finery, lace and jewels. Aunt seems to know quite a few people, though not on very friendly terms, just nodding stiffly.

Outside we were accosted by an elderly gentleman. He was introduced to me as Mre* Falcon, an attorney, an old friend of my uncle's. He inquired after his health, and said he wished to pay him a visit one of these days, but Aunt said her husband was not allowed to receive guests while he was so very sick and weak. She stopped me from speaking when I wanted to contradict her, knowing that Uncle would be delighted to see visitors. She said it was doctor's orders, it would not be advisable to disobey him.

Mre Falcon is a funny little man, very lively and brisk with shrewd eyes that kept assessing me while he conversed with my aunt. He seemed to approve of me. Aunt said she would inform him when her husband was well enough to receive him. She seems to dislike him judging from her flippant remarks when he had left.

We walked across the market where a lot of Negroes, men and women, were displaying their poor merchandise, both fruit and vegetables.

They were mostly slaves. My aunt told me they were allowed to sell the products they had grown on a piece of land left to them by their masters, thus earning the

---

*Abbreviation for Maître; title given to attorneys in France and French speaking countries.

money they needed to buy other food and the bright-colored headkerchiefs they so love. Her own slaves are not allowed to go to town on Sundays as it is too far away, it might encourage them to run away. They are given their weekly ration of manioca, salted beef and codfish, and can tend to the land allotted to them on Sundays to grow fruit and other food for themselves.

Aunt is still very cross because of a runaway. She says if they cannot catch him she will lose a trained field hand worth 2,500 tournois. He ran away to escape punishment. She discovered him hiding behind a bush while she was driving out to the fields.

He said M. Dubrit had sent him to the sick-room, which turned out to be a lie. She was so furious she promised him fifty lashes on Saturday morning. He left work on Friday night with the others, but has not been seen since. As the slaves are free on Saturdays his absence was not discovered before late in the morning when he failed to report to M. Dubrit. Of course, she said, his room-mates will pay dear for not informing the overseer in time. M. Dubrit and his mulattoes started with their dogs to hunt him down yesterday afternoon, but in vain.

She says if a runaway can cross a few brooks dogs will lose his smell, which makes it difficult to trace him quickly. They have been starting again this morning, Charles and the *économiste* from M. Galez's habitation joining them with trained dogs. Aunt is anxious to know if they can catch him alive. I secretly hope they won't find him, poor fellow! She says in future she will have all those to be punished put in chains after work on Friday night to prevent them from running away. She is a hard woman.

We drove slowly along the main streets of the town. So picturesque with the white awnings spread across them to protect them from the sun. Numerous mulatto women in the shadow of fig-trees were selling flowers displayed on long tables. Beautiful, all those many-colored flowers, offered by young women, some of them exquisite, big-eyed, languid, gracious, very attractive with their green and red and mauve headkerchiefs that suit the color of their skin so well. A natural elegance

to be envied. Can understand (though not excuse) any
young white man that gets tempted and seduced by
such refined creatures.

I never saw such a number of coaches in the street,
and elegant ladies with brown and black lackeys in
liveries—negrilloes in fancy costumes, holding bright-
colored parasols above their mistress' head to protect
them from the sun which burns like fire the moment
you enter an open place. César does not look half so impressive in his plain white garments, nor can our two
brown horses compete with the beautifully harnessed
ones of those proud ladies.

Can't help worrying about my situation. What if she
found out? Would call me a strumpet, might drive me
out of her house, penniless. Must consult a doctor—not
Dr. D., by no means. No, better tell Helen, ask her advice. Must make her swear on the Bible not to talk.

SUNDAY EVENING

I am glad they have not caught the slave yet. Maybe
he can hide some place where he can never be found.
Though everyone says he is sure to be delivered to her
because of the reward she is forced to promise. People
that catch runaways often wait for the owner's advertisement in the journal promising 100 tournois or more
to him who secures the runaway slave alive. Poor boy!
I am sure she will have her revenge on him if ever she
catches hold of him.

Uncle says it is wrong threatening slaves. Either
punish them at once, or let them hope their trespass is
forgotten till you think it fit to make them suffer for it.
He says she is responsible for many a runaway case in
the past because of her hot-tempered verdicts.

Read to him a few pages from *Emile*. Makes him sad
and nostalgic. He longs to be back in France. Says he
should not have come to this infernal island, not for so
long.

He remembers his happy childhood in Dublin. Asked
me to tell him about mother, her own recollections of
their early days in Ireland, then in Paris and Lyon.

I was very touched to see him weep silently like a child, poor Uncle. Rather awkward to see a grown-up man cry! Seems to have lost his pride, knowing he is doomed.

Dubrit downstairs with Aunt. He is again invited for supper. I hate his arrogant, bragging rude manners. On Friday night they discussed the whippings to be administered to slaves who had been reported during the week. Such cruel punishments always take place on Friday night to give them time to recover by Monday morning. Serious cases are dealt with on Saturday mornings in the presence of the other slaves in order to impress them.

I am glad there were none yesterday (the one they had picked out having run away, Heaven thanks!). Never, never shall I attend to such a whipping. Revolting, the very idea. Though Denise says she has seen plenty.

Told Uncle about M. Falcon. He was very angry, saying his wife kept him like a prisoner, trying to separate him from the outside world. Said he knew why, but would manage to thwart her. He does hate her. A perfect example of matrimonial bliss!

I had a ride with Charles and Denise again yesterday, but was disappointed they did not take George with them but some vulgar black groom instead. Didn't venture to inquire after George lest they should know I have taken to him.

These beastly mosquitoes again. Seem to be attracted to me more than to anyone else.

"It is your virgin blood," said Uncle smiling.

If it goes on this way they will suck me out to a mummy in no time.

My virgin blood! I wish it would show! God have mercy on me. Could not yet make up my mind to turn to Helen.

MAY 23RD

Thank Heaven my worries are over. I woke up bleeding as though cut with a knife and was relieved. Heaven, was I relieved! As a rule I hate the three, four days every month that keep me to my room with headaches and nerves, but this time I feel happy, so happy! It was a narrow escape. Kept me worrying all the time without knowing what to do. Maybe my prayers in church last Sunday helped. Holy St. Mary, gracious Queen of Heaven! How grateful I am, Your humble sinful servant, never will my thanksgiving prayers to You end. Never shall I trespass again as I did, never!

Told Helen to kill the armies of ants that are invading my room again and again. She put the legs of my bed in pails full of water to protect me. There ought to be a poison against them.

Sent César to Denise to cancel riding lessons for a few days, whereupon she called on me. Said she was never much bothered by her days and needn't even stop riding. I do envy her. They use cotton, raw cotton, here. Very comfortable.

Denise told me shocking things about a woman called Gillet whom we saw in church last Sunday. They have cut her dead for years, and right they are—such a heartless lying bitch of a harlot. Aunt made hints after passing her, but would not give me any particulars.

It seems the husband is an old brute and his wife, twenty years his junior, cuckolds him whenever she can, a lewd man-mad wanton. Once they sent a slave over to M. Galez informing him that one of his Negroes had been caught at night with a slave girl of theirs. They had beaten him so badly that he could not walk.

M. Galez sent his overseer, André, a handsome quarteroon, to fetch the slave in a cart. André was received by Mme Gillet who told him her husband was absent. She offered him a glass or two of rum and had one herself, whereupon she began to become very friendly, too friendly for the poor fellow to keep calm. He started resisting her whereupon she became aggressive, like Potiphar's wife.

André pushed her away and fled, turning to the slave quarters to fetch the injured slave. An hour later both M. and Mme Gillet called on Denise's father accusing André of having assaulted Mme Gillet with the intention of raping her.

M. Galez said he didn't believe a word of it, knowing André was a decent fellow, faithful to his own girl, a pretty quarteroon like himself.

They threatened to call the police and have André arrested and tried. Knowing that a slave would not have a chance in court if accused of such a crime, as his fate always depended on the white woman's evidence, M. Galez sent for André and confronted him with Mme Gillet. But in his presence she calmly repeated her fantastic accusation, in spite of the poor fellow's pathetic denial.

"I want this rascal to be hanged!" cried the irate old man.

M. Galez, who still believed in André's innocence, tried in vain to appease him, offering money or any other compensation.

Finally Mme Gillet interfered saying: "All right, this man may live, but I want him to be gelded. I wish my husband to be present at the operation to make sure our demand is fulfilled. If it is not done by tomorrow night, we shall turn to the police to deal with the fellow."

To spare the poor boy's life M. Galez finally consented, ordering some slaves in to put André in chains. But the latter was so desperate that he jumped out of the window and ran away. M. Gillet, who was carrying a gun with him, shot at the fugitive and killed him before his master found time to interfere. Afterwards M. Galez sued the murderer for high damage, but in the end he lost his case.

Since then the two families have been bitter enemies, catching each other's slaves and detaining them whenever they have trespassed on their ground, and killing each other's dogs and cattle if found on forbidden land.

What a beast of a woman. And she looked so harmless last Sunday, a pious churchgoer, neither pretty nor plain, just insignificant, like hundreds of others. Pale, her nose a little beaked. She had the dignified gait of a virtuous bourgeoise, and underneath she is a cold-blooded murderous harlot!

Maybe it is the climate that breeds such monsters. They seem to be more numerous here than in my home country. M. Rousseau insists man is good. Perhaps he would have changed his opinion if he had lived here for a while. Once I thought wickedness was only to be found among males. How wrong I was. It seems we are all bad to the core, letting the brute in us loose when tempted by the flesh.

Now I know why George is so terribly frightened sometimes. He knows what happened to André, knows that Denise may ruin him in the same way if ever she wishes to. A single hint that he tried to touch her, and he would be lost. I am sure she has threatened him many a time and made him do whatever she liked in that way. She is a bitch, I know she is!

MAY 24TH

Denise's parents are giving a great ball on her birthday, which is on June 9th, and we are invited!

Aunt has promised to take me with her to town next week to have a suitable dress made for me, something better and more *à la mode* than what I have brought from France. Something with stays, which are regarded as indispensable for such grand occasions, though young women seldom wear them on ordinary days in this hot climate. Well, at least I have enough to fill them, not like Denise, whose figure is less developed than mine was two years ago.

Aunt says she is going to town, anyway, to help Dubrit purchase a number of field hands for the crop. There is a public auction there on Thursday, blacks from different plantations for sale, not savages who would be much cheaper but less useful as it takes almost a year to break them for field work and make them understand our language and get used to the climate. She says some get sick and die before becoming profitable, that's why she prefers plantation hands. Savages are sold on board the slave ships, not in town. I am not going to attend the auction. I should hate to see the poor blacks exposed for sale. Must be dreadfully humiliating for them. Women should not be admitted. It is indecent.

Happened to overhear Aunt scolding Louis in the gallery this morning.

"Don't dare contradict me, boy!" she said in a shrill voice. "You stay here and do what I tell you. I have a good mind to sell you the next time you are impertinent. I don't like my slaves to get above themselves. Now behave, and go back to your work!"

He slunk away past me like a beaten dog, poor lad. She is always so rude to him, so full of venom, nagging and censuring him for trifling things. It is a shame.

I told Uncle who grew very angry. He said he knew she hated the boy from his birth because she suspected him of being her own husband's son, which, in fact, he is, as Uncle admitted to me.

I should not have guessed, though he is a little squat like Uncle, but not so handsome. His lips are too thick and his nose too fleshy. But now, knowing they are father and son, I see a certain likeness in their features, though not remarkable. On Uncle's advice, the boy's mother who was one of Aunt's quarteroon house-maids, told her mistress his father was some white visitor who had spent a few nights with them. But Aunt was suspicious from the beginning. In vain Uncle tried to persuade his wife to free the boy.

He says she always refused out of malice and jealousy, and avarice to boot, because Uncle gave the boy a good schooling and has been training him to become an *économiste*, able to run the plantation by himself. Such light-colored slaves get top prices if sold, which she seems to intend to do should Uncle die. He cannot prevent her from selling Louis, nor can he free the boy himself because of their marriage-contract which entitles her to dispose of all the slaves she brought into marriage as her dowry, and all their issue as her life property to her own pleasure.

"It was a mistake," Uncle said. "I should not have told her the truth. I did two months ago, after my accident, when I thought I was going to die. I hoped I could move her to free Louis considering that it was my last request. I thought she could not be so mean as to keep my own son in slavery. But she is going to. Unless I can force her to give in."

I don't know what he has in mind. Being a poor help-less cripple he won't be able to protect his son, though I don't particularly like the boy, his sullen mein and his evasive manners. I do pity him though, especially as he is, in fact, a cousin of mine, his father being my mother's brother.

My uncle was not a very faithful husband, sleeping with a servant-girl so soon after marrying Aunt. At that age she was pretty enough, I am sure. I should never forgive my husband (if I ever get married) such an infidelity, whoring with a brown bastard wench living under the same roof! Men are wicked!

FRIDAY

Helen told me last night why my aunt was so mean to Louis. He had asked permission to ride the horse Uncle had given him some time ago. But she strictly forbade him riding on horseback ever again on the pre-text that she had seen him galloping about instead of working.

"When I send you to the atelier, you make use of your legs like any other slave. You run, sir!" she said.

Uncle had used the boy as his assistant, keeping books and writing letters and checking the weight of the coffee and cotton brought in by the field hands and things like that. But since Uncle's accident Aunt has kept him confined to the house, using him as her sec-retary and book-keeper and *économiste,* which leaves him but little time to see his father. How he must hate her! But she has the whip-hand, no doubt of that.

I am deeply dejected at what happened this morning. Went for a ride again, Charles and Denise having called on me very early. Glad they took George with them. I smiled at him when the others did not see, and how he responded! The sweet language of eyes!

They had a dog with them that kept barking at the stable-boy who was in a hell of a fright. All Negroes are afraid of dogs, says Denise, because they are trained to hunt runaways down.

Slaves had reported that they had seen a family of

wild hogs in the wood. That's why both Charles and Denise were carrying rifles, in case we should find the beasts.

We crossed the wood that borders their estate to the south when suddenly the dog started barking at a tree. Denise stopped and got off her horse. She looked up the tree but could not see anything wrong. Then Charles pointed at a black spot on the ground a few steps from the tree.

"A fireplace," he said. "Somebody must be around."

Denise looked up the tree again, and discovered a black man's foot amidst the foliage high up.

"Come down or I'll shoot!" she cried, turning her rifle upwards.

"Pull the dog away!" shouted Charles. "The fellow is frightened!"

George dismounted and took the barking beast by the leash, tearing it off the tree.

"Come down or I'll shoot!" repeated Denise imperatively. As nothing moved she fired, whereupon I saw a black body slide down the trunk and run away.

"Stop!" she cried. "Stop! Let the dog loose!" The next moment the dog jumped at the fugitive.

"Canst thou not stop when I say stop?" cried Denise approaching the Negro. She had dropped the rifle and seized the crop which she had stuck into the leg of her boot. I had never seen her so furious before. She hit the poor fellow across the face and shoulders and flank till Charles interfered, saying she had better leave that to the slave's master. Like a mad Maenad she behaved, disgusting!

They soon saw from the brand on the Negro's breast that he was not one of theirs, but my uncle's. No doubt he is the fellow who ran away last week. He must have hidden in the wood all the time, feeding on what he found and caught and could steal at night. He looked terribly exhausted, dirty and starved, all rags and skin and bones—a pitiful sight.

They tied his hands behind his back with the leash and told George to take him to his mistress and wait there for us to return. The poor Negro could scarcely walk. There was blood running down his flank from an ugly wound, the dog having bitten him above the hip.

I didn't enjoy the ride after that. Denise is so beastly callous, so pitiless, sometimes. She was not at all ashamed of her outburst of fury. Said she hoped the scoundrel would get his desert, runaways being the worst kind of rotten rascals.

Aunt was very grateful and offered them her reward which they, of course, refused. She said she had not yet made up her mind how to deal with the fellow. Charles advised her to let him recover so as to be strong enough for a severe punishment. Denise again hinted at her father's atrocious penalties. How can a young girl be so heartless!

Poor Uncle looks very pale and tired today. Fell asleep while I was reading to him the sublimest passages out of *Emile*. If everybody were so noble-minded our world would be Paradise.

SATURDAY

Aunt asked me to attend to the prisoners while she was checking this week's accounts and results with Dubrit. That brute! Last night at supper he advised her to keep the runaway in chains for the rest of his life and have him whipped every Saturday morning in the presence of the others in order to impress them. In vain I tried to put in a word for the poor lad. Dubrit's verdict is law to her. She is as dependent on him as if he were her master. It is degrading, that kind of adulterous devotion.

I went over to the slaves' quarters with Helen. An elderly withered Negress unlocked the door of the prison for me. The abominable smell of hot sweat and worse things made me almost faint. I ordered two of the black women present to carry out the pails from which the worst stench rose.

Peering in I was shocked to see two men in chains fixed to the wall. One was the runaway they had caught yesterday, the other a sturdy fellow with a number of open lashes on his bare back. Had been whipped last night in the barn by Dubrit, fifty lashes, which is murderous. For repeated disobedience, Dubrit said, and Aunt consented. They keep him in chains till Monday morning, to boot! I should stop such barbarous measures if I had the power to interfere.

Dubrit is a brute, particularly when he is drunk. I can smell the liquor the moment he opens his big mouth. Helen says twice or three times a month he is roaring drunk, smashing glasses and mirrors and chairs and beating his servants till they lie about unconscious. I wonder Aunt does not stop that, instead of suffering him to stay away from work the next day to nurse his hangover. He is the only person she allows to contradict her, even bellow at her when ill-humored, like last night, the boor! He was bragging about his amorous adventures in my presence and Aunt was laughing instead of stopping him. I was so vexed that I rose and walked out in mute protest. I don't care if she is cross.

I am glad I can make myself useful at last, attending to the prisoners and the sick. I hope she won't interfere when I try to improve things.

I had the prisoners' fetters unlocked and allowed the poor boys to come out into the open and lie in the shade for a while. Helen rubbed their backs with salty water and then with oil she had brought with her.

The runaway's left hip is badly hurt by the dog's bite. Had to strip him to nurse the ugly wound. Embarrassing, but could not be helped. Tried to look calm and indifferent like an expert doctor, used to such sights. Men are monstrous there, perhaps blacks worse than whites. I wonder how their women can stand them without being hurt. The poor beggar's flank was torn open, the raw flesh covered with dirt and blood and purulent discharge. Helen had a bottle of strong rum in her basket. She said it was better than salt water to clean the wound. It must have hurt him terribly. She finally covered the wound with cotton, soaked in rum, and bandaged it. She is an expert. But I can do it myself next time.

In the sick-room there was but one man lying with a bad bellyache. Helen gave him a big spoonful of castor-oil to drink, which made him pull faces like a monkey. I could not help laughing. On Saturdays nobody wishes to be sick, that is why we had so little to do.

I saw a woman with a new-born babe, two days old, sucking at her big brown breast with closed eyes, happy little creature, unconscious of the sad fate to which it is doomed. Negresses deliver them much more easily than whites, and can return to work the next day, so it is said.

I sent the prisoners back in without chaining them to the wall. The can't run away, anyhow, with their ankles carrying heavy fetters. I told the old woman-jailer to keep the prison clean and feed the prisoners well. Threatened to punish her if I found the place dirty next time.

Aunt says a brocade overgown in pale rose would suit me well for the ball, but I should prefer white or dove-blue muslin which is more appropriate to the climate. *Vertugadins* are no longer the fashion, she says, and never were in this island.

She warned me not to be hopeful about Charles courting me. As if I were keen on catching him! Rich planters' sons, she says, may dance attendance upon pretty poor girls, but they will marry rich ones who bring them dozens of Negroes as their dowry. Aunt says she cannot afford to give me more than four or five, but there are enough young planters who will content themselves with such a small dowry. Many a man started his plantation with fifteen or twenty slaves, no more, and succeeded in doubling their number in a few years.

I hate thinking of marriage as a mere business contract. Never shall I marry a man I don't love. I would rather remain unmarried, a spinster, or find a colored husband, a man like George, devoted and faithful to me, and turn back to France with him where he would be accepted as everybody's equal, such a fine, handsome, clever man!

MONDAY

César is a dear little fool. But he is going too far—kissing my feet after drying them, tickling my soles with his caressing lips. Had to stop him, but could not help laughing. Silly little rogue. But I like him. So devoted to me. He admires me like a queen. Would go through fire and water for me, no doubt of that.

I saw a calenda at M. Galez's plantation yesterday evening. Charles and Denise took me to the slaves' quarters where there were a great number of Negroes assembled, about fifty, I guess.

They formed a circle round the dancers, half a dozen couples or more. When some of the dancers grew tired others stepped in from the crowd. They didn't like us whites to watch them, but they soon forgot our presence in the excitement of their wild dance, the spectators clapping their hands, thus emphasizing the rhythmic beating of the drums. But the dancers! I never saw anything so indecent, the men and women clapping each other's thighs and moving their bellies in a way that would make a sailor blush.

Denise was laughing all the time, even joined the black spectators in clapping their hands. I was fascinated against my will. I should have turned away for decency's sake, but seeing Denise so merry I didn't wish to be called prudish. Charles kept by my side, shrugging his shoulders and smiling at me to show he found it ridiculous, no more. Denise afterwards said the verses they sang were very lewd. Fortunately I didn't understand a single word of their gibberish.

Yesterday morning I was angry with Felipe, the runaway, because he had torn off his dressing and allowed his wound to be smeared with dirt again. It looks ugly, festering and badly swollen. Helen cleaned it and fixed a new dressing, partly round his thigh, partly round his waist to secure it. Made him promise to be more careful. He was hot, seemed to be in a fever. I am going to see if he is better now.

MONDAY AFTERNOON

Witnessed a most repulsive scene this morning.
I found Felipe had disobeyed me again, had torn

off his bandage and covered his wound with dirt. He must have rubbed it in on purpose.

I told him I would report it to his mistress if it ever happened again. He nodded his head, no more, listless, somehow unattainable.

On our way back I met my aunt who was coming from Dubrit's house. She looked pale and dejected and seemed to have been weeping. She inquired after Felipe's wound, and I told her of his strange behavior. She was furious and said she wished to see for herself.

We walked back together to the prison, and found Felipe had torn the new bandage off again. Aunt flew into a rage, slapped his face, boxed his nose and mouth and kicked his shin and thigh in a fit of blind fury.

I tried to stop her, shouting that she was killing him! I had to tear her off to put an end to the revolting scene. I never saw her so transformed, her eyes glassy hard like a mad woman's. Then she turned her anger against me, saying I should have chained him to the wall, it was part of his punishment, she didn't like anyone disregarding her orders.

She had the dressing renewed, threatening to torture him if he tried to tear it off again. She ordered Helen and the black women present to bind his hands to his feet behind his back and chain him so that he was forced to keep lying on his right side, unable to touch or push off his bandage.

On the way back home she calmed down, apologized, explained her nerves were overstrained these days. Still, the boy had got his desert, she said, no good pitying him as he had intended to kill himself by letting the wound poison him—out of mere malice, so that she would lose a valuable slave. Sometimes, she said, it was like a contagious disease, these attempts at suicide. If one of the slaves gave an example eating mud all the time, others would imitate him, and in no time she might lost half a dozen of her slaves. It was necessary to strike back to bring them to reason.

I am sure such horrible things would not happen if the poor blacks were treated with more kindness.

I didn't see Dubrit the whole day. There is something

wrong between them, and she is the one that suffers. How strange a woman she is. Hard and soft, hot and cold, frail and ruthless, kind and cruel. Sometimes I hate her, yet I cannot help feeling sorry for that silly infatuated woman. Obviously she is not happy living in sin.

WEDNESDAY

Poor silly Uncle resumed his amatory attempts as soon as we were alone. I let him. Why not? There is no harm in pleasuring a helpless cripple. He is still a handsome man when shaven, his facial traits being refined by long suffering. It is certainly no sin to be kissed and caressed by your next of kin when nothing worse can follow.

I was a little more permissive this time, as a revenge on his hard and faithless wife. He said my bosom is the most perfect he has ever seen. Vain compliments of course. So pathetic, his limp hand trying to explore me. I helped him out of mere pity. There was no yielding to sinful desire on my part and therefore no reason to repent, though next time I had better lock the door. I should not like being caught by Aunt!

I do hope Dubrit will be riding on horseback tomorrow, and not keep us company in the coach. I hate to feel his knees against mine, his hard eyes stripping me like a prospective prey, making Aunt jealous of me without there being any reason. If only she knew how much I detest her beau. I am sure he is a brute in bed, like Pierre. They are all brutes, except George. He would be tender and considerate, all love and devotion. God save him from Denise!

FRIDAY AFTERNOON

I don't feel sleepy, in spite of the tiresome drive home in the sultry early afternoon heat with my aunt again and again impatiently urging the coachman to make haste. I was all dust and sweat when we arrived. I had a cool bath prepared in my room by César. Very re-freshing. I met Aunt again in Uncle's room, already out of her mind with anger and disappointment. But I had better record things in good order, from the start. I am trying to write in my hot chamber, pestered by a million beastly flies swarming around me in the sultry air.

Yesterday morning, when we departed, Aunt told me Dubrit could not escort us as he was indisposed. I know he was drunk as a lord the night before, because Helen had told me. Aunt looked very pale and dejected and was absent-minded half the way to town, then she slow-ly came to life again.

She told me she would have to purchase the Negroes herself as Dubrit could not come.

She said we were staying with a friend of hers, a cer-tain Mme Cartier, a planter's widow who had retired to town with some of her slaves, hiring them out to earn her living. She was sure Mme Cartier would find her a white man to escort her to the slave auction and do the bidding for her. She said it was considered bad form for ladies to go to a slave auction unescorted. She wishes me to keep her company there. Said it was useful for me to learn how careful a planter must be when purchasing slaves, the dealers using plenty of tricks to make valueless creatures look healthy and strong.

We only had two servants with us beside the coach-man, namely César and Aunt's maid, Rebecca. A cart was to be sent to town on Friday morning to fetch the newly purchased slaves from the yard and take them home.

Mme Cartier proved to be a fattish middle-aged woman. She must have been pretty when young. Has a Greek nose and sensual lips and very big eyes, dark and attractive. She is a charming hostess and a de-voted friend of my aunt's. Likes to have a good laugh, which makes her heavy breasts tremble like an earth-quake.

She kept three colored boys busy all the time while she was telling us saucy anecdotes scarcely suitable for ladies' ears. She has trained her slaves to obey mere signals, like clapping her hands, or rapping the edge of the table, of smacking her tongue, or snapping her fingers. If ever one of the fellows failed to respond to such a signal she would pinch his cheek good-humoredly, though hard enough to hurt him, for once or twice I saw the victim wince.

"They are all geldings," she explained to us with a twinkle. "You see, my late husband was much too suspicious to allow virile bucks to serve me. As if I had ever tried to cheat him! If all the wives in this sinful town were as faithful to their husbands as I was to mine, life would be dull: no more scandals, no more gossip. What else could we talk about at table?"

On our arrival we went to the dressmaker, a quarteroon woman owning a workshop with a dozen girls and a few male slaves employed as tailors, a very busy house.

We chose a fine, plain, sky-blue muslin, to be fringed with beautiful white lace, the finest I ever saw.

I was so happy Aunt allowed me such costly finery. The dressmaker made flattering remarks about my waist and bust, said I can wear soft stays and the *décolletage* very low as it is the mode this year. She promised to make six of her slaves work on it deep into the night to have it ready the following week for a second fitting.

On the way back we went to a shoemaker's to have our new shoes made to measure, hers brown, mine blue, both finest buckskin. I never wore such elegant shoes.

After dinner I spent the hot afternoon in the guest-chamber, having a nap and a cold wash. Towards four our hostess escorted us to the slave-market.

"It is one of the rare entertainments we poor women are offered here," she said. "I wonder if there are any fancy slaves for sale. I hope to find some pretty colored wench for Camille. My son will be sixteen next week. Time for any healthy boy to be given a mate. I should not like my son to mix with common harlots. They might ruin him."

Aunt told me later that it is a common practice among the rich to give their young sons colored bed-mates in order to prevent them from getting used to dissipation. Such free liaisons often last till the boy is married to some white girl of good family. As a rule his first girl is rewarded by being freed and paid off with an amount of money and a few slaves. Our dressmaker, too, was once a slave, manumissed by her grateful white lover and now herself the owner of more than a dozen slaves.

Boys are indeed privileged! Imagine us girls being entitled to select our mates among the colored boys the same way! There would soon be more colored brats than white ones. Would that be so very bad?

We were not the only women driving to the slave-market. From every direction coaches appeared in which ladies in tinsel finery sat fanning their bosoms. Other women and young girls were walking by twos and threes towards the entrance of the fenced-in yard, all of them chatting and laughing in pleasant anticipation. They seemed to be the wives and daughters of simple tradesmen who were not rich enough to buy slaves, but wished to satsify their curiosity.

At the entrance, a young man, poorly clad, helped us alight. He had been summoned by Mme Cartier to escort us through the slave-market. An ugly plain little fellow, bow-legged, boorish in his manners, one of the numerous poor whites standing about in town living from hand to mouth, yet feeling superior to even the richest of colored people.

Aunt says Mme Cartier has employed him for years to help manage her slaves, over thirty in number, taking groups of them to the tradespeople and housewives that have hired them from her, finding new employment for them and reporting on their health and conduct.

All the white ladies I saw were escorted by men, only the colored women, walking and standing about, were unescorted. They never mixed with the whites. Whenever we approached one of the slaves whom a mulatto or quarteroon woman was examining with a view to buying she would silently withdraw, respecting our superior rights as whites.

We were welcomed by the slaver's wife whom we had met three weeks ago. This time she was dressed like a fashionable lady ready to receive her guests. She said the slaves for sale belonged to three different owners: the largest crowd, over sixty, to some rich heiress who was departing for France to be married; another group to a planter whose habitation had proved a failure; and a third to a widow who wished to return to her parents in France.

The Negroes were mostly well-broken field hands, with a few house-servants, cooks, stable-boys and coachmen as well. About a dozen colored slaves of different shades were also for sale. They all belonged to the rich young lady of noble family whose name I have forgotten.

All the slaves had been exhibited for sale since Tuesday, but business had been disappointing so far: only twenty-three blacks being sold on the spot, while over ninety males and about thirty females were still waiting for their purchasers.

Aunt says prices are higher here than at the auction where you can often get a Negro a hundred livres or two cheaper than in the open market. That's why most prospective purchasers prefer waiting for the auction. So did Aunt, picking out the ones she wished to buy, noting their number (which was painted on a plate hanging from a cord they wore round their necks).

It was shocking the way the poor creatures were examined like cattle, exposed almost naked to the curious crowd, the males wearing nothing but very short cotton pants while the young and handsome females were all stripped to the waist, their short frocks scarcely reaching to their knees. Only the older women were decently clad.

There were several mean-looking guards standing about, some armed with rifles, others with whips, all watching the visitors from a distance without ever interfering.

The sultry mixture of sweat and perfume pervading the air was repulsive. It was likewise revolting to see so many decent-looking women who would shrink from touching a white stranger's body, calmly pressing a Negro's belly, pinching and squeezing his arms and thighs, making him open his mouth to examine his teeth, ordering him to jump and squat and turn, feeling the skin of his back to probe the scars of whippings, trying to haggle over the slave's price. And my aunt taking part in that shameless bargaining, commenting on a Negro's defects, handling him like a horse-dealer, the young bow-legged fellow standing by, playing the part of an expert slaver, talking deprecatingly of lazy good-for-nothing Bambaras, of obstinate Senegal niggers, of treacherous Arradas.

There was a lot of laughing and giggling and whispering in undertones from many of the young colored girls promenading along the rows of slaves by twos or threes or even fours, watching the white ladies from a distance.

But not all of them were mere spectators. I saw a well-dressed mulatto woman purchase a handsome boy, about fifteen years old, a little darker than herself, and pay his price in gold coins. Carrying his clothes in a bundle under his arm, the boy withdrew behind a high wooden screen followed by his new owner. After a while they both reappeared, the boy having exchanged his short pants for a pair of long pantaloons reaching down to his calves, and wearing a clean white shirt.

Some of the black wenches were sold away to white ladies, but none of the grown-up Negroes, as far as I know. We finally left with a list of about twenty numbers Aunt had selected as worth bidding for the next morning.

Meanwhile Mme Cartier had made her choice among the colored girls for sale. They were all, in contrast to the blacks, decently clad, and so were the colored males, and the ladies talking to them treated them in a much friendlier way than the blacks.

The girl Mme Cartier had picked out was a light-colored octoroon with regular features, quite pretty, fifteen years of age, cost 2,800 livres. She seemed to be indifferent to her fate, looking about listlessly. It is a shame to know she is doomed to pleasure a spoiled whipper-snapper who would do better to be sent to France for good schooling. But his Mama says she couldn't bear to separate from her darling, the silly clucking hen!

On the way back to Mme Cartier's house we passed the Governor's Palace, a big stone building on a place with a fine fountain and palm trees in the center. Quite imposing though, of course, not to be compared with

the palaces I saw in France. Aunt showed me the house
where they play comedies and tragedies and sometimes
even operas in winter.

The streets looked even dirtier than last time. People should not be allowed to throw their refuse into the
open. The stink in some places was almost unbearable.
Like that from a pig-sty. The streets were overcrowded,
everybody promenading in the late afternoon hours, the
heat no longer being so oppressive.

Mme Cartier made malicious remarks about the numerous colored harlots standing about, trying to attract
the white passers-by, exposing their bosoms to the
limit, moving their hips lasciviously at every languid
step. I never saw anything so provoking. I must admit
that some of them look very pretty. No wonder so
many men fall for them. Mme Cartier says they are a
public nuisance, brown snakes poisoning every man
they bite, spreading the ugliest disease on earth.

The boy the mulatto woman bought seems to be a
griot. That is the name they give to the offspring of a
mulatto father and a Negro mother. They treat them
like common Negroes though that one might be taken
for a mulatto. Looked like a younger brother of hers.
Only her features were more refined, almost European.
Mme Cartier says she is a harlot, too. What, then, is
she using him for? It is a wicked, wicked world!

I have learned a lot about Negroes and colored people these two days. Each shade is given a different name.
The offspring of a white man and a quarteroon they call
here *tierceron*. *Métis* are the children of a white father
and a *tierceronne*. The lightest shade is the *mamelouc,*
offspring of a white man and a *métisse*. Some of them
look like whites, but are despised like any other colored
persons. Terribly conceited fools these whites. In France
we judge people by their manners and character and education, here the color makes all the difference.

At supper, Mme Cartier's son was present. An eagle-
nosed, moon-faced, short-legged youth, arrogant and
self-willed, rude language, no manners, bullying his own
silly mother. I pity the poor quarteroon girl delivered to
that ugly young tyrant.

FRIDAY NIGHT (IN THE CANDLE-LIGHT)

This morning we drove again to the slave-yard, escorting my aunt and Mme Cartier. A number of benches had been put up in rows, all occupied by white men, mostly overseers and other representatives of planters I presume, judging from the plainness of their garments. There were only few persons of quality present and no women nor any colored people were seated.

Some free mulatttos were standing in the background, at a respectful distance from the whites. Women I only saw sitting in the eight or ten open coaches that had pulled up, like ours, on either side of the platform where the slaves for sale were being offered to the highest bidders.

The fellow that had escorted us yesterday was seated in the second row. My aunt had handed him the list of numbers she was interested in, so that she could leave the bidding to him after having instructed him how high he was allowed to bid in each case. From her seat in the coach she saw to it that her instructions were obeyed. Other ladies took part in the bidding themselves, giving signs to their male representatives.

In one of the coaches in the background I discovered the mulatto woman who had purchased the brown boy yesterday. She was giving signals to an elderly white man in shabby garments seated in one of the rear benches. I asked Mme Cartier if she knew her. She said the brown woman was the most notorious whore in town, owner of a brothel frequented by rich whites! She called it a shame that such a bastard harlot was allowed to take part in the bidding, competing with whites. Nobody dared send her away because she had powerful protectors.

The blacks were auctioned away by threes and fours, the men getting prices up to 2,200 livres each, women up to 1,500, half-grown boys and girls from 1,000 up to double that sum for the handsomest. Children below ten were much cheaper. My aunt got six Negro males at

2,000 livres each, two hundred less than what they cost in the free market. The mulatto woman secured herself a group of four males at the same price.

While Aunt was settling the payment for the purchase at the clerk's desk I watched that wicked strumpet continue her bidding. All the blacks being sold off, a young light-colored girl was summoned on to the platform. She was not stripped to the waist like the Negro girls, but wore a well-fitting dark brown dress that suited her honey-colored skin beautifully, making it appear much lighter. Her green neckerchief made an elegant contrast to the two shades of brown. I could not help admiring her, but was shocked to see that the mulatto harlot in her coach spread five fingers as a signal for her white agent to raise the bidding price by fifty. Soon she was the only bidder left to compete with a young man who had raised his offer to 3,200 livres.

Mme Cartier was as furious as myself that a mulatto whore should be allowed to purchase a lighter-colored young girl in order to deliver her to her own sinful trade. When that abominable woman calmly went on giving her bidding signals Mme Cartier shouted, "It's a shame!" in such a loud voice that everybody stared at us. I am sure they all agreed with her, but nobody else interfered, either from indifference or because they knew it was no use.

The girl was indeed sold away to that beastly brown slut, an eighteen-year-old maiden, perhaps a virgin, who knows? Sold for 3,500 livres, three hundred more than she would have cost yesterday in the open market! Nobody ready to save her, thought it is against the rule that a mulatto should purchase a slave lighter colored than herself. No other mulatto would, said Mme Cartier, calling that whore's white protectors dirty mean procurers!

She told me that woman had been a slave herself till her rich old master freed her before his death. For some time she earned her living as a common street-walker, but being very pretty she soon saved money enough to buy some girl slaves whom she forced to make money in the same disreputable way as herself.

Today she owns a large house and more than thirty

slaves, most of whom are young females of different
shades helping her to entertain rich clients. Cannot
forget that poor dark lad she purchased yesterday afternoon, a little older than César, very probably still
innocent, suddenly exposed to the rotten shameless vice
of such a place; forced to live among whores and
rakes, perhaps serving them as an instrument of their
infamous debauchery!

Eleven o'clock! Should stop now, feeling a little tired
after writing pages and pages, about twenty altogether.
Never wrote so much at a time, and still such a lot to
remember. But I do want to finish this day's record to
the very end before going to bed. Just the main facts,
no more details. Had to replace the candles twice since
I resumed writing after supper, and they are again
burning low, so I must hurry. César fast asleep in Hel-
en's bed over there by the door (Helen staying with Uncle). Dear little rogue, again and again makes the daily
ritual of washing my feet a tender sport ending in
screams and laughter, funny little buffoon. So comfort-
ing the soft regular sound of his breath. Still a child,
still innocent (though already excitable) and attached
to me body and soul like nobody else in this world.

Impossible to record all the repulsive things I saw
this morning. The shameless way the big fat auctioneer
would handle the females, weighing their breasts, caressing their flanks, lifting their frocks and patting their
thighs to show the firmness of their flesh. Disgusting!
Nor did he spare the poor quarteroon girl. Treated her
like a prize steed, patting and turning her, praising her
hidden charms with a lewd sneer, the fat swine. In her
place I would have died with shame. Strangely enough,
she did not seem to mind. She looked languidly
about, as if bored and indifferent to the stares of the
public, not realising what it meant to be delivered to
that wicked woman.

Then the branding of the blacks! I was shocked to
see my aunt sending hers to the smithy, too, in the far
corner of the yard where groups of Negroes were waiting for their turn. She had brought her brand-irons with
her, I saw César take them out of the leather bag he had
been carrying for her. She laughed at my protest, said it

did not hurt much. In fact it was a little silver plate with
her initials, to be heated and then pressed on to the oiled
skin of the Negro's breast or shoulder. She said it was
necessary, everybody did it, to mark newly purchased
slaves in case they tried to run away which happened
all too often. It helped the *maréchaussée* to catch and
deliver them to their owner.

Saw the mulatto woman again in her open coach,
her quarteroon slave girl sitting beside her, watching my
aunt from a distance. She supervised the branding of
her Negroes. I must admit she looked very elegant, almost ladylike, not at all like a cheap whore that she is.

I noticed that all the slaves, when sold away, picked
up their bundles of clothes and disappeared behind
the wooden screen, as a rule followed by their new master.

Mme Cartier said they all wished to make sure they
had purchased *des nègres toutes pièces* before paying for
them. Embarrassing to see my aunt follow hers, too.
Neither did the other lady purchasers shrink from
that final inspection. At least two of them did, and
then, of course, the mulatto harlot. It seems Denise is
right: everyone is afraid of the infamous Spanish malady spreading among the slaves. A single sick man or
woman can ruin dozens in no time. That's why Aunt
said she could not afford to buy a pig in a poke.

I did not see the end of the auction because of Dubrit
who suddenly appeared alone on horseback. When he
saw me he dismounted and asked where my aunt was,
then walked over to her and had an animated conversation, as far as I could judge from a distance. She
seemed very excited when returning to the coach, said
she wished to drive home at once. Mme Cartier and
Dubrit at last succeeded in postponing our departure, saying midday was much too hot for travelling
and that Mme Cartier would be offended if we deserted
her before dinner. Dubrit took charge of the six Negroes. Said our big cart was on the way to fetch them.
Meanwhile they could be fed from the slaver's kitchen,
at a modest price.

Aunt was terribly upset since Dubrit's arrival. Didn't
tell me why.

We had a gloomy meal, my aunt keeping taciturn all the time, staring at the wall absent-mindedly. We finished eating at two o'clock, then departed at once. Could have melted away in the blasting, stifling heat, sweat running down my cheeks and armpits. Aunt was gruff and irritable all the way and sometimes stared at me as if full of suspicion, even hate! At last she asked me if I had seen Mre Falcon, her husband's attorney, since we met him last Sunday week. Of course, I denied it.

She said he had called on her husband this morning, unannounced. Dubrit being away in the fields. The servants told Dubrit the attorney had been in company with two other men, and they had stayed in the sick man's room for over two hours. She was sure something was wrong. She was going to find out what had happened, what sort of foul play had been started behind her back, and woe to those that had their fingers in the pie! She was on the verge of tears, almost bursting with revenge. Heaven beware me of her turning against me. She is a terrible woman when in a rage.

SATURDAY MORNING

I am going to translate the will into English in case she takes the French copy from me. Good to know the original is in the attorney's hands. She won't be able to destroy that.

It seems that suddenly I am a wealthy woman. If she tries to contest the will, I am ready to come to some arrangement with her through Mre Falcon. I don't want her to hate me. It is not my fault that my uncle has turned against her.

How high-spirited he was this morning. Really happy and talkative like never before. He said that now he was sure she would no longer try to hasten his death. It was in her own interest to keep him alive as long as possible.

It seems they had a violent argument last night, he lying helpless in his bed while she was shouting at him, calling him names, even slapping his face in an outburst of uncontrolled fury when she learnt he had altered his will in my and Louis' favor.

She said she was going to contest the will, that she would never agree to free Louis, that she had ways and means to make that boy deliver her what was her due, and to send me back to where I came from. She called me ungrateful, I had, no doubt, helped to conspire against her. She knew how to find out which of her slaves had informed the attorney, she would deal with that scoundrel appropriately.

Uncle said that, knowing her character, he was not impressed by her threats. In spite of her fits of passion she was, when calmed down, sensible enough to come to terms, accepting the ten slaves she offered her in exchange for his son's freedom. Of course she could force the boy to sign away his whole claim to her, but such a waiver is of no legal value as long as he remains her slave, which will force her to grant him manumission. But the moment Louis is free he can fight any claim of hers exceeding the compensation offered her in Uncle's will.

He said I needn't pity her. As the owner of thirty-two slaves she will be well off. She may buy a house at Cap like so many other widows hiring out her slaves at a good profit. She may marry her lover, though it would mean marrying below her station, Dubrit being a vulgar overseer. Uncle says he does not care. He made me promise to help Louis against her, turning to his attorney whenever advisable.

This is my uncle's will:

1. That my wife, in accordance with our marriage contract, shall receive for her life-time all the slaves she brought to my estate as her dowry: fourteen males and eight females, and all the females' issue, viz. seven boys and five girls below ten years of age. Three of her male slaves and one woman having died since, and six males sold, she is entitled to have them replaced by ten other Negroes (nine males, one woman) of her own choice.

2. That she will receive ten further slaves of her own choice on condition that she will, before my death, eman-

cipate my natural son Louis, born by her late mulatto slave Gabrielle.

3. That my whole estate and securities and livestock, including the rest of my slaves, shall be the joint property of my son, Louis, and my niece, Elizabeth Renault. I wish my son Louis to take charge of my plantation, leaving half of the annual profit to my aforementioned niece, or, should she prefer it, to leave her half of the securities, estate and livestock, including slaves, to be disposed of at her pleasure.

4. That, should my wife refuse to emancipate my son Louis, the whole estate and securities and remaining slaves and other livestock shall be given to my niece Elizabeth Renault, including the ten slaves my wife would have received in exchange for the manumission of my son.

5. That, should my wife die before me, the slaves bequeathed to her shall be given to my niece Elizabeth Renault.

6. That, should my son Louis die before me, his claim shall pass to my niece Elizabeth Renault.

7. That, should my niece Elizabeth Renault die before me, her claim shall pass to my son Louis. In case he is refused manumission, it shall pass to my dear friend Julien Martineau, wine merchant, at Fort de France, Martinique.

That's it. At least the main part of the testament. Have omitted the beginning and the end of it, as they are of no importance. I didn't know our place is called Habitation La Provence.

Date: June 2nd, 1786. Four signatures: the testator's: Henry Martin, two attesting witnesses': Pierre Berry and Jean Calame, both living at Cap François, and, of course, the notary's: Mre Rich. Falcon. Don't know the other two persons, which doesn't matter. No doubt, this testament is valid and cannot be contested. Uncle declares the first testament null and void, the one he wrote when still on good terms with his wife promising her the whole of his estate and livestock.

After his accident she took possession of that document, locked it up in her desk and kept Louis a prisoner in their house, strictly forbidding him to leave it without her consent lest he might summon the attorney to his father's sick-bed.

I never saw a woman so furious, at least not a well-bred one. She seemed to be out of her mind when she learnt she had been outwitted. I am sure she hates me, though she must have realized that I was not in the plot. How could I have informed the attorney, being her constant companion as long as we stayed in town? But who else?

Uncle will not tell me, no doubt he wishes to protect the person that dared help him conspire against her. Hannibal? Certainly not! The coachman is much too servile to risk his skin that way. César? The boy never left us. How could he without my knowledge and hers? The night in town he shared a room with the three house-servants of Mme Cartier's. They would have told their mistress if he had disappeared for a while. (By the way: César says they are not geldings, he saw them close enough! Why, then, did she lie to us?) Rebecca, Aunt's faithful maid, is out of the question. Louis? But he was locked up in the house during her absence. Even if he could have left it, how was it possible for him to go to town unobserved? On horseback? The stable-boy is, and was, strictly forbidden to saddle any horse without her consent or the overseer's. I do hope she won't find out the culprit. She is so terribly hot-tempered and revengeful.

I didn't see her this morning. Everybody in the house seems to be paralyzed by fright, whispering in undertones and gazing at me as if doomed. I am going to the slaves' quarters to attend to the prisoner. I hope he was well cared-for in my long absence.

Louis smiled at me when he passed me after breakfast. He seems to know about his father's will. I do hope she is willing to agree. Ten slaves for one! She would be mad if she refused to accept.

SATURDAY AFTERNOON

I must record something extremely shocking. After translating Uncle's will this morning I went over to the slaves' cabins to look after Felipe. I was angry with the old black jailer because she had again forgotten to empty the pails poisoning the air. I had to leave the door wide open for a while before entering the cabin.

Felipe's thigh was still festering and looked worse than two days ago. I am going to put an end to that stupid cruelty, ruining valuable slaves by ill-treatment. I unlocked his fetters and let him step out into the fresh air and sunshine. If I can save the boy he will never again run away, knowing I am to be his new mistress.

On my return I saw César crouched on the landing in the staircase. He tried to stand up at my approach, wincing and sobbing. I took him upstairs to my room and told him to strip. Was shocked to see that the poor boy's back was covered with ugly red strokes from the shoulders down to his thighs. He burst out crying when I started questioning him. He at last confessed he had been beaten on my aunt's orders because he said he did not know who had informed the attorney.

She threatened to kill him if he did not admit that I had sent him over to Mre Falcon while we were in town. She didn't believe his sobbing protestations of innocence till he had received a severe whipping. Then she sent him away, promising him another whipping to an inch of his life if she found out he had lied to her.

I told Helen to take care of the poor boy while I was away. I ran downstairs and out to the empty barn where the Saturday whippings used to take place. Her butler, Léon, was leaning against the door.

"Ma'am says I must not let anybody in," he said, trying to stop me.

"How dare you touch me. Go away!" I cried.

"Please, ma'am, you must not——"

"Step aside, I say!" I was so furious I slapped his face to force my way to the door. I opened it and ran in, alarmed by the yells and groans I heard. Saw the trembling figure of a boy leaning against the wall, Rex, pale with fright, terror in his eyes. Then, turning round, I saw her and her victim, and so great was my shock, that for a few minutes I watched the scene motionless, paralyzed by the horror I witnessed.

The black man was hanging from the ceiling, naked to his waist, his toes scarcely touching the ground. His wrists were tied together with a rope that ran over an iron hook in the ceiling and one in the wall. When straightened to rope would lift the victim, when loosened it would enable him to stand on his feet.

As the Negro's back was turned to me I could see the marks of numerous lashes crosswise on it. My aunt was standing before him at a table, while her two gardeners were watching her from a distance, each armed with a long whip.

She had not seen me yet, the Negro's groans having drowned the sound of my steps. She was holding something above the flame of a candle. It was a long needle those tip was turning red.

"Still lying?" I heard her say. "But I'll make thee confess! This time it will hurt, really hurt, my boy, and there will be a dozen or a hundred more pricks, till thou confessest or—now tell me the truth!"

"Oh, ma'am, don't, please don't! I should tell you if I knew, I swear I should, but I don't know, I don't know . . ."

"As you like, sir," she said in a mocking voice, turning round to face her victim, the glowing needle in her hand. She seemed to deliberate which part of his body she should choose this time.

"Stop, for heaven's sake stop!" I cried, rushing forward. She looked up and stared at me as if awakening from a trance. She put the needle on the table. Then only I recognized her victim. It was Hannibal, her old devoted coachman! How could she ill-treat him that way, a man over fifty, a faithful servant of hers for many, many years!

"That man is innocent, I am sure he is!" I shouted. "For heaven's sake spare him, I know he is innocent!"

"Take him away!" said my aunt. She looked tired and ashamed, seemed to realize she had done something wicked. Like the day before yesterday, when she had hit and kicked Felipe.

When the gardeners had loosened the rope and freed the old man, the latter broke down.

"Help him out and dress his wounds!" she said, dismissing them.

"I know you think I am cruel," she continued when we were alone. "But I cannot allow my slaves to lie to me. Traitors must be dealt with severely. Everyone has turned against me, even my oldest servants! It's a conspiracy, and you are in it, you, too!" She was on the verge of tears.

"I am not!" I retorted. "You know I am not! I solemnly swear I have done nothing wrong. I never informed the attorney, nor did I send anyone to inform him. I am sure none of the slaves are responsible for Mre Falcon's visit, either. He told Uncle that rumors had spread in town that you kept your husband like a prisoner, not allowing anyone to see him. Remember, you refused to receive Mre Falcon some weeks ago, saying your husband was too weak and ill to see visitors."

"So?" she said. "He is very sick, isn't he?"

"Not so sick as to refuse to see old friends."

"It is the doctor's orders."

"I haven't a very high opinion of your doctor!"

"What are you implying?"

"Uncle feels much happier since he is allowed to breathe in fresh air."

"You seem to care more for his whims than for his health."

"At any rate he looks better than a week ago."

"Wait and see how long this change for the better will last. I wonder if the attorney was wise in putting the cripple's life into the hands of a young girl unknown to him; a girl who may turn out to be a common legacy-hunter!"

"You insult me!"

"Don't tell me you didn't work upon your uncle to have his will changed in your favor!"

"That's a lie, you know that's not true!"

"Oh come!" she said, sneering at me. I was so furious I could have hit her. But I controlled myself.

"You know what I suppose?" I said. "M. Falcon may have seen you in town on Thursday afternoon, or else you were seen by some other friend of Uncle's who promptly informed the attorney. He followed you to the slave-market, coming to the conclusion that you meant to attend the auction on Friday morning, thus giving him the chance to see your sick husband in your absence."

"The cad! But why should I believe you? I have nothing but your word against my own suspicions. Hannibal had plenty of opportunities to play the dirty part of the informer. I wonder if I could not have forced him to confess. My own slaves turning against me!"

"You are wrong, wrong, wrong!" I cried. "And you were very cruel ill-treating innocent servants. You beat César. Very high-handed, indeed! You had no right to touch him. He is mine. Uncle gave him to me as my property, so I must ask you to leave him alone from now on. It is my condition for coming to terms with you."

"All right, he is yours. Any more conditions?"

"You must stop torturing innocent servants!"

"That's no concern of yours."

"I beg it of you, as a favor."

"Why should I?"

"It might help us to come to some friendly arrangement. I don't wish to deprive you of your rights."

"Very friendly, indeed!"

"I mean it!"

She watched me through half-closed eyelashes.

"It is time for dinner," she said, suddenly smiling at me. "Let us go in. I am hungry."

At the table she seemed to have calmed down. She was quite nice to me, which made me agree to help her run the plantation as joint partners. If I should marry I should get a number of slaves, two dozen or even more, as my dowry, the rest I should leave to her for her lifetime or till she wished to give up the plantation. She said she was willing to emancipate Louis on condition that he would leave the whole estate to us, contenting himself with a number of slaves and some money to start a small plantation of his own.

In the afternoon I didn't see her; she was either in the fields or with Dubrit whom I had not met since Friday.

I spent an hour with Uncle. Told him about the cruel beatings. He said he knew she was a dangerous woman when furious, she had killed or crippled half a dozen valuable slaves before, two mulatto girls out of mere jealousy, and once, many years ago, a sixteen-year-old house-boy because he had dropped and broken a precious piece of her china. She had him stripped and beaten till he died under her eyes!

Of course, she was very sorry afterwards, she was always sorry for her outbursts of cruelty when calmed down. She is not worse than so many other Créole women, Uncle says.

From their earliest childhood they have been surrounded by slaves trained to be at their beck and call, to obey every whim of theirs, thus making little despots out of them who have never learned to bridle their passions. He says torturing slaves with a red-hot needle is an often practiced punishment as it does not ruin the slave's skin like a severe whipping.

He married her twenty years ago, when she was eighteen. This is, he says, the average age for a girl to be married in this island. Many brides are no more than sixteen. Girls of the lower classes are often married away at fourteen (to say nothing of slave girls who sometimes get pregnant at the age of twelve). An unmarried girl over twenty is considered an old spinster, so all the parents try to marry their daughters away as young as possible.

When a young girl, my aunt lived at Cap with her widowed mother who owned a number of slaves whom she would hire out to make money. Uncle came to Cap as a wine merchant, fell in love with the pretty girl, and married her after her mother's death.

Aunt was shrewd enough to stipulate in her marriage-contract that all her slaves remained her life-property. She consented to his selling some of them to get the money for purchasing a little plantation. In course of time he enlarged it up to the present size.

He says that, knowing his wife's character, he does not wish her to take charge of it, even as a joint partner. He is sure she would ruin it in no time. Still, there is no danger of her squandering his money as all his securities (to the amount of over 180,000 livres) are held in trust by his attorney. She cannot cash any money without his signature, nor could she pay for the slaves she purchased yesterday in cash; it will all be settled by his trustee.

Uncle is very much relieved to know that his wife at last seems willing to come to terms about Louis. Let us hope for the best!

JUNE 11TH

I haven't opened this journal for a whole week. Was paralyzed by the shock, the terrible events, the heavy responsibility that has so suddenly fallen on my frail shoulders.

So relieved the funeral is over. Never knew she had so many friends—the solemn pomp, the church for once overcrowded, though mostly by the rabble. It reminded me of those swarms of horse-flies that will greedily settle on bleeding wounds. I must have become the gossip of the town, everybody staring at me as if I myself had committed the crime.

Must try to record everything as it happened from the moment I made the last entry.

It is true I was quite confident that afternoon, thinking my aunt had calmed down and was ready for a compromise.

I had supper with her and Dubrit, the rascal! Never liked him from the start, in spite of his good looks. Disgusting his way of sizing you up as if stripping you with his eyes.

He seemed to have recovered well from his indisposition as he called it. She could not turn her eyes from him, poor silly woman, falling for that arrogant upstart ten years her junior. That time he behaved much better towards me than before, quite affable and not so condescending any longer. He paid me compliments that must have vexed my aunt, for she again grew nasty to me, saying I was a clever little thing, laughing, but in a sneering, malicious way that made me blush.

They mostly talked about the work in the fields, the crop and prices, and the field hands to be punished that Saturday night for trifling trepasses, quite a number, at least eight or ten.

Whatever punishment he proposed she agreed to, and when I protested, finding twenty lashes too severe a verdict for disregarding a foreman's order she said:

"Make it twenty-five!" Just to show me she didn't care a rap for my opinion.

Dubrit, of course, seconded her, saying it was necessary to hit hard at the least sign of disobedience among the blacks in order to keep them submissive. There was one case they decided to handle in a particularly drastic way. One field hand had been caught stealing a chicken. Dubrit proposed to have the thief whipped in the presence of all the other slaves assembled in front of the barn on Sunday morning, fifty lashes!

"You will kill him!" I cried.

"All right, make it thirty," she said. "Thirty tomorrow and thirty tomorrow week, and make him work in chains the week between."

"Don't you feel pity for the poor fellow?" I asked.

"Thieves must be punished," she answered coldly.

"At least you should spare him for profit's sake," I retorted. "I think it is silly to ruin a valuable slave worth hundreds of piastres."

"My dear mademoiselle," interfered Dubrit. "I fully appreciate your considerations, but believe me, Mme Martin knows how to handle her slaves better than you. You are new to this island. All newcomers say we should be more lenient, but having spent a few months or years here they all learn to adopt our methods. If we spared that thief, others would be encouraged to follow his example. Better lose one man or two a year if it keeps the others in awe and submission than be forced to kill a dozen to squash a rebellion. You see?"

Of course I did not, nor do I now! Never, never shall I turn to such cruel methods. I am going to treat my slaves with kindness as I am bound to do as a Christian. I am sure they will stop stealing and idling and disobeying orders when they see I am kind to them, trying my best to lighten their burden.

"There is one more case," said Dubrit, turning to my aunt. "My foreman Hector, who replaced me while I was confined to bed, reported to me that his horse was missing on Thursday afternoon. Coming back from the fields at noon to report to me he fixed his horse to a post in the yard for the stable-boy to take care of it. I gave Hector instructions and then sent him to your kitchen to get a meal there. He said he left the kitchen at one o'clock, but could not find his horse nor the stable-boy. He saddled another horse for his afternoon inspection-round. Coming back in the evening he found his horse in the stable. The groom denied having ridden it, said he had found it attached to a tree behind the house an hour or two before.

"Hector reported it on my return from town, but I forgot to cross-examine the groom because of the excitement last night."

"I'll do that myself," said my aunt. "I want to know who took that horse away. Very interesting, indeed!" She faced me triumphantly. Did she really think I knew the culprit? Knew who had ridden on horseback to town to inform the attorney?

Sam, the stable-boy, trembled with fear when he was pushed in. At her call he approached her submissively. She scrutinized him for a while, then frowned and sniffed.

"The bastard stinks!" she said. "Step back!"

He was pushed back to the door by a servant.

"Hast thou not had a wash?" she asked.

"No ma'am, yes, ma'am——"

"He will get ten lashes for disobeying orders. This mudlark knows he must wash and change dress after work like all the others."

That's the way she treated her servants. Disgusting! No wonder they all feared and hated her.

She questioned him severely, but he could not tell her more than the overseer. He had been fetching his meal, so he did not see the foreman nor his horse at noon. When he returned to the yard there was no horse attached to the pole. It was the chambermaid, Julie, who told him to fetch the horse bound to the tree behind the house. That was long before dusk, about an hour before the foreman returned.

She threatened to have him skinned if she found out he lied to her or wasn't telling the whole truth, but he stuck to his story. At last she turned to Dubrit, saying, "Please, remember to serve that slave another ten lashes for not reporting the incident to me this morning, twenty in all, will you?"

He nodded, sending the Negro over to the barn to join the other victims of her despotism.

"And now I want to have a word with that wench Julie," she said, rising from her chair.

She told one of the servants to find the girl and send her upstairs to her mistress' bedroom.

She had the same glassy hard stare in her eyes as that morning. You could see she was mad with vindictiveness. If she found out who had borrowed the horse, she believed she had trapped the traitor she was looking for, the fellow who had informed the attorney. And terrible must be her revenge. She would torture, and kill him if she could.

I should have tried to stop her. If I had not been such a dreadful coward two lives might have been spared—who knows? Now it is too late to regret. And what could I have done?

I felt disgusted and very unhappy. Dubrit had the impudence to invite me to watch the whippings in the barn. I said, "No thank you. I saw enough brutality this morning!" A pity she did not hear that. She was already gone and I never saw her alive again! God save her soul!

I tried to consult with my uncle and tell him what had happened. But he was already asleep. So I went to my bedchamber where César had been put to be nursed by his sister Helen. His back still hurt badly, his cheeks were hot and he was in a fever. I told her to leave him with me overnight.

Later, Helen helped me to hunt the beastly mosquitoes, the maringouins, that are torturing me every night in spite of my mosquito-net which is never quite safe. I was too irritable, tired and depressed to open this journal in the poor light of the candles. Was already half undressed when there was a knock at the door, and cries and shouts outside. In rushed Julie, quite mad with despair, crying, lamenting, throwing herself at my feet.

"He killed her!" she sobbed. "He killed her, he killed her!"

"Who?" I cried.

"Louis!" she answered.

I seized a lantern and ran out, scarcely dressed as I was, to Louis's chamber which was at the opposite end of the gallery. It was wide open. In the dim light of my lantern and a single candle on the table I found her body on the floor, a lifeless pale bundle. Louis was gone.

Léon and Gil and Rebecca rushed in, followed by the other house-servants, all blocking the door. I sent them away, told them to inform Dubrit, rushed back to my room, got dressed and sat down, trying to recover from the shock. The house was in a turmoil, cries, shouts, wails and orders, and then the barking of dogs. Poor boy, poor boy! They were going to hunt him down!

Later I questioned Julie. She confessed she had told her mistress that she saw Louis binding the horse to the tree. She would not have given him away, she said, in spite of her mistress' threats, but Louis had not been nice to her. He had been pleasuring other girls, forgetting about her.

Madame was raving. She told Julie to follow her to Louis' chamber and confront him. Julie carried a lantern, pushed his door open, and in the semi-darkness they saw him lying in bed with Flora, the little bitch. She jumped out of bed and ran out, stark naked, trying to dodge her mistress's furious slaps and kicks.

"Tell her to dress and run over to the barn to get her portion there, twenty lashes, and good ones!" cried Madame, turning to Julie.

"And stop the first two males you meet and send them here with a cow-hide whip, a strong one! Go! Hurry!"

Her mistress closed the door behind her, but Julie listened a while outside before running. She heard an angry dispute, then the boy's voice crying, "Don't! don't! don't touch me, or I'll tell my father!"

And her voice, "You dare threaten me, you insolent scoundrel, whoring about and plotting against your mistress, you dirty bastard of a slave!"

There followed a number of other invectives which Julie did not wish to repeat.

She rushed downstairs and met Léon and Gil and told them what was happening and that they were to fetch a cow-hide whip, and she waited for them to return, and then she heard steps upstairs and saw Louis running past her and out into the night. She could not see him well because it was dark in the staircase, but she was sure he was only dressed in shirt and breeches, no more, and barefoot, too.

They found the horse-whip she had used. It was his own, which she must have seen lying somewhere and had seized in order to attack him. She must have hit him hard, for its handle was broken. It lay on the floor, not in her hand. Perhaps there had been a short scuffle, he trying to wrest it from her. Did he hit her with it? Or did he throw her back against the edge of the table? They found a dark bruise on her right temple. That must have been the heavy blow that killed her.

Louis had managed to flee on horseback, but in the moonshine he was stopped by a patrol of the *maréchaussée* who suspected him of being a runaway because of his strange attire and the fact that his horse was unsaddled. He jumped down and tried to run into the nearby wood. He was shot and killed before his pursuers arrived.

The next day there were a lot of sinister-looking officials in our house, questioning Dubrit and me and all the house-servants, and even poor heart-broken Uncle. His grief was worse than anybody else's. He must have loved his son dearly, else it would not have hit him so hard. He looks like a ghost sometimes, brooding, brooding, scarcely knowing what is going on around him. One often doubts if he realizes one is present. No more willing to remember things, no more able to love or hate, just a brooding, morose, apathetic, dying man.

Charles came over again this morning. So glad he is helping me to settle things. I never knew how much book-keeping, and counting, and ordering, and bills, and answering letters there is in a planter's work. Mre Falcon has taken care of all the legal duties and money matters, thank Heavens!

JUNE 12TH, 1786

Had an argument with Dubrit last night.

I told him he must not allow his drivers to whip the slaves any longer, but this afternoon I saw them all carrying whips as before.

Dubrit does not care a fig for what I say. He thinks I am a stupid young thing, not used to dealing with blacks. He says you cannot make them work with friendly words, it is dangerous for a young mistress to be soft-hearted. It makes them insolent, cocky and disobedient.

He advised me to show them I am as severe as my aunt was, and not to interfere in his domain. He said I had better keep an eye on my house-servants, and tell him if any of them were lazy or disobedient. He offered to help me to curb them.

I hate his patronizing way of talking to me, treating me as though I were a child. If he thinks he can run the plantation as he likes he is wrong! Trying to charm me with his plump flatteries, his false affability, in order to twist me round his little finger! Not me!

I told him I won't allow any of the field hands to work naked. They must wear pants and broad-brimmed hats to protect them from the sun like M. Galez's field hands, upon which he asked me sarcastically if I wished our rams and bulls and stallions to wear pants, too. He said they didn't feel happier in pants, they preferred putting clean ones on after work. As for straw hats there were not any available. They would have to be bought at the market in town, which I mean to do next time I go there to see the attorney.

Felipe's wound looks very bad. I sent for the doctor but he didn't come before yesterday afternoon. An elderly man, very pompous, but I doubt if he knows more about treating wounds than Helen does. He promised to send an ointment to remove the pus, but I am afraid it is too late, the whole leg being swollen. The poor lad is in high fever. I had him carried here for Helen to nurse him.

Uncle is mostly tipsy these days, drinking rum like water. It helps him to forget, and he dozes off even in my presence. The other day he confessed to me that the two mulatto wenches now employed in the fields as drivers were once house-slaves. When his wife found out he made love to them she flew into a blind rage. She would have killed the girls if he had not saved them by promising to send them to the fields. Of course they were too valuable to be used as hard-working common field hands. So he put them in charge of gangs consisting mostly of women and children. It soon turned out that they were as good as any male drivers, because colored women have an even keener sense of superiority towards Negroes than colored males.

JUNE 14TH

Felipe died this morning. I feel relieved rather than depressed, knowing that the poor fellow's sufferings have come to an end. He did not wish to live, he longed for death after the life we whites made hell for him. I somehow feel responsible, too, having witnessed his cruel ill-treatment without interfering in time.

They are digging his grave in the slaves' grave-yard behind the copse. Dubrit says it is no use sending for a priest, he would not arrive in time. They cannot keep the body unburied for so long because of the heat. All field hands are buried, unknelled, in a hurry, almost like dead dogs though they are Christians like ourselves, baptized children of our Jesus Christ!

Why do our priests allow them to be deprived of the last sacraments? Even in death those poor blacks are outcasts. I cannot believe there is any excuse for that.

I do hate that arrogant brute Dubrit! He said again it was no business of mine to interfere with his methods. His contract allowed him to manage the plantation in his own way. Many of the field hands are still naked, and the cracking of whips waked me this morning as brutally as before. Even Charles seems to side with him. He says I had better leave things as they are, lest Dubrit should get angry and desert me. It is very difficult to replace a white overseer in the middle of the crop. Dubrit knows I cannot do without him. That's what makes him so impertinent.

Helen confessed to me that she slept with Uncle last night. He had asked her, begged her, promised to do her no harm, said spending the night alone was hell, he could not sleep, was brooding all the time. She obeyed out of pity and devotion, knowing he is harmless. Didn't even try to be wicked. So let him have his way.

I haven't seen Denise for a whole week. I wonder if her birthday ball was a success. A pity I could not go. Out of the question that night, people dancing and laughing, all happy and gay, while the stench of death was pervading this house. I can still smell it lingering in the staircase where she stood slapping Louis's face.

Whatever I see and smell and hear in this house reminds me of her: the empty chair in the diningroom, the faint scent of her perfume everywhere, the subdued whisper of servants who still seem to live in awe of their bad-tempered mistress. This house is haunted. It ought to be burnt down and rebuilt somewhere else.

I have reason to suspect my servants are getting licentious, lads and wenches mixing at night as they like. I must not allow this house to become a brothel. I'll force them to get married or else separate. A top to each pot. Except mine.

JUNE 17TH

Thank Heavens he is gone! Good riddance! Had a hot dispute this morning, after I found out what had happened.

I had told him to stop the Friday night whippings, made him promise to spare them. Now, this morning, I found two slaves in the sick-room, both badly hurt and unable to walk.

One, a young wench, had been pregnant but lost it after the whipping. She was lying in a pool of blood. The brute! She is a mulatto, served him in his house, was exposed to his dissipation and brutality. She didn't dare tell against him, but Helen heard he was roaring drunk again last night, after whipping half a dozen of the field hands, one of them so badly that they had to carry him to the sick-room. At night his boy heard him smash glasses and chairs, and then heard the girl scream.

After a while he called the boy in, ordered him to carry the girl over to the sick-room and said the bloody bastard had soiled his sheets with her blood. This morning he did not leave his chamber but sent César away, cursing when the boy knocked at his door.

About eleven Helen told me she had seen him turning to the stable. I sent for him, but in vain. He told César to go to hell and said he didn't care for young girls at this time of day. If I longed for him I must wait till night-time!

I was so furious I at once ran out to confront him. Told him to pack his belongings and leave. He said all right, all right, young lady, but it will cost you dear! I said "my attorney will take care of that. I am going to sue you for ill-treating a pregnant girl. I'll make you pay for that!" He laughed at me, saying he had a good mind to spank me, a pity the law forbade him to do, and then lay me!

I haven't seen him since. Helen says he left about noon on horseback. I must make sure the horse is his.

I wanted to tell Uncle, but found him dozing off, his glass of rum empty. I know I am in a mess, but it could not be helped. Sent César over to inform Charles. Hope he won't leave me in the lurch.

SUNDAY

Charles says I made a mistake. Should not have dismissed Dubrit in the middle of the crop. Impossible to replace him. Offered to ask his father to send me one of his foremen on condition that I should give that man a free hand. No white overseer is willing to let himself be controlled by a woman. I am expected to leave the management of Uncle's plantation to somebody who is responsible to his attorney, his legal representative, not to me.

He tried to convince me that slaves cannot be ruled without resorting to the whip sometimes. He said Dubrit had been a severe but efficient overseer, had kept our field hands submissive and hard-working.

Disappointing to see Charles side with that brute, defending him and shrugging his shoulders at the way he ill-treated that poor girl. I didn't accept Charles's offer, not knowing what kind of fellow they would send me. If he is a brute like Dubrit I should have to turn him out too. Better try and put Hector in charge of the management. He is a slave, he must obey me. I can take him to task if he does not.

Must go and see Mre Falcon. I am completely ignorant in money matters. If only Uncle could be consulted. But he is worse than ever. Dozing or brooding or staring at me absent-mindedly.

I wonder why Denise keeps away so long? Charles said she was sorry she could not come, being indisposed. Seems to be a mere excuse for avoiding me. What for? Charles is still very helpful and polite. Too polite to make me feel at ease.

MONDAY

César must be stopped! The wicked little bastard has been trying out a new sport, a very audacious one. Last night while drying my foot he put it on his lap, pressing it down to make me feel his rising hot excitement! A thirteen-year-old youngster! He ought to be spanked. But I cannot help liking the little rogue.

I told Léon to take a mule and ride to town to get fifty straw hats in the market. I wrote him a pass, and sent him to Mre Falcon to deliver my letter, asking the attorney to give him the money he needs.

Then I summoned all the drivers to tell them they must take orders from Hector from now on. He proposed the driver Clément as his assistant. Both seem to be reliable, but I told them if ever they disobey my orders they will be replaced by others.

I strictly forbade them ill-treating their subordinates —no more whips. Instead they shall tell them I mean to reward them all next Saturday with bacon and a barrel of toddy if I am satisfied with their work.

I am sure rewards are better than punishments to make them work. As long as we are short of blacks, my two house-boys, Félix and Roy, will have to take alternate charge of Clément's team. I sent the two gardeners to the fields too. If everybody works hard these two or three weeks, the crop can be brought in, says Hector.

He is very hopeful, perhaps too confident of himself and everybody else. Says yes, ma'am, yes, to whatever I propose to change. Everything is wonderful and everybody happy and content. Smiling at me and nodding and bowing. Reminds me of an eager poodle anxiously watching for his mistress's orders. A little embarrassing, but flattering, his unlimited admiration, as if I were a superior being, a queen.

No doubt he is a good boy, trustworthy, his brown funny monkey face all eagerness and devotion.

Clément is a different type, slow, melancholy, never smiles, but handsomer than Hector, taller. Helen says he was once Aunt's favorite house-boy, then, for reasons unknown, suddenly fell into disgrace and was sent out to the fields.

The other drivers are much plainer, two of them seem to be griots, while the two wenches are fair-skinned mulattoes, tobacco colored, pretty both of them, though one, Flora, is pregnant. I wonder if she bears me a little cousin, Uncle having sown his wild oats among the girls prior to his illness. The wicked old sinner!

JUNE 20th

Mre Falcon is much more understanding than Charles. He promised to find someone reliable to replace Dubrit. He said the latter had already called on him, demanding the rest of his salary, including board and cost of residence up to the end of this year, totalling 3,200 livres as compensation, according to his contract.

It is very difficult, Mre Falcon says, to sue an overseer for cruelties afflicted on slaves. Even if he killed one or two he could pretend he had been resisted or even attacked. Only the evidence of white witnesses might help to convict him, slaves not being admitted as evidence in court.

Mre Falcon will send a reliable doctor (not ours, I am glad to know) to examine the poor wench. The marks of ill-treatment on her belly will tell against that brute. Even should the girl recover we may be able to claim 500–700 livres compensation for damaged property as he is responsible for the abortion.

I asked the attorney what to do about Léon, who has not turned up since I sent him to town yesterday morning. He will inform the *maréchaussée* and promise a reward in the *Affiches Américaines* for capturing and detaining the runaway. But maybe he has not run away. Something may have happened to him and his mule. I am really worried.

At the dressmaker's I tried my new dress on. It fits me so well I am sorry I could not join Denise's party.

Instead I must bear three months' mourning, even though she was not related to me by blood! The dressmaker charged me 320 livres for it. I never wore such a costly garment before. I told her to have Aunt's new robe changed to fit me. Even if full-blown pregnant I could not fill her waist and corsage. When I come out of mourning I shall have a queenly new wardrobe, as good as Denise's. I have hated playing Cinderella's part. It has been long enough. Two pair of fine new shoes, the finest I ever had, Aunt's fitting my feet as if made to measure!

JUNE 21ST

Have been out of sorts since Tuesday night.

It caught me again, two days late, which didn't worry me this time. Thank Heaven it is almost over, headaches and feeling dirty and lying in bed most of the time.

Helen was right: Léon is a scoundrel, must be punished severely. But how? Helen says thieves ought to be whipped in public, she would not spare him such a humiliation. She hates him, says all the house-servants hate him for his mean spying on them, denouncing them to their mistress whose pet servant he was. He made life hell for all of them during the time he was her butler. Well, that's over. I won't have him in the house again. I might send him to the fields or get rid of him, sell him. No manumission for a thief and denouncer.

Mre Falcon informed me this morning that he had been caught and that I could fetch him from the prison yard. I drove there with Helen and César. He was delivered to me in chains, a miserable sight! The jailer asked me if I wished him to be whipped, they would charge me 5 livres for every ten lashes, up to fifty, which is the limit by law. I said I had not come to punish the man but to take him home. They charged me 50 livres for catching and detaining and feeding him, and 20 livres for the fetters, to be restored when the irons are returned.

I was told they had found him locked up in a harlot's chamber, the brown slut having denounced him in order to get the reward.

I drove back with the captive to my attorney. There we questioned him. He confessed he had stolen a set of silver spoons from my aunt's cupboard. He sold the mule and the spoons to different persons unknown to him at the market. With the money he received, totaling 180 livres, he tried to get a forged certificate attesting his manumission which would have enabled him to escape by ship to some other island.

He said he had given the money to a mulatto harlot he had met in the street. She said she knew persons who could provide such a paper for him. But she never turned up at the appointed place. In his despair he picked up another harlot and followed her to her room. Being without money he offered her the only silver spoon he had kept.

She noticed his marks and scars and was sure he was a runaway slave whose owner might reward her well if she delivered the slave. So she treated him to a bottle of toddy, and when he was drunk and sleeping she bound his hands behind his back with the belt of his pants, and tied his ankles and knees with two old neckerchiefs of hers.

When he awoke in the morning she made him confess that he had stolen the spoon, and that he was a runaway slave. Instead of releasing him as she had promised, she calmly dressed saying she would inform the *maréchaussée,* and when he started shouting, calling her names, she gagged him and left after locking him in. Later they came and took him to prison where he spent only five or six hours before I fetched him.

While he was telling his story the mulatto wench arrived who had denounced him, asking for her reward. She didn't look so bad in her gaudy attire, lush and well formed. I would have taken her for a well-dressed young housewife rather than a whore. Confronted her with Léon, she faced his visible hatred with a contemptuous smile. She said he had offered her a valueless trinket which she wished to return as it might, like the silver spoon, be stolen property.

She showed us a small golden ring with a glittering stone which proved to be a pure diamond!

Léon confessed he had stolen it, together with other jewels, from my aunt's jewel-case on the morning after her death. The other jewels he had partly sold and partly presented to the three or four other harlots he had picked up.

Mre Falcon gave the slut 100 livres as a reward. When she had left he said planters depended on such loose women to help them capture runaways. Many of them try to hide with women of that sort. They must be paid well, otherwise they would not be willing to co-operate.

Léon cannot be tried in court. The attorney says you cannot run to the police if your own ox tramples your garden, you are expected to punish the beast yourself.

He advised me to turn to M. Galez or his son and have Léon handled according to his crime. He said a very severe whipping was indispensable. He must not be spared, else others might be tempted to follow his example.

On the other hand, we must take care not to disfigure or cripple or kill him because of his market value.

I was shocked to hear the friendly old gentleman talk like that. Léon may be a rascal, but he is a human being, not a beast! I cannot help pitying him, in spite of all he has done, poor devil! A handsome face and body, but not to my taste; too soft, with womanish features, a weak character. Strange that my aunt should have picked him out and favored him. Helen says she often saw him come out of her bedroom early in the morning.

It was a sad return home, Léon sitting beside Hannibal on the box, his hands still chained behind his back. Helen said he might try to jump down and run away if I unchained him. She is full of venom towards him. He must have been very mean to her to make her so revengeful. She has a fierce passion and hatred hidden behind a mask of kindness.

It was embarrassing the way he behaved when we

came home. Falling on his knees in despair, begging my pardon, imploring, lamenting, sobbing, repenting, promising. No manly pride, all fright and contrition. I cannot help despising him. I had him taken to the prison to be locked in there.

JUNE 22ND

More trouble with Léon. Helen advised me to have him inspected as he might be sick from whoring with those harlots. I sent her to Hector to ask him to examine the man. Helen returned triumphant, saying she was right: Léon is sick, she saw and made sure herself, being present at the close inspection, the shameless wench!

I sent for the doctor, the young one, Dr. Lebrun, who is so much more competent than that old fool Dr. Pellaton. Lebrun had already called on us yesterday morning to see Rosa, the poor maid who had an abortion because of Dubrit's brutish ill-treatment.

He wrote a statement ascertaining that the marks of his kicking, still visible on her belly, caused her miscarriage. He also confirmed that the wounds inflicted to her left breast and thigh will leave ugly scars reducing the market value of the pretty slave considerably. Assessed the total loss (that of valuable issue included) at 1,200 livres, which sum will be deducted from Dubrit's severance pay.

The doctor arrived again this afternoon, examined Léon, and found he had caught the clap, which is, thank Heaven, less fatal than the Spanish malady. The rascal must be kept isolated for at least three weeks, no contacts allowed. Hector says he can make him work in the fields separated from the others. Must be kept chained to a heavy iron ball to prevent him from running away. He has his desert, the fool!

I haven't seen Denise for more than a fortnight. I haven't done anything wrong, have I? She knows I am in no way responsible for Aunt's death. Why, then, should she be cross? Well, I won't run after her, nor after her dear brother. He has not turned up since last

Sunday. Maybe he is angry because I refused his assistance, saying my colored overseers could manage everything all by themselves.

I cannot make up my mind whether I should inform him about Léon, remembering how his father is used to dealing with criminal slaves. It would be too cruel a punishment, even for that fool Léon.

Denise would not spare him in my place, nor would Helen if she had her will. Now I know why she hates him so much: Léon once denounced her to my aunt for having spent a night outdoors with her lover from M. Galez's plantation, whereupon both she and the mulatto lad were severely flogged and the latter was strictly forbidden to approach her again.

She says Léon would spy on all the house-slaves out of mere malice or jealousy, causing many a whipping by denouncing his fellow-slaves. No doubt they feel relieved now, all of them, knowing that I don't mind their nightly love affairs so long as they do their duty in daytime.

I would hate to play the part of a female Peeping Tom. Fancy surprising them in the act! Better them have their fun. We must not spoil the only pleasure left to them in the misery of their bondage. That's why I won't allow Léon to be cut. They may whip him, but they must not mutilate him. I hope Charles will agree with me. If he turns out to be as cold and pitiless as his naughty sister, I'll reject him should he ever try to propose to me. I hate the idea of marrying a cruel tyrant.

Uncle was drunk after dinner, staring into space and muttering confused gibberish, laughing and crying alternately. It was so sad I could not stand it. Maybe I was wrong allowing him to drink rum at his pleasure. But would he be happier deprived of the only consolation left to him beside fondling his bed-mate's breasts?

It seems I am the only person in this house who spends the nights in decent solitude. No, I forgot César. He is, of course, still a virgin boy. But for how long?

This morning his sister told me he complained to her about a pain in his left groin. He showed me a reddish pimple growing there which, she said, might be the beginning of the *pian,* a very ugly disease widespread among the blacks and colored people in this island. This afternoon I had him inspected by the doctor after he had seen Léon. He says it is harmless so long as the boy does not scratch it, the naughty little monkey! His little cock so much handsomer than grown-ups. Everything is pretty in youth, even that! I like the boy. He is so lithe, so gracious, my darling Ganymede, so faithful, so devoted, so wonderfully attached to me. Feigning to be asleep whenever I undress. He wouldn't dare watch me openly, though I would not mind, feeling more like a mother or elder sister towards him.

JUNE 23RD

Charles and Denise called on me this morning. Her fiancé will arrive from France next month and their wedding is to take place in September.

She said she had been terribly busy seeing people, escorting her mother to town, the dressmaker's, the jeweller's, draper's, selecting glassware, china, lace and finery, shoes, perfume, hats, furniture, as well as a hundred things to be bought for the wedding.

I tried to inquire after George in an indifferent way. It seems she must leave him to her father for the future. Thank Heavens! I haven't seen him for weeks.

Denise still looks like a girl of fifteen, not grown up enough to marry and bear children. From a distance, seeing her riding on horseback in breeches and high boots and sitting astride in the saddle like a boy, she might be taken for Charles's younger brother.

As a rich nobleman's wife she will have to behave like a lady, though she may hate it. She told me about their grand ball: more than sixty guests, their own Negro band and one hired from a lady in town, the best performers available. After midnight their mulattoes danced a Chica, another of those shameless dances favored by colored people. Fancy sixteen-year-old girls watching such scenes!

I rode with them out to the fields. I had not been

there for three days. On the way we passed Léon working in the cotton field, hacking and weeding.

Denise recognized him, stopped and beckoned him to approach her, wondering why he had fallen into disgrace. He was forced to lift his heavy iron ball and carry it when he walked. She questioned him, listening with disdain to his awkward confession. She said it was strange that my aunt should have confided in such a rascal, considering him the only trustworthy servant she had. She had treated him as if he were a model slave.

"Lousy bastard!" she commented dismissing him with a switch of her crop across his bare shoulder.

They asked me how I meant to punish him. I said that being kept in chains working in the fields, and spending nights in the prison separated from the others was punishment hard enough to atone for his crime.

Charles didn't agree, neither did Denise. They warned me that all the other slaves would expect the runaway thief to be whipped in their presence, not only once but every Saturday for months to come as a warning towards the rest of them. If I spared him they would lose their respect for me, thinking I was so indulgent a mistress that they, too, might misbehave and go scot-free.

I had to tell them about his ugly sickness to explain why he had been spared so far. Denise said such dirty bastards ought to be gelded. I was relieved that Charles didn't agree. He is, I admit, not cruel out of mere wickedness like Denise, but gives sober and practical reasons for being severe.

Most gangs were busy picking coffee cherries, but Charles said they were all very slow, their baskets still half empty after more than three hours' work.

He advised me to check the daily amount of coffee delivered for drying and compare it with previous results.

He warned me that my drivers and overseers might cheat me, knowing that no white man is in charge.

He thinks I am a stupid simpleton who had better leave everything to him or one of those white brutes like Dubrit. I'll prove to him I can manage my blacks in my own way, as well as any man, by treating them as human beings and not like beasts. I know they like me and won't deceive me, not Hector, who reported to me that everything is all right, and that the crop is good and plentiful. Tomorrow, Saturday, they will get their reward as promised. Seeing that I stick to my word it will surely make them work even better next week. I told Charles I was grateful for his advice but would like to try and do without any white man's assistance, Hector being a very reliable fellow.

Denise said, "Well, you will learn!" rather snappishly.

Charles seems to resent my stubbornness though he tries to hide his disappointment. A nice boy; I must admit I like his good manners, his calm chivalrous way of courting me. I know he is serious and would propose to me at the slightest sign of willingness on my part. But I don't love him, I am sorry to say. After all you have to share your bed with the man you choose for a lifetime.

SUNDAY

I never felt so lonely and helpless before. I should have turned to Charles for help but I cannot make up my mind to do so. It is too humiliating to admit my defeat. I must try and take matters in my own hands and show those bastards I am not willing to let them run things their way, take unfair advantage of my leniency, abuse it in the worst way possible.

They have to be punished, all of them, Hector and Clément and the drivers particularly. They should have stopped the blacks in time instead of joining them in those horrible orgies. They must have known the second barrel was stolen from my cellar. I'll find out who is responsible for that theft and make them pay for it. And the chicken they killed, and two cocks! And four men and three women wounded, bleeding from cuts, out of work for two, three days or even longer!

Charles is right: you cannot keep them in order without resorting to threats and whippings sometimes.

If only I had been warned in time I might have known how to stop them. I could have threatened to open the kennel and let the dogs loose, all eight of them. But Julie, who has been in charge since Léon ran away, was not to be found, nor were the other girls, Rosa, Rebecca and Trisa. They have joined the others, the shameless bitches, forgetting their pride, mixing with the blacks they pretended to despise.

Voodoo, they call it, that obscene drumming and shouting and dancing and twisting their bellies and sucking cock's blood and murmuring magic words and stripping and whoring in drunken ecstasy.

When I arrived it was too late to interfere, all of them were wild drunk, hysterical and dangerous. Helen was right to warn me to keep in the dark lest they should see us, rush at us and rape us, the drunken beasts!

They might have treated me the same way as they treated poor Florence, perhaps Maria too, though she does not admit it. The blacks seem to hate them more than their male drivers, and took their revenge last night. There was no way to prevent them.

I ran away back home and locked and barred my chamber. If infuriated further they might have set the house on fire. There was nobody left to protect us, my helpless uncle and me, but Helen and my faithful César. He was the first to warn me, not Helen, who was in Uncle's bedchamber.

This morning I walked over to the slaves' quarters to see how things were. A shocking sight, men and women lying about in the open, some stark naked, all fast asleep, open-mouthed, snoring and moaning like dying victims of mass poisoning, many couples still in close embrace, others grotesquely disentangled, ridiculous, disgusting, beastly and obscene.

There were feathers everywhere, marks of blood on faces and limbs, and cut and torn-off parts of a cock lying about, its crested head, round dead yellow eyes and beak, feet and withering entrails covered by swarms of flies.

I was so angry I might have obeyed my impulse to beat the drunken swine, to wield the whip if I had had one at hand.

I found Hector in one of the cabins fast asleep, his

head bedded on the bosom of a black woman. I tried to wake him, kicking him till he moved, groaning and muttering curses, staring at me like an idiot.

Then I lost my patience and slapped his face again and again in blind fury! I am ashamed I behaved as though I were crazy, but it worked, made him rise, fumbling for his pants and shirt, trying to hide his ugly nakedness. I told him to dress and wake the others, make them wash and get dressed decently and clean up the compound and all the cabins. Then I would return and inspect everybody and everything.

Helen told me she had found Florence in another cabin, said she was in a pitiable state, moaning and sobbing. Had her carried to the infirmary by Helen and César. She was covered with bites and bruises. It seems she was raped by an unknown number of black brutes, poor girl, nobody protecting her, certainly none of the mulatto drivers present, which makes them accessories to the crime. They, too, will have to pay for that!

I was relieved to find the prison door locked. Thank Heavens they did not release Léon to take part in their orgies! He might have spread his ugly disease in the middle of the crop!

I found him in a poor state, the old jailer having neglected him since Friday night, the stupid slut! She has kept him locked in without any food or water. The poor bastard looked half starved, was almost suffocated in the stench of his unaired prison cell. I unlocked the fetters and allowed him to come over to our house to be washed and fed by César (not Helen, knowing how she hates him!).

I found the kitchen deserted, nobody present to prepare Uncle's breakfast and mine. I told Helen to make a pot of coffee for us and serve us some fruit. No appetite left after what I saw this morning.

Uncle didn't seem interested. He smelled of rum—at nine in the morning! I must not allow him to get drunk day after day, so I took away his bottle, which made him very cross. But I must be strict. I made a mistake in letting him have his own way, encouraging him to make drinking a habit and become a brainless drunkard.

Heavens, what a mess! Everything is going to pieces. But I am ready to fight! We learn from our mistakes. If they think I am a stupid, weak little chicken I'll show them they are wrong!

Charles and Denise must not know what happened, they would laugh at me, despise me, tell everybody I am a soft-hearted newcomer, an innocent in dealing with slaves, full of silly ideas about human dignity and things like that. If I give in it means I admit they are right to treat the blacks like beasts, which they are not, in spite of what happened last night. It was my fault, after all. I should not have offered them toddy as a reward. Never again! No more liquors allowed at this plantation, not for the servants at any rate.

Helen warned me not to let César keep in touch with Léon for too long, which was, indeed, very risky. So I sent for both of them, told César to wash thoroughly, examined Léon and found he had recovered well enough. I allowed him to spend Sunday in the open in the shadow of a tree, strictly forbidding him to walk about or get in touch with anyone, else I should send him back to his prison at once.

He again started begging and imploring me, asking my pardon, weeping and sobbing like a woman, disgusting! Told him he deserved no pity; if a free man he would be hanged for his crime; everybody expected me to have him whipped severely.

I said I might spare him as long as he behaved, but would change my mind if he ever disobeyed orders. He will be kept in chains for a long time, probably for years, and no hopes of ever getting manumissed. Nor will he be allowed to serve in the house again. He will be employed in the fields to the end of his days.

It is easy to be hard on a rascal. Gives you the feeling of moral superiority. Maybe his servile submission helps to provoke my cold disgust.

I returned to the slaves' quarters where the blacks were moving about in dull apathy, indifferent to the approach of their mistress.

I sent César back to fetch my dog Nero to teach them respect. And meanwhile went to the infirmary to see Florence. She was still in a bad state, though, thank

Heaven, able to move and rise and walk about. I hope she will recover soon. She is full of venom, accused the other drivers of cowardice. Said they were scared of the blacks and dared not make them work as they should but allowed them to idle time away.

"Of course," she said. "Whenever news spread that the mistress was on the way to the fields, everybody pretended to work hard, but as soon as you were out of sight they would stop."

So far they had brought in less than half the expected quantity of coffee cherries, each field hand's regular daily portion being four big basketfuls, whereas this year not one had delivered three whole basketfuls a day, and some not even two!

Florence said she had asked Hector to inform me, but he said they must not disappoint me else I might choose to submit them to another cruel white overseer like M. Dubrit. That cheating bastard Hector! I sent for him and told him to summon all the drivers. I told them I had good reasons to degrade them all to the rank of plain field hands and replace them with more trust-worthy men, strong, faithful Negroes I could depend upon.

Of course they all swore they were innocent, and said they had tried in vain to stop the blacks in their disgust-ing orgy last night.

I told them as a punishment they will have to start work half an hour earlier every day, at five next week, and make their hands deliver five basketfuls of cherries a day. Those who fail to fill their five baskets will have to work in the fields next Saturday, when the others are free, and so will the drivers responsible for their work.

I warned them that I shall be present when the bas-kets are being weighed and delivered to see that no cheating is being done.

I do hope I can restore order and obedience and make them work as they should, else I shall be forced to turn to Charles and admit my failure. How Denise would laugh!

Last Friday the attorney promised to send me a new overseer, Laroche by name, to start work on July 1st.

Another week! He said he knows him to be a reliable man, sober, efficient, trustworthy, no complaints. He will come to see me on Saturday morning. Now I am glad I didn't oppose the attorney's arrangements, though at that time I was confident I could run the plantation all by myself.

The attorney said it was against the law to leave the management of a plantation in the hands of slaves. There should be at least two white persons (beside Uncle) able to control them, considering the number of slaves we have. It is a royal ordinance, he says.

When Uncle was in good health there were four whites here, including the *économiste,* a man my aunt dismissed after Uncle's accident, saying he had tried to cheat her. I don't really know what happened, nor does Uncle. Mre Falcon said we must replace him as soon as possible. If I could depend on two decent white men for the field hands and everything connected with the coffee and cotton production, I should be glad to leave it all to them, concerning myself with ruling the house-servants and nursing Uncle, reading, writing, riding and seeing my friends.

MONDAY, JUNE 26TH

I am terribly dejected after my failure this morning.

Had a very bad night, sultry heavy heat and mosquitoes—damned mosquitoes, damned, damned, damned! I heard César breathing peacefully all the time, and I could not sleep. At dawn I heard voices in the yard, not many, though it must have been long past five. It was, in fact, past six when they finally departed for the fields, openly disobeying my orders! I was so furious that I got up, woke César, sent him over to the cabins to see if all had left, as I was not at all sure of that.

I dressed in a hurry and decided to ride out to the fields and take Hector to task. I rushed over to Uncle's room to wake Helen and found her lying in his bed, his cheek leaning against her brown breast.

I sent her to the kitchen to order breakfast. Uncle smelt of liquor. I found a bottle of rum under his pillow, half empty. So Helen, too, has started cheating and disobeying me!

I told him I would punish her for that, whereupon he begged me to spare her. Said he could not do without his regular drink; it would kill him if I refused him now. He implored me to leave him the bottle and began to weep like a frustrated little boy. I tried in vain to convince him how bad it was for him to be half drunk all day. Finally I could not help giving in, leaving him a glass full of the liquor and promising to grant him another one before noon. Poor man. No pride left, no will-power, nothing!

Then César returned, telling me at least twenty blacks were stilly lying about in their cabins! I ordered him to wake the house and fetch my dog Nero.

I had a hasty breakfast, then walked over to the cabins escorted by Helen and César and protected by Nero. When the Negro women saw us approach they ran into the cabins, while a crowd of naked little brats gathered, watching me with round eyes and open mouths.

I sent César into the first hut, telling him to call everybody out. He reappeared with a Negress who said all the men were badly sick. Went in after handing the leash to César. Five Negroes were lying in the straw, moaning.

One, the biggest and strongest, was stark-naked, though he must have known I was coming. I am sure he wished to provoke me, to see how I reacted. He thought I would turn away embarrassed, which they would have interpreted as proof of weakness. But I did not flinch, not for a second.

I asked him in a stern voice why he had not put on his pants like the others, whereupon he answered in mock despair that he was too big for them which made the others laugh aloud.

I became furious, told him I would come back in a minute, and if he had not dressed by then I would have him whipped like a beast, for only beasts lay about naked.

I asked them why they were not working, whereupon they started groaning and lamenting, saying they had ruined their stomachs and bowels and could not move. They were sure somebody had poisoned them.

I knew they were lying, all of them, the lazy rascals! So I told César to run to the infirmary and fetch a bottle of castor-oil. I left and went over to the second cabin, where half a dozen males and two young females were lying, all of them complaining of similar pains in their bowels. Meanwhile César had brought me the castor-oil. Assisted by Helen I forced each of the patients to swallow a good mouthful of it, which made them jump up and rush for the outhouse. A funny sight! Then I returned to the first cabin and made them swallow a mouthful each, with the same result.

The black giant had, meanwhile, put on his pants I am glad to say, but he tried again to make fun of me by grimacing in mock terror at the spoon I was filling, refusing to open his mouth and turning away, spilling the medicine which made me so angry I slapped his face and made Helen force him to open his mouth so that I could push the neck of the bottle in and make him swallow double the portion! I told Helen before leaving to mark the names and numbers of all the idlers.

Meanwhile rumors must have spread of how I was going to cure all the lazy loafers, for when we stepped out into the open we saw a good dozen of them running towards the fields. But I shall punish them all. I shall force them to work next Saturday from dawn till dusk, and keep them imprisoned over Sunday. Spending Saturday night separated from their women will be worse for them than whippings.

When I returned I had my horse saddled and rode out to the fields, escorted by César and the dog, both running beside me.

From a distance I saw a gang of blacks idling about, but at my approach they started plucking cherries with mock eagerness, the driver shouting and cursing as if intent on making them toil to exhaustion.

I alighted, leaving the horse to César's care, and took Nero by the leash and approached the men. All of the baskets were still half empty after two hours work!

I told them if they were not filled four times before sunset they would have to work on Saturday to bring in the full portion allotted to each of them.

They just grinned and smiled and nodded, but I knew they were making fun of me, laughing at me behind my back. I felt helpless and defeated. There was no real resistance to be squashed, just friendly smiles and grins and mock eagerness. It was like striking a soft velvet curtain that gave way, but fell back into place the moment you withdrew your fist. It made me furious. I rushed at the one who dared mutter words I could not understand.

"What did you say?" I asked, provoked by his insolent stare.

"Nothing, ma'am, nothing!"

"Don't dare lie to me, tell me!"

"Young ma'am is very hard on us, makes us work and work and work. Sun is hot, air is hot, skin is hot, face is hot, back is hot——"

"I bought you hats to protect you."

"Hats very good, ma'am, but all is hot all the same, hands and belly and legs and feet, all sweat, all tired!"

"After two hours' work?"

"Knowing work no end, ma'am, work and work and work and work."

"You are given time to rest and eat and drink and sleep, aren't you?"

"Yes, ma'am, but very little."

"Everybody must work, white men, too."

"White men get money for work."

"You get your food and bed."

"What food? What bed?"

"Any complaints?"

"Black man must not complain, black man must sweat."

"What's your name?"

"Rufus, ma'am, but my real name is Mambo, ma'am. Son of a chieftain, ma'am, big chieftain, big hut, big power!"

He looked, indeed, better than the others, though not handsome with his flat nose and swollen lips. But

his dark eyes were sad and proud, not submissive-look-
ing like the others.

I felt a little shy at his bold stare and tried to hide my
embarrassment behind haughtiness. I said things had
changed, he was a field hand now and his duty was
to pick cherries, not to argue and complain. He had
better turn to his work, make haste to fill his basket else
I should make him work on Saturday like the other
idlers. I turned away and saw another fellow sauntering
towards us from behind one of the trees that stood
shadowing the coffee-shrubs. He was stark-naked, and
playful in his dancing gait, as if indifferent to my presence, shamelessly indifferent, which forced me to take
him to task in order to save my face. I would have preferred to ignore him.

I tried to assume Denise's way of talking to slaves,
her sharp voice, threatening frown and arrogant poise.
I asked him what he had been doing there, idling about
instead of working.

For answer he pointed to his private parts, grinning and making faces, swaying his body, legs astraddle.
I got very vexed, knowing the others were watching me,
all smiling and chuckling. I asked him why he had not
put on his pants. He said they were dirty, "Pants no
good, pants very hot!" I told him to take off his hat in
my presence, hold it before him for decency's sake,
which he did, but covered his chest and belly out of
mere roguishness instead of his ugly private parts. Heard
the others laugh behind my back. I got so furious I hit
the fellow with my crop, smacked his face in blind
anger, and then felt ashamed the moment I saw his
face turn rigid, a reddish streak showing across his
cheek.

I turned away, calling for the driver. I ordered him
to punish that man for disobedience, send him back to
his cabin to put on his pants and make him work next
Saturday like all the other lazybones.

I rode back home without having seen the other
gangs. All the way back I had a feeling of helpless
shame at my defeat, saw the ugly black face before me
like a strange beast's, a grinning ape's, unable to grasp
my words, to talk my language, to appreciate my desire

to be liked and acknowledged. It was out of despair that I hit him, admitting my failure to win and bring him to heel by decent means.

For the first time I realized I was capable of the same cruel impulses as Denise, lashing a human being in blind fury. Wasn't it out of mere vindictiveness, because I felt humiliated, that I switched him? Like my father when he thrashed me, knowing I hated him! Heaven save me from restoring to the whip like the other whites, from making it a habit, from admitting I was wrong in hoping to win the blacks through kindness and leniency.

At home I turned to Uncle, hoping he might advise and reassure me, but found him in the worst possible mood.

He said I had no right to take away his bottle of rum. He asked, begged, entreated me to serve him another glass, which I refused to do, reminding him of his promise to wait till midday. He again started weeping, but I was resolved to be adamant. I wanted to prove to myself that I was not so weak as to break my word.

I tried to convince him he could not have it for his health's sake, but he sneered, saying I knew he was going to die soon! He said it was out of mere heartless cruelty that I refused to grant him his consolation, called me ungrateful, hard and malicious. Threatened to send for the attorney to change his will, disinherit me for my cruelty to my helpless dying uncle.

I was so dejected I unlocked the wardrobe where I kept his bottle and served him a glassful, and then another out of sheer despair. His mood quickly changed for the better. When he saw I was on the verge of tears, he started caressing me, invited me to share another glass of rum with him to cheer me up, which I did. I let him kiss and fondle me in his lame, helpless way and listened to his silly bragging about his amorous activities in the past, his secret love affairs unknown to his cold, indifferent wife.

The only thing worth living for, he said, was love, love, love. Looking back he repented, most of all, the many opportunities he had missed of enjoying the raptures of love-making, of touching, embracing and conquering a pretty maiden. At the end of a man's life what remains but the recollection of a smell, a caress, a happy moment of ecstasy? Neither money, nor power nor prestige can compensate for an existence devoid of such ecstasies, he said.

He admitted having deceived his wife many a time, and even when she found out he knew how to outwit her. When she became jealous of the two mulatto wenches he calmed her by sending them to the fields, which didn't prevent him from making love to them whenever he wished, meeting them in a hut or behind a bush.

The more he drank the more he gloried in his sins, as if trying to make me forget the pitiable impotence to which fate has reduced him. Poor cripple!

As I kept silent he asked what worried me. Told him about my failure in dealing with the field hands. He advised me to marry Charles and leave the blacks to his overseers. He said Helen had told him that Charles was courting me. Called him a decent young man, certainly a good match considering his family is so rich. Said marriageable men were rare in this island, so I had better grasp the chance while it was there.

Marriage is always a compromise, he says. The better a wife learns to adjust to her husband, the happier she will be. A pretty young woman like me, he insists, can easily secure her husband's love and devotion if she is willing to offer him all that he longs for in love-making: unconditional surrender, passion and skill.

A man's advice—so typical of Uncle's self-centered point of view! He said we white women could learn a lot from the colored girls we despised and hated out of mere jealousy. They knew all the sweet tricks and ruses and stratagems that make love an art, while white women were mostly shy and reserved, bashful and unresponsive in bed, which spoiled the fun and drove their husbands to foreign playgrounds! Never found him so talkative and cynically frank before. He said a white woman's place was in the house, where she was acknowledged as the undisputed mistress, while the field hands were to be left to her husband and his overseers. If she wished to rule them, too, she should do so through her husband, advising him between kisses and caresses. He maintained I was charming and clever enough to twist Charles round my little finger.

Thus he babbled on with drunken loquacity, feeding me with compliments and platitudes instead of sober advice.

Losing my patience I jumped up, saying it was time I left. I told him I meant to stand by when the blacks were bringing in their baskets.

"Don't leave me," Uncle implored. "Please, keep me company instead of worrying about those beastly niggers. Send for Charles, let him handle them in his own way, stay here with your poor Uncle, I need you, I really need you!"

I promised to send for Helen who was busy nursing the black patients in the sick-room.

I was about to grasp the bottle on the bedside-table to lock it away when I heard my uncle groan. He stared at me so dejectedly, looked so terribly sad and resigned that my heart melted. Oh hell, I thought, let him have his will. So I left the bottle on the table. Let him get drunk and fall asleep, and forget his misery. He cannot be helped.

Now I am sitting here in my room, writing to find peace and strength and courage enough to face them again and prove to them that I mean it when I threatened to punish the lazy ones. If they laugh at me when I am kind they may learn to groan when I am hard. It is a contest of will-power, mine against theirs. If I win today it is a victory for ever! Five o'clock! I must stop. I wonder why Helen has not returned yet. Is she already busy lulling Uncle into sleep?

I bought two new cahiers at the bookbinder's last week, one of which I have already filled to the last page! Writing has become my favorite pastime. It helps me by recording facts, pinning them down like dead insects, wasps, gnats, flies, spiders, to calm down, keep sober and cool and forget that I am in a terrible mess. Hell is no longer hell when you manage to describe it.

SUNDAY, JULY 2ND

I must no longer postpone recording the horrible things that happened last week.

I haven't opened this journal since last Monday, that fatal Monday! I was too dejected, discouraged all the time. But life must go on, whether we like it or not. Charles is so kind to me, so understanding, and so are his parents and even Denise, all trying to cheer me up and skilfully avoid whatever might remind me of my shameful defeat, of Uncle's death, of all the humiliation I suffered afterwards.

I won't return to my house before everything is settled, the papers signed, the marriage contract agreed, everything decided upon. I am fully dependant on my attorney. Knowing he likes me there is no reason to worry about the arrangements.

But I had better start at the beginning, remember things correctly as they really happened, not let them be confused and distorted as often happens when we try to record things long past.

Last Monday afternoon! How hopeful I was I could impose my will by keeping firm. I rode to the storehouse escorted by César, whom I had sent there early during the afternoon to ensure that Gaston was weighing the incoming baskets correctly, refusing those that were not filled to the brim. He had orders to tell the drivers to make each hand fill and deliver his fourth basket by six o'clock, and to warn them that I meant to turn up there myself half an hour before sunset.

César returned about five o'clock and informed me that so far very few of the blacks had delivered more than one or two basketfuls, judging from the small number of red cords they were wearing round their necks as vouchers of each plucker's results.

When we arrived nobody was present, not even Gaston! I sent César over to the fields to find Hector or Clément and tell them to make all the gangs hurry and bring their baskets to the store-house.

I had to wait a long time before the first men arrived, sauntering along like dawdling loafers. Gave them a piece of my mind and asked them if they preferred working on Saturday to being punctual. This didn't impress them at all. They just smiled at whatever I said, smiled and sneered like happy children unable to grasp the meaning of my threats.

I found their baskets were scarcely half filled, and none had delivered more than two before, some only one! They had a dozen lies and excuses in store to account for their poor crop, said it was more than they were expected to deliver, swore they had been working hard the whole day, and they felt sick and terribly tired after sweating in the hot sun so long.

They surrounded me, each trying to make me listen to his voice, half a dozen at a time, their driver standing by smiling, my dog Nero growling a while then suddenly attacking one of them with a snarl, which made them run away in all directions, screaming and shouting.

I had the feeling I was being made the laughingstock, standing alone in the sinking sun, trying hard to hold the furiously barking dog at the leash while the Negroes were staring and sneering at me from a distance, encircling me as if ready to pounce on me any moment.

I felt so helpless and frightened that I lost my composure, started shouting at them, calling them names, the rudest I knew. I ordered the driver to take my crop and serve them ten lashes each, which made them all run away again, laughing, while another group of blacks approached as leisurely as the first, watching the strange scene with growing merriment.

I felt so terribly humiliated, so desperate, so blinded by fury that I let the dog loose. He ran after them, caught the backmost of the fugitives by the flank and bit him.

I heard the fellow yell, saw him collapse, the dog standing over him snarling at the slightest move of his victim. There was deadly silence around me, all the Negroes staring at me in mute hostility like children whose happy game had been spoiled by a cruel fiendish intruder. I was relieved to see Hector approach on

horseback. I told him to take care of the wounded man,
have him carried to the infirmary and then report to me
at the office. I said he was responsible for all that disorder and insolence, he was not fit for his office, had
proved to be a liar, a weakling and a cheat. I had a
mind to punish him hard, send him back to the rows
and replace him by a better man, not a stupid dirty
scoundrel of a good-for-nothing bastard like him! Never
before had I insulted a man that way, pouring all my
venom over him, making him the scapegoat because of
my desperate rage and my own failure.

I took Nero by the leash, leaving the poor moaning
injured fellow crouching in the dust, and rode away
trying in vain to regain my calmness. I felt so miserable
I wished I could run away, back to France, anywhere
away from this hell of an evil, wicked, rotten place.

No sooner had I arrived and alighted than Helen
rushed out of our house crying for help—her master
was dying!

She said he was lying in bed unconscious, waxen
pale, his pulse very weak and his hands and face cold.

I followed her to Uncle's bedroom. Found him snoring as if each breath were painful, wrote a pass for the
stable-boy to ride to town and get the doctor and a
priest.

The bottle had dropped empty on to the floor, some
of its contents had spilt, but very little. A few brown
spots were on the linen, too, but he must have drunk
half the bottle like water, strong liquor, strong enough
to kill a healthy man, a pint of rum at a draught!

Helen said she had entered his chamber a quarter of
an hour before and had thought he was asleep. Then
she grew suspicious seeing he was so waxen pale. It
looked like an attempt at suicide, Heaven forgive him!
I felt responsible myself. I should not have left the bottle on his bedside-table, thus tempting him. I was so
shocked I fled into my bedroom and lay down exhausted. Meanwhile César had returned from the fields,
I sent him to Charles for advice, not knowing what else
to do in my misery and despair.

I must have fallen asleep, for I was awakened by

Helen who told me that young M. Galez was waiting for me downstairs. I met him on the dark staircase and was so weak that I burst into tears, which encouraged him to embrace and caress and even kiss me.

I felt too hopeless to resist him. I needed him, had but the one wish to throw off the heavy load of responsibility on to a strong man's shoulders, knowing that mine were too frail to carry it. I followed him into Uncle's chamber, but it was too late! Poor Uncle had died in my absence. Even in his ultimate hour I had forsaken him! Will God ever forgive me this sin? An hour later the doctor and the priest arrived, both too late. God have mercy on my poor uncle's soul!

Charles, seeing that I was paralyzed by the shock, invited me to spend the night with his family. I have been staying with them all the time, my house being closed and my house-servants moved over here.

Charles has taken over the management of my plantation, assisted by one of his father's overseers who will be replaced by M. Laroche next week.

I didn't ask any questions about the way they dealt with the lousy idlers. I don't care any longer, knowing the blacks do indeed prefer the whip to kind words. I have learned a lot in a few days' time: slapping a drunken Negro's face, hitting another with my crop, ordering a whole gang to be lashed, letting my dog attack and bite a big black fellow. No more reason to blame Denise, having adopted her methods myself. I still find it disgusting, but how can it be helped?

Uncle's funeral took place on Wednesday. I met a lot of his old friends, all unknown to me. He seems to have been very popular among the planters in this part of the island. Most of the men were very kind to me, but their wives and daughters treated me as an upstart, some with haughty reserve, others with feigned affability which didn't prevent them from hinting at the strangeness of Uncle's sudden death so soon after his wife's deplorable decease—as if they suspected me of having quickened it on purpose.

I felt terribly insulted and depressed. Told Mre Falcon, who tried to cheer me up by saying they were just jealous of me for being engaged to Charles whom they hoped to catch either for themselves, or for one of their daughters.

For piety's sake we must postpone our wedding for three months, though Charles says I am cruel to make him wait so long. I am glad I have time to recover, get used to my new surroundings, forget the past and prepare for the future, my wedding-gown, new dresses, all my linen and curtains and tapestry and a hundred other things to be cleaned and renewed and replaced. The whole house will be repaired, perhaps enlarged, and a number of cabins built for Charles's blacks to be added to mine. His father promised to grant him forty of his own, and fifty acres of his estate which adjoins ours. He intends to retire to France next spring and live on his fortune (which seems to be considerable), and the annual profits of his estate, which will be left in charge of some reliable manager.

I do hope he will give George to us, not to Denise. I saw him twice yesterday and once this morning. A nod, a smile, an indifferent word or two, no more. But our eyes talking all the while! Oh Holy Mary, save the poor boy from that little bitch. Help me to persuade Charles and his father to make him our *économiste!* It is not a sinful wish. I mean to be faithful to my future husband. But I do want George to be treated as our equal, a member of our family whom I am allowed to admire and confide in as though he were a handsome, strong, chivalrous, big brother.

As for Charles, I'll try my best to be a good wife, adjusting myself to his character, appreciating his good qualities, closing my eyes to his deficiencies. Uncle said I could learn to love my husband. I do hope he was right.

MONDAY, JULY 3RD

Denise is a gifted actress. In the presence of her majestic father she is the most devoted, humble, obedient, modest daughter: Yes, Papa! Certainly, Papa! Please, Papa! Thank you, Papa! all the time.

But the moment he has left she turns into the wicked

cat that she is, teasing and terrorizing the servants in her arrogant fashion. I am sure they hate and fear her more than any other white person in this house.

I am so glad her father won't allow her to take George with her, though she tries her best to change his mind. He is, thank Heaven, adamant, saying he has educated George to become his assistant. He depends on him, George being clever and trustworthy and as efficient as any white *économiste* for whom he would have to pay dearly. Next year, when he is going to France for ever, she may claim George on condition that her husband consents, which M. Galez doubts. So does Mme Galez. She, too, is decidedly against her daughter taking George with her.

She says young M. d'Argout would never allow his wife to be served by a handsome octoroon boy like George, no white husband would. She will have plenty of female servants in her big house, and a gelding or two her husband is going to give her as a wedding present, but no males *toutes pièces*.

They have postponed their wedding for a month because of her future husband's bad health. Wonder what kind of sickness it is he has caught over there in sinful Paris! At any rate she is not very enthusiastic about her prospective bed-mate. It is a mere business contract. His money in return for her good name, pretty face, proud manners, witty conversation and substantial dowry.

I do not envy her. Charles is, at least, not a rake. Though yesterday morning I saw one of the mulatto wenches leaving his room. One of his mother's maids. What was she doing there? Never mind! All men are hot bucks sometimes, while we women are expected to keep chaste and faithful till the end of our days.

JULY 5TH

M. Galez does behave like the King of France! His word is law! I have never heard Charles contradict him, nor Denise, to say nothing of his mild, soft-hearted wife.

I am glad Charles is not such a despotic character. He can easily be influenced, persuaded, coaxed into consenting. A real cavalier! So attentive and nice-mannered, not insolent like Pierre, nor a vulgar boor like Dubrit. He certainly has his merits and I am sure, in the course of time, he will outgrow his little shortcomings. I do wish he were a little less pedantic though, more lively, cheerful and imaginative. There is no doubt that his sister is brighter and wittier, but of course I prefer his character to hers!

It seems they have succeeded in mastering my blacks, but how they brought them to reason I don't know. Have stopped asking questions.

Charles is an expert at handling disobedient niggers, and so is Laroche, our new overseer. He is a Swiss, served in the royal army, looks like a little uncouth with features hard but honest. If he treats them roughly it serves them right. I gave them a chance and they missed it. Helen says she heard there were some public whippings. This seems to be the only language they grasp, the fools!

Some guests from France arrived yesterday, M. and Mme Larue and their daughter Louise, a girl my age but short and plump with breasts big enough to feed half a dozen babes.

The family are on their way home to France from New Orleans, which is a French town under Spanish rule. M. Larue, who is a solicitor, hopes to find support in Paris for his political aims, namely to return Louisiana to France to which she once belonged. He hates both the Spaniards, and the former English colonies, now called the United States. He says they want to make Louisiana an American state, which must be prevented at all costs by our king. Interesting to listen to his lively political discussions with M. Galez at table.

M. Larue is pinning his hopes on M. Calonne, a French minister who wishes to reform the land tax, while M. Galez fiercely opposes such reforms, saying they would ruin the planters.

It seems we are already being plundered by the State, represented by the Intendant at Port au Prince. We must pay a head tax on each of our slaves, which money is only partly used to compensate us for the loss of slaves killed for disobedience or executed for a criminal offence.

Not only slaves, but plenty of other things are also taxed in our colonies, sugar, coffee, indigo, cotton, etc. Worse than that: we must not export our coffee, rum, tobacco, to other countries. That is the privilege of the French merchants. Neither are we allowed to build cotton mills of our own. Instead we must send our cotton to France and buy the expensive textiles made there, charged with *impôts*.

M. Galez says all the planters in this island are furious about the way we are treated by the arrogant Governor and Intendant and their commandants who prevent us from cultivating vine, and limit our export of rum even to France. We are also forbidden to import cheap corn from the United States, or Negroes offered by foreign traders. Those damned officers, he said, should be packed in a ship, all of them, and sent back to France never to return!

JULY 7TH

Even Mme Galez is not an angel! Last night saw her lose her temper for the very first time. It happened after supper when we women retired to leave the men to their brandy and big cigars.

Coffee and pastry was being served to us in the drawing-room when one of the waiting servants, the mulatto lad Marcel, stumbled, tray in hand, dropping the coffee pot which went to pieces in a black pool of coffee on the flagged floor.

It was a valuable piece of china, the loss of which made Mme Galez so furious that she rose and boxed the boy's ears. He was, in fact, innocent, for Louise Larue, that clumsy fat girl, had turned in her chair while he was passing, pushing him with her elbow and making him lose his balance. But, of course, servants are always wrong, never their masters! Sweet little Denise had risen, too.

"This gentleman deserves a reward," she said. "Don't you think so, Mama?"

"That clumsy, stupid, good-for-nothing!" cried her mother angrily. "Send for Gaston and have this fellow served twenty, and you stand by to see that he is not spared!"

"Yes, Mama," said Denise, nibbling her piece of pastry. She turned to the crestfallen slave, beckoning him with her forefinger. "This way, sir!" she said, smiling maliciously. She followed him to the door, still nibbling her pastry and swaying her little behind with mock dignity as if escorting a poor sinner to the gallows.

When they had left the conversation at once turned to the clumsiness of servants and the punishments recommended, each of the ladies praising her own way of handling cases like this.

Mme Larue said she preferred treating wrongdoers with hot pricks which didn't ruin their hide, while her soft-hearted daughter preferred making them wear spiked iron collars at night for a while.

Mme Monnier, our neighbor's wife, said she hired them out for hard labor to recover the money lost. They knew other women who were used to much more drastic measures, too drastic ones, in their opinion.

They mentioned a lady who sold one of her lackeys to the mines for a trifling trespass, another one who cut her servant's tongue for lying to her.

I am sure there is no atrocity imaginable that has not yet been committed by white masters and mistresses in this wicked island, not to mention colored slaveholders like that fat mulatto bitch in the boat!

I was disappointed to see kind Mme Galez give way to her temper like that. I heard subdued sounds as if someone far away were slowly clapping hands, and a feeble whimpering. After a while Denise returned, flushed and in high spirits, smiling as if having had a good time. She is wicked to the core, the cruel little beast!

MONDAY, JULY 10TH

M. Larue and his family departed this morning.
Mme Galez and Denise escorted the ladies as far as
Cap after M. Larue and Charles had left on horseback,
which gave me the very first chance to have a long
friendly talk with George as M. Galez was lying in bed
with gout.

We felt like daring conspirators, knowing how Denise would react if she knew. I met him in his bureau
and Helen and César made sure that none of the other
servants saw me go there and return. It was hard to
hide our emotions—sympathy soaked in sadness—
yearning checked by resignation.

He still lives in terror of her whims, though I tried
to reassure him by telling him that her father strictly
refuses to deliver him to her after her wedding, instead
may leave him to Charles and myself when he returns
to France. He thinks it is too wonderful to be true.
Poor dear boy—confused by a turmoil of feelings, fright
and hope and humiliated pride and suppressed desire. I
know how he feels. There is an intimacy of mutual understanding between us that needs no words nor bodily
contact to express itself.

The family he came from seem to have lived somewhere near the northern coast, for George does not
remember ever having crossed a mountainous region. I
might ask Mme Galez, but I dare not. It would make
her suspicious. Better turn to Mre Falcon, and ask him
to make inquiries without telling anyone. If it turns out
that his mother was that old widow's daughter, a white
woman, I shall fight for his immediate emancipation.
Mre Falcon said it was against the law to keep a white
woman's child in slavery.

JULY 12TH

I wonder whether Denise lied to me deliberately, or
did she report those horrible lies in good faith? Her

mother was shocked when I asked her if gelding criminal slaves was really common practice here. She stared at me as if my dirty imagination had run wild, then emphatically denied it. Said in twenty years' time only two of their slaves had been punished that way, both for raping light-colored girls, a crime for which they ought to have been killed. Maybe, she said, drivers or overseers referred to these rare cases in order to frighten their field hands.

Denise looks a different person in her new riding-habit, seated side-saddle like a real lady. I admit that frog-green suits her fair hair beautifully. She seems to be growing up, is trying to behave like a *dame du grand monde*.

She has picked up a little mulatto boy, eight or nine years old, no more. Discovered him among a crowd of brown brats weeding the orchard while she was passing on horseback. Told her groom to lift him on his saddle and take him to the mansion. There she had him washed from top to toe and dressed up like a queen's page, white pantaloons and doublet, a golden sash round his narrow waist and a tall, white turban, oriental fashion, quite a masquerade. A handsome little fellow, I admit.

She seems to be quite gone on him, treats him like a pet, a live doll, a toy, keeps him by her side day and night and has him dressed up in a dozen different ways. A strange new whim of hers. Funny to see her fondle a little midget like that, a brown one to boot, bursting with tenderness and playful good humor, quite a different person from that mean heartless little devil who loves to terrorize her servants.

Her betrothed is expected to arrive next month. I wonder what he looks like? She does not behave as if yearning for him. Well, I can hardly reproach her.

They have started repairing and enlarging my house, adding a wing with two more rooms for guests and some more for servants. The large dining-room will be embellished: flagstone floor, mirrors, etc., and so will Aunt's bedroom, which will be ours in two months' time.

I do hope he is not a master snorer like that old fool Courvoisier on board ship. At least he is not a brute like Pierre. Never would I allow him to treat me the way that monster did—never! I am as tall and strong as he is. If ever he should try to handle me roughly I would fight and disarm him the way Helen told me to put any man out of action. He will have to submit to my terms.

JULY 18TH

I visited my house for the first time since that lamentable day. Two dozen blacks are busy repairing it, rooms and staircase and roof and everything, and adding ten yards to the left wing, stone basement and wooden structure as well. It will take them another month to finish their work.

I inspected the slave quarters too, the new cabins they are busy building for our additional hands. All the slaves I met were very respectful and submissive. No more impudent smiles and sneers. They seem to have learned I can strike back if provoked.

Denise escorted me with her inseparable maid, Maria, and her honey-colored pet, little Lutin, as she calls him, this time dressed up like a tiny chevalier, all in white, a silver periwig on top of his pretty little brown angel's face. He looked so innocent and sweet. But she is spoiling him in every possible way, quite shamelessly.

The other day I told her why I had to stop César washing my feet. Mentioned his funny tricks, his excitement at feeling my toes against him. Denise said every little boy would react that way, even her eight-year-old Lutin.

She called him, stripped him, put him on her lap and started titillating him, the shameless bitch. Both were laughing and giggling all the time, the little brat turning and twisting to escape her, his tiny little cock pointing straight to heaven! Last Saturday I saw her sitting in her bath-tub, Lutin scrubbing her naked back. In my presence she made him lick her pink teats with the tip of his tongue, just for the fun of it, giggling like a silly child.

She seems to enjoy such strange sports. I wonder what tricks she teaches him when they are alone. He won't look so innocent for very long. She will spoil and ruin him in no time, and then throw him away like a broken doll.

Charles told me why our new overseer, Laroche, left his former place: got a mitten when courting his master's daughter, though she seems to have encouraged him. He is a proud man, though poor, very efficient and trustworthy in Charles's opinion. He says we must try to keep him, pay him well to make him stay.

JULY 22ND

Have been out of sorts these days. Our inevitable curse! No rides, no walks, just sitting and lying about in low spirits cursing the sullen heat pervading the darkened rooms. Never shall I get used to these beastly flies and mosquitoes and ants and other pests plaguing me day and night.

Helen confessed to me she is pregnant! Does not know for sure who is the brat's father, her present lover or my uncle! Imagine the cripple making love to her! But he did, she admits, several times. Or rather vice versa. She must have played the Amazon's part, riding a lame stallion. What a funny sight! She asked my permission to marry her beau, which I won't refuse to give if his master agrees. The boy looks decent enough. Shall ask M. Galez to leave him to us, we might employ him as a house-servant in order to keep them together. Married couples are sure to be faithful servants.

What if the brat turns out to be a little cousin of mine? Should take care of the child myself, knowing my poor uncle would have wished him to replace his son Louis. Whether boy or girl, I'll give the child the best education possible, manumit him or her when of age, and grant the cousin part of what Uncle would have bequeathed to Louis if the boy had survived him.

JULY 30TH

Yesterday I escorted Denise to town and called on Mre Falcon while Denise was at the dressmaker's. I asked him to make discreet inquiries about George's mother, which he promised to do. Dubrit has accepted our terms, knowing that suing us would be too risky for him. Good riddance!

The attorney read to me the marriage-contract he has drafted to secure my position. All my house-servants are to be put under my sole rule, remaining my absolute property, to be disposed of to my pleasure, no legal interfering on my husband's part possible. Of the annual profits 10,000 livres tournois are to be given to me for my private purse, for paying the dressmaker's and milliner's and shoemaker's bills and whatever I wish to spend it on, in order to protect me from my husband's possible tyranny or stinginess (though, I am sure, Charles is neither despotic nor stingy). But Mre Falcon says better prepare for the worst! You never know!

Should my husband die before me all my dowry shall be returned to me, buildings, estate, securities, slaves and all other livestock, according to their present value. The rest shall go to our common issue. In case of my premature death our common issue will inherit my dowry. If I am childless, I may dispose of my dowry to my own pleasure in my last will.

Denise had a good laugh when I told her about Helen and Uncle. She said I should have to wait at least six months after the brat's birth until I could make sure which of the two lovers is its father, mulatto babes being very light colored the first months.

WEDNESDAY, AUGUST 2ND

Yesterday we had the first heavy rain for months. Everybody felt relieved, though the violent thunderstorm may have made havoc of part of the crop, washing off the soil and flooding the fields. It kept on raining the whole night, but now the sun shines again, hotter than before. The moist steamy heat has soaked my dress to the skin—unbearable! I wish I could walk about like Eve in Paradise, lie and doze in the cool water the whole day, indulging in happy dreams of green pastures and gurgling brooks reminding me of my sweet Irish homeland long, long ago.

SUNDAY, AUGUST 6TH

I caught her in the act, the shameless harlot! Ought to tell her fiancé, or at least Charles or her mother. But for George I would not spare her, not that vicious bitch of a strumpet. Poor George! I am sure he is innocent, was forced to yield to her, knowing she has the power to ruin him if ever he should dare to resist her. Still, I cannot help feeling terribly disappointed, sobered, disillusioned. He will have to confess to me, make a clean breast of everything that has been going on between them. It might turn out to be of great use to me when fighting her claims on him.

But I had better first record the facts. Denise's parents have been absent since yesterday morning, spending the weekend with some old friends of theirs in town.

Denise refused to escort them, pretending she was indisposed. In fact she hates visiting elderly people, finds them dull and stupid, calls their wives and daughters cackling geese.

She was still in bed when her parents departed, said she had a headache. So I went for a ride on horseback all by myself, Charles having left with M. Laroche.

I told César to escort me to the stables. On the way there I saw Denise's maid, Maria, leave the bureau and run back to the mansion. I wondered what she had been doing there. Was she in love with George? I felt a little jealous, considering how buxom and pretty a wench she is.

I watched César and the groom saddle the horses in

the stable. Later, when they were helping me mount my white palfrey outside in the yard, I cast a glance backwards and saw George follow Maria from a distance. I should have stopped and questioned him at once. Instead I rode off, hiding my feelings from César who looked so proud and happy on horseback.

I galloped a long way in order to divert my thoughts —but in vain. I could not help pondering over George and the bastard girl. Or was it her mistress he was going to meet? Denise? That bitch!

I got so jealous I turned back, approaching the house from the rear. I alighted and told César to take the horses back to the stable.

Then I entered the house through the servants' door, ran upstairs and was met by Maria who looked frightfully embarrassed, nay, alarmed, tried to stop me, saying her mistress felt very sick, she was asleep, had told her not to admit anybody.

I pushed her aside and saw the little urchin Lutin pounding at the door with his tiny fists to warn his mistress. When I opened the door I saw two faces staring at me, saw him turn his back to me, stand motionless as if petrified, hiding his shame, while she had dropped back on to her pillows, covering her body up to the bare white shoulders.

I didn't see much as her bed stands in the darkest corner of the shaded room. I was too bewildered to find words. I turned and ran out, back to my own room and fell on my bed as if hit with a hammer.

I met her again at table. She looked indifferent, as innocent as if nothing had happened. And with not the slightest trace of contrition! She prated of a hundred trifling matters before mentioning, in passing, that she had sent for George to tell him she intends to claim him back from her father next spring, make him her butler and supervisor of her twenty or more house-servants. I said I doubted if her future husband would consent.

"He must," she said. "My marriage-contract entitles me to dispose of my own slaves at my pleasure."

"Would you like him to find George in your bed-chamber?" I put in maliciously.

"You are mistaken if you think I let him misbehave," she replied.

"What if your parents knew?"

"I hope you won't tell them. Else I should be forced to inform Charles about those funny games you used to play with your boy César."

"That's a lie! You know I stopped him at once!"

"I doubt if my brother would trust you."

"You are mean!"

"No use getting cross! We had better keep silent, both of us, knowing that nothing wrong has happened. I am still a virgin, as intact as you are expected to be. That's what matters. Believe me, I am not so silly as to lose my head at the wrong moment. I was teasing him a little, I admit, just for the fun of it, no more. After all, he is my servant, not a man worth respecting. One needn't be bashful in the presence of slaves, need one?"

That's what she said, smiling calmly all the while. No use arguing with her. She is so terribly sophisticated she can turn black into white.

AUGUST 8TH

I can no longer feel the same way about George as I did before. Of course it is all her fault. How could he have resisted being her slave? Still—I don't wish to see him again—not for a while. This morning passed him in the yard, keeping my face averted, which now I regret, pitying him, poor lad. But how could I face him, knowing that those lips I once longed to kiss are impure, servile instruments of debauchery. And I have been fighting for that man's freedom! Does he deserve it? If I were not engaged I might still try to take him away from that bitch, make him my overseer, even grant him favors—how could I not help it in the long run, the lad being physically so attractive? But never again on equal terms, my tenderness being poisoned by contempt. I might treat him the same way a man treats his paid mistress or a pretty servant-girl he has fallen for, a fancy slave, a pet to be dismissed when getting tiresome, not a real partner for a lifetime.

But I must not give way to such revengeful thoughts, trying to degrade him instead of helping him. I must never forget that he is her victim. It is that bitch of a girl who ought to be spanked, not the helpless prey of her dirty whims.

Yesterday she told me shocking things about that fat wench Louise Larue. Said Louise had confided to her that she had been intimate with a slave boy of her parents' for years, knowing how to do it without losing her maidenhood. Denise says there are plenty of ways to pleasure a lonely woman who wishes to run no risk.

In her opinion most widows and a great many young girls in this rotten island indulge in such secret pastimes out of mere boredom.

No doubt Denise is trying to lessen her own trespass by slandering other girls. If one believed her, our whole sex is rotten to the core. But I am not, nor are thousands of other girls, decent ones who would shrink from being touched by a man, whether he be free or a slave. Yet—remembering that horrible woman Gillet, or Mme Cartier who pretends her three servants are geldings, which is a lie, or the young twins on board our ship talking of bed-mates and virile bucks and impotent ones in terms that would make a decent girl in France blush, it would seem that Denise is certainly not a rare exception in this wicked island.

It is so easy for a woman surrounded by slaves to give way to her whims, even wicked ones, and go unpunished. Myself, one minute ago, did I not play with the idea of humiliating George the same way as Denise did—out of mere revenge! Dirty wishes indeed, for shame! I am afraid my thoughts are less pure than they were a month ago, more excitable by tempting dreams. Getting married will stop that I hope. I'll try my best to be a loving wife and make Charles happy in bed, adapting myself to him body and soul. So help me God!

FRIDAY, AUGUST 11TH

Our wedding day will be September 2nd, three weeks from tomorrow. It will be a double wedding, Denise and her fiancé, who arrived yesterday afternoon, having theirs together with us. He is a lanky pale fellow, his nose prominent and thin, his eyes cold like a toad's, his Adam's apple moving up and down whenever he talks. It must be irritating for Denise who is so sensitive to ugliness, so critical in judging other people.

He is terribly arrogant and condescending, even when making compliments he behaves as if granting a favor. I never met such a silly conceited ass before. I doubt if he will be strong enough to master her. She is much too clever and self-willed for an empty-head like him. I disliked him from the very first moment—his impudence, assessing me like a prospective prey, resting his cold beady eyes on my bosom as if trying to guess its size and firmness.

He arrived a week early, the fine weather having permitted a speedy voyage. The house is full of bustle and excitement, everyone except Denise being highly impressed with the honor of harboring an offspring of old aristocracy. Even M. Galez has lost some of his royal grandeur in the presence of his guest. To-morrow there will be a number of other guests invited to honor his presence. I am vexed at seeing Charles play the second fiddle all the time. He is too modest to handle that fellow as his equal. There is no reason to envy Denise, Charles is, without doubt, a much better character, serious, faithful, trustworthy and so wonderfully chivalrous!

SUNDAY, AUGUST 13TH

The nearer the great day comes, the more I am worried. What will happen when he finds the door has been opened by someone else? Never will he forgive me if he learns what happened that night on board ship with Pierre. Men are so terribly particular about their first night's privilege—as if crashing a locked door were especially delightful. If deprived of that privilege, all their pleasure is spoiled. It is their ridiculous pride that is hurt, their pride of ownership, not their sense of decency, which is a mere pretext considering their own infidelity, whoring while their wives are expected to keep chaste.

I must try and make it hard for him to work his way in. Some drops of blood might help. I must turn to Helen for advice. She is trustworthy and knows how to handle such problems. How Denise would sneer at me if she knew!

Last night the house was full of guests, invited in honor of our aristocratic dandy. It was the most sumptuous dinner I ever had, partridge and four different courses, and as many wines and heaps of various desserts. A pity I could not enjoy them, feeling fed up like a stuffed goose after the second course. The air was hot and sticky, the ladies' perfumes mixing with the smell of gravy and sweating servants crowded behind our backs, ready for our beck and call all the time.

Some of the guests are still here, for the rain is pouring down in torrents. They were all pompous people whom Denise made fun of as soon as they had retired.

Her beau will leave tomorrow morning. She is invited to his parents' mansion near Môle St. Nicolas, a two days' journey from here, to be introduced to his family. She will be absent a whole week, thus offering me a good chance of seeing George and making him confess.

Thank heaven he is safe for the future. She did not claim him when they made the list of all the slaves selected to follow her after the wedding, twenty-four male blacks and six females for the fields, and seven house-servants, four of them mulattoes, and, of course, her own pets, Maria and Lutin.

I wonder why she has included Marcel in her selection, considering the mean way she has been treating him since he broke that coffee pot, calling him a good-for-nothing stupid clumsy, lazybone whenever he must wait upon her at breakfast, frightening him with her threats or teasing and nagging him till tears ran down his cheeks.

She knows he lives in terror of her and she seems to enjoy it, the cruel cat.

She will only leave him in peace so long as her mother is present, but the moment she is his indepen-

dent mistress he will have a hell of a life, poor boy. And
he is such a docile lad, so fair-skinned that he might
be taken for a quarteroon though he is in fact a mulatto
whom they bought three years ago, at the age of sixteen
while Denise was away in France. He is a handsome
lad. I should like to own him. Mme Galez admits he is
very willing and clever.

But since Denise has turned against him he looks
terribly dejected and frightened all the time, a nervous
wreck, trembling at the very approach of his young
missus.

None of the other house-slaves have been punished
so often as poor Marcel these last weeks. She seems to
be looking for pretexts to have him thrashed all the
time. The other day, while sharing breakfast with me, it
occurred to her to examine his hands. Finding some of
his fingernails black-rimmed she sent him away to clean
them. When he returned she rebuked him coldly saying:
"I must make thee remember for ever that thou hast
ten fingers to keep clean. Go and tell Gaston to serve
thee ten lashes that will leave ten separate marks on thy
back as a record of thy failing. Now hurry, and be
back in ten minutes' time to show me the marks, ten
separate ones, crosswise, and good ones!"

No use interfering. She is too stubborn to revoke any
order of hers, says slaves must be taught the hard way. I
do pity the poor boy. I might offer her one of mine in
his place, but I am sure she would ill-treat that one
the same way. It is her character. It cannot be
helped. I am looking forward to her departure, everyone is, at least all the servants that are not doomed to
follow her.

AUGUST 16TH

I spent the morning in our new house supervising the
Negroes carrying in the furniture from town. Had them
move the big wardrobe from Uncle's chamber into
Aunt's, which will be our bedroom. It is the largest and
finest upstairs. Charles wishes all the mirrors to be left

where they are. A little awkward, rather embarrassing, watching ourselves undressing, lying in bed, even making love. Like a public performance somehow!

They say in brothels there are mirrors everywhere, even fixed to the ceiling. Makes me feel like a common slut! But I must learn to squash my virgin modesty. Husbands expect their wives to stimulate, not spoil their appetite.

Returning I saw Maria and Lutin peering down at me from the staircase, then heard them pounding at a door. I rushed upstairs suspecting Denise of having called George in again.

When I pushed the door open she was sitting at her dressing-table, wrapt in her négligé, facing a young man who was buttoning up his shirt. It was Marcel, not George whom she had been busy with. I felt much relieved when I realized my mistake.

"Get out!" she said, dismissing the frightened boy with an angry wave of her head.

"He was served another portion for being late this morning," she explained. "I sent for him to make sure he got his desert."

I doubt very much if that was the reason for his presence in her bedroom. She looked flushed and embarrassed as if stopped in the middle of an emotional scene.

Why was she again undressed so late in the morning? Her hair tousled, her feet bare! I had met her at breakfast when she was fully dressed in her riding-habit, ready to start for her morning ride. Now her habit and underwear were thrown across a chair and her crop was lying on the floor near the dressing-table.

She is a wicked little bitch, ready to cheat her husband on the very eve of her wedding, the shameless harlot. If her mother knew! But she is away, visiting Mme Robert, their old neighbor's wife.

AUGUST 17TH

Confided my problem to Helen this morning. She says a needle and a piece of thread can mend it. She

will do it herself, having watched her aunt do it to both
colored girls and white ones several times. She practiced
it to earn her living after she was emancipated on her
mistress's death.

Better wait till my sick days are over—next week
some time. Denise will depart for her visit tomorrow.
Hope her parents are going to town on Saturday. I
must see George and listen to his version of the story.
I wonder if Mre Falcon's man has found out something about George's mother. I must see the attorney
next Sunday, after Mass, if possible.

We had another thunderstorm last night, a terrible
one that kept me awake for hours. Once I thought our
house was on fire, so bright was the light and so loud
the noise. César rushed in looking deadly frightened,
and so was his sister. They started praying aloud, the
boy clinging to her as if hoping to find protection in her
arms.

This morning the cellar was flooded, barrels swimming about, and dead rats too. Charles says part of our
corn fields are ruined, but none of the coffee plants in
the protected hilly region. Some of the Negro cabins
are partly washed away but can be repaired in a few
days' time. There was an earthquake too, which,
however, we scarcely realized in the general turmoil.

AUGUST 18TH

Denise left this morning, escorted by Maria and
another maidservant and Lutin. She looked queenly in
her carriage and four, two black lackeys in white liveries on the rear-platform holding golden-tasseled green
parasols above her to protect her from the bright morning sun, and the old coachman in front wearing his
brand-new red livery as proudly as though he were
driving the Queen of France's golden coach.

Now everybody feels relieved. Even poor Marcel
looks happy again, as if recovering from a painful
fever.

I made both Helen and César solemnly promise to
burn all the cahiers of this diary in case anything

should happen to me. They know where the key to the case is hidden. The very idea of leaving this diary to my husband or any member of his family makes me sick. They would be shocked, would call me a slut and a cheat, which I am not. I am just trying to be frank in my records, no more. But people are not judged by what they think and do but by what they pretend to think and do. They are all used to telling lies. Sometimes it seems to me all human relations are based on lies, on pretended feelings, not those we really have.

I have often asked myself why I should write down all this knowing that nobody else will read my confessions. Perhaps it helps me to get rid of thoughts and feelings too dangerous to harbor in my mind for long.

Men are allowed to talk frankly about such matters: love, passion, vice, greed, ambition, envy, hatred and wicked cruelty, but not women.

We are expected to restrain our words, to limit our topics of conversation, talking only of nice things, as if nothing wicked happened around us, pretending to be angels, not human beings capable of strange desires and murderous thoughts like any man.

I often wish I were a man, able to think clearly and describe life correctly. I wish I could write as candidly as M. Rousseau does in his *Confessions,* or Mr. Fielding in his *Tom Jones.* I wish I could create heroes and heroines that are true to life, neither angels nor devils, but the bastards that people are, sons and daughters of Satan and all the Angels in Heaven he raped.

I should make Denise the heroine of my novel, that corrupt bitch with an angel's face, so pretty, so clever, so witty and charming in society, but hard, cruel and lecherous in the private domain of her life.

Unlimited power is apt to spoil all of us, women as well as men. Maybe in France, where there is no slavery, she would have developed a different character with charming traits suiting a well-bred girl like her. It is this social system based on slavery that has corrupted her, the power she has to rule over men and women as their absolute mistress, entitled by law to dispose of them as she pleases.

I admit it is an agreeable feeling, this sense of unlimited power that is given us over slaves. But it is dangerous, I know it is. It makes us arrogant, self-willed and ready to hit at the slightest resistance.

Sometimes I am scared of myself, watching my sudden impulses that I can no longer bridle so well as some months ago, my blunted modesty in dealing with male slaves, my indifference to acts of cruelty and humiliation I am forced to witness every day. I have already got used to such scenes. Maybe I shall soon learn to be cruel myself, and like it. Denise does, and so do plenty of white women in this island, watching executions as a pastime, even inventing new tortures to stimulate their morbid senses.

Remember the lady who cut her slave's tongue, or the one who had her slave buried in the earth up to the neck, stuffed his mouth with salt and watched him moan and whine and slowly die with thirst in the burning sun! These are atrocities committed by women of distinction, still respected, acknowledged as members of society, never prosecuted for their crimes.

Perhaps in many years, when old and lonely, I shall return to France or Ireland and write my book there, publish it under a man's pseudonym, making use of the facts I have recorded in this diary.

But shall I ever see my native country again? A young wife's life in this climate can so suddenly be cut short. She may die in child-bed or may catch one of those murderous fevers that kill thousands every year. She may be bitten by a poisonous snake, or spider, or scorpion, or murdered by a jealous husband or a revengeful slave. If I am doomed to die early may this diary vanish with me, for it is not meant to accuse anybody, nor to cause scandal and disgust among my relatives and friends. It is the most private of my papers. It should be buried with me.

SUNDAY, AUGUST 19TH

Very disappointing news: The man Mre Falcon employed to inquire after George's mother returned without results. He found the place—somewhere near Cap du Môle—where Denise's parents-in-law live, a sugar-plantation owned by M. Chatel, son of that old lady who had treated George like a member of her family. The son denied all rumors, said George was a slave-girl's son, no doubt of that. He grew angry when the visitor tried to question him about names and whereabouts, cut him short and told him to leave. Nor did any of the servants dare to answer his questions. They seemed to be scared.

So our man turned to M. Chatel's sister who is married to one of his neighbors. But she, too, shrugged her shoulders and pretended not to remember the bastard boy.

At last he found an old widow, owner of a small cotton-plantation near by, who turned out to be very garrulous. Said she remembered the eldest daughter very well. The girl had been sent abroad to some aunt of hers, they said. When she returned her brown maid carried two babes in her arms whom she claimed as her own. A few weeks later rumors spread that the young missus had run away with a handsome mulatto boy-servant, taking one of the twin babes with her. No doubt she had been fooling about with the mulatto long before.

Her parents tried to hide the scandal by spreading the news that their daughter had married some Yankee living in Philadelphia. Later she was said to have died there. But nobody knew for sure.

When he asked the old woman if she was ready to repeat her statements in court she flatly refused, but told him to find the brown maid who was said to be the twins' mother. She remembered the wench had escorted M. Chatel's youngest sister to Cap where the latter was married to some wine-merchant, a person much below her station.

M. Falcon's agent has found the man, a certain M. Robin, now an elderly widower, his wife having died in child-bed many years ago. He said he had freed the mulatto maid and married her to a free man the same color, a carpenter by profession, called Chanteclair.

Louise is an elderly woman now. She seemed to be embarrassed, even scared, when our man questioned her. She said, yes, she was the twins' mother, but seemed not to be keen on seeing her son again. Very strange indeed. Have a good mind to see that woman myself. Hope I can make her tell the truth!

AUGUST 24TH

Glad my sick days are over for a while, maybe a long while if Charles proves to be able to stop the bloody mess in time. Still feel a little frightened, though Helen says I needn't worry. She'll do it tomorrow. A matter of five minutes, no more, she says. Must try and make him happy the very first time, maybe decisive for my whole future. I am sure he is not a brute. Would hate him to behave like Pierre. Hope I like his smell. They should not be allowed to hurt us the first night. Just touch and caress us, make us get used to their hairy skin, their tight muscles, their monstrous weapons. They ought to be considerate, tender, slow, not like ferocious bulls intent on killing you with their murderous horns.

I rode over to our house this morning. Caught a dirty swine of a nigger pissing against a young tree in the garden. Told César to serve him twenty on the spot with my crop. Some of them behave like dogs the moment you turn your back on them. Ought to have summoned a strong Negro to warm him up more vigorously.

The new rooms will be ready for us in time. The cabinet-makers were fixing mirrors along the walls. Really bewildering! Charles wishes me to feel like the Queen of France in my new bedchamber, all gold and silver and blue shades and mirrors wherever you turn.

Returning I saw George cross the yard and sent César over to stop and summon him. I treated him with cold sarcasm to show him my scorn. Said I wondered why his young mistress had not taken him with her, using him as her *valet-de-chambre,* which seemed to be his new office.

He was visibly hurt, said a servant must obey orders if he wished to survive. I asked him how long he had been serving her that way, but he refused to answer that question, saying she had strictly forbidden him to talk about her, which made me very angry.

"How can you expect me to help you if you don't confide in me," I said, turning and riding away.

Maybe I was too hard on him considering the risk he runs if she turns against him. No doubt he is very unhappy, constantly threatened by her vicious whims. If ever caught in the act she will coldly sacrifice him in order to save her face. I must try to protect him, though perhaps, he is not worth the trouble. My feelings towards him are sobered and disillusioned. I could never again regard him as my equal, a man worth admiring. Pity mixed with scorn, that's what is left in my heart— nothing but that.

SUNDAY, AUGUST 27TH

This morning I met Mre Falcon in town after Mass. Together we drove to that carpenter, Chanteclair's house in order to question the woman who pretends she is George's mother.

It was a poor dirty street, and dozens of black and brown urchins, most of them naked, danced around our coach, shouting and giggling in the hot clouds of dust— like a gang of little monkeys, all making fun of our coachman who tried in vain to drive them off by wielding the whip right and left but was not quick enough to hit any of the brats. It was quite amusing.

We stopped in front of a whitewashed wooden cabin, windowless. While stepping out I saw dozens of brown faces staring at me from open doors. Inside I had to get used to the darkness before I could see the lean old mulatto man and the woman beside him, both withered and bony and poorly clad, their black eyes fixed on mine, staring at me as if paralyzed, for seldom are white visitors received in a free Negro's house. The warm musty stench of stale sweat and garlic was almost unbearable.

When Mre Falcon told them what we had come for they offered us the only two rickety chairs in the room, which wasn't much better than our slaves' quarters and obviously served them as bedchamber, kitchen and dining-room.

I started questioning her about the twins, told her I was sure she lied when she insisted they were hers. I asked her to tell me the truth and promised to reward her if she confessed. Then I threatened to find means to make her talk, but it was all in vain.

She kept stubbornly silent, nodding or shaking her head at my questions, now and then throwing a furtive glance at her husband who was watching her warily.

They were scared, both of them, as though their lives depended on keeping silent. I am sure she is not George's mother. There is not one single trace of his features to be found in her face. She is plain, dark-skinned, flat-nosed, and in total contrast to George who looks like a European, a handsome sunburnt Provençale or Spaniard, not kinky-haired like that dull, stupid withered brown woman.

He is a white woman's son, there is no doubt of that. But how can I prove it? I wish she were still a slave. I would purchase her from her owner and then whip the truth out of her filthy, pinched mouth. But would that help us? A slave's evidence is of no avail in court.

There is one way left to find the truth, says Mre Falcon. He will employ someone in Philadelphia to make inquiries. If he can find that couple—a white woman married to a colored husband whose eldest son is (or was) George's age, she is sure to claim her second son. Why didn't she do so before? She may have died (but then her husband should have, or friends of theirs who know the facts).

Maybe her family told them the boy they had left behind had died. That would explain his parents' strange indifference to his sad fate. I am ready to pay whatever they ask to find that woman, or her husband, or the other son. Denise will be raving mad with disappointment when forced to release her victim. If he is left to her, she will ruin him in no time.

On Friday morning I made Helen do her little needle-work. One of the pricks hurt like hell, but an hour later I was already on horseback forgetting the fading pain while riding over to my house to meet Charles. I feel more confident now.

Do I love him? We know so little of each other. Just nice words, compliments, small talk, nothing confidential. We are like two strangers ready to join for a long voyage without knowing if they will be a good match. Love takes time to grow. I'll try my best to make him happy.

AUGUST 28TH

César is growing too excitable. I am afraid I must put an end to his silly tricks. He tries to hide his emotions when scolded, but Charles would be shocked if he knew. Even if César learns to behave, my husband would not allow me to keep him upstairs.

Charles's mother has already offered me one of her brown wenches to replace Helen when she is approaching confinement. She asked me what I meant to do with César, which may have been a hint, a nice way of telling me she disapproves of my admitting the boy to my bedroom.

I must employ him downstairs, have him trained to wait on us at table. Or send him to town to be apprenticed to a ladies' hairdresser for a few months. He might replace Helen who is often clumsy doing my hair.

Most married ladies I know keep male hairdressers, so I am sure Charles would consent and grant us half an hour every morning, which would make it easier for us to separate later. Dear little fellow!

I cannot help liking him, in spite of his antics. But he is no longer a child. He ought to be given a pretty mate his own age to tame him. A lad and a lass in their first sap—it must be Heaven for them to make love, bashful approaches, and caresses growing to a final wild ecstasy—innocent, like Adam and Eve before the Fall.

Slaves are to be envied on that score. Nobody cares whether they are married or not: the earlier they start the more profitable for their masters. I'll try and find a suitable playmate for him. Might make her my second chambermaid to keep them all together like a family— mine. Laughter and fun all the time, and Helen's babe playing with mine next summer!

TUESDAY

Denise returned last night. She is not very enthusiastic about her future mother-in-law. Calls her haughty and conceited, but says the moment she is married she will show her who the mistress of the house is. She hopes the fat old woman will depart for France next spring. Then she can move to the big mansion and rule over more than thirty servants like a queen. Till then the young couple will live in a smaller house a mile away, built for the eldest son who died two years ago.

His young widow left for France soon after his death after selling her slaves to her father-in-law. Denise's future husband will receive them as his wedding present. It is a large sugar-plantation like M. Galez's. It seems the young man does not know the least bit about running a plantation and will be completely dependent on subordinates, which makes Denise all the more confident. She is sure she can twist her stupid husband round her little finger and make him consent to whatever she likes, grand dinners and balls and entertainments, and plenty of dresses and jewels and horses and hunting-parties, and a new coach-and-four and pages and dogs and crowds of handsome lackeys in bright liveries.

Our wedding garments arrived this morning to be given the finishing adjustments by the two seamstresses the dressmaker has sent us. They seem to be very expert hands.

Denise looks so sweet in hers, so innocent and virgin. You might think she was the purest young girl on earth, immaculate, incapable of doing anything evil, her soul as stainless as her snow-white wedding dress. If people knew! Never trust the look of men and women you meet. They are all actors performing their part.

AUGUST 31st

One of Denise's field hands disappeared on Wednesday night. He was caught by the *maréchaussée* in the early morning and delivered to Mme Galez, her husband and his overseers having left for the fields.

He said he had not meant to run away but spent the night with a black wench he is attached to, a slave belonging to a neighbor's plantation.

Denise wants him to be treated as a runaway, whipped in public and his ears cut off. Her mother interfered in the poor boy's favor, but Denise insists on a top to bottom whipping. As to his mutilation, she is willing to spare him on condition that her father offers her another black male in exchange. I am sure he will consent.

All the blacks doomed to follow the young lady to Môle St. Nicolas seem to be terribly distressed, even panic-stricken, rumors having spread about the cruel treatment and excessive work there.

FRIDAY MORNING

Denise is afraid there might be other attempts at running away from her. So when the hands returned from the fields yesterday evening she had hers summoned in the yard in order to warn them. At supper she triumphantly said she had thrown such a scare into the whole gang that they sneaked away like a pack of lame dogs.

She had told them that she meant to treat and feed them well so long as they proved to be hard-working, obedient hands, but she said she would punish severely any trespassers, lazybones, liars, thieves or disobedient slaves.

She threatened to have runaways gelded or sold to the mines or the galleys—she had half a dozen bloodhounds ready to hunt runaways down. Then she had the letter D branded on their arms to ascertain her ownership, and they were all locked in two cabins to spend their last night here watched by guards and dogs.

This morning they left in three big livestock wagons, ten men and women in each, all of them chained together in order to prevent them from jumping out and escaping on the way to Môle. Her seven house-servants will escort her to her new home after the wedding.

Helen told me one of the blacks implored his young mistress on his knees to let him take his wife and children with him. But she was adamant. Told him to stop wailing like an old woman. Said he was young enough to find another bedmate in his new home and make nigger brats by the dozens. Fancy such a coarse retort from a young girl's lips. How they must hate her!

Sometimes, passing a group of slaves, you feel their hatred hidden behind a mask of dull submission. Imagine them getting loose, knowing they are hundreds against a small bunch of whites!

Charles says if we are not on the watch a riot may threaten and break out at any time. Perhaps Denise is right to treat them the rough way she does, however disgusting a young woman may look cracking her whip. Remembering my own failure I doubt if we can keep them down in a different way. Denise is a hard woman, but somehow I envy her for her pitiless *sang froid*. I wonder if I shall ever learn to behave like her. I am afraid I am still too soft-hearted for this infernal world of rulers and slaves.

Denise's fiancé is expected to arrive tonight, but not his parents. Denise says they are in bad health, but I believe they are simply too proud to mix with people below their own rank. Never mind: there will be plenty of other guests invited to witness the ceremony in church and take part in the ensuing festivities in this house.

Charles wishes to leave with me as early as possible. We both prefer to spend our first night far away from the noisy crowd. My nuptual bed, which was once Aunt's, is ready for us. May her evil spirit not spoil our matrimonial bliss!

*   *   *   *   *   *

Part II
1790-1791

FRIDAY, OCTOBER 8TH, 1790

I have been reading my old diary, the first eight cahiers, the blue ones that I preserved, thinking they were less compromising than the pink ones written after my wedding. Now I feel sorry I told Helen to burn the pink ones, ten or twelve cahiers. They might have helped me to remember a thousand incidents that will be worth retelling when I prepare my memoirs. For one day I wish to write a book—when I am old and lonely, living somewhere back in France. I shall write under a pen name, of course, to avoid gossip and scandal.

When I told her to destroy them I never thought I had any hope of surviving, forty-two of our blacks and mulattoes having died like poisoned rats and I myself feeling the high fever burning my brains and bowels out like smouldering fire.

I had been told nobody could catch the yellow fever and survive. But I did, and six others beside me, while my husband, who was the last to catch it, was stricken and coffined in three days' time. But when I lay in bed groaning and sweating, he was still healthy and strong, and in my agonies I imagined him reading my journal, my most intimate, most secret confessions about our married life, my disappointments, anger, hate, scorn and resignation at his failures as a lover, a husband, a friend.

I imagined him reading about my wicked revenge, my paying him back by cuckolding him. Facing death I wished him to pardon me, excuse my own deficiencies and remember me as his loving wife, not his enemy.

What a shock it would have been to him and his family had that diary been translated! Denise understands English fairly well. She would have torn my character to rags had she known my confessions.

She did not catch the fever. She watched three dozen of her field hands die away like flies, then her overseer, his wife, her pet Lutin, her maid Maria and her coachman, but she lived, untouched by their groans and the stench of malady and death pervading the house.

There is no justice in the vagaries of fate, just good or bad luck for each of us. The strong seem to have a better chance of survival. Am I strong? I am more callous, harder, less sentimental than when I arrived here, over four years ago. There is no doubt of that. Had I been as sober-minded from the start as I have since learned to be I would never have married Charles knowing I did not really love him. It was a failure from the beginning. That odious first night—so disgusting and painful. His vanity deadly hurt when I stopped his clumsy attempts in time, crying it hurt.

The next night, finding the way open must have made him suspicious, which may have accounted for his stupid jealousy whenever he saw me talking to another man.

I had good reasons to be disillusioned. I wondered why people made such a fuss about one minute's unions, no tenderer, no more passionate than a cock's jumps. I never learned to enjoy his love-making. It left me cold and resentful.

I might have accepted frustration as something no wife on earth is spared in the long run, men being self-centered, conceited egoists, if only he had continued to respect me, and not turned against me with his outburst of blind jealousy.

The trouble began when Denise returned two years ago having separated from her husband after a hot dispute. I don't know what really happened. You never can depend on servants' gossip. But from what Helen learned from her husband Cassius (whose sister, Rose, followed her mistress as second chambermaid) it seems that shameless rake of a bridegroom brought home from Paris an abominable disease as his wedding present. At any rate, they had a doctor installed in their house for months, husband and wife living in separate rooms.

To all appearances Denise has completely recovered, but, after delivering a stillborn babe she had lost hopes of ever getting with child again. There must have been daily disputes between master and mistress. She accused him of having infected two of her brown maids and demanded high compensation for damaged property. She apparently flew into a fit of rage when he laughed, insisting those sluts had been worm-eaten before and had ruined three of his own bucks.

They started calling each other names, and then he slapped her face, whereupon she packed her trunks and left him never to return. How pale she looked when I met her on the staircase that night, after two years' separation. Still pretty, but more adult, harder, her sallow face taut, her cold blue eyes watching me like a prospective enemy.

She took possession of her parents' mansion after M. Gautier, her father's *gérant*, had moved to the old house. For months she kept two solicitors busy fighting for her rights. She won. The *séparation d'habitation* was granted to her in court, her husband was forced to render her all her dowry, including her thirty Negroes and their issue, and of course all her house-slaves, replacing the two wenches ruined by him.

Maria and Lutin were the only servants she had brought with her when deserting her husband. The pretty brown lass was big with child when they arrived. She gave birth a few months later to a fair-skinned boy whose father, Denise said, was a friend of her husband's, a young sea-captain who had spent a night with them. I wish I had known in time who that rascal was!

As to the boy Lutin, he had changed a great deal, had grown almost as tall as his mistress (though only ten or eleven). What a wicked little bastard he was with his insolent sneer, his knowing dark eyes, and his child's face deflowered by vice. I knew from the start that she would ruin him.

I wish she had never come back. The moment she popped up again she started breaking our matrimonial peace, the bitch!

But that is too long a story to be told in a few lines. I'll try and record it tomorrow if I am not too tired after discussing Denise's plan with Mre Falcon, Denise is so optimistic about the financial outlook that I feel tempted to consent. At least 120,000 livres as a net profit! But I must ask Mre Falcon's advice first. He is the only man I can trust.

SATURDAY NIGHT

I was in town this morning, but could not consult Mre Falcon. He has been absent for several days, but is expected to be back Sunday night.

Denise called on me in the late afternoon. Told me she is going to invest 70,000 livres in that profitable enterprise—a share in Captain Basteresse's trade.

He carried blacks from the African coast to Martinique for a group of planters several times and has made so much money that he could purchase a ship of his own, an old one, of course, but still seaworthy. Now he is looking for planters in this island ready to lend him their money for a new enterprise.

He needs a shipload of merchandise to be taken to the Bay of Sierra Leone in exchange for slaves and ivory.

Denise says he has promised her 120 per cent profit or more! She asked me to join her.

At first I was shocked at the idea of taking part in slave-trading, but Denise said there is no reason to be ashamed: Her father invested his money that way many a time and made a fortune. She would be a fool if she left her money in the bank when she was offered ten times the profit by investing it in good business.

I said it was immoral, at which she sneered, asking why, then, didn't I mind purchasing slaves imported by men like Basteresse? If I was infected by the silly new ideas about niggers why didn't I treat them as my equals, grant them their freedom and disclaim all my legal rights as their owner?

I said I did try to treat them as human beings, to be decently cared for.

She just smiled sarcastically, and I realized that her arguments were stronger than mine. Still, I said I could not make up my mind to get mixed up in the infamous trade of slaving. She said I had better consider the matter from a business-woman's point of view.

Of course it is very tempting: 120 per cent profit! I would be rich enough to sell my land and stock and return to France, a wealthy young widow!

I read again a chapter in Rousseau's *Confessions;* enjoyed it even more than four years ago. He was a strange man, weak and vain, but undoubtedly gifted. I cannot but admire his candor in revealing the bad traits of his character. He is one of the rare great men who do not pretend they are perfect. We all have our wicked impulses, we are all sinners. Why not admit it? I hate hypocrites and Pharisees.

Two more hands reported sick. Sent both to the infirmary to be purged. No. 23 is recovering.

Rex confessed he had slept with Lisa last night without my consent. Both received ten lashes. They will be kept separated for a month. Then I'll reconsider their attachment provided they maintain good behavior. I will not allow promiscuity in my house.

SUNDAY

This morning Denise drove up with Captain Basteresse. I was surprised to find he looks like a gentleman, not at all like the villain I had imagined a slaver would be. He was a very affable man of the world, still handsome though middle-aged and a little stocky.

He told us about his travels. He said he had never been shipwrecked in ten years and that trade still prospered in the Bay of Sierra Leone. He is supplied with slaves by several factories up river. Before being bought the slaves are carefully examined, to see there is no defect in any of them. If approved of, he agrees to a price at so many bars and gives the dealer so many flints or stones to count with. The goods are then delivered to him piece by piece, for which he returns so many stones for each, to their denominated value.

I said I thought it extremely cruel to steal and abduct innocent people from their homes and carry them away forcibly into a foreign country to be sold as slaves, upon which he answered that they were mostly either prisoners of war who would be killed if they could not be sold, or trespassers who were sentenced to death.

He is sure that slavery can never be abolished in that part of Africa, because of the hundreds of independent small states and tribes perpetually attacking each other, the natives being of a vindictive and revengeful spirit. When France was engaged in war with England a decade ago, no European slave-ships visited the coast for several years, which resulted in the black slave dealers cutting their slaves' throats or leaving them to perish for want of food.

Listening to him, you get the idea you are obliged to encourage the slave trade for mercy's sake!

He said his slaves cost him no more than 110 or 120 livres a head. He could transport a good 250 Negroes in his vessel that would bring in at least 300,000 livres, costs and taxes reduced, if we advanced a total of 140,000 livres. He is sure he can easily get the money from other planters, but being an old friend of Denise's parents he has promised to give her preference, which, he said, he would be delighted to extend to me, her sister-in-law.

I admit he has a very persuasive way of dealing with women, mixing his compliments with witty remarks and allusions. An interesting man, not to say charming. I said I was willing to consider the matter and would inform him about my decision after consulting my attorney.

I could well afford to invest 70,000 livres like Denise, my funds available amounting to more than 110,000 livres.

Yet, I must make sure that the slaves will be well cared for in the ship, plenty of food and space for each of them. No ill-treatment. And nobody must be told about this business! People might disapprove.

I shall send No. 23 back to the fields tomorrow. Strong enough for light work with the women and children. You never know if a fellow is feigning or really sick. I had him purged with castor-oil (which all of them hate like poison). Must not encourage shirking.

I read Rousseau's *Confessions*. He did behave like a fool sometimes. That new system of musical notation of his! Amusing.

OCTOBER 11TH

I drove to town this morning and had a long talk with my attorney who says he knows Captain Basteresse and that he is quite reliable. Advised me to accept the offer, slaves rising in value because of the rumors that the slave trade with Africa might be prohibited in the near future, not only by the French, but also the English, Dutch and Danish Governments. The moment slave imports are stopped slaves will become very valuable.

He therefore advised me to encourage slave-breeding at my plantation, purchasing a number of healthy wenches to supply me with plenty of brats. Should have to select half a dozen of my strongest and handsomest males for that purpose, perhaps even some of my bastard, light-colored offspring. If slaves are handsome and clever they are so much more valuable. It would pay in the long run, say fifteen years from today. One hundred handsome boys and girls for sale, at 2,000 livres a piece makes 200,000; quite a lot! Purchasing twenty wenches at 2,200 livres a head would do, adding them to the forty or fifty young ones left to me after the terrible loss the yellow fever has caused us. Ninety young women will easily deliver two babes each in two years' time. That makes one hundred and eighty (not including the hundred or more I already own). But where shall I take the 44,000 livres from? I cannot invest my money both ways. I could start with a smaller number of wenches. If I bought ten only, it would cost me about 22,000 livres, which leaves me less than 20,000 in the bank. Too little in case of emergency. Must try and sell ten of my males, pick out the least valuable ones. Must have a list made by Laroche.

Dreadfully hot and damp, worse than last summer. Makes me irritable. I wish I could return to France, to the Lake of Geneva, mountains, snow, cool water and bracing fresh air. Must drop that stupid breeding project, make my deal with Captain Basteresse, cash my profit next year and then sell, sell, sell, and get rid of everything that keeps me chained to this infernal island. Back to France, a wealthy woman, young enough to start a new life!

OCTOBER 14TH

Drove to town with Denise to meet Captain Basteresse at my attorney's. We signed our contract securing first choice of twelve slaves each (free of charge) on arrival of the freight. The rest of the blacks (two hundred of them being warranted as the lowest number to be reckoned with) will be put to public auction in due time.

The net profit of the sale is to be allocated to the three shareholders in the following way: the captain will receive a third of the sum and 50,000 livres extra, Denise and myself, half of the rest. The captain promised not to embark more than two hundred and twenty slaves, (his ship holding below two hundred and fifty tons), and to feed and treat them well. His ship will be overhauled and newly equipped before setting sail in November. It is expected back towards the end of August next year, the voyage taking three or four months.

He showed us a list of merchandise he has to purchase and carry to Africa in exchange for his slaves: salt and spirits and tobacco, powder, sabres, hats, woollen cloths, cotton and linen goods, copper kettles and pans, and a dozen other things regarded as very valuable by the natives. The amount of slaves offered there increasing every year, he can make his choice, picking out young, strong and handsome Negroes only, preferably males.

I made him promise me not to tell anybody that we are his joint partners. Public opinion might disapprove of women taking part in the slave trade. He said we need not worry as there were plenty of other ladies investing their money that way (which our attorney confirmed). In Martinique several of the joint owners of his former slave-ship had been lady planters who, like their male partners, wanted to fill up their stock of field slaves by new supplies from Africa every year.

It is indeed silly to feel ashamed. There is no way of stopping the trade. Too much money has been invested in it, the wealth of this island and the whole of the West Indies depends on it. If I step out, dozens of others, women included, will offer to put their money in this enterprise which is not very risky, both ship and cargo being well insured.

Nevertheless, I don't feel very happy about it. It is dirty. I came home depressed and irritable. I should not shout at my servants, but oh the heat—the moist, damp, heavy hellish heat!

The first thing I did at home was strip and lie down in the darkened bedroom. I ordered a cold bath prepared there and spent half an hour sitting in my bath-tub full of cool water. It was refreshing.

I sent for R. who was very contrite and unhappy. I felt sorry for him and was weak enough to pardon him, even worse, I was carried away by the wicked impulse to yield to temptation, itched by the devil. Relaxed but disgusted at myself. Bitch, bitch, bitch! Impressed on him it had been a whim of mine, no more. Not to imagine things! Made him swear to keep it a secret. He won't talk, knowing what he risks if he should break his oath. Told him he is allowed to meet Lisa twice a week from now on, as long as they both behave well, but each time must ask my permission. Frailty, thy name is woman! It is bad to spoil slaves, makes them lose respect. I must be more careful.

Why not sell everything now and leave? I hate this life. And yet—I can't imagine living married to some dull bourgeois playing the pasha and telling me how to behave. Here I am the queen, not a humble wife forced to obey a lordly husband. Not any more!

Tomorrow I shall have dinner with Denise. Hope to see George and tell him I have extended my inquiries to New York where his family seems to have moved. He looks so sad, so terribly miserable. I wish I could help him to escape her for ever.

I did behave like a slutty bitch this afternoon. Perhaps I would have resisted temptation if I didn't feel so safe from any consequences. That is the only compensation granted to barren women like Denise and me, but it does not make me any the happier.

MONDAY, OCTOBER 18TH

Denise called on me this afternoon, very vexed. George has run away again! It happened this morning, in town. She had pulled up in front of Dr. M.'s house and told George to fetch the medicine prepared there for her. Instead of obeying her he ran away, disappearing in a side street. She ordered her coachman to arrest him, but he was nowhere to be found. She alarmed a group of whites she met. They all helped her to hunt for the fugitive, but in vain. They searched the houses and gardens in the vicinity, but nobody remembered having seen a man answering her description. She said she was particularly suspicious of a free mulatto woman, a dressmaker by profession, whose premises George knew as she had sent him to the woman's workshop several times to have a livery made for him. The dressmaker had once asked her if George was for sale which proves she had an eye on him. Her house was thoroughly searched and each of her slaves questioned, but without results.

Denise is furious and terribly vindictive, says she means to make her horrible threat true this time. Admits she frightened him by telling him she had half a mind to have him gelded by her doctor as a punishment for his last futile attempt at running away. She didn't mean it then, but now she does. Poor boy! I do hope he can escape her for ever, which is, however, not very probable considering he is branded and marked. If he is caught I shall try my best to save him, offering her all the money she asks. This time she won't refuse my offer, realizing she cannot keep him.

A pity I found no opportunity to question him yesterday. There were too many guests keeping him busy all the time. I knew something must be wrong, as he looked so terribly sad and nervous.

Denise is a vicious cat who delighted in teasing and frightening the poor lad whenever she could.

From a child she has had plenty of opportunities to humiliate him. For every trespass of hers, he would receive the blame, and when he was thrashed in her place she would stand by watching the execution. This she told me herself.

M. Gérard was among the guests yesterday, and Colonel V. and his wife, that silly plump old chatterbox Henriette B. with her shameless décolletage (*sans fichu!*) and outmoded coiffure of towering structures of wire and padding. Ridiculous!

Her brother is a fervent opponent of the free mulattoes who claim equality. He took part in some atrocious assaults on several revolutionary-minded *gens de couleur* and seems to be proud of being a bloody murderer. He says a certain Ogé is trying to dispute our privileges in Paris. When he comes back they mean to give him a warm welcome.

I doubt if they can keep the free mulattoes down for ever. There are some well-bred, intelligent men among them, better men than many a blanc, and certainly I prefer George to that murderous fool. But I didn't dare to contradict the others. They are unanimous in their hatred of the mulattoes—even M. Goyffon, that perfect cavalier and charming causeur, a real man of the world.

I met his wife for the first time. She is an attractive Créole of Spanish descent, very elegant, a little conceited but not spoiled like most of them. She had a light-colored slave with her, a pretty young girl with the funny name of Bernardine.

Poor George—it was a shame the way Denise treated him in the presence of all her guests. That constant rebuking and censuring and nagging him, even ironical hints at certain remedies she had in store for him to make him a better servant. No wonder he has run away. I pray to Heaven she will never catch him.

I admit Denise knows how to entertain guests. Everything was splendid and done in a grand style without being ceremonious. And not too many servants; I hate them standing behind your back, watching for your plates to be emptied, glasses to be refilled, signals to be obeyed. They all stand in terrible awe of her, which she seems to enjoy. Still, she was right in sending the one away whose white cotton gloves were not immaculate. I also insist on cleanliness.

Poor, poor George! He cannot keep in hiding for long. Not without friends, not without money. I must do my best to save him.

TUESDAY NIGHT

No news about George. It seems he has found friends willing to hide him. But Denise is ready to pay a high reward, (300 livres) for catching and delivering him. She has her offer published in all the newspapers at Cap and Port-au-Prince. Such a sum will attract denouncers by the dozens.

I feel so terribly sorry I didn't help him to escape at a time when it would have been easier for him. Two years ago, when Denise was still far away, I might easily have prepared his flight, giving him money, providing him with a pass, finding a ship due for Philadelphia or Europe. He could have left while Charles was away for a few days. Afterwards I could have shrugged my shoulders, saying I was not responsible for his subordinates, that I didn't know when George left nor where he went.

But then we were sure she would never return. Charles paid her 500 livres a year for his services as our *économiste*. He depended on George, treated him as decently as any of his white subordinates, never a bad word. Even after her return nothing changed for a long time. She seemed to have forgotten him while fighting for her judicial separation from her abominable husband.

It was not until that wretched Pierre arrived and began slandering me that she claimed George as her property.

Did she suspect me of being on too friendly terms with him? She would have told Charles if she had, but he never mentioned George, not even in his vilest outbursts of jealousy, never! Instead he refused to leave him to her, said she had signed a written agreement, knowing how indispensable George had become as his *économiste*. She didn't insist, so I thought George was safe. But I was warned, and I should have prepared for the worst—except that I felt too downhearted in those days, too miserable to make plans.

How I hated Charles, his stupid suspicions, his mean accusations, his foul revenge! Turning to his brown sluts and spending his nights with them under my roof. Humiliating me before my own servants. Never once have I repented what I did for revenge, not one of those hours in G's arms have I regretted, nor the ruses I practiced with Helen's help to avoid gossip and protect George, keeping all my servants busy downstairs while he would sneak in unobserved, Helen standing outside on guard.

That wonderful man—his golden body, so strong, but so smooth and tender and considerate and tireless—and so intent on obeying me. Those ecstasies of love sharpened by the deadly risk we were running. The hot thrill of it! Melting deep, deep, deep inside. Oh, my golden boy, how I loved him, every inch of his young body!

And later, disentangling myself and looking down at him, stilled, stroking his warm hair, brushing his moist lips with mine, resting my breasts on his chest, watching the warm glow of love in his eyes, in his smile, saddened by fear.

How I pitied him for that animal fear. It rendered him pathetically helpless, like a hunted down stag at bay staring at the merciless huntress. It is strange, but I loved him all the more for his cowardly submission, it was love mixed with pity and scorn, the tenderest of feelings, like that of a mother.

I do feel more attracted to the considerate and tender-minded type of man than by domineering brutes like Pierre or selfish weaklings like Charles—the men who treat you as a cheap instrument of pleasure, no more. George was so different, so wonderfully unselfish, so responsive!

Still, I wish he were a little less of a coward. It is that bitch Denise who has ruined him, made him a nervous wreck of a man always on the alert, like a hunted hare, frightened even while making love which sometimes spoiled our happiness moments. Perhaps, in the course of time, I can help him to recover his self-confidence, make him the perfect lover with whom I might wish to spend my future life, day and night, till death will separate us.

WEDNESDAY

I have been reading yesterday's entry. Very bold confessions indeed! I would not like anyone to open these pages. They would be scandalized, would call me a shameless bitch. But what I wrote is true. It is no use suppressing facts in a journal like this which is meant to be frank and candid, disregarding restraints of modesty imposed on our feeble sex.

I woke in the middle of the night. My mind was busy with plans to save George from her cruel revenge. I have made up my mind to talk to her, persuade her to sell him intact, any kind of mutilation greatly reducing his market value. But she will never be willing to leave him to me, she is so dreadfully stubborn and suspicious.

I must turn to Mre Falcon and ask him to find someone ready to offer her a very large sum for George, a person bribed to sell him to me at the same price the same day she will have signed her bill of sale.

Fancy her wrath, her towering rage when she realizes I have duped her.

I wish I could pay her back for her own foul play. She took the part of Charles's grief-stricken sister so well, she was so kind, so sisterly and friendly towards me—the mourning widow. After the funeral she asked me to leave her George for a few hours, no more. Said she wished him to write some business letters for her, her own secretary having fallen ill. She promised to send him back before dusk. But she never returned him.

The next day, when I called on her, she calmly declared George was her legal property and refused to deliver him to me. I could have murdered her then and there!

My attorney, to whom I turned, said it was no use fighting her, she was entitled to act the way she had, taking her property back after her brother's death.

In vain I offered her whatever sum she asked to return him to me. She said she wondered why I was so keen on getting him back, asked me what reason I had for setting his qualities so high.

"You didn't learn to appreciate them in his office, did you?" she asked maliciously. The bitch!

She must have guessed the truth, though I am sure George never confessed to her. I suppose she hates me for having cuckolded her brother, therefore she would never consent to return George to me, not at any price.

She has made him pay cruelly for my trespass. I don't know what happened after our hot dispute. I should not have shown her my hatred, nor my utter despair. It didn't help him a bit.

It took me a fortnight to realize I must make it up with her, say I was sorry, play the part of the good loser in order to get a chance of seeing him again and plot his escape.

When I finally made up my mind to call on her she was very nice to me, as though never a bad word had been exchanged.

She invited me to dinner, but her kindness was false. How she must have enjoyed her triumph when she saw me stare at poor George, clad in a house-servant's livery, barefoot, and carrying in a large silver dish from the kitchen.

His face was ashen grey and hollow-cheeked, his sad eyes evaded me. She said it was part of his punishment for stealing and running away. He had been caught in town a week before while trying to sell a gold watch to a jeweller. The jeweller remembered having sold the very same watch to M. Galez as a birthday present for his son several years ago, which made him suspicious. He called his servants and had George arrested. He was thrown into prison and later delivered to his mistress. He said he had received the watch from me as a gift reminding him of his late master, a story Denise called a dirty lie.

But it is true, I told her it was true! Charles himself

had wished to reward George for his faithful services, and had asked me on his death-bed to leave him his watch. Yet Denise said I was wrong, giving a slave such a valuable present. He was a thief just the same as a slave could not own anything; whatever he received was, in fact, his owner's property, so it was her own watch he had tried to sell.

For what purpose had he tried to sell it? she asked. No doubt to get money to pay his fare for leaving the island. He had been dressed up like a white gentleman, had ridden to town on horseback without his mistress' consent. Any of her slaves that left her plantation without a pass she treated as runaways, and George was a runaway, no doubt of that.

I don't know how she punished him on his return. I do hope he was spared a severe whipping. She knows well enough that ugly scars would reduce his market value considerably. But there are a lot of other tortures to break a man's will, and she is an expert.

She admits she had him branded to make it easier to catch him if he should ever try to run away again. She has degraded him to the rank of a common house-servant and footman in order to keep her eye on him. She has put him in an old livery with short patched breeches that reach to his naked calves and make him look ridiculous.

The last time I saw him he was better clad, wore a lackey's livery, a new one with fine breeches, but he was still barefoot like all her common slaves. His look was still sad, so pitifully dejected, a doomed man's face. How sorry I felt, knowing I was the cause of his downfall.

He reminded me of poor Marcel who committed suicide soon after she had taken him to Môle. He cut his wrists with a kitchen knife at night and was found lying in a pool of blood the next morning.

No doubt it was Denise who drove the poor fellow to that sinful death. Not by bodily ill-treatment, but by her continuous nagging and teasing and threatening him, which is her favorite means of tormenting her slaves—though I am sure she is vicious enough to resort to worse methods sometimes.

I wonder what she had been doing with Marcel when I stepped in unannounced that morning—her riding habit thrown across a chair, her crop lying on the floor as if dropped an instant before, the thin dressing-gown she was wearing hardly hiding her naked body, facing Marcel who was busy buttoning up his shirt. She was then already a vicious little bitch. She has since grown worse, harder, more deliberate in terrorizing her servants.

Sometimes it seems to me she is stark mad. Her evil malady may have changed her character for the worse. I am sure she would be a much better woman if she had found a husband she could love and admire, a man strong enough to master her, lusty enough to still her appetites and get her with child half a dozen times. She is discontented with life, and her servants must pay for it.

I know for sure, being bad-tempered myself sometimes. It makes me shout at my servants, even punish them when leniency would be advisable. It is this infernal system of slavery that has corrupted us whites, men and women alike, this terrible power we have to treat our slaves like cattle, make them pay for our bad humor, our secret lusts and failures.

I hate this country, have resolved to return to France as soon as I have my share from Captain Basteresse's profits—next summer! I shall sell my plantation, slaves and cattle and furniture and everything that binds me to this hell of an island. Meanwhile I must try and rescue George. I shall take him with me to freedom and happiness. So help me God!

SATURDAY, OCTOBER 16 TH

Laroche is worried about a certain malaise spreading among our field hands. No open disobedience, but mute opposition.

He says you can feel it, but cannot hit and squash it.

Last night we had twelve reports on loafers, one petty theft and nine cases of impertinence, more than we ever had before. He says we must not let that evil spirit grow, we must punish them hard enough to cow them. Proposed to double the number of lashes and administer them on Saturday morning in public to warn the others.

I remembered what M. Gautier, Denise's *gérant,* said the other day about those revolutionary ideas imported from France. Freedom! Equality! Not only all the mulattoes but also some of our blacks seem to be fascinated by those dangerous words. It is like a new religion, a secret sect at first, but in the end it may conquer the whole island and incite them to mutiny and revolt. They would kill us all, rape us white women, cut our throats, drench the whole island in blood. He said we must crush defiance wherever it starts, else we are doomed.

I didn't approve of the drastic measures Laroche proposed, but in the end I gave in and consented to the severe floggings.

I watched them from my window this morning. It makes me sick to remember. I am worried to know they will hate me from now on, thinking I am responsible for these acts of cruelty. But I have never been cruel before. I never liked those Friday night hearings, being forced to pass sentence on a bunch of stupid trespassers like a solemn old judge and see to it that the punishments immediately followed the verdicts.

You get used to it in the course of time, it makes you callous, indifferent to groans and laments. It becomes a matter of routine to be performed as quickly as possible.

They cannot say I was harsh in my verdicts: ten, fifteen, twenty lashes, never more; and pepper-and-salt treatments, fetters, stocks and prison over Sunday, no more. Not one case of mutilation since I had to replace Charles last summer.

Perhaps I would have been wiser not to interfere, but I thought it necessary to impress my authority as their mistress, remembering my failure four years ago. If ever Laroche should fall ill or desert me I should have to replace him myself for weeks, reliable commandants being so difficult to find.

Well, I suppose they have learned to respect me. Not one runaway these three months, not even while the yellow fever still paralyzed our control. Charles was a good master, I admit, decent and just, fed them well, no cruel punishments and few deaths. I do hope I can manage them as well as he did.

Laroche is very dependable, has helped me to replace George on Saturdays, book-keeping, calculations, accounts and all that, together with Rex who has proved to be very useful.

Mre Falcon hopes to find me an *économiste* soon, but he will cost me a lot, 3,000 livres or more a year. George cost us 500 a year! Charles knew how much money he could save by keeping him—such a clever boy—I could murder Denise for stealing him. Making him carry dishes and wait at table!

I hope she will never find him. It seems somebody is sheltering him, someone not willing to denounce him in spite of the big reward she promises. Or has he joined the maroons? Those wretched outcasts, hiding in the bush like wild beasts, living on stolen food, plundering, raping, killing, fighting the better-armed *maréchaussée* till they are hunted down and butchered like rabid dogs! May Heaven spare him such an end!

SUNDAY NIGHT

Had a most disgusting encounter this morning. Called on Denise to escort her to town for Mass. She met me on the staircase in her dressing-gown, and behind her stood Pierre! That dirty scoundrel—smiling at me as if we were the best of friends. I was so terribly taken aback I could not find words but turned round and ran out, jumped into my coach, and off we drove, old Jules obeying my signal as if prepared for it.

He has become her lover—that rotten rake! For one night only, I presume, as he must return to his ship immediately. Well, he does belong to her family, somehow, having fathered Maria's babe. That won't be the only brat he has produced, there will be dozens of them running about in the streets of Cap and so many other ports. I suppose he was her lover when she was still living with her husband. She said he was a friend of her husband's, but it seems he was hers too, and a very close one!

Never shall I forget that first encounter at her grand ball last December, when she was introducing some newly arrived guests to Charles and me.

They must have noticed my embarrassment during his formal bow. He behaved as though we were strangers. Was introduced to us as Captain M., so he must have risen in rank since I met him on board our ship where he served as first mate.

He looked very attractive in his full dress, sunburnt, tall, a handsome man I admit. I should have been so grateful to him if he had acted his part as a polite stranger to the very end. But he got tipsy and started courting me, which forced me to give him a rebuff. I was afraid Charles might interfere, but seeing him approach Pierre turned away smiling.

I tried my best to make Charles believe I had never seen the man before. I assured him he had not been insolent, knowing how touchy my husband was, how easily provoked, how quick to challenge the offender to a duel.

Denise kept silent, but she was inquisitive enough to find out what had happened between us. It seems he told her when drunk, started bragging about his victory, depicting me as the cheap willing victim of his virile charms. The cad!

She didn't keep her secret long. The next night Charles rushed into my bedchamber boiling with rage. Called me a slut, a shameless bitch of a strumpet. Said I had lied to him, cheated him on our first night. No use trying to tell him the true facts, he wouldn't listen, just kept insulting me and left me, never to share my bedroom again.

How stupid men are when jealous. They pretend their heart is mortally wounded—in fact it is their ridiculous vanity that is hurt. It turns them into vulgar, blind, detestable fools. But for my legal rights he would have thrown me out of my own house.

After that there was no day without hot disputes, accusations and bad words. He called me cold like a fish, said no wonder I was unable to get with child, they would freeze in my womb. Whereupon I retorted it was not always the soil that was barren, but more often the seed. Asked him why he was so sure he himself was not to blame for our failure.

He said because little Charlotte was his live piece of evidence.

So she had lied to me, that brown slut Jeannette, pretending she owed her bastard to the overseer. No wonder, I retorted, you were such a poor lover all the time, exhausted from whoring about in my own house. You dare call me a harlot knowing I have been faithful to you all the time while you were busy laying my own servants, you cad, you mean, hypocritical cad!

That is the way we would converse—our matrimonial harmony. How depressed I felt, how utterly miserable for weeks and months. Not for sleeping alone night after night. I should have hated the very touch of his body in bed, so disgusted was I knowing he spent his nights with Jeannette or Rose, openly humiliating me in the face of my servants.

I should have paid him back long before I did. We had two happy months, George and I, before I fell ill, one or two hours a week of bliss, ten or twelve, summed up, and the sweet remembrance and thrilling anticipation between them. That is all life has granted me till now, twelve delirious hours for years and years of boredom, sorrow and disgust.

If that rascal Pierre thinks he can try and win me again I'll spit in his face. He is the cause of all my misery. He ought to be hanged. I hope there is a chance of hitting back at him some time.

Met Mre Falcon after Mass. He told me he has found an agent in New York willing to investigate. He is hopeful as there are but few colored people there. It should be easy to find George's father.

SATURDAY, OCTOBER 23RD

I was in town this morning, at the dressmaker's to have a look at the woman Denise suspected of hiding George.

She is a lot older than he, about thirty, I guess, and pock-marked, but must have been pretty once with large, dark long-lashed eyes.

Her skin is darker than George's. She seems to be a mulatto, not a quarteroon. She keeps busy a good dozen brown and black wenches, sewing and ironing, and three male slaves employed as her tailors, and a boy who reminded me of César, four years ago, the same age, the same slender graceful body, the same soft dark eyes watching in awed admiration. I liked him at first sight and on a sudden impulse asked her if he was for sale.

She said, "Not now, ma'am, but maybe in a few weeks or months, as I intend to sell my business, house and slaves and everything in the near future."

Strange that she should give up her flourishing trade so suddenly. She was evasive in answering my questions. It seems she is going to marry some businessman abroad. Or did she lie to me?

She may be hiding George somewhere, preparing their joint flight abroad. If only she would confide in me, but she was too suspicious to talk, or else she is really in no way connected with George. Still, wishing to keep in contact with her I asked to see her collection of fine crêpe, chose mauve, finest fabric, suits my hair and complexion so much better than any shade of green for a dressing-gown. Arranged to try it on next Saturday.

The boy's name is Henri, but I should call him César, and make him wear breeches and livery. Might help me to replace César in my heart. So sad his early death. Didn't know he had died till Helen told me after my fever had fallen. I was so weak and depressed I could not help crying like a little child.

I felt like a mother who has lost her son. He was the first of my house-servants to fall a victim to the yellow fever. He must have caught it in the stables, two of the stable-boys having died before.

The woman promised to inform me when she is ready to sell the boy. I didn't ask her how much she would charge. Should offer her 2,000 livres which is a decent sum for a colored lad his age. Though prices may have risen for such good-looking ones. What a pity if he fell into the clutches of vice and dissipation!

I had a feeling she was on her guard all the time, as if measuring me as a potential enemy, a spy or a rival. She acted her part well as an officious tradeswoman, very polite, eager to be at the white lady's service, but she was nervous somehow. So were her workers in their *atelier,* busy bending over their needlework, no word spoken as long as I was present. Or was it their mistress who kept them in such strict discipline?

While I was comparing shades and patterns with Helen, she walked over to the adjoining *atelier.* I heard her slap one of the girls and ask her angrily who had told her to take the black ribbons? Then she rushed over to the tailors' table on which her three black males were sitting among heaps of cloth, attacked the eldest, a grey-haired, hunch-backed Negro by boxing his ears, and hissing her reproach in an angry whisper. He received his blows with stoical calm, as if used to such treatment. Then she returned, apologizing with a humble smile, murmuring something about brainless niggers, and resuming her shop-talk with equanimity. A woman used to having her own will. If she has fallen in love with George she may well be ready to take risks to keep him.

Taking leave I said in a whisper, "Tell George I hope he is well. I am ready to do anything to help him, but please be careful!"

She stared at me flabbergasted, not a sign of understanding. It seems I was mistaken. But if she knows where he is hiding she is sure to tell him what I said. It might help to encourage him.

THURSDAY, 28TH

Laroche says we are short of field hands for the next crop. Sixty acres have lain fallow since the yellow fever killed twenty-seven of my strongest bucks and ten of my female hands. I hoped I could do without replacing the heavy losses, but we cannot house the next crop in time without purchasing some strong males, at least ten of them, trained ones, not savages.

It will cost me 24,000 livres or more, prices having risen considerably. Shall send Laroche to the next auction. Must call on Mme S. to make inquiries—24,000 livres! There won't be left much of my cash holdings—no more unnecessary expenses. That boy would cost me another 2,000 livres or more—but in case of emergency I could well resell him at a profit. Or sell the whole plantation after the crop, move to town and wait there for Captain Basteresse's ship to bring me the profit he promised. Then, farewell, thou devil's island!

But Mre Falcon says prices offered for plantations have fallen because of the political crisis in France. They intend to forbid the slave trade, which would stop our supplies for the fields.

In Paris some fanatics say slavery as a whole should be abolished. In fact there is a general unrest among the blacks, as if we were on the eve of open mutiny. Ours have calmed down since we showed them we are still their masters. But we cannot kill the evil spirit this way. Maybe things will change for the better soon, the King having made peace with the crowds in Paris. They say the whole royal family was acclaimed on the anniversary of the fall of the Bastille, which was a prison the furious mob destroyed a year ago.

M. Richard says the army will soon crush the Jacobins, execute their leaders, and restore order and peace in France. He hopes we can sell our coffee, cotton and sugar at much better profits soon, the trade with France being stimulated by new laws.

I don't know which of the rumors to believe. Some say, sell your slaves before they all are emancipated by decree of the French hotspurs, others say keep them, buy more of them as their prices will rise high the moment slave imports are stopped. I am worried about the money invested in that trade. Hope Captain Basteresse will be back in time. I must wait and see how things go. No use being rash.

SATURDAY, OCTOBER 30TH

Called on Mme S. this morning. Her husband was not in, but from what he told her it is very difficult to get any field hands now. She said she was sorry they had not a single slave for sale fit for field work.

So I called on Mre Falcon who advised me to turn to Mme Barthou, a widow living in town who wishes to get rid of her slaves as she intends to return to France as soon as possible.

I paid her a visit. A fat old woman, owns sixteen males and four females, and has lived on the income from hiring them out. The few she could show me didn't look very strong, too old and worn out, none of them trained for field work. But it seems I must put up with them. Told Laroche to examine the whole lot this afternoon, pick out the ten or twelve fittest, paying no more than 1,600 livres a head.

Had a case of open resistance yesterday. Must take drastic measures to bring them to reason. Gave Laroche free hand to make an example of him and his like. Denise said they had to hang two of theirs to cow the rest. She never approaches the slave-quarters without being protected by her two bloodhounds.

Still no news about George, though Denise repeated her notice in the newspapers, offering 500 livres reward for his capture, 200 livres more than the first time.

Mre Falcon says the news from Paris is alarming. Advised me to withdraw my savings from the bank, purchase the field hands as soon as possible, then invest the rest in English or Dutch securities, jewels and English gold coins in order to get rid of those *assignats,* the value of which has become so very doubtful.

He is sure France is on the verge of bankruptcy! There are peasants' revolts everywhere, and general chaos is imminent.

I do hope those rumors are wrong. In any case I mean to take his advice, investing at least part of my money that way.

SUNDAY, NOVEMBER 7TH

One prisoner died yesterday. Blood poisoning, the doctor said. They should have cleaned his wounds with brandy, it might have saved him. Fifty lashes is a punishment few can stand. Laroche should have known. He is responsible for this heavy loss—a strong lad worth 2,400 livres! But I gave Laroche a free hand, so it is no use repenting. I hope the others have learned their lesson. Better one man lost now than a dozen or more later on.

Five males and two women in the sick-room. I doubt if they can be sent to the fields tomorrow. Not the males. We should not punish slight trespasses too severely, else they are lost for field work for a whole day or two.

A quiet week as a whole, I am glad to state. Laroche seems to have brought them to reason. Haven't seen much of them for weeks. I don't like riding out to the fields knowing Laroche might resent it. He might think I was interfering in his domain.

I should be happy to leave everything, sick-room, prison and all, to someone reliable. But which of our mulattoes can be trusted? None! They are all stupid mules! Except Helen. But she is too busy in the house all the time. Rex is too soft—no backbone. Sometimes I resent his submissiveness.

There is no man to replace George in my heart. Nor in bed!

I must not do it again, else Rex might lose his respect. They all grow impertinent if you spoil them. I must show him my scorn for serving me that way. No real pleasure if you don't love the man—his smell, his touch, his voice, his body. Oh, George! My lover! My poor, dear, great lover! Shall I ever see you again? See, touch, kiss, love you again? Will this cool evening breeze carry my thoughts to you? Will you remember me in your hiding-place?

I had dinner with Denise and five other guests: the Richards, the Morleys and M. Gautier. The first time I accepted her invitation since that awkward incident with

Pierre three weeks ago. But it is no use sulking for months and years. Sometimes I do hate her, but she is my sister-in-law and my neighbor. We are dependent on each other in many ways.

She was tactful enough not to mention Pierre. She must realize I hate him more than anyone else in this world. I do not think there will be any more risk of meeting him in her house.

There were hot discussions about the political situation in France. They say all titles and privileges of nobility have been abolished. The National Assembly proclaimed a declaration of the rights of man, which, M. Gautier says, is all right so long as it is addressed to the whites.

The trouble is our free mulattoes claim equal rights for themselves, which, of course, nobody is willing to grant them on this island.

I cannot help taking these people's part thinking of George, but I didn't venture to oppose the others. There have been some mutinies of rebellious slaves in the south, but they were all cruelly quelled. All the men present recommended harsh measures to keep the blacks in awe, else riots would break out everywhere.

I wonder if it is wise to discuss all these things in the presence of our slaves. They will learn a lot, think it over, get rebellious themselves. Mine are too dull to get ideas if not encouraged by others. But I'll see to it that they behave!

NOVEMBER 14TH

Was again tempted by the devilish flesh this afternoon, and yielded! Feel terribly ashamed! Must stop it, else I might turn out as wicked as Denise, enjoying my power to humiliate the man, make him a mere instrument of my pleasure, a male whore!

I cannot help despising him—no sympathy, just scorn —watching him try his best, the cringing worm! Perhaps I hated myself for using him that way, and hated him for letting himself be used. Without a grain of love to spice it, it tastes stale, looks ugly and dirty. It left a beastly feeling in my womb, like those early sinful experiences in my maiden bed so long ago.

I sent him away as soon as it was over. Felt like slapping him with disgust. Later I warned him to keep his mouth shut or I should cut out his tongue! What a beast of a woman I am! I have no decency left! I wish I could run away, go back to France at once, get married again to find peace for my body and soul. But I must stay and find George, save him, take him with me to Europe, marry him and be happy again.

NOVEMBER 20TH

I called on the dressmaker yesterday. She says she is selling out and offered me her young boy Henri for 2,200 livres. We had our transaction legalized by my attorney, signed, and payment secured.

I took the boy with me, happy to have him, such a handsome Adonis. Had him washed from top to toe and dressed to look like César when he still shared my room four years ago. His young body so graceful, narrow hips, tiny virgin cock, perfect thighs and calves, golden brown skin like honey, so smooth, so immaculate, no scars, no branding but her small initials above his right shoulder-blade. She seems to have treated her slaves decently, unlike so many colored mistresses who are said to be even more hot-tempered and cruel than Créoles.

He is still a little timid. Must get used to his new surroundings. But I am sure he likes me as I am kind to him.

She said she would go abroad as soon as everything was settled. To Martinique, she said, where her fiancé was waiting for her. Strange that fellow never turned up to see her, and nobody remembers him.

There is little left of my bank deposit now. The ten slaves Laroche picked out for me from among Mme B.'s cost 16,000 livres. I doubt if they are worth the money I paid. A miserable bunch of old niggers, all over thirty, none really fit for crop-work twelve hours a day. It will ruin them in no time. But impossible to get any better ones. Those owners who wish to return to France sell theirs en bloc, estate, livestock, furniture and all included. Those who wish to stay here keep all their slaves, fearing the imminent stop of imports or doubting the value of the *assignats* they would get for them.

Mre Falcon says I needn't worry for Captain Basteresse's cargo. They cannot abolish the slave trade at once. They must give the slavers and merchants at least a year's chance to get rid of their last imports before stopping the trade.

SUNDAY, NOVEMBER 21ST

Denise confessed to me strange facts about herself and George this afternoon.

I think she was drunk, else she would not have been so frank. I didn't know she liked her brandy so much. She must be very unhappy to take to strong drink at her age. Makes her talkative, moody and repentant.

She said she would not have treated George so badly if he had shown he liked her a bit. But he did not. She knew he hated her, worse, despised her. And she hated him for hating her.

From the beginning, when a little girl, she had wanted him to hold and caress her, but he refused and was indifferent to her yearning which made her cross.

So she started teasing him, finding all kinds of ways to make him suffer for his coldness, and she took pleasure in seeing him thrashed.

She said she had been a tomboy from a child and had been her father's pet. He allowed her to dress and play and romp and behave like a boy, to sit astraddle his knee playing the rider on horseback. He used to call her his little Amazon. Her only playmate was George, her brother being more than three years her senior, too old and too dull to suit her hoydenish temper. At first she adored George, envied him for his strength, his poise, his skill.

"I envied him for everything he had, even for his

pretty cock," she said laughing bitterly. "But he was so terribly cool! Not the least sign of warmth, of brotherly attachment. Rather a kind of wary reserve which infuriated me."

Well, she had the whiphand, and could make him pay for his mute resistance. And make him suffer for it she did, the little bitch!

When about twelve she was told by a woman-servant that one of their Negroes had been gelded for having raped a light-colored girl. She didn't know exactly how that was done, but the next time George resisted her she threatened to tell her father he had tried to rape her. Told George her father would cut his cock to punish him like that Negro!

Seeing how terribly frightened he was she knew she had found her weapon to subject him to her whims and force him to do whatever she asked.

A twelve-year-old girl's curiosity, if not checked by modesty, is as unlimited and reckless as a young monkey's. It must have been a terrible time for the poor boy, constantly exposed to the risk of being caught and punished by her parents if yielding to her shameless demands, or else of being denounced by her to face the most atrocious punishment imaginable.

Her mother seemed to have had some idea of the situation, for she separated them saying George had grown too big a boy for a girl her age. To replace him she was given Maria as her new playmate, while George was apprenticed to the clerk in her father's office. For a year or two he felt safe there, but one Saturday, her parents and the clerk being absent, she managed to enter his office unobserved.

"I had grown a lot meanwhile," Denise said. "Bust, hips and all that, so I hoped he would find me attractive. But he was the same indifferent stranger, as stiff and cold and wary as ever before. He avoided my very touch, pushed me back when I tried to embrace him, which made me so furious that I said I would tear my dress and call for help if he treated me that way.

"But he ran away and that made me breathe revenge the whole afternoon. When my parents were back I flung myself into my father's arms, crying and sobbing.

Told him George had attacked me. He was sent for, but was nowhere to be found. They caught him in town the next day, but Mother pleaded for him because she doubted my story. So he was only whipped and branded, but not punished as I had wished him to be in my revengeful mood."

A few weeks later she was sent to the convent near Paris.

"Strangely enough," she confessed, "I could not forget him there. I longed for that stupid boy, didn't hate him any longer, but wished to see him again, tell him I was sorry, make him confess he loved me. I imagined passionate scenes of reunion, of tears and kisses and embraces and caresses and love-making. What a fool of a silly girl I was, all the time yearning for that wretched brown servant-boy, that common slave who was, by law, my property!"

She said she looked forward to seeing him again so desperately that she hastened her return instead of accepting her fiancé's invitation to spend a few months at his aunt's, the Duchess of P.'s residence in Paris.

George had, meanwhile, grown into a handsome young man. She said she felt shy when she saw him again after more than three years. She wished to tell him how passionately she had longed for him all the time.

She didn't mind his cool reserve in the presence of other persons, but when they were alone she found he was as cool, as hostile as ever before.

"It was such a shock," she said, "being treated like a stranger, nay, like an enemy by the one man I loved! It turned my love into hatred. I wished to make him pay for his stubborn animosity.

"I started humiliating him whenever I could, made him fear and hate me, which, somehow, was better to endure than his indifference.

"I know I was a bitch all the time, driving him almost mad with my threats, treating him like a dog, forcing him to obey my vilest whims. But wasn't it his fault? He made me hit back that way. It was a kind of war we were waging. I had all the strong arms on my side, his only weapon being his passive resistance.

"The lousy beggar dared to defy me!" she shouted

clenching her fists. "Defied me, even while obeying me! I saw his cold disdain, I saw it in his eyes—his mute disdain, his disgust! It made me invent new humiliations. He must have thought that sending him to the doctor's house was a ruse to deliver him to that man's assistants to have him gelded by the doctor. But I wanted to frighten him, no more!"

"Do you think he will return if he knows I am ready to pardon him?" she asked, refilling her glass.

"You may try to tell him," I said, shrugging my shoulders. "Publish another notice in the newspapers. Perhaps he will believe your promise and come back."

I doubt if she will follow my advice. I doubt if he is willing to trust her if she does. I hope he does not!

I never saw her look so unhappy, so defeated, gazing down at her glass of brandy, pale, sad, hopeless.

She is a wicked bitch, but I understand her better now, pity her for all her wickedness. Easy to pity her, knowing I cut her out as my rival. I wonder why she didn't turn against me. Was I wrong thinking she knew he was my lover?

Yesterday put an end to a week of awkward suspense, my regular days having passed without leaving one crimson stain on my sheet. Made me imagine things! Examining my body in the mirror I was sure I was pregnant, my breasts and hips swelling to prepare for the great days to come. Felt motherly saps flooding my womb and was filled with happy hopes of proving mine was not barren soil after all.

Yet I sobered, remembering the man that filled me must be Rex, the miserable cringing servile bastard!

I thought of turning to Helen. She is sure to know how to get rid of such little mongrels. But shrank from committing such a deadly sin, murdering my own child!

I made plans to escape scandal. Decided to find a *gérant* to replace me and prepare for confinement at some hiding-place, then leave the babe to a good wet-nurse and return saying I had been abroad. I could fetch the babe home after a while telling people it was a slave girl's.

Happy dreams, alas! For yesterday morning, while

rising, felt it run down my thighs in gushes, the usual mess! Dropped back into my pillows disappointed, tears trickling down my cheeks. Oh help me!

NOVEMBER 27TH

The dressmaker has vanished!

I wanted to call on her this morning, still hoping to find out about George. I was received by a young quarteroon girl, no more than twenty-two or twenty-three, I guess, who said she was the new owner of the house. She had bought it from the pockmarked woman a few weeks ago, furniture, stock and slaves included, to move in and take charge of the business on December 1st.

But last Monday morning the black coachman called on her delivering a letter written by his mistress, informing her she had been forced to depart sooner than expected. He belonged to the slaves included in the purchase and showed his new mistress his pass, the one his former owner had written for him, allowing him to spend the week's end in town before delivering the letter. She had even given him 20 livres to spend on food and drink and women, told him to have a good time, but be punctual in delivering her letter.

He didn't know when his former mistress departed, nor did the other slaves. They had been told to stay in their quarters the whole Sunday and start work on Monday morning without waiting for their mistress to return.

From all I could find out from questioning the slaves, she had departed on Sunday morning, escorted by the one faithful old servant she had not sold away, a black woman, the only slave that had been allowed to enter her mistress's private rooms upstairs.

But she had left in her coach, so there must have been a coachman, too! Who was the one that drove her away? Why had she dismissed hers on Saturday night?

One of the girl slaves said that, when returning from the outhouse at dawn, she heard the horses outside and later had a glimpse of the coach disappearing round a corner. She saw the black coachman's back, his red livery, and thought it was Rufus.

I wonder who that coachman was. She said she was sure he was black, like Rufus. She saw his neck, his hands, and remembered he was kinky-haired like Rufus. At least he looked so from a distance, judging from a moment's glimpse at dawn.

The new owner, Cathérine by name, is a nice girl, very frank and lively, pretty enough to bewitch an old fool of a widowed master.

She was emancipated after his death and given 100,-000 livres bequeathed to her as a reward for her faithful services which seem to have been limited by his impotence, judging from the fact that she is still childless.

She was shrewd enough to invest her money in this prosperous business, having been introduced to it by her predecessor for months.

Though on very friendly terms with her, she was never invited to enter her private rooms. She remembers her locking the doors upstairs whenever she left and thought it strange for a young woman to be so suspicious. Of course she heard steps sometimes, but thought her old black maid was busy upstairs.

I am sure the black coachman was George. It is so easy to change a man's features, blacking his skin, making him wear a wig. Nobody would think of being suspicious, seeing a black coachman in his livery sitting on the coach-box.

They may have moved to a faraway part of the island, bought one of the many small plantations for sale to live there as a married couple to the end of their days.

There was no ship setting sail for Martinique last Sunday. So the whole story about her fiancé waiting for her there is a lie! She did not trust me. Should I have trusted anybody in her place?

Denise must not be told, else she might draw the same conclusions as I did.

I hope he feels safe now. And happy! Though I am

glad for him I cannot help feeling a little sad. Good-bye, George, fare thee well!

DECEMBER 5TH

M. Nicole, our new *économiste,* says we needn't have been in such a hurry to house this crop, prices having risen up to 4 livres since we sold our coffee at 3¾ livres. Our net profit is about 18,000, only 4,000 less than in May, in spite of the reduced number of hands and so many acres still lying fallow.

A pity we had four deaths this time, three more than in spring. But they all belonged to that gang of rotten old niggers I bought from Mme B. Cost me 1,600 livres each, totalling a loss of 6,600, to be reduced from the profit.

It never pays to buy cheap blacks. Should have known they were not strong enough for crop work. Some planters say a loss of 5 per cent of our field hands is not so bad. It pays if you can sell your crop in time to get a better price. Still, I do feel sorry for those poor creatures.

Laroche should have told me in time that they could not stand it. Next time I'll have them work no more than twelve hours a day.

So glad I am no longer out of cash. M. Nicole says prices are rising because nobody wishes to keep those *assignats* we are forced to accept in place of silver or gold coins. Mre Falcon, too, is very pessimistic about the outlook. He is sure France is going bankrupt very soon.

If M. Nicole thinks he can win me by his ridiculous flatteries he is wrong. Beware of white men! Even if he were more attractive I should keep my distance, knowing he wishes to marry my money.

Remembering George, how could I ever again submit to a white husband's tyranny! Not to mention his short-comings as a lover! Colored mates are so much easier to handle, so much more intent on pleasing you, so grateful if treated with kindness, so tenderly obedient to your demands. And so strong!

Dreamt about George last night! Was accosted by a fruit-vendor at the market, a Negro offering a big basket full of bananas, golden yellow, so ripe, so tempting.

He kept smiling at me, while I was at a loss which to take. Then suddenly I knew he was George, his face blackened with soot. I felt so happy I wanted to touch his hand and told him, but he withdrew, disappeared in the crowd. I felt so sad when I awoke.

Denise is still sure they will find him sooner or later. Has her advertisement reprinted in the papers, this time offering 600 livres for his capture. She is so damnably revengeful.

DECEMBER 11TH

Had visitors from France yesterday, a certain M. Herriot and his wife, owner of a cotton mill near Brest.

They were introduced to me by Denise, whose guests they have been since Wednesday.

They wished to see how our cotton is being ginned.

Myself I never saw it before, because of the insufferable dust pervading the air.

M. Nicole conducted us by way of a gloomy staircase to the logis—the upper storey where the blacks are all employed in one deep room which runs through the whole length of the logis. A multitude of half-naked blacks were skipping about, old and young, male and female, all occupied in preparing cotton by the aid of one faint light, ginning, beating, pulling, carrying, packing the material.

They looked like black ghosts in the semi-darkness, all of them silenced to awe by our presence. It was impossible to stand the infernal smell of sweat and dust, the whole gloomy aspect, longer than a minute. Not at all suitable for ladies' eyes and noses. So we turned and hurried out into the open, breathing in the fresh air, giggling for relief, leaving the men to their technical discussions.

Mme Herriot is a dark-haired little woman in her thirties, very vivacious and talkative. Suffers terribly in the damp air of our rainy season, her face and neck and armpits wet all the time but bravely concealing her exhaustion.

She longs to return to France, though she says the situation is not happy there at present.

The peasants have risen in the south, and the spirit of revolt is growing everywhere. The old provinces have been abolished, replaced by a great number of small *départements* and *cantons,* she says, but doesn't know any particulars.

The King has lost much of his power, the *Assemblée Nationale* makes new laws every day, and both the Church and the Nobles are being dispossessed. But there is still the army ready to interfere and restore order.

DECEMBER 18TH

Mre Falcon was here with his clerk to examine M. Nicole's book-keeping, which proved to be correct.

Nicole is, it seems, as trustworthy and efficient as George was. But I do hate his continuous attempts at courting me—so embarrassing his silly flatteries, his pale eyes fixing me as if hypnotized. Why can he not stop it, seeing that I am displeased?

Laroche is so much more of a real man. Never tried to become familiar, knowing I would not respond. He is much too proud to risk being snubbed. Has been living with his big-breasted mulatto wench, Rose, for years. Seems to treat her very decently, as if she were his wife. She has given him two brats so far whom I promised to emancipate, knowing that he is attached to them.

She is a good girl, very useful, helps him check the cotton delivered by the pluckers. Whenever a driver is sick she can replace him for days and weeks. She is the only colored wench who is really respected and obeyed by the blacks. She can handle any gang of strong males with as much authority as her own master.

Mre Falcon says 1790 was not so bad a year after all, in spite of our great losses in summer.

He advised me to invest my profit in slaves—to

replace some of those I lost. He is sure prices keep on rising because slave imports will be stopped in the near future, maybe by the end of next year.

There is a strong movement in France opposed to the slave trade. But they won't abolish slavery in this island, knowing that the wealth of our colonies depends upon it. So we must breed enough black brats to keep our numbers of slaves at the same level for the next generation.

I don't know what to do. Maybe I can make a lot of money if I follow his advice, buy a dozen more blacks if I can get them cheap, make them house my next crop in spring, and then sell everything! I hope to get more than 500,000 livres, estate and houses and furniture and implements and slaves and other livestock and everything else included, plus the profit from the last crops, cotton and coffee, say 25,000, plus at least 150,000 from Captain Basteresse's profits, make 675,000 livres, enough for me to buy a fine house and park somewhere in France, on the Lac Léman!

A small number of devoted servants, horses and stables and a stately coach, and gardens with beautiful flowers and shady trees, the best *maître de cuisine* available, and books, books, books! And charming friends, men I can trust and confide my thoughts and feelings to, and my cahiers to remember the past.

DECEMBER 19TH

Shocking things happened last night. I feel responsible, at least partly responsible for the cruel killing of one of my most valuable blacks. I should not have left him to that scoundrel. But how could I know what might happen? I was in such a hurry not to be late for supper with Denise and her guests. But I must try and record things in good order.

That fellow Veillon, Laroche's new assistant, had been recommended to me by Laroche himself. He said he could no longer do without a white assistant considering the malaise spreading among the field hands.

I disliked that young lad from the start, his coarse manners, his stupid arrogance. One of those poor whites loitering in the wickedest taverns in town. But we cannot be particular these days.

He brought along his wife, a silly young thing, no more than eighteen or twenty, who seems to be a bastard—not pure white judging from the livid paleness of her skin and the bluish glow in her eyes. Might be called pretty if she didn't squint. Makes her look silly.

Laroche offered them two of his rooms and a servant maid. I agreed to pay him 200 livres a month, and full board, on condition that his wife should take care of the slave quarters, sick-room, prison and all.

They started work last Monday. I didn't see much of the fellow, but the girl soon proved to be rather a nuisance. No experience whatever in handling slaves. An awkward mixture of false intimacy and haughty arrogance.

Seeing they didn't respect her she got nasty and mean. She is the one who started it. If she had not interfered, nothing bad would have happened.

Seeing one of the field hands crossing the yard yesterday evening she stopped him and asked his name and what he was doing.

He said his mistress had sent for him, which is true. Maryse, the brown wench employed in the kitchen had asked my permission to mate with that fellow Brutus, list No. 43.

As she has grown a buxom lass, old enough for mating, I said I wished to see that boy before consenting. So he was sent for. So eager was he to meet his girl that he refused to obey Veillon's wife, who, disbelieving his story told him to turn back to his quarters.

She says he pushed her away so brutally that she fell and hurt her arm.

She yelled for help, whereupon her husband and a number of servants rushed up to protect the woman and arrest the slave.

When Maryse heard about her lover's trespass she threw herself at my feet, imploring me to save him. I followed her down to the yard, silenced the crowd and questioned the prisoner who proved to be one of my handsomest Negroes, a young strong griot worth at least 2,500 livres.

I told him he had committed one of the worst crimes, raising his hand against a white lady. In court he would be sentenced to death, but considering he had meant no real harm I was willing to spare him. Told Veillon to punish him severely but not kill him; said I would take the matter in my own hands tomorrow. I took Veillon aside and in a low voice told him to serve the slave a good flogging and put him in chains afterwards.

"Not too hard!" I said. "Remember that the fellow must be fit for work on Monday morning!"

I was in a hurry because I was already late for that supper with Denise. So I departed without making sure that my orders were obeyed correctly.

This morning Helen told me something dreadful had happened. Opening the prison at dawn they found Brutus lying dead in his chains.

I hurried over, and was shocked to see the poor fellow's body naked, his back and buttocks one big dark wound, even his private parts badly hurt! A monstrous sight.

I sent for Veillon, called him a murderer, had him arrested and taken to the cellar of my house and imprisoned there in spite of his furious protests.

Both Laroche and M. Nicole being absent, I sent for my attorney, the doctor and the police. The latter arrived this afternoon, questioned Veillon, his wife and the servants who had been present last night. She swore the slave had hit her (which is a lie, else she would have told me before!), said his crime made the punishment inflicted by her husband justifiable. I myself had ordered him to punish the slave hard. She had witnessed the flogging, which was not excessive, considering the gravity of the slave's crime, fifty or sixty lashes, no more, and the slave had been alive when they left, had groaned and lamented as they all are used to do when thrashed.

The officer said I should not have arrested Veillon who seemed to have obeyed my orders, no more! Veillon left with his wife after threatening to prosecute me for deprivation of liberty.

Then Mre Falcon and the doctor arrived together. The latter examined the body, said he had died of internal hemorrhage, must have been whipped and beaten most cruelly, one hundred lashes or more, no parts spared, the wickedest torture imaginable! Mre Falcon said it was of no use prosecuting the scoundrel, considering he is penniless.

In court the couple would swear I myself had given orders to punish the slave that way! The judge would be sure to acquit him, public opinion favoring drastic measures against dangerous Negroes.

I had better claim indemnity from my insurance. They would pay me 1,500 livres, 1,000 less than the fellow's market value!

I feel terribly depressed. It will spoil the whole of Christmastime, rouse the slaves' hatred and rebellious spirit. They will hold me responsible for that murder, will say I ordered him to be ill-treated that way! Laroche and Nicole, whom I met at supper, are of the same opinion as my attorney. Laroche says he is sorry that fellow Veillon turned out to be such a stupid brute. He is sure he was spurred to that pitiless beating by his revengeful wife. I don't wish to see them again. I shall set the dogs on them if they dare return.

CHRISTMAS 1790

Attended Christmas service this morning, all my slaves assembled in the yard and a priest from Cap officiating, which cost me 500 livres for the greedy Capucins.

Each of the field hands received a new shirt and pantaloons, the women chemises and frocks, 1 lb. of sugar, 12 oz. of tobacco for the men, stained glass pearls for the women, cost me 1,150 livres altogether.

They will get two barrels of toddy this afternoon— half a pint each, and bacon and mutton as a Christmas treat. Tomorrow and Monday will be free for all of them.

My female house-servants got pretty necklaces and rings and bandanas, the males fine shirts and hats, belts and tobacco.

In spite of all the gifts there was no real happiness among the blacks, no means of brightening the dull apathy that has silenced them since Brutus's death. So sad to know they hate me thinking I am a heartless tyrant. It is no use trying to be friendly.

Last week I questioned the servants who had arrested Brutus.

They said the young master and his lady told them to take the prisoner to the "threshing floor" (*aire!* that's what the blacks call the barn where the Friday night whippings use to take place).

There they were told to strip him and stretch and fasten his limbs *à quatre piquets,* which is a torture I have strictly forbidden to be practiced on any of my slaves, however great his trespass may be.

Then the young lady told them to wait outside. She shut the door and bolted it. So none of the servants could tell what happened in the barn. They heard the young master and his wife talk a while in undertones, then lashes and yells and moans, again and again interrupted by the master's voice and the young lady's, and long pauses when nothing could be heard.

After about half an hour the door opened, the lady called them in and calmly told them to take care of the slave, carry him to the prison and put him in chains there, which they did. It seems Veillon and his wife had applied the *rigoise* to him, judging from the blood-stained cowhide lying on the floor.

Helen, who was sent for to nurse the victim's wounds, said they both looked tired and pale in the dim light of the lanterns, especially the young man, who seemed to be embarrassed, as if repenting what he had done. He didn't utter a single word, but silently put on his jacket, watching the servants unfasten his victim.

His wife was leaning her back against the wall, her raised hands busy dressing her badly tousled coiffure, dark blotches of sweat showing under her open armpits (so typical of Helen to observe and mention such details). She grew angry at the sight of Helen, forbade her

to nurse the Negro on the spot or have him carried to
the infirmary. She said my special orders were to throw
him into prison and keep him there in chains.

That way they put all the blame on me, made me
responsible for what they had done.

In the slave-quarters rumors are spreading that Veillon and his wife did no more than obey my orders, some
of them having seen me talking to Veillon in a whisper
before I left on that fatal Saturday evening.

They say I told Veillon to serve the slave a hundred
or more, knowing such a whipping must kill him. What a
monstrous lie! There is but one way left to prove to
them I am innocent: that scoundrel and his wife must
be prosecuted, whatever Mre Falcon may say to warn
me. Must turn to him at once, ask him to take steps,
else I am stamped for ever as a cruel murderous tyrant.

SATURDAY, NEW YEAR'S DAY

I spent a noisy, sleepless night, the blacks having
drunk their toddy. My own servants were in high spirits
till dawn, singing and dancing and laughing in the yard
all the while, each wench finding her bed-mate by the
end of the evening. No use interfering—they would
have hated me for spoiling their fun. They still respect
me, perhaps even like me considering I have tried to
treat them decently all the time.

Poor Maryse knows I am innocent of Brutus's death,
and so do all the others. Helen told me they know the
facts. But not the field hands. There is no use telling
them I was shocked, and feel as sad about Brutus as
any of them. I should prosecute that wicked couple to
prove my innocence. But Mre Falcon again warned me
most emphatically against such a course of action. He
said we must avoid scandal by all means.

If this case were brought to trial, it might arouse
public controversy. Even the hotspurs in Paris might
hear about it, might call it another piece of evidence
which proves how cruelly we treat our slaves.

He said Veillon and his wife would be sure to put

all the blame on me. The judge would have to weigh my word against theirs, and even if he believed me the benefit of the doubt would be in their favor. The whole would cost me a lot without giving me any hopes of proving my innocence. On the contrary the whole town would start gossiping about me. People would say that's the woman that whipped one of her Negroes to death. What a rotten world this is!

Looking back, 1790 was one of the saddest years I remember, and also the happiest, weighing a few blissful hours against heaps of misery. I see the scales rise and sink depending on what I remember most vividly. If George is still alive, maybe his thoughts are joining mine this very minute, recalling a happy hour in my arms, sweet memories uniting us in the same hopeful dream in which I find solace whenever I turn to you, my lover, my beloved unforgettable lover!

JANUARY 9TH, 1791

Tempted again by the flesh and sinned! Yet this time no pricks of conscience, but a sweet feeling of relief after so many weeks of growing tension and irritable moods.

We are so much more prone to weakness when we feel unhappy. We long for love when we know the world has turned against us.

I didn't mean to seduce the boy. On the contrary, I was angry with him at first for still being so maladroit at hairdressing.

He has been apprenticed to Helen for more than a month, has assisted her in doing my hair every morning and sometimes in the afternoon too, before replacing her this morning, Helen being busy in the sick-room.

I was nasty at first, bad-tempered and impatient, called him a clumsy bastard for dropping the comb, which made him so nervous his hands trembled.

He made such a mess of my hair that I turned and slapped his face and the next moment repented what I had done when I saw tears running down his cheeks.

I tried to soothe him, pulling his head down to my

bosom, stroking his kinky black hair, caressing his wet cheek, kissing him.

What followed was like a slow fall into a bottomless abyss, with closed eyes, sweet, sweet surender to shy touches and caresses and rising strength.

How could I have foreseen a boy his age would react this way! César had been more than a year older when he started playing his amorous antics. So disarming—his inexperience, that strange mixture of shyness and daring curiosity rising suddenly to blind raging passion. The little savage—an untamed colt in his first sap! So virile the smell and touch of his young body, so slender, so graceful, so perfect. So innocent and exuberant in his lust and ecstasy!

Later he confessed to me that he had not been initiated by me, but by his former mistress who had been very kind to him, and kept him in her private rooms upstairs for weeks.

But one morning, on returning from an errand, he was strictly forbidden ever to go upstairs again. That was about three or four months ago, he said, on a Saturday.

It may well have been the day when George escaped. Now I am sure she managed to hide him in one of her rooms, though Henri insists he does not know. I didn't question him, for I quite appreciate his unwillingness to talk. It proves he is a good boy, trustworthy. Wishes to protect his former mistress.

I told Helen, Henri will be my hairdresser from now on. She may draw her own conclusions, knowing I have certainly not promoted him for his professional skill.

She has been a little jealous of him from the start, realizing that I wished him to replace her brother César. She never liked my calling him César, asked me not to change his real name Henri, which was a nice name, and better suited to that clumsy boy than César.

I didn't wish to make Helen unhappy about a boy's name, so gave him back his old name of Henri—my handsome colt Henri.

It is so amusing to tame this young stallion, to teach him to obey my reins and the touch of my spurs. He is still much too impetuous, too raw and unskilled, but he does not lack strength nor blind devotion, nor that animal grace which is the most precious gift of adolescence.

SUNDAY, JANUARY 23RD

I forgot last week's entry. I was too busy entertaining my guests, Denise, and Col. V. and his wife, and Laroche and Nicole and M. and Mme Richard and her young brother, who seems to be Denise's new lover, judging from the way she would return his glance whenever he fixed his fine dark eyes on hers. Such a captivating fellow, so handsome, witty and well-mannered. A pity if he should fall a victim to that shameless bitch.

In February he will return to Port where he is employed at the Government Palace as a secretary.

There were some hot disputes about the *Déclaration des Droits de l'Homme* which Denise tried to make fun of. But it is too serious a matter to be ridiculed, the free mulattoes claiming equal rights which the whites are not willing to grant.

What if the *Assemblée Nationale* turns against us? Col. V. says anything may happen, we must be prepared for the worst!

On Denise's plantation they arrested two Negroes who had tried to incite the blacks to open rebellion. She had them tortured to make them confess, and they were hanged in public, which is against the law, but Denise says it was necessary to make an example of them in order to frighten her other blacks.

If she had merely delivered them to the police, the others would not have been impressed in the same way. Mine have been quiet for weeks—but you never know.

Mre Falcon has promised to find me another white overseer to replace Veillon. Laroche says he can no longer trust our mulattoes, so we must be on our guard.

Denise said prices for blacks are still rising. They charge you up to 2,800 livres for a strong lad below thirty! The reason is there have not been any imports since last spring, so we can hope to get high prices for Captain Basteresse's load next summer, provided he brings in a good supply from Sierra Leone—perhaps the last to arrive before the abolition of the slave trade.

Denise hopes we can sell them at a much higher profit than expected. On the other hand, mulattoes are offered everywhere at bargain prices, a colored boy of twenty costing no more than 1,200 livres or less!

Everyone wishes to sell his or hers before they are all emancipated by the new rulers in Paris.

I cannot make up my mind to sell mine, fourteen in number, though it is a lot of money I risk if I keep them all.

Must ask Mre Falcon what to do. For my prettiest wenches and handsome boys such as Louis or David (not to mention Henri!) I could still get good prices, no doubt of that. But I am not willing to deliver them to vice and ruin. Denise is so unscrupulous as to offer hers to brothels if she can make more money that way!

The good wine made us all high spirited and gay. So I had my group of black dancers and musicians called in to perform a real Chica, both males and females naked to the waist, an attractive sight, the lasses being shapely, the boys muscular and strong, and their oiled skins glittering in the light of a hundred candles.

I could not help feeling fascinated by their barbaric music, their monotonous time-beating, the crude indecency of their gestures and their rising ecstasy—as though ready to jump at their enticing partners and rape them.

Even Denise admitted she had never seen a better performance—said it was a pity I didn't let the males do it in Adam's dress! I am sure she would not have minded telling them to strip if they had been her slaves.

Later she asked me how much I would charge her for the tallest of the boys, a handsome griot called Léon (No. 53), but I said he was not for sale. She already has more blacks in her house than mulattoes—calls them her bodyguard—ready to protect her in case of a riot, but I wonder if she has not selected them for other purposes!

There is no limit to her appetites—a harem of black bucks as her latest pastime! But how can that little bitch stand any of those monsters and remain unhurt? It must be like a snake devouring a prey double its size!

AFTER DINNER

Reading my last entry I feel a little ashamed. I should not have slandered Denise on mere suspicion. Though she is wicked enough not to care what people think about her as long as nobody knows for certain. None of her servants would ever dare to talk, knowing what they risk.

Whatever she may do to pass her time she is not happy. It seems she cannot forget George and imagines cruel ways of punishing him if he is ever returned to her.

But the other day she said she was willing to forgive him if he should return of his own free will and beg her pardon.

Last Monday the young couple whom Mre Falcon sent to replace Veillon and his stupid wife arrived. Jeanne Carpentier is Mme Sarraud's daughter, the one I met on my arrival at Cap so long ago—five years next spring!

She has changed a lot, grown into a ripe woman, round and high-breasted, and is nursing a babe.

She refused to accept the wet-nurse I offered her. She said she liked suckling it herself, it was the latest fashion in Paris—even ladies of high aristocracy were nursing their own babes. Maybe it is a mere pretext for exhibiting her shapely bosom in the presence of men.

It makes me feel sad sometimes, seeing her kiss and fondle her little brat, a motherly bliss denied to me for ever! While all the women around me, black and brown and white, get filled up year after year, bearing children and nursing them, I have remained as barren as a mule! Something must be wrong within me, four men having tried their best to fill me, nay, five, not to forget my wild little colt Henri!

Helen says I can still be hopeful. She heard of a white woman who got with child in the tenth year of her married life. Some slight change in a woman's womb may make it work as it should.

Helen says black magic might help. But I had better wait till I am married again. There are plenty of women who envy Denise and me for our failure. It renders other pleasures so much more enjoyable!

But it makes you cynical and lustful, knowing it is of no consequence if you yield to temptation. One looks upon love-making in the same way that men look upon it.

It seems modesty is a mere weapon, to protect woman from the risk she runs if she succumbs. If all women were barren they would be as immoral in matters of love as most males are. What a wicked world that would be! I had rather bear a child or two and then live chaste for ever than make love every night without results.

Jeanne married below her station, her husband being employed as her father's overseer when he got her with child. Her parents were thus forced to accept the ill-bred, penniless fellow as their son-in-law. But because slave dealers are facing bad times—their slave-yard has been empty for months—the young couple were compelled to look for a place elsewhere.

I do hope they are better than Veillon and his wife. At least they are both used to handling slaves, they should know how to make them obey without ill-treating them.

I strictly forbade them to administer more than ten lashes in cases of laziness or disobedience. Those who deserve a warmer treatment must be sent to Laroche or myself.

Jeanne seems to be an expert in nursing the sick. So glad I can leave the sick-room and the prison to her and Helen's care.

Yesterday she went to town to fetch four of her father's dogs, strong, well-trained animals, cost me 120 livres, but for safety's sake I had to replace some of my dogs. Now I have sixteen, all trained for hunting up runaways and idlers, and ready to defend us whites against any attempt at opposition or violence.

To show me her dogs' cleverness, Jeanne summoned four Negroes and told them to run away in different directions. After a while she sent the dogs after them. They caught up with the fugitives in no time and forced them to stop and return.

None of the slaves were hurt as I examined them myself; only one man's pants were torn because he had tried to resist the dog that had caught him.

It has been raining the whole day. Rain, rain, rain! Felt like a captive in my house. Sent for Henri and spent part of the afternoon with him. So tempestuous when in heat, quite unmanageable. Hurt me, the young savage! Should not allow him to disrespect me that way. But it is my fault for spoiling him all the time.

FEBRUARY 13TH

I haven't opened this diary for weeks! So many things to do—invitations, neighbors to be visited, guests to be entertained, money matters to be settled with Laroche and Nicole and Mre Falcon.

Two deaths have occurred, two males belonging to by the political tension, Mre Falcon says.

I might have saved a good 4,000 livres if I had resold them in time, considering the high prices they pay even for second-rate blacks nowadays—well, no use repenting! I was consoled by the good profits we made from selling our last cotton crop: 8,500 livres, which is 1,500 more than last autumn's profit. Coffee, too, is rising in value, British competition being almost stopped by the political tension, M. Falcon says.

We had an earthquake one night last week. No harm done except one Negro cabin collapsed: three slaves slightly injured, nothing serious.

After the great rain that started on Candlemas our fields were flooded for three days—all the field hands idling away their time in the barns and store-houses because their own cabins were standing knee-deep in water. That's where the two poor fellows caught the pneumonia that killed them.

Jeanne is a funny creature, full of roguish humor and such a good mimic.

Both Denise and myself had a good laugh at her performance the other day, acting the part of a mistress, her black maid, and her coachman all by herself: the mistress questioning her sobbing maid, forcing her to admit she had been thrashed by her lover, the coachman. This one is summoned and threatened and slapped for lying till he confesses he licked the wench out of jealousy because she had been laid by her master, which revelation infuriates the mistress so much that she tells him to beat the maid again, so thoroughly that she can no longer waggle her buttocks for weeks.

It was absolutely marvellous the way Jeanne managed to change her voice and mien, acting the part of the furious mistress, the moaning maid and the servile lying male slave with his hoarse voice, his stammer and his blurting out the truth.

She is great at mimicking our Negroes' vernacular, with their vulgar vocabulary so rich in lewd words that are too coarse to record.

She knows more about Negroes than any of us. Can tell at first sight what part of Africa a fellow comes from, the physical marks of his tribe, his good and bad traits, his market value.

Even the most intimate facts she will mention as if referring to bulls or stallions: she knows which tribes are said to be equipped best of all (the Mandingoes—up to 8 inches, the size of a small boy's forearm!). She insists some can do it twice a day for months without tiring!

Denise thinks she exaggerated, but she was highly amused. Jeanne also knows all kinds of punishments which her parents used to practice instead of whippings, which scar the skin and reduce the slave's market value.

She recommends one as particularly effective, more than the hottest flogging but without its visible consequences: strip and fasten the fellow *à quatre piquets,* then pour a liquid she knows how to prepare down his crotch. Makes him jump and squirm and yell like a wounded boar, so you better have him gagged before applying that medicine.

If punished that way on a Friday night the man will have fully recovered on Monday morning, no damage done, no scars, no bad effects.

It can also be applied to females with similar results. Those who have suffered that way will be frightened for a lifetime.

Denise, of course, was interested, and asked her to prepare a bottleful for her own delinquents!

Jeanne is a nice girl, in spite of her callousness in treating the blacks. In her opinion, they are not human beings but mere cattle.

She is not unfriendly towards them, just a little too quick at slapping a slave's face for the slightest trespass, quite calmly, as a matter of routine, no harm meant.

I am glad she keeps me company whenever I feel downhearted, such a merry young woman, always happy and gay and garrulous, though a little vulgar at times.

The frivolous anecdotes she likes to tell us are most indecent, but you cannot help laughing at her frankness, and the innocent angel's face she will wear while telling the lewdest stories!

Denise seems to like her very much. Invited her for next Sunday's dinner—a mere overseer's wife! As a rule Denise is terribly haughty. Treats all the whites on her estate as mere subordinates, never allowing any of them to enter her house unless summoned to discuss business matter with her.

FEBRUARY 27TH

The saddest news to record! Denise has recaptured George! Helen told me, rumors having spread among Denise's slaves, and through them to Helen's husband.

I drove to Denise, who triumphantly confirmed the rumors. She said she had caught him in town dressed up like a white gentleman. Realizing that he could not escape he obediently stepped into her coach to avoid the humiliation of being arrested in public.

She said she had not yet made up her mind what to do with him. She keeps him chained to a wooden block, degraded to the rank of a common field slave and forced to toil in her garden, separated from the others.

I saw him from afar, poor man. He was half naked, barefoot and toiling in the rain, his wet pants sticking to his thighs. From a distance I could see marks of ill-treatment on his pale back.

Once, looking up, he saw me and stared at me as though I were a stranger—so hopeless.

I have been pondering since what to do to help him. Better not show her what I feel. It might worsen his fate if she found out about us. I must try to talk to him unobserved, which is not easy considering she can watch him from her window.

The bitch seems to enjoy her triumph. She prefers a slow, long lasting revenge to a quick one. She enjoys the daily sight of his humiliation which she may lessen or worsen to her vile heart's content.

I feel so sad, so terribly unhappy all the time. Can no longer turn to Henri for consolation. I hate the idea of touching another male—regard it as an act of disloyalty, as though committing adultery, though I know G. was not faithful to me.

What will that other woman do now? Is she looking for him? If I knew where to find her I could get in touch with her and together we might find a way to rescue him. Perhaps find a third party ready to offer a big sum of money for him, money paid by us without her knowing the facts.

I shall consult Mre Falcon tomorrow. Hope he can help me. But she must not get suspicious. She would rather kill George than leave him to me or that other woman.

MARCH 3RD

I don't know what to do. The man is not George, though the likeness is astonishing. It might be his twin brother, the one taken by his parents to the free American States. I must find a means to make him talk. He didn't open his mouth when—knowing that Denise had gone to town—I tried to question him this morning.

He looked up when I approached him and stared at me without recognition, just apathy and sullen hatred distorting his face.

"George, George!" I said. "Don't you know me?" But he didn't move, just stared.

Then I noticed the difference—there was no scar above his left eyebrow! However small George's was, it could not have vanished altogether. So I turned him round and examined his back scars, none of which were similar to George's.

I cannot be mistaken. I know George's body better than mine, having touched and caressed his scars many a time. Those were a stranger's scars, all of them new, and so different. Nor are his brands the same. George's marks were smaller, older, and had grown almost unreadable in the course of so many years. This man's brand is big and red. Must have been done recently. Not with the ordinary plate used for branding new slaves, but each letter separately: D and then G. No doubt she tried to imitate George's old brand-mark in order to make people believe the man is George. She knows that none of her slaves would dare to denounce her.

This is the foulest crime imaginable, catching a stranger, a free man if he is George's brother, reducing him to the rightless state of a slave. It cannot be tolerated! Mre Falcon will tell me what to do to save the man and take her to task.

The poor fellow is much too frightened to trust me. "You are not George!" I said. "Who are you?" But he just stared, as if deaf and dumb. "Tell me!" I said. "I order you to answer my question!"

Instead of obeying he turned round and resumed his humble work, hewing the soil, no doubt frightened by the approach of the giant black gardener, the one Denise sends for whenever she wishes one of her house-servants to be thrashed. He is devoted to her and might tell her if he realized I had grown suspicious. So I played the part of the angry mistress.

"This fellow seems to be mute," I said in an indignant voice.

"He must not talk, ma'am," he answered. "Else Madam will have his tongue cut, that's what our mistress said."

I was much too shocked to find a retort. Turned away, not knowing what to do next.

I have been pondering all the time about that poor fellow. If he is George's twin brother, which is very probable, he has no doubt come here by ship in order to find George, Mre Falcon's agent in New York having informed him of the facts.

Jeanne told me she has six males and two females in the sick-room, all of them down with fever and aching bowels. I do hope it is not contagious. I sent for the doctor, who promised to come tomorrow morning.

SUNDAY

Went to town to consult Mre Falcon yesterday. He said I must not be rash and suggested I keep my discovery a secret considering how difficult it would be to prove in court that the man is not George. All her slaves would give evidence in her favor, and so would most of her friends and neighbors.

Even the victim himself might be so cowed by her threats that he would confirm her statements. Still, my attorney promised to investigate and collect evidence proving that the man is George's brother, a free citizen of the United States of America.

He thinks it will be easy to find out which ships have arrived from an American port in the first six weeks of this year, certainly no more than two or three. Returning from the islands they will all lay anchor here again in a few weeks' time. By examining the passenger lists he hopes he can find the names of those who debarked at Cap.

The captain and his crew are sure to remember all of them, which might help us to prove that a free American citizen has been trapped by that criminal bitch of a woman and forced into slavery by threats and ill-treatment.

Maybe we can find the inn where he stayed before she caught him, and make the innkeeper give evidence in court after being confronted with the victim.

There are a number of highly placed Americans at Cap and Port. We might turn to them for help, which would strengthen our case considerably as our authorities would certainly not allow a free American citizen to be treated that way. If things turn out as we hope they will, she is sure to get her just desert!

The doctor is alarmed over my sick hands. He says it may be typhoid fever! We must keep them all separated from the others, else the fever might spread and kill them all. What a calamity only eight months after the yellow fever reduced my livestock to little more than half its original value! I should have sold the rest at once instead of waiting for new disasters to ruin me. Jeanne has left the sick blacks in the care of three old Negresses who are strictly forbidden to get in touch with anyone but the invalids. Heaven save us from the worst!

MARCH 12TH

Things are not as bad as I feared a week ago. All my sick Negroes are recovering, two of the males are already fit for light work with Clara's gang on Monday. I told her not to work them too hard for the first few days.

I am so happy I managed to make Denise's captive talk! All my suspicions were confirmed. He is, indeed, George's twin brother—called Tom.

Knowing Denise was away on Friday morning I sent Helen to the gardener to tell him his mistress wanted him. When I saw him cross the yard, armed with his whip, I entered the garden. I told Tom I had sent the gardener away and that it was safe to speak frankly, because the young mistress was in town.

I said I knew he was George's twin brother and was being kept a captive illegally. I said he must trust me if he wished me to help him. I told him I was George's friend and had asked my attorney to employ an agent in New York to find George's parents.

At first Tom watched me suspiciously, then I saw a

gleam of hope brighten his sad face—so dear to me though unshaven like a savage's. He dropped his hoe, seized my hand, pressed and kissed it.

I was so touched I felt tempted to embrace him, forgetting he was not George but a stranger. I do feel attracted to him in the same way I am to George. I cannot help it. Pity and love all mixed in the one delirious tenderness I felt for George so often, but oh so long ago!

Tom told me he had come to Cap to find his brother, had arrived on February 22nd and his ship's name was the *Mirabelle*.

The inn he chose at Cap had been recommended to him by the ship's captain himself. He said it was near the big market, so it must be Mme Rolland's *Auberge de la Couronne d'Or* where he was arrested the same afternoon, claimed as her runaway slave by Denise herself. He was beaten, bound and gagged for trying to protest and shake off her big Negroes, then carried downstairs a helpless bundle, thrown into her coach and taken away by her in the presence of a dozen witnesses, none of whom interfered for they all thought he was indeed a runaway slave whom she had recaptured.

Knowing the ship and the inn we are sure to find plenty of persons ready to give evidence against her. I have already informed my attorney. He, too, is very hopeful but he says we must be careful and not turn to the police too soon. They would arrest him and keep him imprisoned as long as his identity is disputed by Denise. She might even bribe the guards and poison him to get rid of the main witness.

She is so unscrupulous that she would turn to the wickedest means to save her face. Better wait till our evidence is so strong we can force her to accept our terms: release Tom at once, restore his stolen property and manumit George! Otherwise we prosecute her. If George's emancipation is advertised in the newspapers we can hope to find him soon, so everything may turn out the best way possible.

But Mre Falcon is right: we must be very careful and patient. She is so devilishly shrewd! The second time I met Tom he wore a ragged shirt, no doubt to cover his scars. The gardener seems to have told her I tried to talk to the prisoner, which may have alarmed her. She wishes to hide his back from my eyes, realizing the scars would make me suspicious.

MARCH 14TH

I called on Denise yesterday hoping to meet Tom. I could only see him from her window—still toiling in her garden, no longer chained to the wooden block but wearing his ragged shirt that reached to his knees, and no pants! He must have been exposed to the heavy rain that had poured down an hour before.

I was so shocked that I told her it was a shame the way she treated him. He might catch a bad cold and die.

"How touching to see you pity him," she said smiling coldly. "I know you have always protected him, perhaps a little too obviously, considering he is only a slave. You even tried to talk to him the other day, though he is strictly forbidden to speak to anybody without my consent. Please don't do that again. It helps to strengthen his rebellious mind if he knows you pity him. Remember he is a runaway, a very stubborn one."

"You are revengeful!" I cried. "You are cruel!"

"I don't think I have been too hard on him," she answered. "Some of my neighbors mutilate their runaways, or sell them to the mines or the galleys. You wouldn't like me to do that, would you?"

"I should turn to the police if you did," I retorted. "Even slaves have some protection under the law."

"I am entitled to punish my runaways."

"But not this way! Remember, he is not a common Negro, but almost white and as well educated as we are."

"He is my property! I can deal with my property as I like!"

"You are wrong," I said. "Times have changed. The new rulers in Paris are said to favor the general emancipation of all our mulattoes. They may force you to release George in the near future."

"That's why I must punish him as long as I have the whip-hand. I simply hate the idea of letting him go scot-free after what he did, the stubborn impertinent fool!"

That's what she said. I have tried to record her words as faithfully as possible. It is no use arguing with her. She is too spiteful to listen to reason.

MARCH 18TH

She has moved him in. She keeps him in close confinement in one of her upstairs rooms—in order to watch him better she says.

She seems to be employing him as her secretary, charging him with letter-writing and other clerk's work. I could not see him, his door being locked. I am worried for he may be ill, though she said he was not. Perhaps she lied to me, not wishing me to know she has ruined the poor man!

Yesterday I met the man Mre Falcon has employed to make discreet inquiries at Mme Rolland's auberge. He found the young chambermaid who denounced Tom to her mistress. Mre Falcon's man seems to have spent the night with her (though he tried to hide this fact from me) in order to be able to question her without rousing suspicions. She turned out to be one of the mulatto wenches Denise sold away last month when rumors spread about the emancipation decree for mulattoes being imminent.

She sold her to Mme Rolland—though her auberge has a rather bad reputation, being not much better than a brothel where the chambermaids are forced to pleasure the guests for money. (A bad joke of the captain's to give the *ingénu* Tom that address!)

The maid recognized George when she saw him, and she confessed she would not have given him away had she not resented his cold indifference to her—he treated her as though she were a stranger (which in fact she was).

So she told Mme Rolland the stranger was her former mistress's runaway slave, whereupon the landlady at

once sent a servant on horseback to Denise informing
her that her erstwhile slave was taking a siesta in his
chamber.

In the early afternoon Denise arrived escorted by her
maid and a big Negro. The landlady took her upstairs
to Tom's room and knocked at the door. When he
opened it, half undressed, the landlady asked him to
come out, there was a visitor waiting for him. The same
moment Denise stepped forward, facing him with a triumphant smile.

The chambermaid said that meanwhile all the servants had rushed up to watch the scene, rumors having
spread about a runaway slave hiding in their house. She
said the lady welcomed him with mock courtesy saying:
"Bonjour, Monsieur le déserteur." But he just stared at
her surprised, then said in a foreign accent: "I am
sorry, ma'am, I don't know you."

"Monsieur does not know me? He pretends he does
not know his own mistress!"

"My name is Shattle, Tom Shattle, ma'am. I am an
American citizen from New York."

"Stop acting, my boy," she retorted in a sharp voice.
"You are not clever enough to deceive us. Get dressed
at once and follow me!"

"I am sure you are mistaken, ma'am," he said.
"You are taking me for somebody else."

"That is the limit!" she cried. "Arrest him!" Whereupon her Negro and one of the landlady's male servants rushed at him. There was a fierce struggle, Tom
trying to push and kick them off, but in the end they
succeeded in knocking him down.

On the landlady's order one of her servants brought
ropes with which the captive was tied in to a helpless
bundle, and as he went on protesting loudly and shouting for help, Denise had him gagged with one of the
stockings they found in his room. Then he was carried
downstairs and out to her coach and thrown into it.
Nobody interfered, all the servants and guests thinking
he was a runaway slave recaptured by his mistress.

Denise thanked the landlady for her assistance and
promised to send the reward she owed her. They
watched her step into the coach, the captive having been

pushed to one side to make room for her feet. The bitch!

Maybe she did not realize her mistake before he was untied and stripped and his papers examined. After that she must have known she had committed an abominable crime which could only be atoned for by apologizing and offering the victim whatever compensation he might claim. Instead she has kept him a prisoner, ill-treating and branding him like a runaway slave—as though he were the meanest of her dirty blacks! By God I'll make her pay for that crime!

APRIL 2ND

Had three cups of coffee in order to keep awake while at his bedside. Now Helen has replaced me for the night watch, but I cannot fall asleep. I am much too excited to calm down so soon. I have opened this diary in the candle-light to record the main happenings of this memorable day.

Early this morning I was awakened by great commotion outdoors. Helen rushed in and behind her Denise in a man's breeches and shirt, her blond hair tousled and unkempt, her face waxen pale.

She said her field hands were rioting—she had been wakened before dawn by shouts and cries and barking and shots. Then her maid rushed in saying the slave-quarters were in wild disorder, some of the blacks had run away while others were preparing for an attack.

Rumors spread about hundreds of maroons approaching the plantation intent on killing the whites, plundering the house and raping all the women.

Knowing how much her slaves hated her Denise hastened to put on a man's disguise, which made escape on horseback easier.

Her sole escort was her black gardener who was the only one she could trust in such an emergency because the other slaves hated him as much as herself. His fate was linked to hers like a scoundrel's to that of his accomplice.

Never have I seen her in such a fright, the proud

lady turned into a trembling coward. She didn't look pretty any longer, her face distorted by fear, the same panicky scare in her eyes as in a hunted-down animal's. It reminded me of the way that poor runaway stared at her when she hit him after shooting him down from the top of the tree. So shocking a scene that I can never forget it. Félipe was the poor creature's name, I remember.

Of course I at once sent for Laroche to inform him. But he bluntly refused to help her crush the riot. He said our own slaves were sure to get restive too, the moment rumor spread about a riot at a neighboring plantation. We must prepare for ourselves, arming all the whites and the drivers with pistols and rifles and allotting a dog to each of them as their escort.

All the white and light-colored women he advised to gather in my house for protection by the most trustworthy of my colored servants, all of them armed too. Roy was sent to town to inform the police while Helen's husband rode over to Denise's plantation to watch the situation there.

Denise confessed she may have caused the uproar herself by interfering in matters she should have left to her *gérant* and his drivers.

Out of mere boredom she had driven out to the fields yesterday, and got angry at seeing so many hands idling away their time staring at her in mute hatred. So she turned to one of the drivers and ordered him and all his fellow-drivers to pick out half a dozen of the worst loafers all to be thrashed this Friday night as an example. The stupid bitch! There is one rule we women must observe strictly: leave the field hands to their drivers and the drivers to their superiors. Nobody likes us to interfere in matters concerning the field work.

After a hasty luncheon Denise retired to rest saying she had a headache. An hour or two later two riders on horseback appeared: M. Charon, her *économiste*, escorted by Helen's husband.

They told us the riot had been quenched quickly. About two dozen slaves escaped but were recaptured after a few hours—three of them killed, five wounded, the rest unhurt.

The only fugitive still uncaught was a house-servant of hers, the light-colored mulatto called George!

The moment Denise knew how things stood she turned nasty again. Tom's flight seems to worry her more than the heavier losses she must face—three males killed, five wounded! She at once had her horse saddled and rode home, escorted by M. Charon and her gardener.

No sooner had they disappeared than Henri knocked at my door to tell me Rex had caught a runaway belonging to Mme d'Argout. The captive insisted on seeing me, he said. So I called them in anticipating a happy reunion.

Sure enough the captive was Tom. But what a sight! He was wrapped in a soiled sheet which turned out to be his only garment. He looked like a skeleton, poor boy, you could see he was in high fever—so hot and wet his body—all in a sweat.

I made Helen and Rex promise not to tell anybody about the captive, even threatened to cut their tongues if they talked! Helen helped me to wash and dry his body and face and put him into a clean shirt. Then I laid him in my own bed and prepared a hot drink for him made of herbs that Helen is sure will help to cure him.

I have prayed to God, our Lord, and His Holy Mother, Virgin Queen of Heaven, to have mercy on our poor dear patient and save him. Promised in my prayers to offer one hundred candles to the glory of our Lord and His Holy Mother as soon as Tom is recovering. Never again shall I miss the Mass on Sundays, nor the monthly confessional, knowing how sinful a woman I am.

Rex told me later he had discovered the runaway hiding behind a bush near the house. The captive turned out to be too weak to walk unassisted, so he had almost carried him indoors, where he met Henri who came up to inform me. So glad no other servants were about, all of them having escorted the women back to their dwellings.

MONDAY, APRIL 4TH

How glad I am I got rid of her so soon this afternoon. Imagine her discovering him in my bedchamber!

It is inflammation of the lungs, the doctor says, and there is little chance of saving him since his poor body is already weakened by hill fever. He must have been very ill for weeks. That's why Denise took him upstairs.

When he ran away naked but for the sheet he was already in high fever. It was the desperate escape of a doomed man.

I feel so empty and sad, though Helen tries to comfort me saying she is still hopeful. I lay down beside him this morning after a long watch and at once fell asleep, so tired. Awakening I felt his hot body beside me, his wet hand grasping mine, still tumbling from one delirious dream to another. Such a pitiful sight. He must have gruesome visions in his agony judging from the terror in his eyes and the faint shrieks and groans he utters in his tormented sleep. The doctor says the crisis is approaching; if he lives another night there is a slight chance he can recover. But I could see he was sceptical. We must prepare for the worst. I feel like a burnt-out stove: empty and useless.

APRIL 7TH

This morning he opened his eyes and, seeing my face bent over his, he smiled. Very faintly, but smile he did! So happy he recognized me after lying unconscious for so many days and nights. His night-shirt was all soaked in sweat. I washed him from head to feet, and softly dried and rubbed his poor emaciated body, which seemed to relieve him.

His breathing has calmed, so weak, but regular again. Helen says he is sure to recover, but she has been confident all the time. Still, he drank a whole cup of beef-tea she gave him before relapsing into sleep. May be a good sign, but I must not give way to wild hopes too early.

Yesterday I sent a note over to Denise telling her I was in bad health and unable to receive guests for some time. Must keep her away from my house as long as possible.

MONDAY, APRIL 11TH

Tom is recovering visibly. He ate his breakfast with a good appetite, though still too weak to talk long. But I can wait. I am so happy to listen to his regular breathing at night, to feel the warmth of his skin, press my cheek to his when he awakes, rest my hand on his still skinny chest and respond to his shy caresses.

He said she had been kind to him while he was sick, and had helped to nurse him herself. She seemed to be sorry, knowing she would be responsible if he should die. She had his sick-bed put in the chamber beside hers and watched over him day and night.

I wonder if I can hide him from her much longer. No doubt Henri and Rex will keep their mouths shut, but we cannot keep our doings a secret from our servants much longer. There are doors and peepholes and smells and sounds and footsteps and whispered words and restrained laughs—all treacherous enough to give us away.

I know I have been watched and discussed in a whisper by my servants from the very first minute I arrived here. They know before breakfast if I rise in a good or bad temper, if I smile or snarl at any of them, what orders I give to whom, what question I put, what remarks I make, how long it took to wash my feet or dress my hair. The most intimate things about their mistress are common knowledge in a trice, even when she gets her blood and when it is over.

The moment I started favoring Henri he rose visibly in their esteem. They treated him with envious respect, which spoiled the little rascal so badly that I was forced to drop him.

Well, I don't mind their stupid gossip so long as no one else is informed, which I doubt as each of my servants knows what he risks if he is caught slandering me. Nor could Denise's servants ever be induced to give their mistress away, whatever secrets they may harbor. None of them would dare to give evidence against her in court, they all are much too frightened to talk. It would not even be admitted in court. Never mind! We shall have plenty of other witnesses to prove her guilt.

FRIDAY, APRIL 15TH

Now she knows! It was inevitable, so let us fight. She is wrong if she thinks she can frighten me with her threats. I am prepared to strike back if it comes to the worst.

It happened this morning. Suddenly she was in my bedchamber unannounced, not noticed before she faced us, hiding her fury behind a malicious smile.

I was sitting on the edge of my bed, still in my chemise, feeding Tom, which was great fun, for he made faces like a little fool. We were giggling and laughing and did not hear the door open. What a shock for both of us when she stood in the middle of the room, watching us, her face pale like a ghost's.

"So sorry I have interrupted the love-birds," she said with a sneer.

"It would have been decent to knock before intruding," I retorted, trying to hide my confusion.

"I didn't expect a slave of mine to lie in bed with you."

"Don't dare say that—you know he is sick. When he came here he was a dying man. I am the one who has saved his life."

"I know your ways of nursing your bed-mates!" she answered laughing spitefully.

"Get out of here!"

"Not before recovering my stolen property! You have hidden and harbored my runaway slave! That's a crime, and I'll make you pay for it!"

"He is not your slave, he is George's twin brother, a free citizen of a free country," I retorted.

"You believe the absurd lies of a runaway bastard slave!"

"We shall prove it in court."

"In court? All right! But it is you who will be brought to trial, not me. You, you, you filthy slave thief! I know dozens of people ready to swear this fellow has been my slave since I was a little girl."

"My attorney has found other witnesses ready to swear this man's mother is a white lady. Their home is in New York, which is a town in the United States where he grew up a free citizen. He has plenty of friends there ready to affirm these facts."

"Lies, lies, dirty lies!"

"There is a certain sea-captain with his crew who will remember him debarking at Cap."

"Maybe somebody resembling him."

"We know a certain landlady and her servants and guests who were present when you had him beaten and tied up and gagged and carried away! You will have to answer for that in court!"

"I'll show them his brandmarks and his scars, the ones he received for running away before. And all my friends and my servants will give evidence against you, you little hypocrite! Playing the part of a chaste widow, and all the time whoring about with my runaway niggers like a rutting bitch!"

"Get out of here!" I cried.

"I am going to send for the police!" she shouted, turning round.

"Do send for them! They will be interested to learn the true facts about you!" I shouted while she was rushing from the room.

Well, she has not made true her threat as yet. But you never know. I informed Mre Falcon—I sent Rex to town to implore him to come to my rescue at once. I do hope he will be here in time.

SATURDAY, APRIL 16TH

Mre Falcon is very confident. He says she is sure to realize what risks she runs if she should turn to the

police. The *Mirabelle* is due to arrive next week. Mre
Falcon hopes he can bring the captain and some members of his crew here to confront them with Tom in the
presence of other witnesses and make them sign a written statement to ascertain his identity.

He told me to send for the doctor and ask him to
attest that Tom is much too weak to be taken away. By
all means we must prevent the police from arresting
him before those main witnesses can give evidence in
his favor. But I do hope they won't interfere. She is a
vicious bitch, but she is shrewd enough to know she has
already lost her stake.

MONDAY, APRIL 18TH

She must have lost her head, else she would not
have played that ugly trick on us. Was it out of mere
spite? Or did she really hope I might consent to her
stupid proposal? But I must record the facts first:

This morning L. sent word to me that our driver
Camille had disappeared. We all know that fellow has
fallen for Denise's little maid, Pia, and has spent all his
Saturday and Sunday nights with her for months. We
didn't mind as long as he was back in time for work on
Monday. He had never been late before so I was worried
and sent a man over to Denise's house to investigate.
Two hours later he returned with a note from Denise,
which read:

Dear Elisa,
    In order to put an end to our dispute I have taken
your mulatto man, Camille, in exchange for George. I
am sure you will consent realizing you are getting the
best of the bargain, George's market value being much
higher than this stupid dark-skinned fellow's. But for
friendship's sake I am willing to leave the better man to
you. Please tell your attorney to prepare the deed to
make the barter legal.

                                              Denise

I at once drove to town to consult Mre Falcon. He
promised to write her a letter, telling her he would be

forced to turn to the police if my slave Camille should not be returned to me before dusk this Monday. Sure enough, the fellow was back in the late afternoon, but in what a state! Scarcely able to walk, so cruelly had he been whipped. She had kept him confined in a narrow room the whole day before telling him he was going to be thrashed for sleeping with her maid without having asked her mistress' consent.

I doubt if he will be able to work tomorrow. At any rate, some of the wounds will leave ugly marks on his back. I might sue her for damaged property, the man's market value being reduced by those scars. But I had better leave it at that. I don't ever wish to see that woman again!

SATURDAY, APRIL 23RD

It was a black Friday for Denise yesterday! I wonder if she can bear humiliation without somehow hitting back. She is so proud, so arrogant a woman, so used to having her word undisputed. For the first time she was forced to stoop, to admit she had made a bad mistake, to beg her victim's pardon and ask for his mercy!

I was glad I had prepared the dining-room for the conference, though I was not prepared for so many guests, such a crowd of witnesses, some of them so unfamiliar—the burly old captain, and his red-haired first mate, sturdy and virile.

The third of the crew was a plain sailor, the few teeth left in his filthy mouth yellow and big like a horse's —disgusting! And then that fat-bosomed woman, Mme Rolland, the landlady, and Denise's solemn-looking stout attorney, and the police officer, who never talked, just watched and listened, and Mre Falcon of course, with his officious little secretary.

And, apart from us, all seated round the table, the main witness, the victim of her detestable crime, Tom, still too weak to sit, listening to the testimonies from the bed I had placed near the table.

At first Denise had refused to come, had sent her

attorney to represent her. She had had to be fetched by the latter who made it plain to her she must obey or else she would be arrested.

How embarrassing for her to listen to the witnesses giving their evidence, then to be forced to add her signature to all the others verifying the written statements, and at last to sign her own confession, admitting all her illegal actions and promising to duly indemnify her victim.

Then Mre Falcon turned to Tom, saying he would not advise him to spare her but for considerations of political importance.

If brought to trial her atrocious crime would be sure to arouse public scandal that would prejudice the interests of all the slave-holders in this island, good and bad alike even for instance those of the young lady who had so gallantly rescued and protected him.

"Still," he added, "it is left to you to decide whether to forgive the wrongdoer or not."

There followed a deadly silence, all our eyes were fixed upon Tom. He had fallen back on to his pillow, and he stared up at the ceiling as if ignoring the attorney's words.

"You had better ask the gentleman's pardon," said Mre Falcon at last, addressing Denise who was sitting at the end of the table, waxen pale, a defiant smile about her lips. Her attorney moved close to her and talked in a whisper.

"All right," she said, shrugging her shoulders. "If you insist." She rose and walked to the sick man's bed.

"I made a mistake," she said, turning to Tom. "I should not have done so if I had been able to tell you from your brother at once. Now I am sorry, I beg your pardon."

It was the very first time that her voice faltered. I had the feeling she was about to burst into tears and I could not help pitying her for a moment. But Tom was still unmoved, and kept staring up at the ceiling.

"Tell me, what are your terms?" she said regaining her poise.

"You will have to manumit George," I put in. "You

will have to do it now! Ask my attorney to draw up the document and sign it in our presence!"

"This is no business of yours!" she snarled.

"The lady is right!" I heard Tom say. "This is what I demand, beside the recovery of all my stolen property, trunk, clothes, money, papers and the rest of my belongings. And ten thousand livres damages," he added, "to be delivered to my brother the moment he turns up." He spoke in a firm voice, so different from the soft tender whispers to which I was accustomed. It was the more impressive as he had kept silent before, never said a word, just listened.

There was another whispered dialogue between Denise and her pompous attorney, which ended in her consenting to the demands stipulated by Tom.

Then the two lawyers and the secretary were busy for a while dictating and writing the document which made George's manumission legal and irrevocable the moment we all had signed it, Denise, the lawyers and the witnesses present.

Denise was the first to rise and leave, proud and upright like a queen, no nods, no farewell taken, the great lady disgusted at the insults she was exposed to by the rabble!

SATURDAY NIGHT

Late this afternoon Tom's valise was delivered to him and an envelope containing her promissory note for 10,000 livres payable before June 1st. Quite a sum!

It has cost her dear, that stupid crime of hers, and she must add that amount to the fee she will have to pay my attorney as well as hers. Also there is the definite loss of George, her most valuable slave, whom she could have sold for 5,000 livres last year had she minded her profit, instead of driving that poor man to desperate escape.

It seems none of Tom's papers are missing, nor did she touch his money or clothes. So she lied to him when she said she had burnt all his belongings. She was trying to discourage him.

Perhaps she was really taken aback when she saw him stripped—no brand, no scars—realizing she had made a bad mistake. She may have been ready to apologize had he behaved differently after recovering from his ordeal. But she could not expect her victim to take it as a joke. I can well imagine how exasperated he was considering the way he had been treated, lying bundled up in her coach, gagged, exposed to the murderous heat of midday, the continuous jolts of the coach on the rough road, the kicks she dealt him whenever he dropped against her foot, the pain he felt growing in his arms and legs from being bound tight together for almost two hours, and all the time forced to listen to that woman's vile reproaches, insults, threats and scoffing humiliation.

He says she called him an ungrateful scoundrel and promised to give him a hot welcome when back at home, one that would leave its mark for the rest of his life. She said she would keep him in chains for months and send him to the fields to be treated like the meanest of her blacks.

She had a mind to have him gelded, she said, a pity she had spared him so long. It seemed to be the only means to break his rebellious spirit and make him a useful servant who would obey and respect his mistress.

It was an endless torrent of filthy language, he says, the more disgusting as it came from the lips of a refined-looking young lady, pretty and well dressed, not a vulgar fishwife. He could not see much of her, only the lower part of her skirt beside the maid's bare feet, and now and again, whenever she bent forward to watch him, her angry face in the shadow of a parasol.

After a while she had thrown off her shoes and started kicking and tickling his face with her bare toes. When tired of that pastime, seeing he was gasping for breath, she removed the stocking with which he had been gagged.

"Don't dare to start reasoning!" she shouted the moment he tried to find words. "Keep quiet or I'll stop up your filthy mouth again!"

To emphasize her warning she pressed the whole weight of her bare foot against his open lips. He must have fainted, for when he opened his eyes again he was lying on the bare wooden floor of a dusky room, stripped to the skin, his right ankle chained to the wall. He tried to get up but felt too weak to stand. The clatter of his iron fetters must have been heard outside, for a door opened and a brown woman's face popped in and disappeared.

After a while he again heard steps. This time it was the terrible blonde woman who stood in the door-way. She must have had a bath, for she was drying her hair with a towel while she watched him. Ashamed of being exposed naked to a woman's stare he turned his back on her.

"Who are you?" he heard her ask in a perplexed voice.

"I wish for my clothes!" he retorted. "Haven't you any modesty?"

He felt something soft drop on his shoulder; it was her towel she had flung at him. Binding it round his hips he turned, facing her with cold hatred in his eyes. She had approached him, and walked around him in embarrassed wonder, scrutinizing his back and gliding her fingers across it.

"Who are you?" she repeated. "I see you cannot be George."

"So I told you from the start," he answered. "But you would not listen to me, ma'am. There is no excuse whatever for the shocking ill-treatment I have suffered, for the way you have insulted and degraded me. I'll make you pay for all that, believe me, you brainless little beast of a woman."

He lost his self-control—all his wounded pride exploded in an outburst of raging hatred. Of course it would have been wiser if he had kept calm, but there are moments when we cannot help giving way to our feelings unrestrained. He called her names, a monster, a shameless bitch of a female despot, and threatened to turn to the police and have her arrested.

He said he was sure the man she had mistaken him for was his own twin brother whom he was looking for because he was held in slavery against the law, being a white mother's son like himself. He said he pitied his poor brother for having fallen into the claws of a tigress, a woman who should be spanked and then hanged or shot like a beast!

Knowing Denise I can well imagine her reaction to such words, her rushing out thirsty for revenge. A minute later she reappeared, followed by two giant Negroes of hers who fell upon him and whipped him mercilessly till he lay motionless on the floor, groaning with pain.

Maybe it was then that Denise realized she had gone too far. The former ill-treatments of her victim could have been excused on the ground of her having mistaken Tom for her runaway slave. No court of justice would have considered her trespass a grave one. But this last whipping was a deliberate abuse of her power, it might cost her very dear.

In her panicky fear she lost her head and made things worse by trying to make people believe he was, indeed, her runaway slave George whom she had rightly punished after recapturing him.

Tom's subsequent branding, her forcing him into mute submission by threats and daily maltreatment and humiliation were all a means to an end: to prevent him from finding a chance of escape and prosecution. Moreover, it was a kind of revenge on George: If she could not take her vengeance on the latter, his next akin was to suffer in his place. The loss of her most valuable slave was outweighed in the simplest way possible, by making use of and replacing him with his twin brother.

I am sure it was frustrated love—perverted into hatred—that also played its part in the hidden motives that drove her to commit such a crime. I am trying to explain, not excuse her abominable offence. She is wicked, but she is not a monster. I well remember that afternoon when she confessed to me, half drunk, how unhappy she felt about George. If she had met a man of equal birth worth admiring I am sure her frozen heart might have melted into that of a tender-loving woman. She has not met such a man so far and I am afraid it would be too late now. She has grown too hard a woman to be helped.

APRIL 24TH

I am starting this new cahier, the former having been filled to the last page during the recent weeks, no wonder considering the great events I have had to record.

I forgot to report so many other important things. For a while, nothing else mattered but Tom's case. No diary can give the whole truth. Remembering is like picking floating scraps of wood from a broad river at random—letting other fragments pass unobserved, things too familiar to us to be minded, all the disagreeable things of daily life we have learned to put up with, the sultry heat, the beastly insects, the stupidity and laziness of our servants, their dirty habits, superstition, disobedience—all these are forgotten along with our own shortcomings, daily failures, rash and arbitrary verdicts, outbursts of bad temper, impatience and irritable moods.

We women are said to be more disposed than men to yield to our whims and the changing caprices of our heart. It is impossible to recall all those little daily incidents that force us to impose our authority; to say nothing of our secret feelings and thoughts.

It would take a whole book to register one single day's happenings if I tried to record everything, routine life and desires and hopes and apprehensions and physical appetites and pleasures and dislikes and discomfort, the thousand intimate reactions of my mind and body to what happens around me in the course of a day.

How naïve I was when, five years ago, I promised to write the truth and nothing but the truth!

The whole truth? What about those wicked experiences I never mentioned in this diary because I was ashamed of remembering them? Ashamed of myself! It is so hard, so painful, to be candid with oneself. We hate to realize we harbor wicked urges that may awake and change us into beasts at any time!

I hate to remember that coarse itch that made me turn to a vulgar servant once and again and abuse him as a mere instrument of beastly pleasure—a strange mixture of scorn, scare, thrill and brutish lust reversed into disgust and hatred when exhausted, and then bitter shame and remorse and loathing towards the wretched male. What a bitch of a slut I felt! Impossible to record such experiences without despising myself.

Or those outbursts of rage that, more than once, drove me to hit a servant with my own hand or crop in order to break his mute resistance. It was unpardonable lack of self-control and dignity I would repent as soon as I calmed. (Though I am sure there is no white woman in this island who can rule a pack of slaves without ever resorting to the whip. Even softhearted Mme Galez did when that fellow Marcel broke her china.)

Of course it is very bad manners for a lady to castigate a slave herself, but which of us does not forget at times she is a lady? In this hot climate we often feel so irritable we cannot control our temper the way we should. We resent the very look, the very smell of a stupid servant with his boorish grin at a rebuke, as if daring his mistress, doubting her authority, defying it, gauging how far he can go in braving it. Another sign of impertinence, a grimace, a saucy gesture, may raise our anger to blind fury: We start boxing the slave's ears, and when he tries to dodge our hands we make him kneel so that we can hit him with redoubled force, right and left and right and left, to quench the stubborn spite still lurking in his eyes, force him to complete submission, body and soul. It is a wicked drunken lust to hurt and destroy, slap, slap, slap, till exhaustion stops us all in a sweat, followed by a shame and regret as mortifying in its way, as the resentment we felt before the punishment.

Maybe it is my old hatred of Pierre that makes me turn against other males, helpless ones, so savagely at times. The wickedest, stupidest kind of revenge imaginable!

I think I never mentioned these disgusting trespasses of mine before in this journal. Felt much too ashamed to record them. Well, here at last I have made a clean breast of them.

I am sure it won't happen again. We feel so much more placid and kindly disposed when we are happy. No greater happiness than to love and be loved! We have not made any plans so far. I don't wish to urge him to talk about marriage before he has completely recovered. Perhaps he is just too proud, or thinks I am too conceited to marry a colored man. Or too rich for a man of his station. Silly boy!

I should tell him I am ready to follow him wherever he likes. Get rid of my house and estate and slaves and everything to start a new life at his side, as his loving faithful wife till death does us part.

MAY 2ND

Jeanne warned me to sell all my mulattoes at once.

She says her father knows for certain that all slaves of partly white origin will be declared free in the near future.

I cannot make up my mind to separate from them, rather shall I emancipate them of my own free will. None of them would desert me, knowing how hard life is in town for poor, unskilled bastards.

Tom would be pleased. He would regard it as proof of his good influence upon me. He says slavery as a whole is wrong, and he wishes me to manumit all my slaves, Negroes included. In vain I told him they depend on me, could not earn their living if driven away from their cabins and the little plots allotted to them for growing their food.

He cannot expect me to lose all the money invested in my slaves—quite a fortune—out of mere magnanimity. It would leave me a poor woman, reduce me to the shabby life of a little bourgeoise dependent on her husband's income. I am ready to sell my plantation, but no prospective purchaser will take it without the necessary stock of slaves to work it.

Laroche says our hands are getting restive again.

That uneasy feeling, that malaise so difficult to explain and so much more difficult to suppress is back with us again. It is in the air, you feel it, you see it lurking in their eyes, their faces, but you cannot strike back because nothing serious has happened—yet Laroche warns me, says we must be prepared for the worst at any moment, rumors of riots at other plantations having spread among our blacks.

Bad news from France! They say the Royal Family is no longer allowed to leave Paris. They must feel like prisoners. It is high time the army interfered, restored the King's authority, and brought order and peace to our poor France.

MAY 9TH

Have resigned my owner's rights on all my fourteen mulattoes! I do hope Tom will appreciate my decision, which cost me a considerable part of my fortune, for though market prices for bastards have fallen badly a certain woman would have paid me 3,000 for each of my prettiest wenches and for some of my handsomest lads, too. I might have saved 15,000 or more, that way. But I should be tormented by pricks of conscience to the end of my days, knowing I delivered the poor creatures to vice and prostitution.

Denise would not care, but my heart is not of stone like hers. Tom would hate me, turn away from me if I had sold one single servant. Really, I do feel better now it is done.

Even Mre Falcon said manumitting my mulattoes might prove profitable in the end. Their gratitude may secure me their faithful protection in case our blacks should start rioting. I offered to pay them monthly wages, 20 livres the males, 10 livres the females, on condition that they won't desert me as long as I stay here. Even Rex says he wishes to stay.

I told him he had proved a good boy all the time, said I was sorry I had not always been very nice to him and asked him to forget. I promised him a reward for

his faithful services, a decent sum of money to be given
him this summer to help him to start a trade in town.

I wonder what thoughts he harbored in his thick
brown skull, his only answers being, "Yes, ma'am;
thank you, ma'am," all the time, his eyes fixing mine
with a sad stare.

I asked him if he bore me any grudge, which he
denied, hiding his true feelings behind a mask of respectful equanimity. I felt embarrassed remembering
the shocking secrets we share like conspirators acting
the parts of strangers. Does he hate me? Or is he attached to me the more for knowing I am ashamed?
There is an intimacy between wrongdoer and victim no
mask of indifference can efface.

We advertised George's manumission in *Les Affiches
Américaines* and in two newspapers in Port. If he is
still living in this island he is sure to be informed sooner or later. We must repeat our advertisement again and
again.

I am so glad Tom has promised he won't leave before
finding his brother, though I don't know how I will
manage when Captain Basteresse's ship arrives in August if Tom is still my guest. Imagine him learning I
have invested my money in the slave trade! But he
cannot expect me to lose that money, too! Of course,
slavery is ugly. But as long as it is established by law
we are bound to make the best of it. My blacks are fed
and cared for, and do not starve like so many thousands of poor free families in Ireland and France. If
there were no cheap hands available to work our plantations, prices for sugar and cotton and coffee would rise
to such heights that no one could afford to buy them
any longer.

It is no use arguing that way with Tom. He expects
me to manumit all my Negroes, renounce the best part
of my property and leave this island a poor woman. I
love Tom, but I cannot help getting impatient whenever
he starts propounding such tomfoolery. It is the only topic I must try to avoid; it is like touching red-hot iron:
it burns and makes us yell at each other.

MAY 16TH

Emancipating my mulattoes has had a bad effect on our black hands. It has awakened wild hopes about imminent freedom for all of them, the silly creatures.

Friday night they sent a deputy of three men who asked permission to talk to me. Maybe it was unwise to receive them. Laroche said I should have sent them away with a stern warning. It is no good permitting slaves to claim any rights. It makes them think we acknowledge such rights, which we do not as, by law, they are considered as part of the livestock, like cattle, my undisputed property, not under contract like free persons.

Well, I didn't wish to be taken for a tyrant, so I called them in, three of my oldest Negroes.

One of them—called Rufus—I remembered as having talked to me before. On that fatal day when they had all torn my authority to shreds, he was the fellow who had complained of hard work, had said he was the son of a chieftain. He might turn out to be dangerous —he must be closely watched.

They asked me to grant them free Fridays to be added to their Saturdays so that they could work their own plots with better results.

It is impossible to grant them a whole day more. I tried to explain it to them in a kindly way, said if they worked only four days a week our crops would be late. For such late crops I should get little money which would force me to reduce their food and clothing— perhaps even sell some of them to pay my debts. In a few years' time I should be ruined, another white planter would replace me, would make them work harder than ever before.

I promised to talk to their commandant. Maybe, between crops, the most diligent workers among them might be granted a free Friday afternoon at times, as a special reward, but it was to be decided by their commandant, M. Laroche, who knew better than myself what to do.

Afterwards Laroche was very cross that I shied from blank refusal, but in the end he promised to try it out if the concession I proposed proves practicable. He is afraid it may turn out to be disastrous, rousing envy and discontent among those excluded from the privilege of a free Friday afternoon.

It is so difficult to decide whether to make concessions or not. Both ways may prove fatal.

No news about George. Maybe he is suspicious and thinks it is a mere ruse of Denise's to trap him. Tom wishes our attorney to insert a new text in the newspapers of Cap and Port, advising George to answer and secure a happy reunion with his brother and mother.

Tom didn't know he had a twin brother till the agent turned up and made his mother confess she had run away from her parents with his dark-skinned father twenty years ago. She said they had been forced to leave George behind because he was very sick. Later she tried to recover the baby but was informed by letter he had died. Her husband she lost when Tom was twelve.

MAY 23RD

Jeanne told me she had met Denise in town yesterday. She said she looked as high-spirited as ever. Denise invited both her and her stupid husband to be her guests on June 9th, which is her birthday.

Jeanne asked me if I minded her accepting that invitation. Of course I do! It is a deliberate affront to invite my paid subordinates while cutting out her own sister-in-law!

But curiosity prevailed. So I told Jeanne it was all right, she was sure to have a good time being such a good dancer.

She knows why Denise and I are on tenterhooks. It has become common gossip everywhere, even in town, thanks to Mme Rolland and so many other scandalmongers there. Strangely enough, people seem to admire rather than disapprove of Denise. They laugh at her boldness, call her a shrewd little devil of a woman.

Well, Jeanne is a keen observer, she is sure to tell me everything about Denise she can find out.

I am glad Tom is so clever he can replace my arrogant *économiste* so easily. Nicole left suddenly last Monday. Said he had found a better place. I refused to pay his wages for the last weeks, considering he deserted so abruptly.

He seems to disapprove of my relations with Tom—hates me for preferring a colored man to him. It is their stupid vanity that is hurt when a white woman rejects them for a mulatto. I don't care a pin for their disapproval!

Laroche told our drivers to select one man in each gang to be granted the first free Friday afternoon. He says the others obviously resent being refused the privilege.

It is no use trying to be nice to them. They are like little children who need a spanking in order to learn. If we are too complaisant they get saucy, while harsh measures might turn them more stubborn and rebellious. But for that odious Captain Basteresse and his cargo I would sell everything on the spot and leave with Tom, for I have given up hopes of ever finding George.

MAY 30TH

This time twenty-three hands were granted free Friday afternoons, almost a dozen more than last time. Laroche says the general feeling is still doubtful, so many being disappointed at being left out. I told him to promise them all a free afternoon next Friday, except the dawdlers. We must try to convince them they are better off when working well.

I told Jeanne to stop hitting the slaves. No use humiliating them that way for trifling reasons—even blacks wish to be treated as human beings, not as dull brutes.

Jeanne is a nice girl, but sometimes she is too blunt in her handling of the servants. No wonder, considering she is a slaver's daughter used to regarding blacks as two-legged cattle. Tom resents her rough manners. He told me he saw her slap my groom's face after stopping him in the yard. He threatened to spank her on the spot if he ever caught her hitting a man again. I wonder how she would react to being thrashed by a colored man—would raise hell to get her revenge, that's what she would do. Heaven protect us from a scandal like that!

I do wish I could leave with Tom. He does not feel happy here, calls it terrible the way we treat our slaves. I dare not rebuke a servant in his presence any longer lest he should call me a despot. Must keep him away from the fields. He would be shocked if he saw our drivers carrying whips. I am afraid, sooner or later somebody will tell him about the Friday night thrashings. Impossible to explain to him that we cannot do without them, no planter can.

Tom is so terribly thick-headed in these matters, such a fanatic! Though I like him all the more for his noble-mindedness. Wasn't I myself shocked when I came here five years ago by the sight of that fat mulatto woman in her boat rowed by her two wretched blacks? And my aunt examining a group of slaves for sale . . . that first slave market I attended.

Of course, he, too, would get used to things like that in course of time. Everybody does. But it would take years. And meanwhile I might lose his affection for ever!

It makes me sick, the very idea of losing him! Oh, Tom, dear, silly Tom! I love you, love you, love you the way I never loved anybody before, not even George. I confessed to him about George. He just listened, no comments! Maybe I was wrong to tell him. It will certainly not help to make him love me the better, knowing how weak and profligate a woman I am.

Sometimes I feel so down-hearted, realizing I am not worthy of him, not even able to bear him children! How, then, can I expect him to marry me? Yet I can no longer live without him. I feel so happy in his arms, so terribly unhappy when alone, the fears of losing him haunting me ever in my dreams!

JUNE 6TH

I saw Mme G. and her daughter in church, but they openly ignored me, cut me dead as if I were a complete stranger. The stupid fat old cow and her ugly offspring! Rumors seem to have spread fast about my liaison with Tom. A white woman attached to a bastard lover—what a scandal! I don't care a copper sous for their stupid gossip. Tom is a free-born citizen of a free country, isn't he? Well educated and much handsomer than any of their own stupid white sons and brothers, to say nothing of his character and intelligence which makes him a king among beggars.

It is not the first time I have felt hostility rising against me. But so far nobody has dared offend me so brusquely. Even Jeanne is no longer nice. She avoids me, watches me disapprovingly from afar.

She knows Tom dislikes her for her rough ways of handling slaves. No doubt she would like to treat him in the same way to show him how superior she feels to any colored man, however wealthy and well-educated he may be.

It is hard to brave the whold world around us, to see our friends and neighbors turn away from us. But weighing their disapproval against Tom's love is like weighing dust against heaps of gold! Let them slander me to their heart's content. The very touch of my lover's golden skin makes me forget the scandalmongers, all of them. You hear the nightingale, and all the sparrows' silly chirping stops.

FRIDAY, JUNE 10TH

She is a devil of a mean creature! Intent all the time on spiteful revenge—slandering me that way!

Of course Jeanne tried to deny it, said she had not listened to the silly chitchat, nor believed a word of what the captain said, seeing he was as drunk as a lord.

But I could see she was embarrassed. She tried to

avoid me, not knowing how to behave. It is obvious
Denise invited that scoundrel for the very purpose of
making him drunk, hoping he would start bragging
about his easy victory over me, telling all the guests how
eagerly I had opened my door and legs to him that
night!

It seems I was the main topic of their gossip from the
beginning of the evening—the shameless bitch living in
open sin with a mulatto man, a slave's brother. A little
whore, every man's bed-mate, who had managed to
cheat poor Charles into marrying her, thinking she was
an innocent virgin! There was no doubt she had duped
her husband from the start, turning to his own slaves,
the lewd bitch!

That's the way Denise would malign me in public,
knowing there were no friends left to defend my honor.
It seems I have become an outcast, having committed
the worst crime imaginable for a white woman in this
island: making love to a bastard. Of course there are
hundreds of other women who have done that before
and will do it again. But none is so stupid as to admit it
and defy the holy rules of this horde of hypocrites.

That bitch! I am sure she has been whoring with half
a dozen of her own slaves, not only bastards but blacks
as well, in every way possible. But who cares—as long
as nobody knows? She plays the part of the haughty
mistress so well that people think she would shrink
from the very touch of a colored man. If they knew!
But she goes free, whatever crime she may have committed, while they are ready to stone me for loving a
man who is their equal.

She is setting them on me, intent on ruining me,
that's her revenge! But I won't care. I am prepared to
defy the whole crowd of them, the stupid pharisees!

None of them was shocked in the least by Denise's
disgusting lack of decency. They enjoyed that lascivious
Chica performed by her black dancers, all of them
stripped to the skin, their parts so poorly covered that
the males could not hide their rising heat. (I am re-
peating Jeanne's statement.) Quite embarrassing for
the ladies present. Jeanne seems to have broken the ice
by making a funny remark which caused a peal of

laughter and encouraged the others to comment in the same strain on the display of savage virility.

Later, when a little drunk, Denise started bragging about one of her blacks whom she claimed to be the strongest fellow in the island. This was doubted by some of her guests, one of whom offered to prove that his own black servant was better at wrestling. They bet 1,000 livres each on who owned the stronger man, and the other guests joined in the wager.

The two blacks were ordered to strip and oil their skins. Denise and her challenger agreed on acknowledging the other's victory the moment he or she thought it wise to stop the fight.

Jeanne said Denise talked to her Negro in a menacing whisper before giving the signal for the start. It was a ferocious fight, each of the black wrestlers being encouraged by his backers again and again. But in the end Denise's man was paralyzed by a foul kick from his opponent, was knocked down, choked, disfigured, and his arm sprayed. But Denise didn't admit his defeat until he lay there unconscious, his face smashed to a bloody pulp, so that he had to be carried away like a corpse.

After that animating interlude their ball was resumed, Denise acting the part of a good loser. If the fellow is ruined, she has lost a good 4,000 livres on her birthday, 1,000 the bet and 3,000 the Negroe's market value, strong Mandingoes being offered at no lower a price anywhere at present. Serves her right!

SUNDAY, JUNE 12TH

I feel very depressed, knowing how deeply he resents my "pitiless cruelty" as he calls it. But what else could I do? Runaways must be dealt with severely, otherwise deserting becomes a habit.

Yesterday morning, while Tom was on his way to town (to see our attorney), Rex told me two of my hands had run away during the night, but had been caught by the *maréchaussée* and delivered to us early in the morning.

I refused to have them whipped in public. Imagine Tom watching such a scene. Instead I ordered them to be served a good lick, twenty lashes each, with pepper and salt treatment afterwards, and then have them chained to wooden blocks for a month or two and employed in a distant field, far away from the road, so that Tom should not see them. It is the least punishment imaginable for such scoundrels. Still, I was glad Tom was absent while they were being punished.

But we ought to cut our servants' tongues to stop their gossiping! I don't know which of them told Tom, but last night he took me to task—said he knew I had ordered them to be whipped and had been present when they were beaten. It proved I was a cruel tyrant. No decent woman would enjoy ill-treating human beings!

I said I had witnessed the whippings solely to prevent any wanton cruelty. I saw to it that their waists were protected by broad leather belts in order to avoid injuring their kidneys.

"So they were stripped?" he cried indignantly.

"Well, how else could we warm up their hides?" I retorted.

"Don't you feel ashamed!" he shouted. "A young lady watching males being stripped naked!"

"My dear Tom," I replied laughing, "if you think I am interested in watching nude males you are wrong. As a rule they are a very ugly sight and not at all attractive. But you cannot expect me to behave like a prudish maiden after having been responsible for the health and bodily fitness of a hundred black males for years."

"Your slaves' health!" he cried. "Is their health improved by ill-treating them?"

"What do you propose to discourage runaways?" I asked.

"Grant them freedom, treat them as human beings, not as rightless animals!" he retorted, returning to the one and only subject of our daily disputes. No use arguing—he is so terribly stubborn.

SUNDAY, JUNE 19TH

I still feel paralyzed by the shock. Like the time when my aunt was killed. The news came like a bolt from the blue and it takes time to recover.

I thought I hated her, yet I cannot help feeling crushed, and I pity her for all her sins. She was not so thoroughly bad, after all. I remember many happy hours we spent together, her laughter still rings in my ears. She was so bright and clever a girl, so witty, so charming when in high spirits! But was she ever really happy? Certainly not in love matters. She was much too self-willed, too arrogant and demanding. She had no willingness to surrender and submit herself to the man she loved.

Did she ever really love any man? Her husband? She despised and detested him. George? Remembering her words that afternoon when she was drunk I am convinced she was attached to him in a strangely perverted way. Had she fled with him as his mother had done with her lover years before she might now be his happy wife, somewhere in France or in one of those free American states where slavery is unknown. She would not be lying in her bloodstained bed, a disfigured, strangled corpse. What a horrible end!

They found her yesterday morning, lying across her pillows, already cold, a hideous sight, with slashes across her naked breasts and belly. Her bluish face was swollen into an ugly grimace, her blue eyes fixed in a cold stare.

When I arrived the police were already busy questioning the house-servants. No one had thought of covering the mutilated corpse. It was left to me to close her legs to a decent position and hide her poor body under a clean white sheet.

They suspect the gardener, the most faithful of her servants, of having committed the crime, killing not only his mistress but two other black servants as well. I hope they will hunt him down and make him suffer for his atrocious crime. All our neighbors have joined in the search. I sent Jeanne's husband with two of my best dogs to assist them; promised him 200 livres if he can catch the murderer alive.

JUNE 21st

Heaven be thanked, it is over! That ghastly funeral! What an ordeal from beginning to end. I never felt such an outcast before—waves of hatred and disgust surrounding me wherever I looked.

There were so many people who had been my own guests, or whom I had met with Denise all avoiding me, turning their stony faces away as though I were a complete stranger, worse, a common harlot whose very presence was embarrassing.

The church was crammed with mourners and prying rabble, Denise's scandalous death being everywhere the gossip of the week.

Even while kneeling and praying I knew a thousand eyes were staring at me. I could feel them like poisonous darts piercing me from all sides. "That's the white whore who is living in open sin with a brown bastard!" I could sense the words—could hear the frenzied whispers.

As soon as it was over I drove home in a hurry, rushed to Tom's room, embraced him and encouraged him to make love, drowning my rage and despair in a torrent of delirious passion. I felt so relieved afterwards, even happy again for a while and ready to face the whole crowd with scorn.

It seems the murderer has succeeded in joining the Maroons. All the planters demand radical measures to hunt them out. They say military forces should be used to support the police and search the mountainous parts to the east that offers innumerable hiding-places for outlaws. There is still a great commotion among the whites, Denise's horrible death having roused general alarm, especially in town where she was well known and admired in spite of her doubtful reputation.

This is what we have found out by questioning the servants:

Last Saturday morning Denise became suspicious while watching her young maid Claire. She made her admit she was pregnant. The wench confessed she had slept with the gardener, had yielded to him like most of the other wenches in the house. She said they all feared him, knowing he was their mistress' favorite who could make them suffer if they refused to pleasure him.

Denise was furious, for she had strictly forbidden her male servants to sleep with any of her females without her consent. So she sent for the gardener, told him she had a good mind to have his hide flogged to shreds and then banish him to the fields. She dismissed him, saying she would deal with him in the evening.

After dinner, when she had retired to her rooms for her siesta, her maid told her that she had overheard the gardener saying he would kill the person who dared raise the whip against him, whereupon Denise sent for two of her strongest Negroes and told them to fetch the gardener.

The maid said her mistress sent her out the moment the three men entered the lady's chamber. For a while she listened outside. She could hear the lady's angry voice, then a scuffle and bangs and moans and a terrible shriek. She rushed downstairs to tell the other servants the gardener was getting his punishment. They all gathered on the stairs listening, but could not hear a sound.

After a while the door opened, the gardener stepped out, his shirt bloodstained and torn, his eyes and lips swollen, blood oozing down his chin. Seeing the crowd of prying servants on the staircase he told them to resume their work, said the lady had a headache and wished to be left undisturbed the whole afternoon, nor did she wish to have supper in the evening. It was not the first time she had given such an order.

The servants knew the two Negroes were still inside, so they did not ask any questions, no business of theirs to find out what was happening in there. It would have been dangerous to be too inquisitive. Those who had been called up to her rooms before never talked. Nor did any of the maids dare enter the lady's chamber in the evening if her bell didn't summon them in.

It was not until late the following morning that one of her chambermaids plucked up sufficient courage to knock at her door. As not a sound was to be heard she opened the door, saw the two Negroes lying on the floor motionless, and rushed downstairs to call for help.

The *gérant's* wife was summoned; she was the first to enter the bedchamber. They soon saw the two Negroes had been stabbed. One was still alive, but unconscious. He died when carried downstairs. The bed was covered with blood-drenched pillows. They found her butchered body when removing them—a shocking sight that drove the women into hysterical fits. When the police arrived more than twenty hours must have passed since the crime was committed. The murderer had plenty of time to escape to the forests in the hills. It will be difficult to track him down if he found aid and shelter with the Maroons.

JUNE 25TH

This morning Jeanne and her husband left us.

They said they were bound to help her parents to prepare a slave auction on July 5th. But that's a lame excuse. Those slaves are the poor remainder of old Mme Richard's, who died a month ago. There are no more than eighteen in number, a bunch of miserable wornout Negroes, none below thirty, all second-rate blacks she used to hire out to earn her living. Jeanne's parents could easily handle them unassisted.

Why did she not tell me frankly that public opinion has forced her to leave me? Well then, good riddance! Though I don't know what I shall do if all the whites desert us. If Laroche, too, leaves me in the lurch I shall be forced to sell everything in the middle of the crop. And it takes time to find a purchaser ready to offer a reasonable sum and pay cash.

I must turn to Mre Falcon for advice. I ought to get a decent price considering the value of my estate and houses and slaves and all the rest; say 200,000 the landed property, buildings included, eighty black males at 2,000 a head, makes 160,000, sixty-five or -six females, and old and useless ones included, at 1,500 on average makes about 100,000. One hundred and twenty brats below twelve, at 500 a piece—60,000. My other livestock, horses, cattle, dogs, etc., 20,000; furniture and machines and tools; 20,000 totalling 560,-000 livres. Quite a sum! Maybe I must reduce it to 500,000 or less, considering it is an emergency.

If I can't sell it as a whole I'll put all my blacks up for auction, which may prove even more profitable in the end, and offer the land to my neighbors to be purchased by the acre. Or find a *gérant* to run the plantation in my place and have the annual profit transferred to me in France or New York through my bank. I must consult the attorney.

At any rate I had better tell Tom to return to New York soon. He would raise hell if he knew I am going to sell my slaves instead of emancipating them as I almost promised to him when lying in his arms weak and defenceless last night. Frailty, thy name is woman!

What would he say if he knew about my contract with Captain Basteresse? I'll have to take care of Denise's share too, all her property and legal claims returning to her widowed mother in France. Mre Falcon told me nothing will go to her former husband, nor to me since Charles died before her, leaving no offspring.

Mme Galez will certainly be happy to leave the awkward business to me and my attorney. It will take time to pick out my share of the blacks and put them up for auction in town. Might bring me in another 150,000 livres or more, prices for male savages *toutes pièces* having risen up to 2,000 a head!

I hate the idea of separating from Tom. It makes me sick to have to send him away. Those weeks of loneliness to be faced after his departure will be bitter. But when all is settled I'll follow him to a happier life in a happier country, whether married to him or not. I am rich enough to brave the world. We shall find a place where nobody cares if a white woman is married to a brown man. Money makes people color-blind, thank Heavens.

SUNDAY, JULY 3RD

I am in an awful plight. Laroche intends to return to his country, Switzerland, towards the end of this month. But for Tom, I should be left unprotected in my house, one white woman among a crowd of discontented blacks. Even the mulatto drivers are unreliable, may side with the slaves in case of a riot. Nor do I trust my house-servants. They are getting lazy and disrespectful, knowing I can no longer punish them the same way as before their manumission.

They know I wish to sell the plantation, which does not help to strengthen my authority. If I cannot find a purchaser soon I'll have to look for a trustworthy *gérant*. I suggested to Laroche that he should take care of the whole estate, offered him a third of the annual net profit, which he refused, saying it was high time he left.

He is sure war between France and England is imminent. The English will prevent our trading with France, which will ruin us in a few months' time. He predicts slave riots and starvation, says he has saved enough money to return to his country and buy a farm there.

If things really grow bad I'll call for military protection, ask the soldiers to take my Negroes to town and keep them in prison until I can put them up for auction. Tom will be furious, but meanwhile he may have learned his lesson as I learned mine five years ago.

He says if I emancipate my blacks and grant them a weekly pay they are sure to work better. He is convinced it will turn out to be more profitable for me in the long run. I told him he might try and rule them his way for a while and reward them for good work, but I warned him not to promise too much too early.

He is being trained for his new office as superintendent by Laroche. I wonder if he can handle the blacks in this way, by treating them as his equals. His failure may help to bring him to reason. I wish he were more sensible, considering the major part of my capital is invested in slaves. It would mean throwing away a fortune if I decided to manumit them. Even Tom could not persuade me to be so foolish.

JULY 11TH

Bad news! They say civil war is imminent. The free mulattoes are claiming equal rights more loudly than ever before, rights which the whites stubbornly refuse to grant them.

It seems the new rulers in Paris side with the mulattoes and intend to interfere with military force in their favor, some of their leaders having been cruelly murdered by groups of furious whites.

The blacks, too, are getting more troublesome. There are new rumors about riots in the south and a number of plantations that have been plundered by black marauders. Military troops are marching south to protect the planters.

There are gruesome stories about atrocities committed by rebellious slaves, of white families butchered, women raped and strangled. M. Calame, who is known to be a good master, was forced to execute three of his Negroes for mutiny; he admonished me to keep a watchful eye on mine and punish the slightest sign of insubordination pitilessly. Monetary compensation is promised to those who are forced to kill rebellious slaves.

It seems Laroche is right: I should not have waited so long. It is impossible to find anyone willing to invest his money in a plantation in troubled times like this.

Neither can I hope to find a reliable *gérant* to replace Laroche, though Mre Falcon says he is still hopeful. He has received news from Europe that England and Austria are ready to interfere in France, restore the King's power and reestablish the old order.

He advised me to wait a month or two before selling my slaves, prices having suddenly fallen considerably because of the critical situation. So many people wish to get rid of their slaves and return to Europe that Negroes are being offered in town at bargain prices. The moment order is restored, prices for blacks will rise again, imports being most difficult to get. If he is right, Basteresse's savages can be sold away in a few days' time, and should bring me in a fortune providing we choose the right time—when demand is rising high.

Meanwhile Tom may do his best to treat my blacks as well-bred free citizens. *Liberté, egalité, fraternité!* I do hope his inevitable débâcle will sober him. Mre Falcon has promised to approach Major Labiche who is a good friend of his. In an emergency he can send me fifty soldiers to protect us and drive my blacks in to town for sale. It will close me 3,000 livres a day, but will save me a fortune in the long run. Poor Tom! I wish I could spare him his humiliation, but it cannot be helped. In such matters he is like a little boy. He does not believe hot iron will hurt until he has touched it and burnt his fingers.

He is so difficult to handle at times. He is no longer the devoted admirer but is torn between love and protest which may rise to naked animosity in our daily disputes.

Even his love-making has changed. There are no longer those sweet playful preludes, tender waves carrying us dancing to Paradise. He has become terribly fierce, as if angry at me and intent on breaking my will and killing the last trace of self-assertion in me. He behaves like a conqueror, reduces me to a helpless victim of his terrible pounding passion. I hate to see him turn into a savage, but I cannot help being carried away by the surf each time it flows over me.

Thank Heavens I am still strong enough to resist him in other domains. When all is settled he will realize I was right in rejecting his silly demands.

So glad Laroche has promised to stay till the end of July, his ship setting sail on August 2nd or 3rd.

JULY 18TH

I had another hot dispute with Tom, so hot I was afraid he might hit me!

He discovered the two runaways chained to their

wooden blocks, a sight that shocked him so much he ran home and gave me a piece of his mind.

He said I was a cruel despot and a liar, having assured him the two fellows were only whipped and not otherwise punished. I was so terribly cowed by his wrath that I gave orders to release them though I knew it was wrong, wrong, wrong!

I felt sick with despair, which made him feel sorry. He tried to embrace me. I pushed him back, but could not resist him long. I burst into tears but was soon lulled into sweet oblivion and surrender by his caressing hands and lips. That's the way all our fights should end —from anger, rage and despair, to reconciliation and caresses and bittersweet ecstasies that lead to exhaustion and blissful peace. But in the morning when I awoke I remembered everything. I watched his brown back turned towards me, a slave's back, scarred, branded, and I felt resentment poisoning my thoughts again.

I repented having yielded to him, knowing how stupid it was to pardon the two field hands. They are sure to try and run away again, and will encourage others to join them seeing how little their punishment is if caught. How could I hunt them down unassisted? I have no white man to protect me, no neighbors ready to help. Tom would refuse to arrest them, and the *maréchaussée* are too busy keeping the roads safe. Even my drivers cannot be trusted any longer. Nor could I spare any of my dogs for the man-hunt as I need all of them here to keep my blacks in check.

How sorry I am I didn't sell everything before Tom came here. But then I should not have met him! No, I ought to have got rid of my plantation and slaves while he was still hiding from Denise. At that time he would not have interfered, so humble was he and grateful, so devoted to me. It might have saved me a lot of trouble —and money, considering the market value of all my mulattoes I manumitted on his request instead of selling them. Well, it is no use regretting now. But this morning I could not help hating Tom for a while, hate mixed with love, a rebellious feeling which drove me to wake and tease him, excite him while still half asleep and unable to resist my lust. I wanted to pay him back, watch his warm lips slightly parted, inviting me to drop down on my handsome prey, my golden stallion, again so strong and this time so obedient—unflagging to the blissful end of our ride.

What a bitch of a wicked woman I am at times! Acting the male's part as a revenge! A minute's triumph, no happiness left—rather disgust because I know this is not real love. I am too self-willed, too intent on domineering instead of abandoning any thought of ownership in our loving embrace.

He won't be able to replace Laroche. He is much too mild a master to be respected by the blacks. They are already restive again, says Laroche, as if expecting a great change. Rumors have already spread about their master's imminent departure.

Knowing Tom will succeed Laroche they are looking forward to happier days, freedom, which to them means everyday is a Sunday with plenty of food and merry music and dancing and making love.

Helen says they are still convinced that Tom is a slave like themselves, and that he belonged to the young lady from the neighboring plantation. Some swear they saw him serve as her humble coachman or groom. They think I bought him from her to use him as my pet and bed-mate, which does not help to raise his esteem. They are sure to sneer behind his back and whisper dirty jokes about us, for slandering their superiors is their favorite pastime, their weak revenge on those who keep them down.

JULY 25TH

Had two visitors last week. The first was a handsome blue-eyed fellow, quite attractive, but too unknown a quantity to be trusted as a prospective *gérant*. No money and no experience either, having traded in timber all his life.

The second, an elderly pot-bellied man, was only interested in my slaves, offered a ridiculously small sum for the whole crowd of them: 200,000 livres to be paid in cash by the end of August. I can get almost double that amount if I put them up for auction myself. They all think because I am a woman I can be cheated and duped like a duffer!

Thank Heavens there have been no more attempts at running away. It seems my blacks are all so hopeful about their future that they feel as happy as little children. There are few complaints. Laroche says they have never been so cheerful before.

I wonder how long this change for the better will last. Maybe Tom is right and does know how to handle them. He is certainly kind and friendly all the time. We have had no more disputes, all is happiness and matrimonial bliss. I do feel married to him though we shall have to postpone our wedding until we arrive in New York because of the rising animosity against mulattoes in this wicked island. They might molest us, might even attack us if news spread that a white woman of the ruling class was marrying a mulatto.

Tom says he is looking forward to presenting me to his mother. She is sure to be an exceptional woman considering she braved public opinion by running away with a bastard slave. I feel like her companion in arms, though Tom is a free man, not a slave like his father.

The other day when I told him I have lost all hopes of ever bearing him children he said he didn't mind. He said why not adopt a baby or two? The more I know him the better I love him, the dearest, kindest, noblest man on earth!

It really seems everything is turning out for the best. I was right in choosing Claire to replace Jeanne. But for her and Helen I should be lost, being the only white woman left on this plantation. Maryse may be trained to assist them, but she is too young to be relied upon. At seventeen you cannot impose your authority on a crowd of black women and brats, to say nothing of the males in the sick-room and prisoners kept in chains over the weekends.

Fortunately there has been only one prisoner left for several months, the brute that raped André's wench. He spends his nights and Sundays in chains and will have no more women for a long while, a much more severe punishment than a sound whipping. Even Tom agreed when I told him, knowing what penalty the brute would risk if he were a free man.

I doubt if we can leave Claire's gang in charge of her young brother. Laroche says he is too quick at cracking his whip and shouting at the women and children all the time. It makes them mulish and discontented. I warned him to stop acting the part of a despot, silly fool!

Claire knows how to handle her gang. Even the few males in her group respect and obey her. There are seldom any complaints and no cases of open resistance. Perhaps she is a little too haughty, too proud of her light color. She walks like a queen, though heavy with child. M. Nicole fathered it, she admits, and is quite happy to bear a white man's bastard.

That fellow was sowing his wild oats in many a furrow while he was here, the rutting ram. And so conceited! Expected me to fall for him like any of my bastard wenches!

AUGUST 1st

Laroche left yesterday morning. Could not help being moved to tears, the last white friend deserting me, the only one I could depend upon.

I didn't realize before that I felt so strongly attached to him though he always kept his distance, and never tried to court me—such an honest man, so efficient and respectable. But for him I could not have kept my plantation in good order and prospering so long, in spite of so many calamities.

I promised to take care of his sobbing mate and her brats whom he seemed deeply sorry to leave. Such a moving scene to see them all cling to him, no end to his kisses and caresses and tender words. A good husband and father, no doubt of that, but impossible for him to take that family of bastards with him back to Europe.

He will marry a white woman there, some Swiss peasant girl, and father plenty of blond, blue-eyed children with her and feel happy and forget his brown mate and brats in this far away island, like imaginary creatures in a fading dream.

I might adopt one or two of her children. She has a pretty little daughter who is sure to blossom out into an attractive beauty, like her mother before she grew fat from lack of physical exercise. But for my daily riding on horseback I could not have kept so slim, though my breasts and hips have grown heavier. Tom says they are perfect, but never trust an excitable lover's compliments!

I'll tell her to move in here with her children. She can help me to rule my servants, keep them busy, and improve on my menus which have become so dull because my cook is too lazy to care.

I should like children in my house. Makes us feel a real family. Tom is sure to consent.

Our hands seem to be behaving well. No complaints so far. I pray to Heaven Tom can keep them tractable long enough.

AUGUST 7TH

A week full of sorrows, disappointment and bad news from France. They say the Royal Family tried to escape to Brussels, were arrested and taken back to Paris like common prisoners.

The Jacobins call the King a traitor and want him to be dethroned and put into jail! If that rabble comes to power we are all lost. They will declare all our slaves free and encourage them to revolt, plunder, rape, murder all of us!

It is high time we left. If I cannot sell this plantation or find a reliable *gérant* by the end of this month, I'll have all my Negroes taken to town and put up for auction there whatever Tom may say to change my mind.

He has been so irritable these days. It is impossible to discuss our problems calmly. He says I had better mind my household. It is no business of mine to interfere in anything concerning the field work, which is man's domain.

From Helen I know the hands are getting difficult again though he has granted all of them the whole of Friday free without asking my consent. He has also promised to pay them wages if they work well. When I took him to task he got angry, called me names for having amassed a fortune by sweating and ill-treating so many human beings who had as much right to freedom and happiness as myself.

He made me feel like an evil parasite, a vampire feeding on the blood of my slaves, making them toil to exhaustion for my profit's sake. I was so depressed I turned my back on him at night, but when he said he was sorry I was again weak enough to surrender.

My own servants are getting more and more troublesome—so lazy and negligent. Last night, while undressing me, Lydia was so clumsy I slapped her face, and this morning I again lost my patience when that stupid fellow Paul kept me waiting at table and then grinned when I rebuked him. I boxed his ears instead of remaining calm and dignified.

Captain Basteresse's ship may arrive any day. Must ask Jeanne's father to take care of the cargo and prepare the public auction of the savages. Must make him promise not to mention my name to anybody, not even to Jeanne, but deliver the sale's profit to my attorney. I do hope Tom is too worried by his own problems to get suspicious. With Mre Falcon's assistance it should be possible to settle that awkward business discreetly. But if Jeanne talks I'll again be the gossip of the town. Even Tom might be told, and he would raise hell and hate me if he knew. The very thought of it makes me sick.

Better leave it all to my attorney who is sure not to disclose my name to anyone. Disastrous—the low prices offered for Negroes at present because of the bad news from France: No more than 1,000–1,200 livres for a strong male! That is less than half of what I could have made a month ago. I shall lose a fortune. But I cannot wait any longer. Better drop half my profit than leave this island a beggar.

AUGUST 14TH

Our blacks are out of hand.

It was to be expected. I warned Tom but he would not take my advice. The more we offer them, the more they demand. It will end in open disobedience. It is all his own fault, silly boy! And mine! I should not have yielded to his demand to fetch the money he promised to the hands, a bag full of coins, three for each (cost me 360 livres). It would ruin me if I had to spend so much money on them every week of the year.

I told him giving money to slaves was against the law. If my neighbors knew they would raise hell. News spreads fast enough which may cause trouble at other plantations. All the whites will hate me for having roused the slaves' appetite for money.

Claire says most of them spent it on toddy. Heaven knows where they got it. I haven't signed more than five passes for a three hours' stay in town on Saturday afternoon. Claire swears they all returned in time, their baskets full of food and no bottles. They seem to have hidden them from her somehow. It is no use cross-examining them as the rascals will swear they are innocent. A sound whipping might make them confess but Tom would never allow me to resort to such drastic measures.

Now they are lying about like dead corpses after a noisy night of drinking and dancing and orgies that remind me of that horrible night five years ago. Tom behaves as though he does not know what has happened, but of course he does. He is just too proud to admit his failure.

I drove to town to call on Mre Falcon last Wednesday. I gave him the written inventory of my livestock, furniture, machines and tools, and consulted him about values and prices to be charged.

He promised to arrange everything, to prepare for a public auction to take place on my premises at the beginning of September. I must leave Rex and Claire and a dozen of my blacks to take care of my house and animals after my departure.

I am so glad I needn't be present at the auction. All my neighbors will turn up, without doubt, and their nosy wives and sons and daughters, for mere curiosity's sake. Never mind! The larger the crowd the higher the bidding! Including all the slaves in the auction I estimate my net profit at 380,000 livres, or more if I can get rid of the whole lot to one buyer.

As for my landed property, Mre Falcon intends to offer the different fields and buildings to my neighbors before preparing a second auction.

I am sure M. Gautier is highly interested in the cotton fields bordering his. He might purchase this house, too. It would suit his son and daughter-in-law as their residence after the wedding.

The Morleys may take the rest, or the Richards who have always envied me for my profitable coffee-crops. But no underpricing for them! Either they pay the sum I ask, or they leave it.

Mre Falcon is sure they are both keen on securing as much as possible for themselves, and so are the Gillets, though I should hate to leave anything to that disgusting woman.

With Helen's aid I have already started packing my trunks. It will take me a week or more to be ready for a sudden departure. One never knows! I must leave part of my wardrobe, leave it to Helen and Claire. And there are such a lot of other things too heavy to be carried so far. But not my diary! Though it has become quite a burden—so many cahiers—I wish to keep them, read them when old and lonely, perhaps consult them while writing me memoirs which might turn out to be more interesting than many another book of recollections.

I hope they can house the rest of the crop this week so that it can be included in the auction. May bring me another ten or twelve thousand.

*   *   *   *   *   *

OCTOBER 19TH

On board the *Flore* on the way to Charleston.

I haven't opened my diary for many weeks. It has been quite impossible to find time to record the terrible happenings that have made a hell of my life and reduced me to the miserable existence of a homeless fugitive.

My heart is so empty I feel like a dried-out well, no tears, no friend to comfort me, just brooding, brooding, brooding all the time. Perhaps it may help to divert my thoughts if I return to the past, recording what has happened since I wrote my last entry. It is high time I overcame the dull apathy that has paralyzed me since I read his cruel letter.

Oh Tom! Have I deserved to be treated like this? Don't you remember the sweet nights we spent together, the tender words of love and everlasting faith you whispered in my ears? If you really cannot love me any longer—isn't there any gratitude left in your cold heart? Don't you remember who it was who saved you from the clutches of that ruthless woman? But for me you would never have recovered your freedom, you would have died a miserable slave, and nobody would have cared! You could not even have saved your skin when the riot broke out.

But for my presence of mind we should all have been lost, massacred like so many others. Nor were you safe in town, later, considering the general hatred turned against colored people.

You owe it to me that you are now safe. I protected you from the bloodthirsty fools, both you and your brother. And what did I get in return? One word of gratitude? Nay, you insulted me, called me a monster, a greedy slaver, a heartless female despot! What have I done to deserve such gross insult? Aren't you a monster yourself? A monster of ingratitude! Oh Tom! How could you hurt me that way?

Remember, I am still your wife, I belong to you to the end of my days. I cannot believe nor accept your cruel word that it is for ever that we parted. I'll write to you again and again, and one day you will pity me, pardon me, answer my letters and invite me to join you —for ever, your poor loving wife.

But I must try and keep calm, must try to report the main facts soberly, bring order into the turmoil of my recollections that have become a chaotic nightmare haunting me even in my dreams.

I have retired to my narrow cabin to find solitude. So glad I managed to bribe the steward to leave it to me alone. I should hate to share it with any of the other women on board. They are mostly nosy, garrulous creatures. Privacy cost me 100 livres extra!

Thank Heaven I kept the cahiers in my handbag, together with all the other important papers, and my jewellery. Otherwise I would have lost my diary with all the other valuable things I put in the big black trunk. They stole it while I was talking to the captain, persuading him to admit Tom on board. I did not realize the loss before the ship had already weighed anchor. Never mind—I departed from Martinique with a substantial cheque: 34,000 livres. Much more than I had hoped for, prices for savages having risen at Fort de France up to 2,500 a male *toutes pièces*, females up to 2,000 a piece! Might have got even more, up to 3,000 a strong buck, had we found time to fatten them up for a while with plenty of oatmeal and gallons of weak beer.

Some looked like skeletons, though the captain swore they had been fed well all the time. He reported only twenty-eight lost on the way from Africa, which I doubt remembering the heaps of empty handcuffs lying about when the males, still wearing theirs, were driven naked on deck for medical examination.

I got a cold reception when climbing on board, all the sailors staring at me as though I were an impudent intruder into their sanctuary. A fine sanctuary! Stinking like a pigsty, a delicious mixture of sweat and piss and disgusting male odors!

But I didn't wince. I examined them calmly, as if used to such sights and smells from my girlhood! I am glad the doctor helped me to pick out the fittest males, all of them, in spite of the captain's protest.

Mre Oliva showed him my contract, which gave me free choice.

Such a pity we were not allowed to take them ashore but were forced to expose them for sale on board the slaver. Strange rules they have in Martinique! The following day there were plenty of visitors climbing on board from morning till dusk. I never saw such a crowd of men and ladies on the deck of a ship. They frightened the poor blacks by touching and turning and sizing them up haggling in a language they could not understand.

I sold away mine in four hours' time at a net profit to deliver to Mme Galez. Deducting my expenses it to deliver to Mme Galez, and deducting my expenses it will leave me about 12,000 livres cash.

I don't know how much Captain Basteresse got for the rest of the cargo. If he sold all of them, about two hundred, but forty females included and not counting the sick and worthless ones, he may have earned about 350,000, after expenses, which would secure me another 100,000—no, 90,000, deducting the attorney's fee.

Mre Oliva promised to transfer the money to New York, exchange it for American Dollars (which, he said, are safer than French money at present) and deposit the whole sum in a trustworthy bank there. It seems he is helping to save another fugitives' money in the same way.

100,000 livres plus my shares, and a few jewels, that's what is left of my fortune. I lost 100,000 or more —much more, if prices for Negroes rise again when the riot is crushed—adding the value of my slaves to my estate and buildings and livestock and all the rest I left to the rioters.

It makes me sick to think of it knowing I could have sold away the bloody blacks at 2,000 a piece a month before the rebellion started! Meanwhile they will have burnt down my house, ruined my crop and ravaged the whole plantation like all the others. All that lost for ever.

Tom knows I am ruined, yet instead of pitying me he expected me to tear up my contract with Captain

Basteresse, renounce my claim on the shipload of savages and leave the whole profit to the captain and Mme Galez! The very thought of it makes me angry with him all over again.

If I had yielded to him I should now be a penniless beggar without having improved the fate of any of the poor blacks imported from Africa. Why can't he see I was forced to claim my share, my legal rights on that cargo, in order to save a small part of my money. I do hope he will come to reason when back in New York, will realize he was wrong. I am sure his mother will take my side, appreciate my steps, tell him he was a fool to desert me for a *chimère*. Women are so much more sensible than men!

If it had not been for that abominable Créole bitch on board the ship he would never have guessed I was mixed up in that trade.

She fell for him at first sight, was so keen on getting him she asked me point-blank how much I would charge for him, thinking he was my property. She seemed to be rolling in wealth, offered me 5,000 livres or more—got angry when I refused. So typical of those spoiled rich Créole women who are used to getting what they want and if their whim is denied, get nasty and revengeful.

Though no more than twenty or twenty-one she was a widow (or said she was). She had been at Cap on a visit and was on her way back to Martinique. It would have been so much easier to snub her if Tom (and George) had not been forced to act the part of a slave belonging to me—on Mre Falcon's advice.

He warned us that no free mulattoes were admitted on board, all of them were being arrested and pressed into military service to fight against the rioting Negroes. Of course we could testify that, in spite of his scars and brand, he was indeed a free American citizen, not a runaway slave trying to escape with forged papers, but it would have taken days or even weeks to verify that in court. Meanwhile our ship would have set sail without us.

So I pretended he was my slave, and that poor George and himself were one and the same person. But that is another story which must be told in detail to explain the rest. It takes too long to record it now. There is plenty of time to continue my report tonight or tomorrow and the day after tomorrow—so many empty days.

I feel tired, the air is being so terribly sultry in here. Though stripped to the skin I am sweating as if in high fever. I ought to get dressed and climb on deck for a breath of fresh air though there is no hope of finding a seat in the shade, the sun standing high and burning hot like fire at this time of the day. I wish I could have a bath in the cool sea and dream and sleep and sink and never awake again.

OCTOBER 20TH

What a mess I made yesterday trying to record the frightful events that drove me on board this ship. I ought to start by telling the main facts in logical order, which may help me to see things more soberly, perhaps find out what mistakes I made, what measures I should take to win back Tom.

My last entry before the flight was dated August 14th. It was a Sunday, I remember, an hour or two before we had another violent dispute.

Tom called me a cynical bitch of a despot reducing my slaves to the state of shameless beasts! The fact is he was shocked to see the results of his silly complaisance, their drunken orgies, their mating in the open air, the wenches behaving like whores, each pleasuring several males in turn. So silly to expect them to behave like decent Christians.

He was scandalized when I admitted that none of them were married. In vain I explained to him that we were short of women so the males were forced to share those available, love-making being one of the few pleasures left to them. It made their hard life bearable, each looking forward to the week's end when they were allowed to mate with their women.

Tom is so terribly ignorant of our problems. He said I ought to have provided the males with an equal number of females to make decent marriages possible. Didn't realize how unprofitable large crowds of women would be for us. They are unfit for hard work because of being heavy with child again and again. Many young mothers die in child-bed, the rest of them are worn out and useless by the age of thirty, while males can keep fit for hard work on an average five years longer. Maybe married couples would feel happier, would never try to run away. But on the other hand they would make trouble if ever we were forced to sell a husband or wife or their children away. What heart-breaking scenes to be faced if they had to be separated!

No, it was so much better not to encourage family feelings among them, to keep them ignorant of which brats they had fathered. Of course there were quarrels and ugly fights now and again out of jealousy and revenge, but we were not forced to interfere very often as they knew we would put the squabblers in chains and keep them away from their women for quite a while as a punishment.

It was different with my house-servants whom I encouraged to get married. Three of my black maids I allowed to marry field hands. They had the privilege of spending their Friday and Saturday nights together in the servants' quarters downstairs. It also served as a source of information for me about everything that was happening in the fields and slave-quarters.

I remember how unhappy I felt after that dispute. It was the first quarrel that didn't end in reconciliation and love-making. At night he turned his back on me as if he were scared of the very touch of my skin. I felt so sad I wished I were dead.

The next morning he left early, and didn't return before dusk. He was sad, mute and visibly depressed. I knew the hands had been troublesome again, an hour or more late at starting in the morning, slow at work and restive. Long before noon they had begun complaining of the heat, dropping their tools and returning to their cabins.

Helen reported that they had demanded higher wages, a whole livre more a week, which Tom finally promised to grant them if they went back to work, and were prepared to house the rest of the crop by Friday night.

Later, news spread that one of the drivers had been attacked and maltreated by some hands. Tom stopped them, but instead of arresting the culprits he sent the driver home and replaced him with one of his subordinates.

The victim turned out to be Claire's brother. The fool! It served him right, but things like that must not be tolerated—slaves openly attacking their superior! They ought to be hanged, or at least whipped in public and then kept chained to the end of their days, or sold to the galleys.

Tom's leniency was inexcusable. It will encourage open disobedience, uproar and revolt. He must have realized he had made a bad mistake for he did not protest when I said I meant to send for the police and have the rebellious slaves arrested.

That night he did not shrink from touching me. For weeks he had not been so sweet, so tender, so intent on making me happy. And again at dawn: so hungry for love as though anticipating there was little time left for us. There was a touch of sadness spicing our most blissful moments, the knowledge that it could not last.

Before he left he made me promise to wait one more day, to give the blacks another chance to behave before alarming the police. But later in the morning a deputy of three blacks came in and said the master had sent them to me because they had a request. They claimed 6 livres a week for all the hands and no more separation from their women on the nights between workdays.

I felt a little disappointed in Tom, seeing how his self-confidence had shrunk like an empty bag.

I gave them a piece of my mind and said they would be given their pay with the horse-whip next Friday night if I heard any more complaints. I threatened to resort to the old-established means of keeping order: the driver's whip and the Friday night thrashings if they did not make haste to house the crop in time.

As for the women, I said, spending every night of the week with them would render them even more tired out and sleepy, completely unfit for the day's work. I called them a horde of slackers and lazybones whom I meant to lock apart from the women over the next week's end if they failed to bring in the crop by Friday.

I dismissed them, cowed to mute submission, which I am sure, was the only way to keep them in check for a while. Any sign of forbearance would have made them even more arrogant.

Returning from the fields Tom looked terribly dejected. He advised me to gather all the drivers and mulatto servants, men and women, in my house, arm the men with pistols and keep all my dogs ready for a nightly attack. The blacks might try to set fire to the house, assault and kill us.

We kept awake the whole night, alarmed by the fact that Claire and Maryse were missing. Didn't dare to look for them in the dark of the night, but at dawn Tom and some of his men repaired to the slave-quarters, found the women's cabins deserted, the prison door open, the prisoner gone. Claire and young Maryse had been brutally murdered. When informed I at once sent Paul to town on horseback to alarm the police and call for military support.

Never shall I forget that horrible morning, Tuesday, the 23rd it was. There were ghastly rumors about riots having broken out everywhere, as though a signal had been given. The first reports came that Denise's house was aflame, all the whites and free mulattoes had been butchered, and similar atrocities had been committed at M. Gautier's plantation, and M. Richard's, and the Gillets'.

Realizing what risks we ran if we waited any longer we prepared for flight. The small velvet bag containing my gold coins and jewels I hid in my bosom, my legal documents and cahiers I had put in a leather case which was fastened to the saddle of my horse. Riding on horseback seemed much safer than travelling by coach, considering marauders might assault us on the way to town.

My coach was filled with trunks and then Old Jules and Helen climbed into the coach-box waiting for my order to depart. It was too late!

I remember a woman's voice shouting: "They are coming!"

I rushed to the window. There, in the bright sunshine they stood, the whole crowd of Negroes, some armed with sticks, others hiding their fists behind their backs, a sullen, menacing horde. If they saw us leave they might think we were frightened which would stimulate their aggressiveness. So from somewhere I plucked up courage to face them. Disregarding Tom's protests I stepped out into the sunlit yard, Tom following me, and my drivers, each with two dogs at his leash, a small group confronting a hundred who might attack us any moment.

Remembering the situation I wonder how I managed to keep my sang-froid. I told young Henri to run over and tell Rufus his mistress sent for him. I was sure Rufus was their acknowledged leader and it was him I had to deal with.

I watched the brown boy hurry across the empty sunlit yard and then stop, facing the crowd of blacks from a distance. His thin voice shouted something at them. There was a commotion, then slowly one tall man separated and started walking leisurely towards us. Henri turned and ran back to me.

"They said he must ask for a cask of brandy, a big one!" he reported, gasping with excitement.

"Brandy on their backs!" I shouted, no longer frightened, but furious as I watched that big fellow sauntering along. When he was near enough I clapped my hands, which made him quicken his steps. He stopped at a respectful distance.

"Come here!" I called. "One more step! Kneel down so I can face you better!"

He didn't move, just stared at me defiantly. But I did not flinch. I repeated my command in a menacing voice, intent on humiliating him. At last he obeyed, though reluctantly. I seized him by the ears and twisted his big black head.

"Are you used to walking when your missus sends for you?" I asked severely.

"No, ma'am. I must run." He was all submissiveness again. I knew I had already broken his resistance.

"Did you run?"

"No, ma'am."

I slapped his cheek, told him to stand up and run back and return running, mind running! Or else my dog would teach him how to run!

"You are carrying things too far," Tom whispered watching the Negro run back.

"Please leave it to me," I retorted. "I know how to maintain my authority. The moment they think we are intimidated they start getting impertinent. That would be the first step to open rebellion."

Rufus was doubling across the empty yard. When he reached the others they seemed to stand motionless, as if paralyzed by the defeat of their leader. He turned and raced back towards me.

"You see?" I said triumphantly, turning to Tom.

"They will hate you the more," he answered.

"Of course they hate me, they hate all of us. But as long as they fear us, too, we are safe," I said.

When Rufus arrived, I let him pant a while before speaking.

"Tell the others," I said, "that we are expecting soldiers from town. They may arrive any minute. Meanwhile I order you all to turn in at once. If any of you is seen loitering outdoors he will be punished severely. Run and tell them!"

I knew I had won even before the Negro had reached the others and told them what my orders were. We saw them move, and slowly turn towards their cabins.

AFTERNOON

It is embarrassing, my report on that incident, glorifying myself as a heroine, though, in fact, I was as frightened as any of my servants. I just hid my mortal scare behind a mask of calm authority.

I remember how proud I was of my victory. I thought I had impressed Tom in my favor. Had I? Maybe he found me disgusting, humiliating a man in public that way. Maybe he thought I was a cruel despot like Denise, enjoying treating my slaves like dogs.

But had I shown the slightest trace of scare we should have been lost, all of us. I wish he realized that I saved his life as well as mine. But should I wish him to marry me out of mere gratitude? Oh Tom! Please don't forget our happy hours, your lover's oaths whispered in ecstasies of bliss. Remember me as your devoted, humble, loving wife, not as a cold-hearted tyrant, which I am not and never was!

It is impossible to report all the ensuing incidents as minutely as this one. We rode to town, Tom and I and six of my mulattoes escorting the coach, the rest having refused to join us.

A gang of black runaways or marauders we chased away with pistol-shots, killing or wounding at least one of them. We heard distant shouting, cries and moans when crossing the wood. Then the sound of clattering hoofs approaching us—whites on horseback suddenly surrounding us and the relief of knowing we were safe.

The streets in Cap were overcrowded with fugitives, mostly women and children. The men were trying to organize armed groups assisting the military forces in the defence of the town. I called on Mre Falcon, who said news was very bad: most of the plantations in this part of the island were already in the hands of the mutineers who seemed to be well organized, probably instructed and directed by clever mulatto leaders.

Mre Falcon disapproved of our plan to depart together for New York and get married their. Broad-minded though he was, and acclaiming the bold ideas of the Revolution in France, the old man could not help being shocked at my intention of breaking the most sanctified law of our society by marrying a colored man. He said the town was full of light-colored runaways who all hoped they could escape on board a ship. The police had orders to arrest any person whose features betrayed the slightest trace of Negro origin. If they stripped Tom they would see the brand and scars on his back which would convince them he was a runaway slave regardless of his American papers.

He advised us to pretend Tom was my slave. That way, he said, I might manage to take him aboard our ship although strong young slaves were, as a rule, not allowed to follow their master or mistress abroad. They were forced, instead, to join the little army that was being formed to fight the rebels.

I was relieved to see how good-humoredly Tom played his new part as my submissive slave, with a twinkle in his eyes when unobserved by others, but all servile obedience in the presence of any third person.

Returning to our inn I was shocked and dismayed when Helen sobbingly reported that her own husband and all my drivers and male servants had been arrested and taken away by the police, even my youngster Henri who is little more than a child!

I told Tom to hide in my bedroom. I locked the door and returned to my attorney hoping he could help to redeem my servants. But he said it was no use trying, they were better off that way than if they had been caught by the white rabble who were killing all the mulattoes they met in the streets.

He advised me to go on board a ship that was preparing to set sail for Martinique on Thursday. Told me to stop Captain Basteresse's ship there and tell him to sell his shipload of savages at Fort de France.

He said I should turn there to Mre Oliva, a reliable friend of his, and ask him to assist me in dealing with the Captain and all the authorities, and prepare the sale of the blacks which, he said, was sure to bring me a considerable profit, prices for Negroes being even higher in Martinique than anywhere in this island. I was so glad I could hope for that money after having lost the rest of my fortune.

Leaving Mre Falcon's office I noticed a lady sitting in the antechamber. When she saw me she rushed at me with outspread arms, as though I were an intimate friend. She embraced me, a cloud of perfume rising from her vast bosom.

"How glad I am, my dear, to meet you safe and sound!" she cried. "Poor Denise! Everybody pities her. What horrible, horrible monsters! I hope they will catch them all and skin them, those ogres, those beasts!"

At last I remembered where I had seen her before:

at a ball my sister-in-law had given last winter. Some
Colonel's wife, a silly garrulous chatterbox, plump and
baby-faced, a fat, grown-up baby.

I had to tell her everything about my escape.

"What about your runaways?" she interrupted.
"Haven't you looked for them in the prison yard? They
are bringing in dozens every day for us to examine. I
am used to going there every morning hoping to find
my coachman that ran away a month ago. If ever I get
him back I'll give him a warm welcome. You know
whom I discovered a few minutes ago? One of Denise's slaves. The rascal pretended he was a free man
calling himself M. So-and-so, but of course he had no
documents with him to verify his fairy-tale. I recognized
him at first sight as Denise's butler, having seen him
waiting on her six months ago. I have a very good
memory for faces, you know, particularly handsome
ones. And handsome he is, that fellow; we all envied
Denise for such an attractive fancy slave. Looks almost
like a white man, blue eyed under black brows, very
exceptional among slaves."

"I want to have a look at him!" I cried, alarmed by
that description.

"They are already giving him his desert," she said,
chuckling. I pushed her aside and rushed out, jumped
into my coach and drove over to the prison yard where
people were streaming in and out.

I asked one of the guards where the whippings took
place, offered him a silver coin, and followed him
across the yard to where a little crowd of men and
women were passing along a line of black and brown
prisoners. Then I entered the building, turning left along
a corridor, and heard muffled cries from somewhere
below.

"They are busy at present, ma'am," the guard explained. "Some runaway. Seems to be a dangerous fellow. A stubborn liar. But they know how to make him
confess. You wish to see?"

"Tell them to stop it at once!" I cried. "The man is
mine, I won't have him ruined!"

"Come here, ma'am," he said. He opened a door
leading down to the cellar. I heard the sound of the lash

and a moan, then the guard's voice downstairs telling
them to stop. I rushed down and saw the naked body of
the victim hanging from the ceiling. His ankles were
chained to a heavy iron ball as big as a man's head.
Blood was running from a dozen reddish streaks covering the man's back and buttocks and thighs.

"Leave that man to me!" I cried. "I am his owner!"

"Can you prove that, ma'am?"

"Of course I can. But let him down first! I won't
have him ill-treated that way any longer."

They released the rope lifting the victim. He dropped
on the blood-stained pavement, unable to keep upright.
One of his torturers kicked him in the hip.

"Stand up!" he shouted.

"Let him lie a while," I said. "You see he can
neither sit nor stand. You have ruined him! I am going
to sue you for damaged property!"

"Not so fast, ma'am," said the oldest of the three
brutes. "Can you prove he is really yours?"

"Tom!" I said. "Turn round, look at your missus
and tell them who I am!"

As he still did not move one of the men seized him by
the shoulder and turned him round. I stared at him
aghast, stared at the old scar running across his left
thigh, the small one above his eyebrow, his emaciated
face and chest. It was not Tom, but his brother
George! George, no doubt of that! He gazed at me
stupefied and I knelt down stroking his hair and patting
him like a wounded dog.

"You are my servant Tom, tell them you are! I won't
punish you for running away, you silly boy. Just promise never to do it again!"

His rigid features moved, a faint smile was visible.
He nodded his head.

"Yes, missus, you are my missus, sure you are!" he
whispered.

"His own fault!" said the foreman. "Why did he not
tell us the truth? It might have saved him plenty of
trouble."

"I myself am responsible," I said. "I threatened to
punish him severely for some slight trespass. When angry we often say things we don't mean. The silly boy

took it in earnest, was frightened to death and so he ran away."

"Runaways must be punished, ma'am."

"Well, he has got his portion, has he not? Now let him get dressed so that I can take him with me."

"We must charge you fifty livres for arresting your runaway slave, and ten for feeding and whipping him."

I paid the tax and gave each a silver coin as a tip, whereupon they became quite affable, helping the poor boy to get partly dressed and carried upstairs and across the yard to my coach.

On the way back to the inn I told him he must stick to my tale and play the part of my slave Tom. I said someone was sure to be happy to see him, a very good friend of his.

The poor fellow was too exhausted to find words. But his eyes were expressive enough to tell me what he felt—immense relief, gratitude mixed with bewilderment, and lingering fright. Could he trust me? After all, I was a white woman, I belonged to the enemy class of merciless despots who had been hunting him down.

When we drove up the servants rushed out of the inn and watched the stumbling man following me in assisted by Old Jules. I had given George my handkerchief to hide his face.

"What's the matter with the fellow?" asked the landlady approaching us.

"This silly slave of mine tried to run away," I replied. "So I was forced to inform the police. They soon caught him and served him a good thrashing. But I am afraid they handled him too roughly. I'll take him upstairs and have him nursed by my maid. I wouldn't like him to be crippled or killed. He is too valuable a slave."

"Have a look at that fellow, boys!" the landlady cried triumphantly. "That is how they deal with runaways!"

Never shall I forget Tom's bewilderment when he was confronted with his own self, reduced to a skeleton!

"It's you! It's really you!" he whispered. "My brother! George! I've been looking for you so long! And now we have found you, my poor little brother! They treated you badly, the scoundrels! But I'll take care of you, take you home to our mother who is waiting for you in New York, far away from here. Ever heard of New York? It is a big fine town in a big fine country, a free country, where you will be a free citizen like myself, George! Brother! Look at me! Don't you believe me? Don't you?"

He was bending over the naked, lacerated body, gazing into the staring eyes of his wounded brother. He caressed his cheeks and hair, he patted his chest. Helen sobbed, and my eyes, too, were moist.

Later, when George had recovered his strength, he told us the strange story of his adventures as a runaway slave. But that is too long a tale to be reported now. I'll record the main facts tomorrow.

OCTOBER 25TH

I was terribly sea-sick for three long days and nights. Our ship tumbled like an empty barrel all the time. Now the sea has calmed down and I feel better after the first substantial meal I have had since Saturday. Most of the other passengers are still lying sick. That's why I have retired to my cabin. The very sight of such a crowd of vomiting people, the stench and filth around them might turn my stomach again.

Now let me resume my report. This is what George told us about his adventures.

When Denise's maid told him about their mistress' intention to have him gelded he decided to run away at the very first opportunity. That afternoon, when she took him to town he knew what to do the moment she told the coachman to drive up in front of the doctor's house. He was sure she had already told the surgeon to prepare everything for that dreadful operation. So when she sent George in on the pretext that he should fetch a remedy for her he ran away through the narrow streets which were almost empty at that time of the day. He took refuge with the mulatto dressmaker whom I later rightly suspected of hiding him.

She must have been very much attached to George, else she would scarcely have found courage to conceal him in her wardrobe considering the risk she ran if he was found.

For three months she managed to keep him hidden in her bedchamber, locking the door whenever she left it. The only confidante was her black maid, Rachel.

None of her other slaves realized that a young man was constantly living upstairs. Though well fed and tenderly cared for George felt like a prisoner whose fate depended on his female guard's good-will.

He must have done his best to satisfy her insatiable demands. The bitch! I knew she had a lover; no woman can hide such a secret from another woman. The warm gleam in her eyes, the contented smile around her lips, a dozen things betraying her.

Then something happened that changed his situation for the better. When his protectress realized she was pregnant she turned to an agent who found her a small cotton plantation in a distant part of the island.

She sold her house and slaves (except for her black maid). Disguised as her black coachman he drove her out of town.

After a three days' journey they arrived at their destination. George cleaned his face and hands of the soot that had transformed him into a Negro, and in a white gentleman's attire he, from now on, played the part of the mulatto woman's husband and ran the small plantation all by himself.

The house proved little more than a shack, and the fields were barren and dried out. There were only four-teen skinny blacks crouching in front of their miserable ramshackle cabins patiently waiting for their evening portion of flour for baking their bread.

A fat black woman whom George discovered in the kitchen gave him the key to the store-room where some dried-out hams and a sack half filled with flour were left by the former owner, provisions that would scarcely last them a few days.

It was a poor beginning. His mate Carmela was on the verge of tears when confronted with the bleak poverty surrounding her.

But George managed to re-establish order and tidiness in a few days' time.

He called on all his neighbors, buying food and clean linen and other things indispensable for the near future. His long prison life in Carmela's dark bedroom had rendered his complexion so pale that everywhere he was taken for a white man and therefore was received as everybody's equal.

But when he introduced his alleged wife they at once turned haughty and unfriendly. It was a disgrace for a white man to marry a colored woman. Perhaps he was not white himself! The moment they realized he was a "white nigger" they cut him. So they were forced to live a lonely life full of hard work. The cotton fields were too small to be profitable, so he started growing corn and sweet potatoes instead, which enabled him to feed his slaves well and sell the rest of the crop at a decent profit.

The constant open-air life quickly strengthened his health. He became more and more self-confident, knowing that Carmela could no longer control him as her subordinate. She was forced to stick to him whatever might happen, for, if he were discovered as a runaway, she too would be lost. She slowly became accustomed to the changed relationship and, in spite of everything, they were moderately happy.

Last May Carmela had an accident. She stumbled while groping her way downstairs in the dusky staircase and fell so badly that a few minutes later she was in labor.

George at once saddled his horse and went to fetch the nearest doctor who lived a few miles away. But the doctor was absent, and the only midwife to be found insisted on being taken to the expectant mother by coach. When they finally arrived Carmela had already died.

She was lying in a pool of blood while her black maid was trying in vain to rock the baby back to life. George buried them both in the small flower garden Carmela had managed to grow by the house. It was a shock to him, for he had grown very attached to her in their time together.

For months he lived the lonely life of a widower, try-ing to forget his grief in hard work. His little plantation prospered and his neighbors began to respect him.

The only woman who kept him company was Rachel, the black maid. It seems he liked her though she was not pretty. He says she was the most good-natured and cheerful creature he ever met. It was Rachel who saved his life when the spirit of mutiny started spreading in that part of the island. Trusting in his reputation as a good master he was little impressed by the news of the atrocities committed by slaves on some plantations in the neighborhood. His own Negroes would never do him any harm.

But one night Rachel rushed into his bedchamber, woke him and implored him to flee. Looking out of his window he saw dozens of burning torches approaching his house, and red flames illuminating the horizon.

It was too late for him to saddle the horse. He ran downstairs and out into the darkness of the night turn-ing towards the wood where he could hide from his pur-suers. Three days he spent hidden in woods and ra-vines, under bushes and rocks, living on berries and eatable roots. At night he would move northward to-wards Cap, avoiding any human contact for he feared the whites even more than the blacks.

On the morning of the fourth day he was caught by a group of white soldiers. When they stripped him they discovered the old scars and brands on his back, which were proof enough that he was a runaway.

They took him to town where he was, like so many other suspects, exposed to public inspection. His fate seemed doomed when Mme Monnier recognized him, said he belonged to a young lady who had been mur-dered by some of her slaves. But for my intervention he would no doubt have been tortured and finally killed.

Even now he was not safe, nor was his brother Tom, for rumors spread that many mulattoes were joining the Negro rebels, offering them their help against the whites. Therefore every mulatto or octoroon in town was suspected being either an enemy spy, or a runaway slave.

It was going to be difficult enough to smuggle Tom on board my ship undetected, and now there was George. We discussed several plans till we agreed on a project that seemed to us the least risky. But it is time I stopped. I feel tired after writing six pages at a stretch.

OCTOBER 26TH

The sky is so blue, the sea so calm. There is no wind to fill our sails. The captain says we haven't covered more than a few miles since dawn.

Most of the passengers seem to have recovered. There is no room left for me on deck, not in the shade. So I have returned to my narrow cabin where I can sit undressed, unmolested, and devote my thoughts to the past, happy hours gone for ever, bittersweet recollections that may soothe my grieving heart for a while.

I must report the way I managed to smuggle both Tom and George on board the *Bretonne* that morning. Of course, if arrested, George too, could have proved he was a free man, our attorney having provided him with the legal documents attesting his manumission. But knowing that no free mulatto was allowed to leave the town we were forced to pretend he was my slave, and he and Tom were one and the same person.

La Bretonne was a handsome brig, small enough to lie at anchor in the inner harbor along the pier. When I saw the crowds of people on board on the morning of the ship's departure I had little hopes of being admitted, let alone my servants! So many fugitives, mostly women and children, were filling the deck, shouting, crying, running up and down the wooden stairs connecting the deck with the pier.

Two constabularies were watching each person going aboard. They refused to admit us and told me to approach the captain who was standing nearby talking to some officers in uniform.

"I am sorry, ma'am, we have no room left, we cannot take any more passengers."

"But there must be a way . . ."

"If you are willing to spend the nights on deck together with the crowd——"

"I am sick, I must have a room for myself. I am willing to pay any amount."

He shrugged his shoulders, then turned to one of the men in military attire. They had a whispered conversation, after which the captain turned to me politely, saying he might persuade the first mate to give me his room if I was willing to pay him a decent sum, say 200 livres! I said I was ready to pay that sum on condition that I could take my servants with me. He said your maid, yes, but not that fellow. He looks strong and healthy, you must leave him to these officers to be recruited. They need men like that for the army.

"But he is the only male slave they left me," I retorted. "I have already delivered them all my other mulattoes, six good men, and a boy, to join your army. I have lost all my fortune, my house, my crop, my livestock, more than two hundred blacks, everything. This fellow Tom and his wife are the only slaves left to me, the last property I own. I am going to sell them in Martinique in order to get the money for my fare back to France. I am absolutely dependent on the money I hope to get for him."

"He looks almost white. Aren't you afraid he might run away?" he asked.

"Not this man. He is too much attached to his wife. He would not think of deserting her, would you, Tom?"

"No, ma'am!"

"I promised to sell them together, not to separate them."

"I am sorry, ma'am——"

"I am willing to pay another two hundred livres if you allow me to take him with me." I opened my purse filled with glittering gold coins.

"You are not penniless, ma'am," said the captain smiling.

"I sold my jewels."

"It would be against the strictest rules, ma'am," put in the officer. "We need fellows like that, every single man is important. It is wartime, ma'am, we have to squash a rebellion!"

"But you could not rely on him. He might desert you, run over to the blacks."

"You are contradicting yourself, ma'am."

"I said he won't run away because of his wife. But if you separate him from her he will desert you at the first chance. Please leave me that man! I won't give him away simply to be shot as a deserter. A lad worth five thousand livres! If you refuse me, I'll turn to the governor himself whose wife is a friend of mine!"

He turned to the other officers. They talked in a whisper. I saw him shrug his shoulders, nod his head. Then he again approached me.

"All right," he said. "I'll make an exception. But don't tell anybody. You might get me into trouble."

That is how I got Tom on board the ship. It cost me a lot of money, bribing first the officers, then the captain, then the first mate—the whole pack of greedy rascals. I left Tom in my cabin, locking it to make sure nobody could see him. Mixed with the descending crowd and drove back to the inn, hoping that no one on board had noticed that I entered my cabin with two servants but left it with one only, Helen. She had been moody since her husband was taken away and forced to join the military troops defending the town. She was very anxious to see him again or at least get news of him.

When we were back in my room where George was waiting for us, she burst into tears, asked my pardon for refusing to follow me, and said it was her duty to stick to her husband, wait for him to return to her when the rebels were beaten.

I felt disappointed at her disloyalty—deserting me when I depended on her more than ever before. But when I saw George trying to console her and persuade her to join us—his voice soft like a lover's, his hands caressing her cheeks and hair, I felt jealous. It was strange, considering I didn't love him any longer. I could not bear to see him caress a common servant of mine and maybe fall in love with her after having shared my bed.

I grew angry and said she was right, it was her duty to stay in town and wait for her legal husband's return.

I said goodbye to her in a cool voice as if she were a

stranger, unmoved by her sobs and tears. How beastly
I behaved, so heartless and ungrateful! I lost the only
human being who was blindly attached to me, the only
one I could completely depend upon, my dearest faithful friend and confidante. What a fool I was, what an
idiot to treat her that way. It makes me sick to remember.

I didn't realize my mistake, then. I was too much
preoccupied with the comedy I had to play to smuggle
George aboard the ship.

I raised my voice and rushed out calling for help, told
the landlady's servants to arrest my slave. I said he had
refused to follow me. I had his hands chained behind
his back and ordered him to precede me to my coach.
Then I paid my bill and drove with him to the port.

I said goodbye to Old Jules after telling him to return
to my attorney who had promised to take care of the
old Negro and my coach and horses. Such a dear old
man, so devoted to me all the time. I do hope Mre Falcon can protect him from the stupid rabble who are
making every black-skinned person suffer for the rebels'
crimes.

It was, no doubt, a strange sight—the slave in chains
followed by a lady and two porters carrying her
trunks and bags. I remember the curious crowd
watching us in mute astonishment, the passengers on
deck staring down at us, the officer I had met before
stopping me at the bottom of the gangboard.

"What's the matter with that fellow?" he inquired.

"You were right," I said. "I should not have trusted
the beggar. He ran away with his wife. We caught him,
but not the woman. They gave him a good thrashing
as a reward for his escapade, but I am afraid they
served him a little too well. He can barely walk. I hope
he will recover soon for I cannot offer a sick slave for
sale."

Up on deck I told the mate the same story. I paid him
another 100 livres for providing me a mattress which
they put in the small dark compartment that usually
served as a storeroom for trunks.

"We must keep this fellow locked up for a while,

else he might try to jump overboard before we are out of the port," I said turning the key.

When alone again we all laughed, Tom stepping out of the wardrobe in which he had been hiding, and George rubbing his wrists after I had removed his manacles.

OCTOBER 27TH

It was not very comfortable, that twelve days' voyage to Martinique. It was also an awkward situation: myself sharing a narrow cabin with two lovers!

Of course George was much too sick and weak at first to claim his old-established rights from me. But I could not expect him to keep calm and indifferent if he saw his brother make love to me.

Tom, too, was frightfully embarrassed; at night he refused to undress, turned his back to me and never touched me for fear his brother might hear us.

The second evening George said he felt much better and would prefer to spend the nights on deck, the air being too stuffy in our cabin, Tom immediately insisted on sleeping in the open air in his stead. It seems he wished to show his brother he was not jealous. Knowing George had once been my lover he wanted to avoid hurting his feelings.

That night George never approached me, though I doubt if I would have been strong enough to resist him considering how angry I was at Tom for deserting me. It was so wrong of us not to be honest from the beginning! Pretending didn't help to ease the tension, that mute resentment we felt growing against each other though we tried our best to hide it.

It was no use telling Tom the next morning that his brother had behaved like a sexless angel. Jealousy makes them all so ridiculously suspicious.

The next night he said it was George's turn to sleep on deck. When we were alone he sulked and quarrelled, even hit me, repenting his rudeness at once, asking my pardon in the usual way and ending in kisses and violent love. Dear silly brute! It was his stupid suspicion that, at last, drove me to what I should never have done had he trusted me.

I was so furious that afternoon, the day before we arrived at Fort de France, so terribly disappointed at his rude manners, his insults, that I burst into tears when he rushed out at the sight of his brother who was returning from the deck.

George asked me what had happened and tried to console me. His soothing voice, his soft caresses made me lose my head. I was simply overrun by his growing passion—like a sudden tidal wave whirling away all the protecting dikes. I swear I was imagining kissing and loving Tom. I was not unfaithful to him in those passionate minutes; it was Tom's body and skin, and smell and voice, his soft strength, his ecstasy, his melting force—sweet, sweet oblivion in my lover's arms. I fell asleep relieved, and awoke unable to repent. I don't know what might have happened if Tom had caught us in the act. Thank Heaven he did not return before late that evening.

Maybe it was not only jealousy that made Tom turn so nasty. He must have resented being forced to act the part of my obedient slave in the presence of others. Hurt his pride. But I had to treat him that way, order him about in a cold commanding voice to make people believe that, in my eyes, he was nothing but a slave.

The slightest sign of friendliness would have roused doubts. Women observers are so quick at drawing conclusions. "A young widow admitting her male servant to her private cabin!" they would have said, wondering what happened behind the locked door. Instead they all took me for a cold-hearted despot and felt sorry for my servant, rumors having spread that I had had him whipped for running away from me. They also believed I intended to sell or put him up for auction in Martinique.

That's why that impudent Créole woman asked me how much I would charge for my slave because she was willing to purchase him. I replied I was sorry but the fellow was already promised to a friend of mine at Fort de France. She insisted on offering me 1,000 livres more than my friend was willing to pay. She got angry when I refused to strike a bargain, said she pitied the poor boy, everybody could see how badly he was treated, even whipped like a common Negro.

"I am not responsible to you, ma'am, for the way I choose to deal with my servants," I said haughtily.

The next morning she again stopped me on deck.

"I wish to apologize for my rudeness," she said with an ingratiating smile. "I'll no longer annoy you with my purchasing offers as you refuse to sell him to me. But may I ask you one little favor?"

"I am at your service, ma'am," I said, "if it is possible."

"It concerns my maid Rosita," she explained. "She is a very pretty girl, isn't she? I have not allowed her to mate as yet, but seeing that she admires your servant very much, I should be willing to grant her the pleasure of a little tête-à-tête with him provided you would consent."

"But the fellow is married to my maid."

"I heard she ran away from you, so it would not matter, would it? We would only borrow him for a night or two."

"You expect me to encourage adultery?" I replied angrily.

"Adultery! Aren't they slaves? I'll pay you whatever you charge."

"Am I to play the part of procuress?"

"Please, ma'am, don't use such nasty words for a mere business proposal! I want my wench to produce a fine offspring, something worth breeding, not a mere mongrel. I think your man would suit that purpose excellently. It would not hurt him, would it?" she asked, smiling and winking at me.

"You wish to use him as a stallion for covering your mare?" I retorted.

"In a way, yes, certainly. Why not?"

"Because he is not a stallion, but a human being with human feelings. Even a slave has his dignity, particularly a well-bred one like Tom."

"If you are so considerate, why don't you stop ill-treating him?"

"Who says I am ill-treating him?"

"I can tell when a slave has been beaten. By his looks and his gait."

"Perhaps you are wrong."

"Whipping slaves does not suit a lady," she said.

"You are insulting me!"

"I see we cannot come to terms."

"Certainly not!"

I turned round, furious. The insolent bitch! But I was the one who had taken pains to make them believe I was a female brute. No wonder I was stared at whenever I went on deck.

Yet was I not forced to play that part? I am sure there were people on board who remembered the rumors about my mating with a bastard. Only by treating Tom as the lowest of my slaves could I refute that gossip. What a perverse world it was that would sooner believe a white woman was a heartless despot than a colored man's sweetheart!

Looking back I wonder how we managed to make people believe for so long that there was only one servant attending me.

It is true Tom and George looked as similar as two eggs the same size. They were dressed the same way in plain linen breeches and shirt, and were barefoot. Sometimes even I could not tell Tom from George at first sight: the same voice, gait, movements—identical. They had to be cautious all the time, and obey the strict rule of never leaving our cabin except in turns. Fortunately it was separated from the next by our small storeroom, a big wardrobe covering the opposite wall. So our voices could not be heard by our neighbors.

Nor did we run any risk of being overheard by people outside considering the constant commotion on deck and below, sailors shouting and cursing, women calling, children running about, yelling, laughing, crying.

Trouble started when we debarked at Fort de France. That bitch of a woman! But I'll record that incident tonight or tomorrow, for it will take me pages to do it. It is time for a breath of fresh air and a walk, if there is any room left for that on deck.

OCTOBER 28TH

I had a long talk with M. Raffael before turning in last night. An elderly Jew, but charming and a real gentleman. I never knew they could be so charming and well-mannered.

He told me a lot about Philadelphia and New York. Said he preferred New York—not so stiff and puritan, more open-minded, cosmopolitan he called it, a term new to me. Yet marriages between white and colored people are disapproved of there, too, he said.

I wish I could change Tom's mind, tell him I am still his faithful, humble, obedient wife, ask his pardon, persuade him to follow me to France where he would be respected as everyone's equal. It's hard to bear this terrible loneliness. I feel too dejected to mix with the noisy crowd. I prefer to stay in my cabin and remember happier days past and gone.

Six more pages left in this cahier. Must try and come to an end reporting the past. Impossible to get any writing paper here on board. But I mean to resume my entries in New York, or back in France, who knows?

Those days at Fort de France—we knew Tom was safe the moment he stepped on land, his papers proving his American citizenship. But George was still in danger of being arrested. News of the great rebellion in S. Domingo had, no doubt, put the authorities in Martinique on the guard, so every colored man arriving from our island was sure to be suspected of being a runaway rebel. That's why we thought it wise that George should go on playing his part as my slave for a while.

We all hoped my attorney's friend, Mre Oliva, could help us to provide George with the papers necessary to attest his manumission and permit him to leave Martinique a free man.

So I wrote a slave's pass allowing him to debark with some of my trunks. He was to find a coach and drive to a recommendable *auberge* to reserve rooms for us there, then send the coachman back to the harbor to fetch Tom and me with the rest of our luggage.

I did not wish George to return himself lest the captain, or the shipmate or anybody else we knew, should see the twins together.

But when we arrived at our hotel George had disappeared. The landlord said two men had come and taken him away. Of course we were frightfully worried and turned to the police. But they said no foreigner had been arrested that day. Nor could Mre Oliva help us. George had vanished as though spirited away by magic. Tom was so depressed that he remained locked in his room. It was as if he held me responsible for George's disappearance.

The next morning there was a knock on my door. I jumped out of my bed, hoping it was Tom. But when I opened the door—what a surprise! It was George! George, dressed like a perfect chevalier, a lover's smile round his lips when he saw me cover my breasts. Later he told us what had happened to him.

The two strangers had, indeed, ordered him to follow them to the police. But instead they had stopped in front of a fine house in parklike surroundings. They delivered him to two giant Negroes who took him in and left him in a big room with a marble floor, carpets, costly tapestries, majestic armchairs, chandeliers, etc.

After a long while the door opened, and in stepped Mme de Torres, the Créole woman who had kept molesting me on board ship.

He says she treated him like a guest, offered him a glass of brandy, started questioning him about me, asked him how long he had been my servant, if he was really married and why had his wife run away? And how did I punish him when he was recaptured?

He tried to answer in an evasive way, asked her permission to leave and said his mistress was sure to be very angry if he kept her waiting any longer. She replied he need not worry, she knew for certain that there was another servant replacing him, a man so similar to him that he must be his twin brother. She forced him to admit she was right, whereupon she said she had half a mind to inform the police and have his mistress arrested for smuggling in a colored runaway. It depended on him whether I was spared an inquest or not. That way she forced him to stay.

George says she proved a charming hostess, offered him a hot bath, and when he wanted to dress again his poor servant's clothes were replaced by fine and costly ones which, she afterwards explained to him, had belonged to her late husband's wardrobe. She said George reminded her of the deceased, his features, size, voice. She had been married nine months only when her husband died, a few days before she lost her babe in childbirth.

George never admitted she made love to him that night, nor did he ever mention her pretty maid, just said they were very nice to him and treated him well.

I cannot help feeling jealous, remembering how much he was impressed by that shameless woman. He must have met her again later, for who else could have told him about my business with Captain Basteresse? I know who told her. I knew an hour or two before my departure, when I met her with Mre Oliva who introduced her to me as his own daughter!

I wish I had known in time! Fate seems to have so many malicious coincidences in store for me. Remember that scoundrel Pierre who spoiled my married life. What an evil trick of providence that he should have been acquainted with Charles's sister! If there is any angel shuffling my cards it is an evil one, a devil, not an angel!

The triumphant smile she gave me, that little bitch. Makes me sick to know she managed to bewitch George. Not so very attractive, after all, her beady black eyes, her Jewish nose. I wonder if Tom would have liked her too. Maybe he did. You never can tell!

He must have met her, talked to her, otherwise he could not have known so many facts and details about our contract with Captain Basteresse—He made a terrible scene, calling me all kinds of names, a merchant in human flesh, a pretty-faced monster, a greedy hypocrite, a money-minded, heartless, double-faced bitch of a slave trader!

He refused to listen to me or let me explain. He wanted me to disclaim my rights on that cargo, renounce the only fortune left to me, a shipload of blacks worth 150,000 livres or more—all my share.

I got so angry I lost my temper, called him an idiot, a stupid brainless bastard! I repented that ugly word the moment it had slipped my tongue when I saw how much it hurt him. What a fool I was not to shut my mouth in time!

I saw him turn round and rush to the door. I should have run after him, have stopped him and begged his pardon. He might have calmed once more, as on so many other occasions. Instead I stood there, stiff as a poker, unable to move, not realizing how fatal a minute it was, the last glimpse I had of him. I never saw him again. Nor George, for when I returned from Mre Oliva's office their room was empty, their trunks gone. Tom's letter was lying on my table, cold words informing me there was an English ship setting sail for Jamaica that evening. He invited me to join them on board. If I could not make up my mind to do so, it was goodbye for ever! He thanked me for all I had done for him and his brother, but even gratitude had its limit, he added.

I was so shocked I dropped on my bed unable to shed a single tear. I wished to run down to the port and stop them, but I was too proud to follow my heart's call.

Mre Oliva had told me Captain Basteresse's ship had dropped anchor outside the port waiting for permission to enter. How in Heaven's name could I be expected to depart before having met the man I had been awaiting so long!

Now I realize my fatal mistake.

I ought to have put my attorney in charge of the whole business. Could even have asked him to give me a decent part of my profit in advance and transfer the rest to New York without anybody else knowing about the deal. At least Tom and George might have been kept ignorant of it. What a fool I was not to do so! But I did not trust Mre Oliva. He might have made a deal with Captain Basteresse to cheat me.

But weighing my full profit against what I lost, Tom's love and George's love too—it is like exchanging gold for dull, gray lead. Heaven forgive me, I know I was wrong, I'll tell him I am sorry, offer part of my profit to the church or an orphanage or the poor—anything to prove to him I mean it. He cannot be so hard as to reject me, remembering he swore I was the only woman he ever loved. Oh Tom, don't desert me, let me return to you, serve you as your faithful, obedient wife till death do us part.

AFTER DINNER

No use whining like a repentant sinner. The past is gone. I wish they had at least left me Henri, my dear little colt, so graceful, so charming, so dear to me once, before I loved Tom. I should have known how untrue grown men are, all of them, stubborn heartless beasts! Henri would have stuck to me, faithfully, unconditionally. Would have spared me a world of grief, disappointment and despair. Looking back it seems I have for ever made a mess of all my life.

A Special Preview of
a compelling opening section from

A COWARD FOR THEM ALL

The tumultuous saga of a proud
Irish-American family

by
James Kavanaugh

John Patrick Jr., called Jack, was born in Chicago in 1926 and Grandma Kate was happier than anyone had seen her in years. Three days before his delivery she had dreamed of mice running over an empty cake pan, but despite the fearful omen, Jack's broad shoulders and almost orange hair on a large Irish head reassured her. John Patrick bragged of a triple-threat quarterback at Notre Dame, and Margaret thanked God and Saint Anthony, but she was further distressed the night before Jack's baptism when she herself dreamed of an old man in a long coat standing on a highway in the moonlight. However, she dismissed the disturbing portent when the priest washed Jack's soul clean of sin. John Patrick Maguire could not stop smiling.

Margaret recalled the awesome signs a few months later when a bloated Kate dropped dead of a second stroke.

Over the protests of the Irish matriarchy, Johnny Muller draped his wife in a white silk dress and placed in her hands, along with her rosary, the sack of soil Michael O'Brien had given her the day before she sailed from Ireland. More than forty years had passed since Michael had made his promise: "The land is all yours. It won't be long now."

John Patrick received notice of a promotion to manage a new office of the Audit Bureau in Kirkwood, Michigan. His superiors agreed that marriage and a young son had settled the wild, gifted Irishman into a new maturity. It was a rare compliment to a Maguire, and Daniel, his father, stayed drunk for three days in celebration.

Margaret was delighted to leave Chicago. A smiling John Patrick bought drinks at a South Side speakeasy and promised to return only when he could pay cash for all of Marshall Fields. They left late in 1927 with their Tin Lizzie and a stocky year-old-Jack, who had his father's red hair and Margaret's light blue eyes.

Kirkwood, a prosperous town of forty thousand in southwestern Michigan, was a strange, angry setting for Margaret Ann, daughter of Kate and grandchild of Michael O'Brien. Neither she nor John Patrick had ever known the sordid religious bigotry of a small midwestern town.

Kirkwood was a Dutch Protestant stronghold, and the young Maguires arrived there when Alfred E. Smith, "the Happy Warrior," was running for president, the first Catholic ever to do so. Assuredly, Kirkwood was no extension of Chicago's South Side. There were no First Ward politics or illegal hooch at the Knights of Columbus, no boisterous White Sox games and Irish camaraderie that battled niggers and insulted Polacks. Almost overnight, the Maguires were the "niggers," and the pride of John Patrick's promotion was turned to bitterness. Three times they were unceremoniously refused access to Dutch neighborhoods. They finally rented a small frame house, purchased simple oak furniture, and unloaded Jack's crib. Margaret sprinkled the rooms with holy water as John Patrick struggled with boxes. They were crushed to see anti-Catholic cartoons splashed in the *Kirkwood Gazette,* depicting Al Smith welcoming an owl-eyed, salami-nosed pope to the White House. Crosses were burned in front of Saint Raphael's gabled brick rectory, and crude jokes about lusty nuns conceiving priests' fat babies in drunken orgies—Smith favored the repeal of Prohibition—drew lunchtime laughs in the Victory Cafe and in John Patrick's office.

It was a rude awakening for a proud Irishman and his shy wife who had known only the security of a giant city where twenty percent of its three million inhabitants were Irish Catholic.

John Patrick had come to Kirkwood with the dreams of a young businessman on the way up, and his dreams were magnified when he surveyed the dozen young women who seemed delighted by the handsome charm of their new manager. Although the fierce bigotry against Catholics outraged him, he tried to ignore the snide attacks, only snarling back when the remarks were too crude to tolerate. . . .

Although a few hundred Irish had settled in Kirkwood almost a century before, the Dutch had come in greater numbers with much more money and the finer skills of successful artisans and experienced farmers. They also possessed a historic hatred of Catholics that was born of Europe's religious wars and the fury of the bloody Spanish Inquisitions. These same Dutch Reformed had emigrated to Kirkwood, bought its rich black land, built it up to its present prosperity, and even named it in honor of God as a "church in the woods."

It was no wooded church to John Patrick Maguire, but a concrete coliseum where he was daily fed to mocking lions who soon learned to circle him at a safe distance. The Dutch believed Tammany Hall to be a papal plot, and they despised Franklin Roosevelt as a turncoat for supporting Smith against Herbert Hoover. But even when Hoover won the 1928 election and the Dutch of Kirkwood rejoiced, John Patrick knew that his own Irish victory was only a matter of time. He knew it especially when he watched his fearless infant son gleefully raise his fat fists to battle his own father. Then John Patrick lovingly buried Jack in awkward arms and told the boy his favorite story again and again until he kissed his beautiful son good night.

Margaret was apparently content to bathe her infant with hymns to Mary and the baby Jesus, and she nursed him for over a year until he bit her breast fiercely a third time. She knew little of angry politics, yet she shared John Patrick's bitter pain, especially when neighbors shunned her or suddenly talked in Dutch and laughed together in the grocery store at her pregnant belly when Jack was not yet a year and a half old. Remarkably, she reported none of this humiliation to her husband, sharing it only with God in whispered aspirations all day long and during the daily six o'clock mass she attended at Saint Raphael's. She begged heaven's forgiveness for not entering the convent, not convinced that an ambitious, handsome husband and a healthy son had released her from God's wrath.

Early in 1928, a great shame came to Saint Raphael's parish in Kirkwood. The soft-spoken and kindly Irish pastor, an uncomplicated farmer from rural Sligo, was shot to death at the dinner table by a crazed monk from Europe. The *Chicago Tribune* reported it as an unspeakable tragedy, but the *Kirkwood Gazette* kept the scandal alive with a disgusting prurience that delighted the Calvanist bigots.

Was it a love triangle with a nun? An illegitimate baby in the rectory basement? A Vatican assassination? All the historic crimes of Rome and its infamous popes were recalled, and wild-eyed ex-priests appeared in Dutch Reformed pulpits to recount in sordid detail the horrors of Roman Catholicism.

The Irish community was numb and embarrassed, and the Saint Raphael parish became divided: hostile cliques wanted vengeance, and passive groups prayed to ignore the new persecution. School attendance dropped, Catholics were denied jobs and publicly ridiculed, students left the seminary. Margaret cried for an entire week and she was terrified to go to the grocery store. John Patrick read the *Kirkwood Gazette* to shreds and swore bitterly at each new accusation. When his regional supervisor at the Audit Bureau, J. R. Harris, a tight-jawed WASP with thin lips and rimless glasses, hinted at a drunken orgy, John Patrick felt the blood rush to his head and had to leave Harris's office lest he break his jaw.

The scandal could have destroyed Saint Raphael's parish had not the bishop of Detroit, the archdiocesan seat for Kirkwood, appointed James Michael Doyle as pastor six weeks after the tragedy. A stocky Irish American with a booming voice and dark brown eyes glaring under bushy black hair, Doyle whipped the parish back into shape within two months. The parish council was fired, the ushers disbanded, the ladies guild terminated; James Michael Doyle was to be consulted about everything from altar boys to the menu at the Saint Patrick's Day banquet. Pockets of resistance were threatened with excommunication and wiped out; the editor of the local paper was threatened with legal action as well as receiving anonymous phone calls in a thick Irish brogue predicting a long stay in the hospital. James Doyle himself invaded a luncheon meeting of Dutch Reformed ministers and promised an all-out war if "God's more peaceful ways are not observed." His muscular body rippled defiance and commanded such respect that he was finally applauded when he quoted Jeremiah.

Almost overnight, the parish had its pride back. The high school football team got new emerald green uniforms and were informed that any missed blocks or "gutless" tackles would be dealt with in the rectory office. Sports, always significant, now became a religious crusade. James Michael Doyle conducted pep rallies personally. During the half time of a game Saint Raphael's was losing to Bay Harbor Central 6–0, he slapped a star halfback, knocked two powerful tackles over a locker room bench, and watched his team win 27–6. The team was undefeated the very first year, and schools twice the size were not only defeated but humiliated. John Patrick roared his approval from the sidelines with Jack on his lap. Even Margaret, on the brim of delivery, cheered her support. The *Kirkwood Gazette* called the team the Fighting Irish, after Notre Dame, and gave the games more space than was given to a mediocre Kirkwood Central, three times the size. When the Fighting Irish humbled Central 42–7 and four Dutchmen were carried from the field, a special mass of thanksgiving was offered by James Doyle. John Patrick smiled proudly at J. R. Harris and thereafter ignored his pompous initials, calling him "Jimmy boy" in front of the office staff.

Nor did it end with the football team. Ushers began dressing in tuxedos. A new statue of Saint Patrick with bishop's miter and green robes was placed in a special grotto, and evergreens were planted around the church. School attendance shot up. James Doyle preached eloquently that his parishioners were engaged in a holy war to save civilization, just as the Irish monks had done ten centuries before. The pastor soon became a legendary hero—even among the men.

Irish men traditionally were not fond of priests. Too many men remembered the stories of the famine when the priests had upheld England's right to tax the peasants to death. In the eighteenth century, priests had been persecuted heroes who defied English law to say their masses in caves and secret glens, protected by thick Irish shoulders bearing clubs, but when the clergy were reprieved in 1829 and permitted to conduct their services, a fearful new conservatism scarred their ranks. Most, as in Clare, supported landlords' rights from the very pulpits, and the brooding Irishmen would never forget. Even as they tipped their hats, begged a blessing, or permitted their own sons to enter the seminary, they cursed under their breath.

The women were more tolerant, almost obsequious, not because they truly loved the clergy, but because they recognized them as the only real defense against the total chauvinism of their oppressed and angry husbands. The women knew instinctively that the Holy Mother Church was a matriarchy as fierce and domineering as their own real control of the family. They well understood the clerical arrogance, and they also knew that the priests ate and drank better than most parishioners. They saw the expensive clothes and vestments, the lavish episcopal dinners, the extravagant rectories and cars, the vanity and selfishness. But they also saw the true shepherd who would give his life for the flock, who cared about the poor and gave his every waking hour to console the sick and lonely. They knew his devotion came from God himself, and they kissed his hand or the hem of his cassock in genuine love. They felt his tenderness and understanding in the confessional, his compassion at times of tragedy and death. He was the same priest who had defied the landlords, blessed the people's defiance, and died with his flock in the Great Famine of 1845. There probably was no finer or nobler love among the Irish than that lavished on such a priest.

James Michael Doyle did not know that kind of love. His was the respect given to a leader in war. Even the men knew they could not survive without him, and his powerful word became law. No one was to date a non-Catholic; every child was to attend a parochial school; and a boy who didn't go out for football needed a doctor's exemption or congenital blindness. Anyone who hadn't voted for Al Smith was in serious danger of excommunication.

There were twelve babies christened James Michael that very first year, and to have a vocation to the priesthood, always an honor, was suddenly a mark of divine preeminence. Even to be appointed an usher was an invitation into a sacred oligarchy controlled personally by James Doyle. In such an environment, John Patrick became an exemplary Catholic and a bellowing threat to every careless referee who officiated at a Saint Raphael game. He was James Doyle's kind of man, and at the baptism of his second son, James Michael Maguire, John Patrick was asked to be an usher. Of course he accepted, and he doubled his weekly donations. Only Margaret knew that he had never actively practiced his faith before he met her.

James Michael Maguire was born at the end of 1928 at the edge of the Depression, and he was the opposite of Jack. A small baby with no Maguire traits, he had light brown hair and serious, almost frightened eyes that gradually became hazel. He seemed docile and unprotesting from birth. He seldom cried. A week before his delivery, Margaret felt a shadow fall across her face, and a strange black bird stared at her from a cherry tree close to the house. Nor did it move when she emptied the garbage. She was afraid to mention it to John Patrick, and she rejoiced when the delivery was an easy one and the new baby seemed reasonably healthy. But James Michael Maguire was an anomaly, and even a two-year-old Jack, freckled and boisterous, twice slapped him in his crib and had to be restrained from tormenting Jim when he first began to crawl.

John Patrick made light of it. "It's the Maguire blood. Jimmy will learn to defend himself."

Actually John Patrick was thrilled with both sons, wrestling for hours with the feisty, oversized Jack and patiently teaching a tentative Jimmy to fight back. Jack was the powerful exemplar of what it meant to be a Maguire, and James Michael was expected to measure up. There were subtle signs even in infancy that he would withdraw from the impossible contest, but John Patrick was too happy to notice. Margaret, too, was never happier, fussing endlessly over the children and preparing her husband's favorite roasts with mashed potatoes and thick, rich gravy the way Johnny Muller had instructed her. Baking bread and Parker House rolls and apple slices with white frosting, and trying as best she could to satisfy her husband's strong sexual appetite although she didn't understand it and was embarrassed when he fondled her enlarged breasts while she was nursing Jimmy.

Curiously, in the early years, when success at work absorbed him and the joy of children was a novelty, her very shyness about sex excited him. He was satisfied to be the aggressor, charming her little girl's fears, and well pleased to feel some minimal compliance. She gazed at the bleeding crucifix on the wall or the serenely cold china madonna on the dresser, but she never refused him, for she knew that his salvation depended on her service and prayers, and that her own sanctity, like the Blessed Virgin's, was measured by the performance of God's will. God's will was of far greater concern than even John Patrick.

Thus she left her husband's bed every morning at five to attend the early mass with the nuns; her closest friend, "old maid" Mary O'Meara; a scattered two dozen other devout women; and two or three effeminate men she did not admire. At first John Patrick had protested her daily departure, not admitting his need to feel her warmth next to him, but insisting protectively that she required more sleep.

"I can sleep for all eternity," she said softly.

She would have honored any other request, but God came first, and there was no way on heaven or earth to dissuade her. At times he held her tightly and feigned heavy sleep, but she fought her way free. Occasionally he pretended sickness, and then she would attend to his needs quickly and go off to mass in the new Oldsmobile he had taught her to drive. Finally, he gave up and accepted her going to mass as he did his own job.

She was transformed when she entered the old brick church. With its vaulted arches and huge plaster pillars, the smell of incense and the creaking of oiled wooden floors, it gave her a few moments of peace, without interruptions or babies to attend or coffee to make. Her face became like that of a child. Her lips, normally thin and drawn tight to hide an overbite that had always embarrassed her, relaxed with the fullness of a passion John Patrick would never know. The blue eyes glowed and stared rapturously at the giant crucifix suspended behind the altar. She readied her missal like a teacher preparing for class, read the special prayers on holy cards gathered since childhood in Chicago. Then came the organ and the ancient Gregorian melodies of the Kyrie and the Gloria and the triumphant preface chant that had startled Mozart, the solemn Pater Noster that brought her close to tears. There was no greater joy. She made her way to communion, calling out in her heart *Domine, non sum dignus* and thrilling to the soft strum of the organ's Adoro Te . . .

The office transformed him as the church did her. His booming good-morning and always new Irish palaver about "so much beauty in a single room" or "how lucky can a man get" reduced the female office staff to giggles. Even his firmness, when reports were late or quarterly rating charts incorrect, made him attractive. He had an incredible mind for figures, could multiply or divide complicated problems in his head, and stored endless statistics of insurance rates and projected costs almost effortlessly.

His private secretary, Doris, was secretly in love with him and found his dramatic dictations of letters an eloquent delight. Although forced out of school in seventh grade to help support his family, John Patrick had an impressive vocabulary and perfect grammar. He was exceptionally clean, had manicures with his twice-monthly haircut, and dressed handsomely. Always a fresh white shirt and appropriate tie, shoes shined, rusty hair flattened as much as the stubborn curls would allow. He held his head proudly, tilted almost arrogantly, and usually opened his mouth when he smiled. He liked his own looks, especially the proud, prominent nose that gave immense character to his face and justified a touch of swagger when he walked . . .

A month later he bought a house despite the alarmist talk of troubled economic conditions and an end to prosperity. He surprised Margaret one evening after work by inviting her and the children out for a ride.

"Dinner's in the oven—"

"It'll keep," he said. "I feel like taking a ride on such an evening."

She feared he had been drinking with his new friend, Mike McNulty, a short, stocky ex-middleweight he had met at a football game.

They drove to a Dutch neighborhood in the south end of Kirkwood, hardly two blocks from where J. R. Harris lived, at the fringe of Protestant affluence.

"Beautiful houses here," he mused aloud.

"That's not important," she said. "We have everything we need." She didn't admit that she wanted a refrigerator to replace the dripping old icebox that was rotting the linoleum.

He stopped the car in front of a corner house that had brick wainscoting and an enclosed front porch. There was a front and side yard and a separate garage. A neat hedge surrounded the entire property and a peach and a cherry tree bloomed gracefully in separate yards. Small evergreens flanked the front porch and contrasted elegantly with the fresh white paint. It was two stories with an attic and basement and half again as big as the house they were renting.

"That's a fine house," he said. "Let's take a look."

"My God in heaven, John. You might get shot just wandering around." Now she was certain he had been drinking.

He picked up Jack and walked to the front entrance. Margaret did not move from the car, and little Jim was crying. She prayed aloud when John Patrick walked up on the porch.

He shouted to her. "It's empty, Margaret, let's take a look." He disappeared inside with Jack.

Still she did not understand, and she feared for his welfare. She slid out of the car with the baby and walked nervously up the front steps, reassuring herself that the children afforded protection. Her heart almost stopped when she saw the open door and realized he had stepped inside.

"For God's sake, John," she hissed. "What on earth has happened to you?"

Then he came to the front door with the beaming smile that had won her love at Lake Winnebago.

"How do you like it? It's empty. I think I'll buy it."

"Don't talk foolish, John, we never could afford it." She walked inside cautiously, as if she were robbing a bank.

"Dear God, it's beautiful," she whispered.

There were refinished hardwood floors and a living room fireplace with an ivory painted mantel. A formal dining room with double windows and wide window seats, a bright kitchen, and three bedrooms upstairs. The basement was large, though unfinished, with a fruit cellar and a coal bin.

Margaret was speechless, giggling like a little girl now, delighted by the daring escapade that reminded her of their courtship, still not realizing that the house was hers.

When he used the toilet upstairs she was frantic. He put his arms around her and smiled that proud smile again, and then she burst into tears of joy.

"O John, John, but so expensive!"

"It's too late now," he said. "We'll move in next week. And I've ordered a refrigerator."

There was no brooding that night as he ate seconds of pot roast and peas, gravy and apple pie. After a third cup of coffee and another cigarette, he helped her bathe the children and they talked till almost midnight about the business he would have, all his own, and the place in the country besides.

For once she only listened, delighted that they had room for all the children God might send and worrying if her lust for a refrigerator had been sinful.

"I only wish my mother had lived to see it." It was one of the rare times she made such a request.

Then they went to bed and he made love to her. With special gentleness and as much pleasure as she had ever allowed herself. When he was finally asleep, she slipped from bed to ask God's forgiveness for her enjoyment and thanked Him for the new house. Then she cuddled next to her husband and set the alarm for early mass.

She prayed more fervently when the Depression came crashing down in October 1929. Although Kirkwood, with its furniture factories, paper mills, and chemical plants, its apple orchards, dairy farms, and celery marshlands, was not nearly as scarred as the larger Michigan cities that depended on the automobile, the impact was, nevertheless, dramatic. The Audit Bureau cut back employees and with them John Patrick's salary. Still he did not admit his concern as he brooded in the new leather recliner he had bought along with Margaret's refrigerator. "A chair worthy of Doyle himself," he had joked.

Now he was not joking. It was a tense struggle to survive from day to day. Gene Tunney's retirement from boxing and a vacant heavyweight throne seemed inconsequential although Notre Dame's continuing dominance of college football under Knute Rockne gave John Patrick consistent energy to hold up his head in Kirkwood. No Depression could change that, nor could it ever force his fierce pride to admit aloud that he was frightened. He even permitted himself to gloat over the bungling "medicine ball" administration of pudgy Herbert Hoover with his Quaker background. Al Smith would have handled it all.

Somehow, with the money they had saved and Margaret's fierce management, they were able to endure and keep the new house. But there could be no thought of starting a new business or buying an old one. Or of having more children. Margaret did not agree with his decision about children as he uttered it one brooding evening as he sat in the brown leather recliner. To have a dozen children was, for her, a small enough sacrifice for ignoring the convent. Yet, to her credit, she would never have disputed her husband's judgment if he had not introduced a condom into their bedroom the week after Jim was weaned. Although she had never seen one, she instinctively knew it was evil, and she blessed herself nervously.

"My God in heaven, John Patrick!"

"It's a way of not having children for a while."

He was embarrassed, but it had never occurred to him that it was really wrong.

There had been no discussions in Saint Raphael's pulpit about birth control. Informed Catholics may have known the law, but Margaret was too naïve to have wondered, and John Patrick believed he only had to be a faithful husband and a good father. He had never heard the pope's opinion, nor did he care about it. Thus when Margaret turned from him, as much perhaps from fear as from any spiritual rejection, he became furious. The condom shriveled and fell on the sheets and Margaret grasped her rosary.

"For God's sake, Margaret, I'm a man!"

"We can deny ourselves and be grateful for what we have."

"Damn it. I am grateful, but we're entitled!"

"If Father Doyle says it's—"

He shouted, ripping the condom to shreds, "Doyle doesn't run my bedroom! You're my wife!"

She was trembling, then crying, and the two boys were crying besides. "What's it all worth if we go to hell?"

He charged from the bedroom and slammed the door. The crucifix fell to the floor and Margaret gasped in horror. As she arose to replace the crucifix and sprinkle holy water from the small ivory font by the door, John Patrick poured himself some bourbon, smuggled from Canada by McNulty's brother, and sat for several hours in his recliner. The sadness engulfed him until even the beautiful new house had lost its luster. Tears formed in his eyes but would not fall. Then he heard Jim crying and brought him in and held him tenderly, rocking him in the chair until he gurgled softly in his father's arms. He put his son back in the crib and fell asleep on the couch.

That night, something changed in their marriage.

Several other children are born to John and Margaret including one son who will enter the priesthood and be torn between the calling of the spirit and the yearning of the flesh.

Read the complete Bantam Book, available September 1st, 1979, wherever paperbacks are sold.

THE LATEST BOOKS IN THE BANTAM BESTSELLING TRADITION

RELAX!
SIT DOWN
and Catch Up On Your Reading!